Finchley ... ch End

D0727573

USA... ... bestselling a ...
nominated author **Caitlin Cre** ... ...ing
romance. She teaches her favou...e romance novels
in creative writing classes at places like UCLA
Extension's prestigious Writers' Programme, where
she finally gets to utilise the MA and PhD in English
Literature she received from the University of York in
England. She currently lives in the Pacific Northwest,
with her very own hero and too many pets. Visit her
at caitlincrews.com.

BEAUTY AND HER ONE-NIGHT BABY

DANI COLLINS

CLAIMED IN THE ITALIAN'S CASTLE

CAITLIN CREWS

MILLS & BOON

First Published in Great Britain 2020
by Mills & Boon, an imprint of HarperCollins*Publishers*
1 London Bridge Street, London, SE1 9GF

Beauty and Her One-Night Baby © 2020 by Dani Collins

Claimed in the Italian's Castle © 2020 by Caitlin Crews

ISBN: 978-0-263-27818-7

MIX
Paper from
responsible sources
FSC™ C007454

This book is produced from independently certified FSC™ paper
to ensure responsible forest management.
For more information visit www.harpercollins.co.uk/green.

Printed and bound in Spain
by CPI, Barcelona

BEAUTY AND HER ONE-NIGHT BABY

DANI COLLINS

For Phil, Eva and your adorable boys. Thank you
for showing us such a wonderful time in Madrid. There
aren't enough heart emojis to express our love for all of you.

CHAPTER ONE

HER WATER BROKE.

Horrified, Scarlett Walker hoped that if she didn't look it wouldn't be true. She stared at the hook on the back of the stall door where her handbag hung and prayed she was wrong.

She knew what had happened, though. There was no mistaking such an event and no, no, *no*. This was supposed to happen *next week*, at the island villa that had been her home for the last six years. Or last week, when she'd been sitting vigil at her employer's bedside. Anytime but *today*.

Not now.

Please not now.

It was a futile wish. In fact, she should have predicted this would happen. She had so many butterflies in her stomach they were knocking her baby clean out of her right before she walked into a boardroom to face a small but extremely volatile group of personalities—including the baby's father.

What would he say?

She'd found Javiero Rodriguez dynamic and powerful and intimidating *before* she'd slept with him. For nine months she'd been dreading and anticipating the moment when she would finally face him again.

Now she had to rush off to the hospital.

Thanks a lot, baby, she thought with a fleck of ironic hysteria. She wouldn't have to face any of them. Saved!

But how was this her life?

The Walker colors were shining brightly in her today. If there was a way to turn an everyday, natural occurrence into a trashy satire, the Walkers were there to make it happen. Scarlett wanted to sit back down on the toilet and cry her eyes out.

No time for that, though. With a sob of desperation, she fumbled her phone from her handbag and texted her best friend, Kiara.

My water broke. Help!

She pulled up the skirt she had so recently wriggled into place over her hips. Only her maternity underwear and one shoe were wet. She wrangled herself out of the unflattering cotton knickers with the stretchy front panel and discarded them in the bin.

Don't need those *anymore.*

Shakily, she left the stall long enough to wet a hand towel and grab a small stack of the folded ones off the shelf. Thank God it was empty in there. She edged back into the narrow stall and closed the door, then dropped the towels on the floor to blot up the puddle while she gave herself the quickest of bird baths.

She had let her doctor's "any day now" yesterday go in one ear and out the other. Had she really expected this baby would stay inside her forever?

Kind of. She'd had so much going on that she hadn't let herself think about anything other than ensuring her healthy pregnancy. She certainly hadn't envisioned the moment when the baby would actually arrive—or how that event would unfold.

Who had time for labor when she was facing a ton of work finalizing Niko's burial arrangements and continuing to manage his estate? Then there was Kiara's show in Paris. She had promised to help her with her artist's statement and had somehow deluded herself into believing she could attend.

Really, Scarlett? Due next week, yet planning to fly to Paris in three?

Denial was a wonderful thing—until it stopped working. It was screeching to a halt while she stood on the hand towels, waiting for Kiara and deliberately avoiding thoughts about how Javiero would react to everything he would learn today.

To *this*.

Not for the first time, she tried to will herself back in time and make a different decision. She'd been processing her employer's refusal of further treatment and frustrated with certain decisions he had made with regard to his errant sons. Maybe those two men didn't deserve much consideration, given their mulish refusal to see their father in his last days, but Scarlett had been compelled to prod them one last time.

Valentino Casale had never been cooperative with her so she hadn't expected any better than the brush-off he'd given her. Javiero, however, possessed a more solid sense of family. A heart.

At least, that was what she wanted to believe.

Maybe it was wishful thinking on her part.

What Javiero had in spades was a magnetism she had barely been able to resist the handful of times she'd met with him. It had taken everything in her to keep from betraying her reaction to him.

He must have known. He was too smoldering and sophisticated and experienced to not know when a woman was swooning over him. Maybe he'd even privately laughed at her for it. Maybe that was why he'd made a move that day. He had probably sensed she'd mentally slept with him a thousand times and was dying to make it reality.

She hadn't expected it to happen, though. Not really. Seeing him at all had been a rare overstep on her part, moving beyond the tight constraints of her employer's dictates and acting of her own volition. She was still trying to explain to herself how she'd been in Madrid at all, let alone how she had wound up in Javiero's bed.

A quiet sense of injustice had driven her. She knew that much. Had she also been affected on a basic level by Niko's failing health? Had she longed to assert the beginnings of life to hold off the shadows closing in on the end of one?

Or had it been as simple as a secretive yearning on her part to have a final connection with a man she would never have an excuse to see again once Niko was gone?

She hadn't expected Javiero to give her the time of day after his father's death. As it was, he only tolerated her in deference to his mother. Javiero's attitude toward Scarlett had always been…not hostile, but disparaging. He hadn't liked that she worked for his father. He couldn't respect her for it.

She'd had no idea how he might react to her pregnancy. Perhaps she'd been in a bit of denial then, too, not expecting their passionate afternoon could change her life—or create one! By the time she had suspected and had it confirmed, though, she had not only desperately wanted this baby—she had seen a poetic sort of balancing of scales in her carrying Javiero's child.

Not that Niko had viewed it that way. He'd been a hard man. A nightmare to work for, actually, and suddenly cynical of her motives. They'd had an extremely rare disagreement when she told him—rare because, until then, Scarlett had made a career of acting on his command.

You went behind my back, he had accused her.

I told them you were dying because they deserved to know.

She had stood by that decision even though he'd been angry at her for it.

Surprisingly, her pushback had earned his grudging respect, proving her tough enough in his eyes to take control of his holdings. He'd added her baby to his will, too, ensuring Javiero's child would inherit the half of his fortune that Javiero had declined.

And life altering as this pregnancy was proving to be, she didn't regret it. She patted her swollen belly, excited to meet him or her.

Just. Not. Today.

Where was Kiara?

Into her ruminations a strange sensation accosted her. A faint, dull ache in her lower back grew more insistent. Tension wrapped outward until it squeezed across her middle.

A contraction?

Well, duh. Of course that was what was happening, but, *come on*! She nearly pounded her fist against the wall in frustration.

What had she thought, though? That she would still go into that meeting, bare as a Scotsman under her skirt while she looked her baby's father in the eye and admitted...

She hung her head in her hands and bit back a whimper.

The main door opened. She lifted her head, relief washing over her. As she started to call out, however, she realized the person she could see through the crack in the door didn't have Kiara's voluptuous figure or curly black hair.

Oh, dear Lord. That slender woman in a bone-colored skirt suit was Paloma Rodriguez, Javiero's mother.

Scarlett never swore, but she tilted her head back and mouthed a number of really filthy words at the ceiling. She texted Kiara again, suspecting Kiara had silenced her phone for the meeting.

Javiero's mother was smoothing her hair, checking her makeup, unconsciously betraying how important it was that she appear flawless to the rest of the people in that boardroom, most particularly her rival for a dead man's affections.

Scarlett had to make a split-second decision. No matter how this day played out, Javiero would finally learn she was having his baby. She wanted him to hear it from her.

As his mother started to leave, Scarlett forced herself to speak though she could hear the quaver in her voice. "Señora Rodriguez? It's me, Scarlett."

Paloma's footsteps paused, and she said with guarded surprise, "Yes?"

"Is Javiero waiting for you in the corridor?"

"Yes."

"I'd like to speak with him. In private. In…um…here."

Global warming ended and the modern ice age arrived in one glacial word. "Why?"

Shifting to open the door was awkward, given her full-term belly. Scarlett wrestled herself around it and watched Paloma's gaze drop to her middle. Her eyes nearly fell out of her head.

"I need to speak to him," Scarlett said as another contraction looped around her abdomen and squeezed a fresh gasp from her lungs.

Javiero Rodriguez was unfit to be in public, not physically and not mentally.

He'd showered, but he was unshaven and should have gone to his barber before leaving Madrid. He had blown off the nicety, which wasn't like him. For most of his thirty-three years, he had passionately adhered to tradition and expectation. He'd had a family dynasty to restore, his mother's reputation to repair and his own superiority to assert.

He had achieved all those things and more, becoming a dominant force in global financial markets and one of the world's most eligible bachelors. He was known to be charming and intelligent, and an excellent dancer who dressed impeccably well.

Despite all that, a sense of satisfaction had always eluded him.

Javiero had come to accept this vague discontent as just life. Happily-ever-after was, as anyone with a brain in his head could deduce, a fairy tale. He had experienced the bleakness of financial anxiety and the bitterness of powerlessness. He'd had a father who belittled him and abused his trust, one who didn't so much as offer a shovel to help him dig himself out of the hole he'd been shoved into. He had tasted grief when the grandfather he'd revered had passed away. All of that had taught him ennui was the best one could hope for.

World-weariness was a luxury he no longer enjoyed, however. Three weeks ago, he had nearly died. He had lost an eye and was left with scars that would be with him forever. He looked like and felt like a monster.

As he ran a frustrated hand through his hair, his fingertips reflexively lifted in repulsion from the tender line where his scalp had been sewn back on. He shouldn't be inflicting his gruesome self on helpless receptionists and unsuspecting coffee-fetchers. It was a cruelty.

His mother needed reinforcement, though. She had stood by him when nearly everyone else was giving him a wide berth. His uncles and cousins, people he financially supported, were taking one look and keeping their children away. His *ex*-fiancée, whose idiotic idea of being interesting was to keep an exotic pet menagerie, had dropped him like a hot potato once she'd seen the damage.

Not that he was stung other than in his ego by her rejection. Their proposed marriage had been an effort to *rescue* his pride. He saw that now and it only made his foul, obdurate mood worse. What a pathetic fool he was.

Grim malevolence was his companion now. It had become as entrenched in him as the deep grooves carved into his face and body. It clouded around him like a cologne gone off. It had sunk into his bones with the insidiousness of a virus or a spell, making his joints stiff and his heart a lump of concrete.

Staring with one eye down at the streets of Athens, a city and country he had sworn never to set foot in again, he dreamed only of burning this whole place down.

Your family stands to inherit a significant portion of the estate, his father's lawyer had said. *All parties must be present at the reading of the will for dispersal to move forward.*

Javiero didn't want any of his father's money. He didn't want to be here in his father's office tower and couldn't stand the idea of listening to yet another version of his father's idea of what was fair.

For his mother's sake, and what she stood to gain, he had relented. She had been treated horribly by Nikolai Mylonas and deserved compensation. If Javiero's presence could help her finally gain what should have rightfully been hers, so be it. Here he was.

He didn't have it in him to muster pretty manners, though. His already thin patience was tested by the prospect of listening to his mother chase principles his father had never possessed. She would argue one more time that *her* son was Niko's *legitimate* heir and *Javiero* was legally entitled to everything.

Then he would have to listen to his father's onetime and always scheming mistress, Evelina, arguing that his half brother, Val, was two days older than Javiero, and therefore all the money should go to them.

Mine, mine, mine.

The sickening refrain continued despite the instrument being dead.

Javiero wished the damned jaguar had finished him off. He really did.

As for Scarlett…? His grim mood skipped in and out of its channel, sparking and grinding at the mere thought of her.

She had called once while Javiero was in hospital. *Once.* On behalf of his dying father. His mother had informed her that Javiero would survive, and that had been all Scarlett had needed to hear. Not another word, no card or flowers. Nothing.

Why did that bother him? Until the last time he'd seen her, she had always been a very businesslike and unflappable PA. Almost pathological in her devotion to his father. She would turn up in one of her pencil skirts, blond hair gathered at her nape, delicate features flawlessly accented with natural tones, and she would irritate the hell out of him with her one-track agenda.

Your father wants me to inform you that he's aware you're behind the hostile takeover in Germany. He is willing to give you control of his entire operation if you come back to Athens and run it.

No.

Or, *Evelina has made a specific request for funds. Niko has granted it. This is your mother's equivalent amount. If you would like to speak to him about—*

No.

And then that final meeting. *Your father has run out of treatment options. He is unlikely to survive the year. Now would be the time to come see him.*

No.

She had finally cracked and it had been fascinating.

She hadn't understood how he couldn't care one single rat's behind about his father or his father's money.

You don't want what is rightfully yours? What if it all goes to Val?

That had caught his attention. If it was up to Javiero, Val could have every last cursed euro, but his mother would be devastated. *Was* Niko planning to leave it all to Val?

No, Scarlett had assured him, but that hadn't been the whole truth. *Come and see him*, she had insisted, looking ready to take him by the ear to accomplish it. He hadn't understood what had driven her so vehemently. It wasn't love for his father. She had never said a harsh word about Niko, but she'd never said a kind one, either.

There had been a mystery there—Javiero had felt it— but he had refused all the same, annoyed that she was instilling a genuine temptation in him to solve it. He wanted to go with her when he had sworn nothing would ever induce him to see his father or visit that island again for any reason.

He'd sensed a finality to her visit, though. There'd been a futility in her that told him he wouldn't see her again after this. It had added a layer of desperation to their power struggle. The tension had become sexual and had burst into a passionate encounter that had left him reeling.

But only him, it seemed. He had continued to think about her months later. She had left before the dinner hour, choosing to go back to work for a man Javiero hated with every fiber of his being rather than remain with her new lover.

That had been before he looked like hell. Would she be repulsed by his injuries when she saw him? Indifferent?

Why should he care what she thought?

He didn't. But he entertained a small, malicious fantasy where he pointed out his disfigurement was only physical. Scarlett had *character* flaws.

"Javiero." His mother's voice behind him held such heightened emotion that the hair lifted on the back of his neck. Shock and urgency and something bordering on triumph?

He swung from the window in the small sitting area and almost had to reach for the back of a sofa to catch his balance. He was still getting used to his lack of depth perception.

His mother had insisted on rechecking her impeccable appearance. Her black hair was still rolled into its customary bun, but she was pale beneath her makeup. Agitation seemed to grip her while there was a glow of avaricious excitement in her blue-green eyes.

"Go in there." She nodded toward the door to the ladies' room.

Javiero lifted his brows and felt the pull under his eye patch against scar tissue that hadn't fully healed.

"Is there a problem? I'll call maintenance." That came from Nigel, the assistant who had met them at the south entrance. He had taken one aghast look at Javiero's face and had kept his attention on Paloma ever since.

"No," his mother said firmly. She stepped aside and waved at the door, prompting. "Javiero."

With a snarl of impatience, he strode past his mother and shoved into the women's toilet, halting abruptly at the sight of Scarlett turning from the sink.

Distantly he heard the door drift closed behind him while he took in her appearance. Her blond hair was gathered at her nape, her face was rounder, her blouse untucked and her tailored jacket open to allow for—

He cocked his head, widening his one eye, not sure he was seeing this correctly.

He yanked his gaze back to her face. Her expression was frozen in horror as she took in his shaggy hair and eye patch and gashed face poorly hidden by an untrimmed beard.

The word *pregnant* landed in a pool of comprehension deep in his brain, sending a tidal wave of shock through his entire psyche.

Scarlett dropped her phone with a clatter.

She had been trying to call Kiara. Now she was taking in the livid claw marks across Javiero's face, each pocked on either side with the pinpricks of recently removed stitches. His dark brown hair was longer than she'd ever seen it, perhaps gelled back from the widow's peak at some point this morning, but it was mussed and held a jagged part. He wore a black eye patch like a pirate, its narrow band cutting a thin stripe across his temple and into his hair.

Maybe that's why his features looked as though they had been set askew? His mouth was…not right. His upper lip was uneven and the claw marks drew lines through his unkempt stubble all the way down into his neck.

That was dangerously close to his jugular! Dear God, he had nearly been killed.

She grasped at the edge of the sink, trying to stay on her feet while she grew so light-headed at the thought of him dying that she feared she would faint.

The ravages of his attack weren't what made him look

so forbidding and grim, though, she computed through her haze of panic and anguish. No. The contemptuous glare in his one eye was for her. For *this*.

He flicked another outraged glance at her middle.

"I thought we were meeting in the boardroom." His voice sounded gravelly. Damaged as well? Or was that simply his true feelings toward her now? Deadly and completely devoid of any of the sensual admiration she'd sometimes heard in his tone.

Not that he'd ever been particularly warm toward her. He'd been aloof, indifferent, irritated, impatient, explosively passionate. Generous in the giving of pleasure. Of compliments. Then cold as she left. Disapproving. Malevolent.

Damningly silent.

And now he was…what? Ignoring that she was as big as a barn?

Her arteries were on fire with straight adrenaline, her heart pounding and her brain spinning with the way she was having to switch gears so fast. Her eyes were hot and her throat tight. Everything in her wanted to scream *Help me*, but she'd been in enough tight spots to know this was all on her. Everything was always on her. She fought to keep her head and get through the next few minutes before she moved on to the next challenge.

Which was just a tiny trial called *childbirth*, but she would worry about that when she got to the hospital.

As the tingle of a fresh contraction began to pang in her lower back, she tightened her grip on the edge of the sink and gritted her teeth, trying to ignore the coming pain and hang on to what dregs of dignity she had left.

"I'm in labor," she said tightly. "It's yours."

Fresh shock flickered over his scarred face, and his

gaze dropped to her middle again. "I'm supposed to believe that?"

"My water broke. It's a textbook sign."

"You know what I mean." His aggressive stance didn't soften, but a tiny shadow flickered in his eye as he watched her draw in a long breath.

She was trying to bear the growing intensity of her contractions without a grimace, but it wasn't working.

"Is it my father's?"

"No!" She should have expected that, she supposed. Pretty much everyone believed she was more than Niko's long-suffering PA. She closed her eyes, wincing in both physical and emotional anguish as the pain peaked. "I don't have time for a lot of explanations." She tried for calm when her voice was still tight from the fading contraction. "Whether you believe this baby is yours by my word or after a DNA test doesn't matter." It mattered. She hated that he was so skeptical of her. It ground what little self-esteem she possessed well into the dust. "I have to go to the hospital, but I wanted to be the one to tell you that this is your baby. That's what you would have learned in today's meeting, along with the fact that…"

He would never forgive her. She had known it even as she was staring at the positive test. Even as she was telling Niko and watching his eyes narrow with calculation. Even as she had sat in meetings that secured her baby's future and her own.

Even before she told Javiero what Niko had done with his will, she could see stiff resistance taking hold in Javiero's expression. He would never forgive her for any of this, including abiding by Niko's wish that she hide her entire pregnancy from him. She hadn't wanted to, but Niko had been dying at the time. She had agreed to delay telling Javiero because revealing her pregnancy would have caused the sort of war that Niko wouldn't have been able to handle in his weakened condition. She had known that everything would come out now, after his death, anyway.

So what was one more secret kept for nearly three years?

It was *one more*. When it came to Niko's relationship with his two sons and the two women who had birthed them, every misdeed was a blow against someone. Getting between them meant getting knocked around herself.

It was going to hurt no matter what, so she waded in.

"You won't inherit anything," she said bluntly. "Exactly as you wished. Instead, Niko has split his fortune equally between his grandchildren."

"Grandchildren." It was strange to see his brows rise unevenly, one broken by the claw mark, the other still perfect and endearingly familiar. "Plural."

"Yes. He has a granddaughter. Aurelia." Who was adorable, not that Scarlett could say so. "She's Val's."

Javiero's gaze turned icy at the mention of his half-brother. "Since when does Val have a daughter?"

"Since her mother, Kiara, gave birth to her two years ago. They've been living on the island with us since the middle of her pregnancy."

"That's not possible." Javiero spoke with the cynical confidence of a lifetime of dealing with his father's other family. "Evelina would have used a baby to influence Dad. You haven't shown up with any equal opportunity checks for Mother."

"Evelina doesn't know about Aurelia." Scarlett didn't bother explaining how Evelina had dropped the rattle and Niko had picked it up. "Val doesn't know, either. Niko didn't want any of you to know. It would have caused fresh battles and he was too sick to weather them. Evelina and Paloma will each receive one million euros and the rest goes to Aurelia and…" She set her hand on her belly, willing the tingle in her back not to manifest into a fresh contraction.

"Well, isn't that darling," Javiero bit out. "He continues to treat us so *fairly* that he kept our own children from us and burdens them equally with his damnable fortune. No wonder Mother looked so thrilled when she walked out of here. Did you tell her Val's kid is getting half and she's only getting one million?"

"No." She struggled to hold his venomous glare.

"Coward," he pronounced, but laughed harshly and shook his head. "More of his stupid, stupid games, right to the bitter end! And you're still helping him." He pointed in accusation. "You knew all of this when you came to Madrid that day. *That* day."

He pointed at her middle. His contempt was a knife to her heart, and despair threatened to encase her. She shoved it away.

"I don't have time to justify his actions or mine." She teared up as she said it though, doubting he would ever see her side. He hated her. She could taste it on the air. "I have to go to the hospital."

She glanced at her phone on the floor, face down and possibly cracked, definitely a million miles away when she could hardly breathe let alone touch her toes.

"Kiara is my birth coach. Will you get her for me? She's not answering my texts."

"The mother of Val's baby is your birth coach?"

His derisive tone got her back up. She might not have much moral high ground to stand on, but she would die on this particular mound.

"Don't disparage either of them. Aurelia is an innocent child and Kiara is the best friend I've ever had." Her only friend, really. Better than a sister because they'd chosen each other. "Hate Niko and Val if you want to, but don't you dare attack my friend and her child."

Javiero's hand smacked on to the marble that surrounded the sink, making her jump. He leaned into her space, looming like a terrifying raptor as he thrust his marred face up close to hers.

"Look me in the eye, Scarlett." His breath was dragon fire against her cheek. "Is that my baby?"

His eyes had always been so fascinating to her, sea green with flecks of blue. Shifting and moody. So beautiful.

Now there was only one. She'd been in agony since she'd learned the extent of his injuries, desperate to go to him. If he hadn't survived…

She pushed back desolation and bit her trembling lips, huskily saying, "It's yours."

He snorted with skepticism and shoved to straighten away from her, his retreat so full of contempt it felt as though he took a layer of her skin with him.

"I'll give you the benefit of the doubt, but the DNA test had better prove that baby is mine. And if that is my child, there is no way it will start its life defiled by that misbegotten half brother of mine. *I'll* take you to the hospital. Let's go."

CHAPTER TWO

"I'M SORRY I didn't come to the hospital after the attack," Scarlett said in a low voice when they were in the back of his car.

Mentally, Javiero was in the pen, her pregnancy having struck him as unpredictably as that big cat, leaving him wrestling under the bite of words like *his*, trying to evade the claws of *The money goes to...*

As her apology penetrated, he bristled and sat straighter, refusing to let her see how much her indifference had stung. He shouldn't have cared either way.

"Why would you?" he asked distantly. He had asked her to stay and she'd made her choice, turning their torrid encounter into a one-afternoon stand. He knew how those worked.

And he hadn't been fit company in hospital any more than he was today. That hadn't stopped his mother from showing up every day, but as her only child—and her only link to his father's fortune—Javiero had no illusions about the breadth of her maternal concern. Paloma was no Evelina Casale when it came to unadulterated greed; nor was she willing to let go of something she believed wholeheartedly belonged to her.

Paloma had gone to her hotel in a huff after they emerged from the ladies' room and told her the terms of the will. She'd been *very* unimpressed by her entitlement to one million euros. It was nothing after all these years, but Javiero supported her financially. She wouldn't go without. Any incidental funds she received from Niko were hers to throw away on an impulse trip to the Riviera or a vanity purchase in Paris. She could do the same with today's top-up.

"Your father was extremely ill when I heard," Scarlett continued in that subdued voice, making it impossible for him to remain detached—not that he'd ever exceled at ignoring her. "I was keeping everything running in his stead and coordinating all his care workers."

"You didn't have time. I understand." He kept his tone arid and emotionless yet conveyed how pathetic he found her excuses to be.

She flinched.

Good. He wasn't about to sympathize or forgive her choice to continue working for a tyrant.

"And I was—" he heard her swallow "—showing."

"You're something else," he muttered on a cynical laugh. "You want me to empathize with what a difficult position you were in? Because coming to the hospital would have revealed to me that you were carrying my child?" He'd been at his absolute lowest! Today wasn't much better. "Did you get pregnant on purpose?" It was the one question that kept pounding behind his brow. "To deliberately try to get your hands on his money?"

"If that's all I wanted, I could have slept with Val," she threw at him.

"Have you?" He would kill him. He really would.

"*No*. And Niko's money isn't coming to me. I'm entitled to an allowance to raise the baby in suitable comfort and I earn a salary for managing Niko's estate, but the bulk will be held in trust for—"

Her mouth tightened, and she sucked in a great breath, holding it.

Concern breached his wall of anger as he watched the color in her cheeks fade. Perspiration appeared in a sheen on her upper lip.

"Aren't you supposed to breathe or something?" he asked gruffly. That's all he knew from the few programs he'd happened across that had featured a birthing scene. Usually it was a comedy that played the whole thing as a roaring joke.

She flashed him a glare of outrage, but after a moment her breath hissed out and her tension began to ease.

"You refused to see your own father," she bit out. "How would I know your feelings on becoming one?"

"Ask," he muttered, accosted by too many emotions to identify.

Did he feel guilty at not going to see his father? Not at all. Niko had cost him too much of his youth. All of it. Not just the innocence of childhood or the hardship his extended family had suffered after his mother divorced Niko, either. There had been the engineered conflicts with Val and the responsibilities he'd had to shoulder while watching his grandfather fail. The bleakness of a mother who was embittered and broken, incapable of being a real mother.

Now Niko had denied him his own *child*.

Javiero wanted to roar out his anger. He was furious that Scarlett had been by Niko's side all these months. Niko should have died alone, the manipulative son of a bitch.

They arrived at the hospital. His driver had called ahead, and a nurse was waiting with a wheelchair.

The nurse glanced at him with startled apprehension as he stepped from the car, a reaction he was getting used to, but it still made him want to snarl. He turned his back on her as he leaned in to help Scarlett shift across and out.

Bureaucracy ensued. Questions were asked and forms completed. Nurses took Scarlett's blood pressure and temperature, and helped her change into a hospital gown.

It gave him time to absorb that he was about to become a father. He trusted Scarlett on that with instinctive certainty. She was too distraught to scheme. Besides, the timing worked, and his father wouldn't have named her baby his heir if he hadn't been convinced that baby was his blood.

With acceptance of that came an avalanche of duty and anticipated sacrifice, the weight of it so heavy and voluminous that Javiero's chest felt tight. He didn't have room in his life for more. Time wasn't a commodity in a well he could draw on when he needed more. How was he supposed to fit child rearing into his already tightly packed days? The physiotherapy after his attack was a challenging addition to his calendar.

And what did he know of fathering? He spent the occasional hour with children of his cousins and other relatives, but they had proper, decent parents to go home to. The only example he'd had, an acrimonious mother and a domineering father, would have him breaking his child's spirit before it could talk. Damn that old man and his continued manipulations!

Niko must have known what sort of hornet's nest he was building by leaving his money to his grandchildren, but when had Nikolai Mylonas cared one iota for the suffering he caused? Javiero's grandfather had been on the ropes, barely hanging on to his properties in Spain when he had brokered the marriage of his eldest daughter to Niko. Paloma had been young and naive and beautiful, and determined to save her family.

Niko, however, hadn't given up his mistress while they'd

been engaged. In fact, he'd kept seeing Evelina right up until the night before his wedding. He hadn't seemed terribly concerned about birth control either, trusting Evelina's attachment to her modeling career to keep her from getting pregnant.

Evelina had conceived Val with malice aforethought and turned up pregnant with her hand out as Paloma was testing positive with Javiero.

"You were setting me up for the same nightmare I grew up in," he accused Scarlett, when she was settled on the bed and the nurse had left them alone. "Were you going to wait until I was *married* before you told me I had a child on the way?"

"Your wedding wasn't scheduled until next year," she mumbled, throwing off the blanket and swinging her legs to the edge of the bed. "Niko asked me to wait until he'd passed before I told you. It was essentially a dying wish and he needed me there, running things while he declined. He knew you'd insist I leave if you found out. I knew he would be gone sooner than later so I did as he asked." She tried to keep her gown from riding up while her foot searched blindly for a slipper.

"Where are you going?"

"I want my phone. Kiara is probably worried."

"Screw Kiara." But he fetched Scarlett's handbag from the cupboard, waited while she rummaged in it and returned it after she'd retrieved her phone.

She glanced at the screen and quickly dropped it to the mattress as her expression crumpled. She groaned with suffering, doubling forward over the ball of her belly.

Despite his foul mood, his heart lurched in alarm.

"Should I get the nurse?" He moved to open the door, prepared to yell the place down.

"She won't do anything. I said I want to deliver naturally. She said this is *normal*," she groaned, her knuckles sticking out like broken teeth as she gripped the sheet beneath her.

This didn't look very damned normal to him. He hovered in the doorway feeling uncharacteristically useless.

"Why the hell would you want to put up with that? Take something."

After a moment, her tension dissipated. She released a pent-up breath with a few pants, but she was trembling and licking her dry lips.

"Kiara delivered naturally." She rattled a paper cup and shook an ice chip into her mouth, holding it between her teeth as she spoke around it. "I'm sure I'll be fine."

Even so, her hands bracketed her belly as though trying to keep it from splitting while a keening noise emanated from her throat.

The pain that gripped her was so visceral he felt it twist through him. He stood there in empathic torment, paralyzed by the tension of watching her expression flex in agony, waiting for it to ease. He didn't breathe again until she did.

"I don't understand how this is happening," he muttered, referring to the entire event. Not in his wildest dreams had he seen this coming when he had climbed out of bed this morning.

She shot him an incredulous look and pushed her hair off her face. "You didn't use protection. Not every time. You know you didn't."

That *last* time.

Stay, he had ordered. Pleaded, maybe. Either way, he hadn't wanted her to go back to his father, and she had worn a look just as conflicted as the one on her face right now.

I can't.

Their final kiss had turned into something that had nearly pulled the soul from his body. She'd moved her clothing aside. He'd wound up thrusting into her against the wall of his entryway.

He'd been so shaken by the experience he'd still been hot under the collar half a year later, loosening his tie as he overlooked the cat pen at his fiancée's home, hoping the breeze would clear his head of Scarlett. The jaguar had leaped at his tie and dragged him into a fight for his life.

"I didn't mean to sleep with you," she said in a subdued voice. "Niko took a terrible turn when I got back. Things were very unsettled, and I didn't even think about repercussions until I was facing a positive test."

He dragged his mind back from the brink of death to Scarlett on the edge of the bed. She looked incredibly fragile, as though she hugged a cushion rather than his unborn child against her middle.

"Why did you come to me at all? You had to know I wasn't interested in seeing him."

Guilt creased her expression. "I knew Niko planned to leave everything to Aurelia. I was sworn not to tell anyone about her, but if you had come to the island, you would have met them and learned everything."

"Seems a dirty trick on Kiara. I thought she was your friend."

"She *is*. And I only wanted to give you the chance to learn what he planned so you could make an informed decision about rejecting his money. My conscience demanded I do that much! What happened between us was completely unexpected."

"It was *unexpected*?" he scoffed.

The sexual tension between them had simmered for years. He had ended a longtime relationship immediately after the first time he'd met her, convinced he would sleep with Scarlett by the end of that week. He'd been too proud to chase her, though, and she'd been tied too tightly to Niko to visit him more than once or twice a year. Each time she had left a wake of what-ifs until that last time when their chemistry had burst into flames.

Then she had *still* gone back to Niko.

"Ask yourself how you would be feeling right now if everything was going to Val's daughter," she challenged softly.

"I'd feel great." But his mother would have had a stroke. Even so, he said, "Don't pretend you did me a favor, Scarlett. You're as bad as he is, making choices for people that *change lives*."

"I'm being punished for my poor judgment, trust me," she choked. "Maybe if you're lucky, I won't survive, and you can ride your high horse forever."

"Too far," he snarled, appalled she would think he wanted her to die. He wasn't enjoying her suffering. He sure as hell didn't want anything tragic to happen to her or his unborn child.

Her phone rang.

"Kiara," she said as she answered with shaking hands. "I'm in labor, what do you think? How did you *do* this?" That might have been an effort to make light, but her arm was trembling as though the phone was too heavy for her to hold to her ear. Her voice didn't disguise her fretfulness as she added an urgent, "No, wait."

She glanced at him, doubt and distress clouding her blue eyes along with a question.

"Javiero wants to stay with me."

He did. He stepped closer without hesitation, as if he could physically oust anyone from trying to get between them. He wasn't sure where that compulsion came from. So far this had been a hellish reunion for both of them and it didn't promise to get better, but this was exactly where he would stay until his baby was born.

Then he didn't know what he would do.

He was close enough to hear the woman's voice ask, "What do *you* want?"

"I don't *know*." Scarlett rubbed at the crinkle of anguish between her brows. "I had to tell him everything. Now he thinks you shouldn't be here. Because of Val." She sounded bereft. Anxious and deeply vulnerable and... Was she *crying*?

Scarlett was tough as nails. She argued with reason, stuck to her guns and kept her cool. That was why he had always found her so infuriating. And compelling.

The sight of a tear leaking from the corner of her eye down her cheek snapped his roiling emotions into a new pattern, one that drew her firmly behind the shield of protectiveness he'd been wielding against her.

The flip of mind-set happened so fast it made him dizzy, but one thought crystalized—whatever else was going on between them had to wait. Right now, Scarlett was in genuine distress.

He touched her bare knee to get her attention. She apprehensively met his gaze and he held it. He shoved all his anger and resentment into compartments behind his breastbone and deep in the back of his throat. He conveyed confidence he had no right to because he had no idea what they were in for, but here he was and here he would stay.

A fraction of her tension eased, and her mouth trembled while the woman's voice softened. He only caught the gist that Kiara was promising to book into a nearby hotel. She said that Scarlett should call her if she wanted her.

"Thank you," Scarlett said in a quavering voice. "I'm a wreck and— Oh, here comes another one."

He gently took the phone. "Breathe?" he suggested gently.

"I *am* breathing." She sounded petulant. Persecuted. "What do you know about it? Oh, my God, I *hate* you for doing this to me."

That stung, but he ended her call and set the phone aside. Then he stepped between her knees and took her weight as much as he could while she pinched his biceps in biting fists and pressed her forehead into his shoulder.

He rubbed her back, trying to ease the rigidity in her.

After a full minute, she slumped weakly against him. Her hands still clung to his sleeves and her head rested against his heartbeat. Her tears dampened the front of his shirt.

"We're not going to fight anymore," he promised as he continued to rub her back. "Not right now. Our baby won't be born into a war zone the way I was."

As far as Scarlett knew, Niko hadn't been present for the birth of either of his sons. She hadn't expected Javiero to be here for this. She probably should have drawn back when the pain passed, but she stayed leaning on him. It felt too good to be held by him.

"I'm scared," she admitted. Terrified, more like. "I was Kiara's birth coach and thought that meant I knew what to expect. I convinced myself it would be different for me. I would handle it better because I've had more practice at keeping a stiff upper lip. She's kinder and softer in all the right ways, but I'm starting to think she's the bravest, strongest person I've ever met."

He continued the soothing run of his hand up and down her back. It felt really nice, but as she allowed herself to remember Aurelia's arrival she knew it was only fair to let him off the hook. Witnessing a birth was pretty over-whelming.

"Kiara said she would come if I need her. You don't have to stay if you don't want to."

"I want to." His tone was firm and sure. He didn't ask if she wanted him there.

She did. It didn't make sense. Their relationship had been stoic, if laden with undercurrents. Then it had been volatile and intimate. Then radio silence while she'd been swimming in a miasma of mixed emotions for months. All of that had imploded in the last few hours, tearing her up while she headed inexorably toward the massive event that was taking over her body and her life.

In this very moment, however, they occupied a serene pool of affinity. She sniffed, not knowing how to handle his tenderness.

If anything happened… Well, she didn't want to think of that. She was just glad he was willing to stay.

"I should have asked Kiara how it went with Val," she murmured to distract herself.

A reflexive tightening in Javiero's body rejected his half brother's name.

"Tell me what I can do to help. Do you like when I rub your back?"

He was changing the subject and maybe that was a good thing. She nodded against his chest. Her hair was pulling at her scalp and falling apart, but when she reached to pull out the pins, he gently set her arms around his rib cage and removed the pins himself, pausing when a new bout of pain arrived.

"Don't be afraid of it," he murmured. "That's what I learned. Fighting pain makes it worse. When you accept it and let yourself feel it, you discover you can bear it."

Easy to say, but she tried not to tense up or worry about

anything beyond taking slow, measured breaths as she waited for the contraction to subside. It helped a little.

"Okay?" he asked when she was breathing normally again.

She nodded and he resumed taking pins from her hair, then combed his fingers through the strands, making a soothing noise as he massaged her scalp.

Time passed in a blur after that. She paced and had a shower and paced some more. She sat and knelt and stood and swore. She cried and said awful things to him about his libido and the patriarchy and that Niko's money wasn't even close to being worth what she was going through so how dare he accuse her of wanting a penny of it.

Javiero patiently endured her vitriol, repeating stupid platitudes the nurse had given him to say like, "You're doing so good. I'm so proud of you. I'm here for you."

"That's a lie," she said at one point, elbows on the edge of her bed, his palm making circles on her lower back. "No one has ever been here for me. Not when it counted. *No one.*"

Even Kiara had abandoned her—which wasn't fair since she had told her to stay away. Maybe she had pushed Kiara away so she wouldn't risk being disappointed by the one friend she truly cherished. She could test that friendship—pick up her phone right now and beg Kiara to come—but Kiara couldn't do anything to help her. Not really.

No one could.

Which was pretty much the way her entire life had gone. Her parents and her schoolteachers and social services had all let her down. She had always had to save herself along with everyone else. Maybe that had meant pledging undying allegiance to Niko, who had, at least, kept his promises. And if she hadn't worked for him, she wouldn't have met Javiero. Did he realize that?

Maybe he did and it was one more reason he reviled Niko. And her.

Because he might be here now, but he wasn't here for *her*. He was here for the child she carried. When it came down to it, she was utterly alone in this world. People surrounded her and acted like they cared, but she was the one who suffered and labored and pushed and cried.

Finally, even her baby left her.

For one long moment, she was weightless and numb and wondered if she even existed.

Then a warm, damp weight settled on her chest. He was tiny and flushed and so helpless she was flooded with the need to shelter and comfort and nurture him. His eyes squinted open once before he clenched them shut and made an unhappy squawk. It was laughable the way his own noise seemed to surprise him.

She didn't care that he was one more person who would rely on her instead of the other way around. She was enraptured. Instantly, utterly, completely in love.

She lifted her gaze to Javiero's gleaming eye and breathed, "Thank you."

CHAPTER THREE

JAVIERO HAD WRESTLED an overgrown house cat for less than five minutes until it had been lured away by a fresh cut of meat. His two weeks and four surgeries in the hospital had been acutely painful, but the morphine drip had ensured he slept through most of it.

Scarlett had struggled in agony, her final hour of pushing intense and fearsome to witness. He'd never felt so helpless in his life or so humbled. Reverence gripped him as he took in the dazzlingly tender light in her eyes and her smile of serene joy.

"You were incredible," he told her as a nurse took their son to measure and swaddle him. Javiero carefully brushed away the tendrils of hair stuck to her temples. Nothing in his life had prepared him for such an internal upheaval.

Shadows came into the dreamy blue of her eyes. Her mouth trembled. "I know you're still angry."

"I am." He wouldn't lie to her. "But all that matters right now is that you and our son have come through this alive and well. I didn't expect to be a father when I woke up this morning, but I'm grateful, Scarlett." The word wasn't big enough for the swell of thankfulness in him. He was incredulous and dumbfounded and deeply moved.

"I love him so much and we've only just met." Her wet lashes blinked as she looked for him, the sweetest smile trembling on her lips. Javiero wanted to set his own there to steady them.

"Does he have a name?" the nurse asked.

"I thought Locke for a boy," Scarlett said tentatively. "But you can think on it." Her eyelids blinked heavily. "I need to tell Kiara. She'll be anxious."

"I'll do it," he promised, continuing the rhythmic caress of his thumb across her brow, bemused that she could think of anything beyond this moment. "You should rest."

"I haven't slept properly in months," she admitted on a yawn. "Will you wake me if he needs me?"

"Of course."

"Thank you." Her voice was fading and her eyes stayed closed on the next blink. With a small sigh, she drifted into sleep.

He straightened, and the nurse handed him the bundle that was more blanket than baby, far lighter than Javiero expected, and such a punch in his chest he had to sit down to absorb it.

The lens through which he had viewed his life had completely inverted. He was no longer a son with a father, but a father with a son. He was overcome with pride, and also responsibility and an unmistakable fear. One day this infant, who was at this moment unmarred by life, could turn on him with abhorrence and tell him to go to hell, the way he had done with Niko.

I will do better, Javiero swore compulsively even though he wasn't sure what "better" would look like. He had only ever thought of himself as a parent in the vaguest of "someday" terms, not the immediacy of *every day.*

His psyche leaped on the words. He wanted *every day* with his son.

He wouldn't be a father in name only, as Niko had been. An imposing stranger who enforced a handful of visits a year, someone who provoked fear and insecurity, resentment and rebellion. He would not fill his son's ears with disparagements of his mother.

Javiero moved his gaze from the eyelashes against a delicate pink cheek to the longer, blond lashes on Scarlett.

It seemed impossible that the two of them had made this fragile miniature person. Oh, he remembered every second of the act. A stir of the infuriating attraction he'd always felt toward her teased him even now, calling up wispy memories of a lush breast in his hand and the incredible sensation of sliding into her heat. She had smelled of sunshine and crushed flower petals and had held back nothing.

At the time, it had seemed so deliciously spontaneous yet inevitable.

Given his father's behavior, Javiero had always guarded against letting his nether regions take control. Scarlett had tested his resolve from their first meeting.

He wasn't sure what had driven that depth of attraction. Her classic beauty, obviously, but she had worked for his father. He'd wanted to shoot the messenger as badly as he'd wanted to seduce her. He'd sent a message to his father by barely giving her the time of day, but he'd always had a sense of possibility where she was concerned, certain she would one day turn her back on Niko and come to him.

There'd been something in her self-possessed demeanor that had intrigued him. She wasn't a doormat. Hell, no. From the first moment, he had seen she was intelligent and witty and capable of withstanding high stress. She hadn't let him or his father's complicated love life get under her skin.

Maybe that had been the draw. Val and the war between their mothers had always been a stain that Javiero couldn't erase, yet Scarlett had disregarded it. Or regarded it as normal?

Either way, the far more interesting reaction was her betraying awareness of him. She'd done her best to hide it, but he'd seen it in a lingering look or a poorly disguised blush.

He had fought his own sexual tension, suspicious of her even then. When he had ultimately lost that battle, it had been a deeply humbling experience. Not only had he succumbed to his primal instincts and discovered his perfect sexual match, she had left him afterward. *For his father.*

He'd been ripe with self-disgust then, angry with himself for giving her the upper hand.

He had followed his mother's suggestion that he propose to Regina as a means of moving on from Scarlett. To firmly closing off roads back to the madness he'd shared with her.

Yet here he was with her, holding the baby they'd made that day.

The baby she had kept secret out of loyalty to a man he despised—possibly to gain control of that man's fortune.

On the other hand, her anxiety through her labor had been for the safe delivery of their baby. Her maternal connection to their son was indisputable. They would both want "every day," so how did he proceed?

His mind leaped to marriage, the historically presumptive course of action when a couple shared a child. His mother had been after him to provide an heir and here the boy was. Did Javiero *need* to marry?

His libido rushed to vote in favor of every night with Scarlett, but he made himself ignore the tantalizing thought and consider the idea more dispassionately. Marriage came with no guarantee of success. His mother had married Niko in good faith and dutifully conceived Javiero, only to have Evelina emerge pregnant as well. Paloma had been so humiliated she had divorced Niko. The ensuing hostilities and financial hardship had become Javiero's blighted childhood.

Javiero had always wondered how different his life might have been if he'd had united parents who eschewed others for the sake of providing a stable foundation for their offspring. Could he provide that for his son? Javiero would honor his vows if he was legally bound to Scarlett, and he experienced a possessive thrill at the idea of his ring on her finger—one he shied away from examining too closely.

He couldn't trust her, he reminded himself. The deep knot of betrayed fury that he'd ignored while she'd been writhing in labor tightened into a harder lump in the pit of his belly, but his acrimony was as much reason to marry her as not, he rationalized. Keep your enemies close, and all that.

One way or another, he decided, as he transferred his gaze from her innocent-looking face to the tiny blameless one peeking from the swaddle, they were coming home with him.

"Sir?" A nurse entered the private room and spoke softly, noting with a glance that Scarlett was fast asleep. "There's an inquiry from a woman downstairs. A friend of Miss Walker's." She glanced at a pink slip in her hand. "Kiara O'Neill. She's wondering if there's news. May I pass along a message?"

For a moment, he had expected his mother was there. She hadn't responded to his text that she had a grandson, but she'd had dinner plans with old friends tonight. She would likely check in with him later.

"I'll speak to her." He rose and settled Locke—it was a strong name and he liked it—into his bassinet, then went down the corridor to the elevators.

He could have dismissed Kiara with a message through the nurse, but he had promised Scarlett he would inform her, and Scarlett had called Kiara the best friend she'd ever had. Plus, there had been genuine caring and respect in her voice when Kiara had asked Scarlett, "What do *you* want?" He appreciated that she hadn't pushed her way between them or forced Scarlett to take sides when she'd been in such a state of heightened anxiety.

Maybe he was also looking for insight into how Scarlett had remained so devoted to Niko. What sort of troll-like spell had Nikolai Mylonas cast over two seemingly sensible women, compelling them to live with him and keep their children a secret?

Whatever mellow mood had fallen over him with the birth of his son dropped away as the elevator doors opened and the first thing he saw was Val. His half brother's cover girl face was nothing but chiseled cheeks and trademarked brooding sulk. His black shabby chic jeans and shirt were tailored for his lean frame by his personal design house in Milan.

Javiero almost hit the button to close the doors, but he would be damned if he would allow that bastard to affect him. He stalked forward, his fuse beginning to burn.

Val recoiled infinitesimally as he took in the evidence of Javiero's mauling.

Javiero didn't falter, but he might as well have been going for round two with the cat. Val was every bit as dangerous as a jungle feline, attacking on a whim, bordering on sociopathic in his propensity to torture for the fun of it.

If Val had ever demonstrated a conscience or an ounce of reason, he and Javiero might have moved on from the bitterness of their early years, but Val hadn't been willing to leave their rivalry in their report cards or on the track. No, he had insisted on making things personal—and as devastating as possible.

They'd been thirteen when Val had gotten himself expelled from boarding school and had thrown Niko's financial support back in his face. Val had had that luxury. He'd already been drawing a six-figure salary looking pretty for magazine photographers. As he departed, he'd made a point of taunting Javiero with the fact he didn't need their father's money.

Have it all. You need it more than I do.

Javiero had needed it for the same reason Paloma had, but Niko had always been pathological about treating his sons with precisely equal measures of tough love. By Niko's sense of twisted impartiality, if Val was leaving school to work at thirteen, Javiero ought to be able to support himself as well. His tuition payments to the exclusive boarding school were halted.

Val's immature desire to rebel had thrust Javiero into years of struggle. Javiero had spent the next five years eking out an education while working alongside his maternal grandfather, fighting to turn a profit on an energy corporation that had been impacted by a massive downturn and breaking his back in the fields with his uncles and cousins, trying to retain properties they'd owned for generations. They had hung on to the family assets by their fingertips, but those long days and the heavy weight of worry had prematurely ended his grandfather's life. Javiero had shouldered everything alone ever since.

And why had Val hit out at him like that? Because he *could*. Selfish, malignant tumor that he was.

Everything in Javiero congealed to a gritty ball of antipathy as he faced Val. At least their father was dead. This was the last time he would ever have to so much as look at him.

"Javiero." A warm, lilting Irish accent sounded on his blind side, but Javiero wasn't stupid enough to take his eye off his enemy. "It's nice to meet you. I'm Kiara." He caught a glimpse of an extended light brown hand.

Javiero had an impression of voluptuous curves and a

flash of a white smile in a light brown face, but Val swept his arm out and shoved her behind him in a protective move that was insulting as hell. All Javiero glimpsed now was masses of curly black hair and dark brown irises blinking wide-eyed from around the width of Val's shoulder.

"For heaven's sake," she grumbled as Val moved her out of Javiero's reach. Val's entire body had hardened with unjustified, pumped-up aggression.

Javiero returned his loathing tenfold.

"No comment?" Javiero taunted into the thick silence, suddenly thrilled to look like a street thug who'd lost a knife fight. "Not going to say you like what I've done with my hair or something equally banal?"

"How is Scarlett?" Kiara asked brightly, still behind Val.

"Fine." Javiero told her they'd had a boy and Scarlett was sleeping, all without wavering from his locked stare with Val.

"I'd love to see him," Kiara said with a pang of yearning in her voice.

"No," Javiero said, silently conveying to Val *he* was the reason for the refusal.

"I'll stay here," Val said grittily. His unblemished features twisted into a frustrated sneer. "Let her go up."

Wow. That sounded almost as though Val possessed a conscience inside that pinup exterior. Javiero wasn't fooled. He took supreme pleasure in delivering a second, implacable, "No."

Val gathered himself and Javiero did the same, distantly thinking it was a good thing they were in a hospital.

"It's fine. It's late." Kiara's arms wrapped around Val's waist from behind, as if to hold him back. Or to protect him? She was wasting her energy either way.

"Tell Scarlett to call me when she's up for a chat," Kiara added with forced cheer.

Javiero walked away. His win against Val felt empty, but it was a win and that was all that mattered.

A muted hum intruded on the best sleep Scarlett had had in ages. She frowned without opening her eyes, resisting coming back to consciousness.

"A boy. Well done," a woman's voice said. "Did you do it deliberately?"

Paloma? *Ugh.* She'd drifted into a nightmare. She tried to redirect to something pleasant. Clotted cream and strawberry jam on freshly baked scones. *Mmm...*

"No." Javiero's quiet rumble was a staple in her dreams—sensual and invigorating and fantasy inducing. Very *mmm...*

"At least that would have made sense." Paloma's sharp voice faded as though her volume had been turned down. "What were you thinking, taking up with your father's mistress?"

What? Scarlett scraped her eyes open, barely comprehending that the golden light was a night-light and the metal bar was part of a hospital bed.

"She was not his mistress. Never repeat that."

"I don't have to! The rumor mill will do that for us. They'll rake up every misstep all the way back to my father's lack of foresight during the oil shock."

"Gossip is an unpleasant reality of life, like death and taxes."

"As is the fact you'll have to marry her? Because you can't let Val and Evelina waltz away with half the money that should be ours and leave the other half to *her*. You have to take control of our half."

That snapped the last of the drowsiness out of Scarlett.

She shifted and, as she did, heard a mewing noise. She glanced at the bassinet, which was empty.

"I have to go, Mother. Scarlett's awake and Locke is hungry." Javiero was in the recliner, their son in the crook of his arm. He clicked off his phone and set it aside.

"What time is it?" She fumbled for the button that would raise the head of the bed.

"Nearly midnight." If he felt guilty for what she'd overheard, he didn't look or sound it. He lowered the footrest and brought the baby over, back to being the effortlessly compelling yet infinitely intimidating man she'd always known.

"Can you look out the window or something?" she asked as she started to fumble with her gown.

He moved away and she latched her son, then draped a receiving blanket over him. With a shaky sigh, she tried to relax, but now that she was awake, she was absorbing the fact her entire life had made one more turn on the kaleidoscope. All the pieces had dropped into a completely new pattern. Niko was dead. Javiero knew about the baby. Her son was *here*.

And Javiero's mother wanted Javiero to marry her to take control of Niko's money.

Scarlett longed to blink herself back to the villa and familiar surroundings so she could catch her breath.

"Did you text Kiara?" She glanced around for her phone, wondering if she could go back to the island with her in the morning.

"She was here a few hours ago."

"Oh?" A rush of pride zinged through her. "I wanted to see her when she held him for the first time. She kept saying she was excited to have a baby in the house, especially one she didn't have to deliver herself."

He didn't laugh. "I didn't bring her up. Val was with her."

"Oh." It wasn't her fault that her friend's baby had been fathered by Javiero's detested brother, but she still experienced a stab of guilt. "Did you tell her we'd had a boy?"

"She asked his name and I said we hadn't decided, but Locke suits him." He turned his head, voice warming exactly two degrees.

"Locke," she whispered as she peeked under the blanket. He'd fallen asleep so she fumbled him off her nipple and caught the blanket to hide her breast. "Can you hold him? Kiara made this look so easy."

He took Locke and used the pad of his thumb to dry the boy's shiny chin.

She tried to gauge his mood with a surreptitious glance as she tucked herself back in. The tenderness he'd exhibited during the hours she'd been in labor was gone. Because of his altercation with Val?

"How did she seem when you saw her?" she probed lightly.

"Kiara? Ordinary."

"What's that supposed to mean?" She held out her arms to take back Locke, wanting to cuddle her baby now that she was awake and feeling her new station in life. *Mother.* It wasn't so much a title as a compulsion. Why hadn't Kiara told her about this intense craving to cosset?

"I don't keep tabs on Val's love life, but his world is nothing but supermodels. His ex-wife ticked all the boxes for "fashionable heiress." When you said Kiara had kept his baby a secret, I imagined she was a calculating socialite. Instead she was very…"

Scarlett stared, daring him to say a wrong word.

"Understated. No flashy makeup or jewelry. Val doesn't have a subtle bone in his body. I don't understand how she caught his attention long enough to make a baby with him."

"She's very sexy! Don't you think?" Kiara was average height with doe-brown eyes in an oval face that some might call cute instead of beautiful, but she was also very sensual looking with her masses of corkscrew curls, and full lips and ample curves.

"Is that a trick question?" He lifted a brow, one that made her realize she didn't want to hear how attractive he found other women right now. Probably not ever. "I expected someone more hardened is all I'm saying."

"No, Kiara's a very gentle sort." Scarlett latched on to thoughts of her friend, the one person in her life who at least tried to be supportive. "She's very loving with Aurelia. She's an artist. An extraordinary one." Scarlett had always been envious of Kiara's creativity. Her own life had necessitated she become starkly practical. Any ingenuity she possessed was confined to spreadsheet formulas or a database programming language. "Her first gallery show is in Paris in a few weeks."

Scarlett knew she wouldn't be able to attend. A deeper melancholy stalked her, one stemming from the fact that she and Kiara had both known their lives would change after Niko passed. They had talked about it in hushed tones while sitting at Niko's bedside, wondering what would happen once Val and Javiero knew about their children.

Maybe nothing will change. Maybe they won't care, Kiara had said in a whisper at one point.

They had joked that staying on the island, raising their children as a celibate same-sex couple might have its perks. At least the toilet seat would always stay down.

They both desperately wanted the fathers of their children to bond with their babies, though, no matter what that meant for their own futures.

"When I asked how Kiara seemed, I meant with Val.

Was she upset? How did he seem to be taking the news about Aurelia?"

"I have no idea. It was all I could do to be civil to him. I turned them away and came back up here."

"You turned her away? I can't make you like your brother, Javiero, but I expect you to be nice to Kiara. From the time I told her I was pregnant, she's only ever been happy for me, even though she knew it meant Aurelia's portion of Niko's fortune would instantly be cut in half. She and I have always agreed we would never behave like your mothers. We won't fight over that money."

Her superiority was wasted.

"She can have it, as far as I'm concerned," he said flatly.

"Really? Because the conversation I overheard made it sound like you were anxious to get your hands on it."

A chill like the creeping fingers of frost emanated off him to invade and stall her heart.

"What you heard was the lifetime of ravenous insecurity Niko instilled in my mother with his cruel dangling of that money only to snatch it away. His fortune has caused so much pain and strife for me and people I care about, I refuse to poison my son with a cent of it."

She really had underestimated his hatred of his father. It made going to him nine months ago seem almost an act of maliciousness, embroiling him further in Niko's affairs rather than allowing him the clean break he obviously preferred.

Recognizing that left her shaking at her core, but she had to make the situation clear. "It's not your choice whether Locke gets it. Niko's assets will be managed under a trust until Locke and Aurelia are old enough to decide what they want to do with their portion. There's an allowance for me to support him—"

"*I* will support you and Locke."

Scarlett licked her chapped lips.

"We can discuss that if it's important to you, but I don't expect you to support us. I might not have told you about my pregnancy, but I never intended to keep you from your son or use him to get anything from you. I have the means to give him an excellent life. Along with my allowance, I draw a salary for managing the trust. Plus, Kiara and I have the use of the villa. There's a stipulation to maintain its staff and upkeep. Any material support you offer is strictly at your discretion."

"I won't live on the island and neither will he," Javiero pronounced with every ounce of the implacable, single-minded stubbornness she'd witnessed in him over the years. "Your allowance can stay in the bank. You're coming to Madrid and I'll provide everything. You won't need to work, either. We're getting married as soon as it can be arranged."

A nurse heard their voices and came in to check on them. Gently she encouraged Javiero to return to his hotel, insisting Scarlett needed her rest.

Scarlett tried to sleep, but Javiero's pronouncement pressed on her, making it hard to breathe. She couldn't marry him. It wasn't just about fighting for her right to control Niko's fortune—which she would do—or how thoroughly marriage would impact the freedom she had finally been granted by Niko's death. There were things in her past that Javiero and his mother definitely did not want to be connected to. Things she didn't want to confess to if she could avoid it.

They didn't circle back to his proposal—could she call it a proposal?—until the following day. Javiero arrived in time to speak to her doctor as he was making his rounds.

"I've arranged for a private nurse. Will that be sufficient to discharge them early so they can travel to Spain with me?" Javiero asked. "We'll hire a nanny once we're in Madrid," he added in an aside to Scarlett. "I have a designer working on plans for the formal nursery, but a temporary one is being organized for our arrival."

"A *formal* nursery. Like, one where ball gowns and tails will be worn?" Scarlett wasn't sure where the sarcasm came from, but he'd put her on the defensive with his railroading tactics. That sort of behavior had been standard with Niko but, among other good reasons to tolerate his bullish tendencies, he had paid her salary.

Javiero gave her a sharp look but didn't respond. He listened carefully as the doctor promised to check with the pediatrician, who was likely to agree to early release so long as she had proper care.

The doctor left and Scarlett folded her arms across the draped front of the pretty print dress Javiero had arranged to be delivered first thing this morning. He had ordered her a small wardrobe from a shop that specialized in maternity wear and clever styles for nursing mothers. He'd also organized a kit of newborn items, a top-of-the-line infant car seat and a basket of personal care items made with organic ingredients.

Since Scarlett had been admitted without so much as a toothbrush, she had been grateful. This morning's shower and new clothes were a step toward feeling like her old self.

Since her old self knew how to hold her ground when she had to, she put on her unfazed expression and her most matter-of-fact tone. "Niko is no longer at the island villa. There's no reason you shouldn't come wi—"

"No," he cut in.

She had known it was a long shot; still, she bit back a sigh.

"You said you weren't intending to shut me out of his life," he reminded.

"I'm not," she assured him. "I want you to have as much opportunity to bond with Locke as I have. I just thought we would spend time discussing all the options open to us, then make a decision jointly, not crash straight into the train wreck of a loveless marriage."

"The fact we're not lying about our feelings is the reason it won't derail at the first pebble on the tracks."

"And your feelings are?" she prompted, holding tight to a blasé expression while her lungs seized on either side of her trembling heart.

"Unashamed," he said in a level tone. "But protective. I would have married you immediately if you'd informed me sooner."

"People don't care about illegitimacy these days," she argued.

"Some do. Val was teased partly because his mother's affair with our father was such a notorious scandal. I didn't participate or encourage it. I fight my own battles with him," he said, as though it was important to clarify. "And I didn't come away unscathed. I was mocked for being schooled alongside my bastard half brother. So you and I will do whatever is expected to ensure Locke doesn't needlessly suffer. On that note…" He reached into his pocket. "My team informs me it's customary these days for new mothers to receive a 'push present.'" He held out the square velvet box.

"Resorting to bribery?" She shoved her fists deeper under her elbows. "You gave me clothes. Flowers." She indicated the obscenely extravagant bouquet.

"And this." He opened the box, revealing a necklace of intricate platinum links. It held a charming pendant shaped like a padlock with diamonds inset in the hasp and around the keyhole. A miniature skeleton key hung next to it, lined with diamonds with a blue-for-a-boy sapphire decorating its head.

It was too beautiful to refuse, too extravagant to accept.

"It seemed appropriate." A hint of gruffness entered his tone. "But if you want something else—"

"No! It's beautiful. But I didn't expect anything." She didn't know how to reject it gracefully so she spoke the truth. "Accepting it makes it seem as though I really did get pregnant to enrich myself." She bit her lip in misery.

The corner of his mouth twitched in cynical agreement, the small action like a flick of a whip against the center of her heart.

"Your motive doesn't matter. You did the work," he said darkly, none of yesterday's solicitude in his demeanor.

"I did the work so I could have a son, not so I could have *that*."

His mouth tightened. "Nevertheless, inquiring minds expect you to wear it." Carefully he drew the necklace from its nest and circled his finger to indicate she turn around.

She remained facing him, her chin jutting out with hurt.

"Paparazzi are gathering outside. That's why I requested the early departure."

"To Spain," she choked. "I'm supposed to go with a perfect stranger—"

"Far from perfect. I'm sure we agree on that."

"Well, you're strange enough I don't want to marry you!"

A thundering silence crashed between them, so voluminous it should have knocked their sleeping son from his bed. Her internal heat became embarrassment. *Shame*.

"That wasn't what I meant," she mumbled, looking to

her feet in the low sandals he had provided her. Forceful he might be, but he wasn't stingy. Or repulsive. "I'm not saying I would *never* marry you. Just that we should wait to make that decision."

"After you see what can be accomplished with cosmetic surgery?" His crooked lips gave a cynical twist.

"After you quit thinking my motives are purely materialistic and superficial." She fought to make herself understood. "We don't know each other, Javiero. I know a version of you that your father told me. You know nothing about me." Once he did, he would thank her for refusing him.

"We'll learn. Marriage isn't complicated. Like any partnership, you bring your strengths to the table and work toward advancing mutual interests."

Was that how he had regarded his engagement? She'd been informed that his arranged union was about financial compatibility, not affection or passion. It had still made her sick to contemplate him being tied to another woman. Sleeping with her.

He wasn't offering love here, either. That shouldn't sting when it was unrealistic, given the circumstances. They really were strangers, but she'd like him to *like* her. To *want* to like her at least.

She cleared that yearning from her throat.

"What I know about partnerships is that they require compromise." As opposed to being controlled by your husband until you were too exhausted to fight anymore, the way her mother had been by her father. "I'll agree to go with you to Madrid. In return, you agree to hold off on marriage."

"No." Just that. The same aggravatingly pitiless refusal he'd always given her.

She wasn't Niko's envoy any longer though. This was

about her and her son. She narrowed her eyes and tightened her ponytail.

"*If* we ever marry, I want Kiara and Aurelia there." On that, she would not budge.

His expression hardened, exactly the reaction she expected.

"You don't have family?"

"I do, but…" If she thought her mother would come, she would make the arrangements. The rest of her family was a wedding photo he didn't want. "We'll discuss the guest list if we agree to marry—which I haven't. I have my hands full, in case you haven't noticed."

Locke had begun to fuss so she picked him up and sank into the rocking chair, but that wasn't the reason an unsteady wobble accosted her stomach. What if he agreed?

"What do you really want?" he asked grimly. "This isn't about a guest list."

"No, it's not," she allowed shakily. "I want you to trust me."

He snorted, telling her how far-off that was.

Which was the crux of her reluctance, and each time she pushed back, she undermined what little regard he might have for her. It made a future with him impossible.

"Let's table marriage until we see how we get along as parents," she said in a conciliatory tone. "We may decide killing each other is preferable to sharing our lives."

"I'll table it until we get to Madrid." He moved behind the rocker and stuck his foot in the rail so the chair stopped moving. The hair on the back of her neck stood up.

"I don't want to delay the rest of our arrangements with an argument I'll win." The pendant flashed in front of her eyes, then settled as a cool weight against the base of her throat. His fingertips brushed the sensitive skin of her nape and his hand nudged against her ponytail, sending a sensual tingle across her scalp and down the front of her chest.

She hugged Locke to breasts that began to ache.

Javiero moved in front of her and centered the pendant. His smile pulled at the scar across his lip and became more of a sarcastic sneer. "Compromise is fun."

CHAPTER FOUR

SCARLETT STILL HAD a thousand concerns about her future with Javiero, but she wanted to coparent in good faith. She climbed aboard the private jet that would fly them to Spain.

She thought she would finally see Casa del Cielo, the Rodriguez estate south of Madrid. The sprawling villa had been featured in architectural magazines and overlooked hills covered in wine grapes. His family owned properties in Valencia and Seville, too, obtained generations ago and retained by the skin of their teeth after Paloma's divorce from Niko.

All Javiero's estates were profitable and worth millions now, but the bulk of their fortune had always been in telecom, energy and infrastructure. The corporate offices for those were in Madrid, ten minutes from the family apartment in the city center.

The scene of the crime, as it were.

As they arrived, she thought back to the first time she'd met Javiero here. Paloma was too proud to ask Niko for money, but Evelina had demanded funds once or twice a year. Niko had never simply transferred a balance. He had liked to make a statement of his "generosity" and use his supposed benevolence as an opportunity to lure his sons back into the fold.

Mere weeks into her employment, Scarlett hadn't yet

realized the murky history between all the players. Niko had sent her to Evelina first—a stunning, scorpion of a woman whose son hadn't even bothered to show up for the meeting although Scarlett had gone to great lengths to accommodate his schedule.

Then she had arrived here expecting to meet Paloma, but the broad-shouldered, square-jawed Javiero had opened the door. He'd been unhurried, shirt open at his swarthy-skinned throat, charming and hospitable as he invited her in—yet intimidating as he issued an order that had somehow come across as an understated threat.

"Never approach my mother directly again. Come to me first with anything Niko wishes to convey. I will decide if she needs to hear it. And don't get your feminist feathers in a ruffle." A cynical smile had widened his masculine lips as she sat straighter. "I'm protecting her from a conscienceless tyrant, not controlling her. How do you come to work for such a monster? Do you need help? Blink twice."

She'd been stunned, utterly out of her depth; her blood felt thick in her veins, her skin oversensitive, and her entire being throbbed with a sensual beat. Somehow, she'd stammered into her spiel about Niko wishing to entail Javiero's birthright on him with the caveat he come to Greece to claim it.

"No," Javiero had stated before she'd even finished.

Minutes later, he'd dismissed her. She'd left feeling as though she'd barely escaped with her life, yet she'd been brimming with excitement and sexual fantasies.

The handful of meetings she'd had with him in the next five years had all been held here in this six-bedroom residence. It was a stunning home that took up the top floor of a complex built in the 1800s. The ornate decor reflected its history, but the building was impeccably maintained, with the layout of the minimansion airy and bright. There were three fireplaces and fully six balconies—two big enough to dine on—all of which overlooked the lush greenery of El Retiro park.

Every inch of this place became a salacious memory of *that day* as they entered. She had experienced the familiar, nearly irresistible pull when he'd opened the door. Her heart had plummeted then soared when he'd served the coffee himself, casually mentioning the staff had been dismissed for the day. Wicked temptation had kept her here to argue her point when she could have said her piece and left. She had been frustrated on so many levels that she had stepped into his space, pretty much *daring* him to make a move.

He had. He'd taken her by the shoulders and kissed her. Moments later, they had fallen onto that striped sofa before they moved into the bedroom for the most intimate type of communication. It had been silent except for words of erotic encouragement, and utterly spectacular.

Afterward, they'd showered, still barely speaking, and returned to the bed to make love again, less frantically this time. As the sun had set beyond the closed blinds, she'd insisted she had to leave, but they'd had one final, desperate, life-altering interaction right here in the foyer, against this wall.

Her soul stood outside her skin as her feet found the same spot, making her feel obvious and utterly defenseless. She searched his grim expression as he hung her jacket without removing his own.

His gaze tangled with hers. The iris of his one eye seemed to flare like a ring of blue-green flame, telling her he remembered every second of that day as clearly as she did.

She caught her breath. She hadn't felt sexy in months,

but a shiver of awareness swirled into her middle and sent echoes of pleasure into her erogenous zones.

Whatever had driven them into a frenzy that day was still there, lurking and circling under the surface, teasing her to let it swallow her again.

Apparently, he was impervious. "Get settled. I'll be back in an hour," he said, and abruptly left.

It was a kick in the face. A profound rejection that left her floundering in a sea of abandonment. Never mind the nurse or housekeeper hovering behind her. They seemed nice and well-meaning enough, but she wasn't about to hand over her newborn to strangers. She didn't want to.

She asked to be shown to Locke's room, where she changed and fed him.

Self-reliance had been drilled into her from her earliest memories, when her father had been surly and hungover, her mother nursing a bruised jaw or a wrenched shoulder, unable to do much. Scarlett had made the breakfast, and gotten herself and her siblings to school. When she'd begun needing female necessities, she'd found herself a job to pay for them. When she had gone to social workers, her mother hadn't backed her up and things had almost returned to the way they'd been—only worse. When she'd had to stay home to nurse her mother, teachers hadn't given her a break on exams.

There'd been no concessions at university, either, when she'd had to drop out to help the family. Niko, demanding and vainglorious as he was, had made her work herself to the bone for the job she held. Kiara had promised to show her the ropes of new motherhood, but their talk of rearing their children together at the villa had been a fantasy. Texts from Kiara revealed she was off to Italy with Val while Scarlett had come to Madrid.

Despite having no one to rely on, ever, Scarlett had

thought things might be different with Javiero. He'd been so considerate yesterday. He had sounded so determined to be part of their son's life. When he'd talked of a partnership, she'd heard *team*.

But this relationship would be as one-sided as all of them, she supposed, ignoring the fog of despondency that manifested around her. She would manage. She always did.

When Javiero returned two hours later, Scarlett had just settled Locke in his bassinet and was at the door, taking delivery of the parcels she'd ordered.

"Why aren't you resting?" Javiero's hair and beard were freshly trimmed. It was a startling change, exposing more of the discolored claw marks, but reinforcing his natural, commanding air.

He took all the bags from the intimidated young man and gave him a few euros to send him on his way.

"I thought you were going to your office." She gazed at Javiero, once again struck by what a close call he'd had yet rather taken with the clean-cut version of his brutish looks. "You look nice."

His flat stare refuted her compliment. "It's a haircut. I couldn't blame you for rejecting my proposal when I literally looked like something the jaguar had dragged around its pen."

"Javiero!"

He brushed away her pang of hurt and dropped the bags into a chair. "I spoke to my doctor about a prosthetic eye. I need more reconstruction before I can be fitted. He wants another week of healing before I go for the consultation."

"Your scars have nothing to do with my reasons for putting off marriage. I've…" She faltered with self-consciousness, then pressed on. "I've always found you attractive. I still do." Her voice faded, not from a lack of sincerity, but from the way he trained his one eye on her and made the floor go soft under her feet.

"Really."

"Why do you sound so skeptical?" she asked crossly. "You're very…" Virile. He must work out like a demon because he had a chest and shoulders like a stevedore. His biceps were equally powerful and his thighs were like tree trunks. She would bet any money that his strength had saved him, allowing him to fight off the jungle cat.

She swallowed and looked away as heat came into her cheeks. The sensual awareness she'd always felt around him was back with a vengeance, now coupled with the knowledge of how making love with him really felt. Their connection through their son magnified it, leaving her defenses in tatters.

"Really," he said in a tone heavier with speculation and traces of the charisma that had drawn her so inexorably.

"Well, I wouldn't have slept with you if I *wasn't* attracted, would I?" she defended hotly, unable to look at him.

"The jury is still out on your motives." His voice turned flinty. "Val would have slept with you if you'd wanted him to. He and Evelina would have loved to screw my side out of Dad's fortune completely. I can't believe he didn't offer."

"Of course he did," she said with a snort of *obviously*.

A flash of something murderous flickered in his expression. "When?"

"In the early days." She hugged herself. "Before he learned that I would keep talking about your father until his libido shriveled back into its shell." She shrugged off what had been a minor annoyance in the big scheme of things. "Val wasn't serious, just testing me the way you're doing right now. You're trying to see if you can disconcert me into saying something that will prove I'm a liar. You want me to admit I found Val attractive so you can hate me for it. I did," she said, her heart pounding at the risk she was taking in being so blunt.

He snapped his head back.

"In a very objective way," she clarified. "Who wouldn't? He made his fortune in fashion because he epitomizes fashion's idea of masculine beauty. And he knows it. Which is why I'm not genuinely attracted."

He studied her. "You don't find arrogance attractive?"

"No, I don't. That's why I never slept with your father. Or *you*. Until you quit talking down to me." That was a prevarication. She had always found Javiero compelling. Val hadn't stood a chance after Javiero had set the bar. No man had.

"Did I talk down to you?" he asked blithely.

"You're doing it now." She copied his humorless smile.

He made a noise of false regret and ambled closer. "I can't help it if you're shorter than I am."

He wore his customary tailored pants and a crisp button shirt, sans tie, with the collar open at his throat. He also wore his particular brand of superiority that she found enormously exciting. He'd inherited that authority from his father, same as Val, but Niko hadn't had any humbleness in him and Val's conceit was too self-aware. Javiero's confidence was *earned*. He hadn't made his fortune by gambling with other people's money in the stock market or applying his good looks to an ad campaign for cologne. He *built* things.

The aura of cool assurance that surrounded Javiero enveloped her as he came closer. His steady gaze dared her to look away, and part of her wanted to. It was far too revealing to let him read her expression and the effect he had on her. He had always had this ability to disconcert her and she feared he always would. But even though holding his gaze was like dropping all the defenses she possessed, allowing him to see her flaws and broken dreams and cheap foundation, she also knew she couldn't flinch from him, not without losing whatever respect he had for her.

She compromised by studying his face the way she had allowed herself only once, when she'd sleepily opened her eyes and found him dozing with repletion beside her.

Javiero was not classically handsome. His face had held character marks before the attack. He had a bump in his nose and a strong brow and a wide jaw. His rugged features weren't refined. They were rough-hewn and all the more mesmerizing for having been scored by that cat.

"Still attracted?" It was a light taunt, but she saw the tension that invaded behind his indifference. He was bracing for criticism or rejection.

She couldn't lie. She had to tell him the truth even though it made her feel as though she had stepped off a cliff blindfolded and trusted him to catch her.

"Yes," she whispered.

He touched her chin, tilting her mouth up a fraction while he looked from her eyes to her mouth and back to her eyes.

"I'd say that's a point in favor of marriage, wouldn't you?"

Had she thought about spending her life in his bed? Only a million times and well before she'd carried his baby.

Those fairy tales were supposed to stay in a book on a shelf deep in her personal library, though. For one moment, however, she opened those pages, peeked and glimpsed them falling in love and making a life together.

Whatever dreams softened her expression seemed to have made up his mind. He dipped his head.

She had wanted this, she acknowledged as his mouth covered hers. She had hated herself for walking away nine months ago. Or, rather, she had hated that she had had no choice but to do so.

For every waking minute of every day since, she had wanted to return to this moment. To one more kiss. To see what might have been.

He played his lips smoothly across hers. It was a lazy return to a place that was familiar. He settled with ownership, with a long, leisurely taste that made her sigh in welcome. Her toes curled and her hands splayed across his stomach, feeling his abs tighten.

He rocked his mouth over hers with more purpose, deepening the kiss by degrees until she was sliding closer, into the sensual pool he conjured so effortlessly.

His arms went around her and it was like coming home. She melted, feeling the stir of his firming flesh against her middle while her arms climbed to curl behind his neck. She moaned with pleasure and skimmed one hand into his hair.

Her finger caught against the band on his eye patch, not dislodging it, but startling them both.

He jerked his head up and she dropped her hand to his shoulder.

The heat of their kiss dissipated, leaving a chill that grew more strained by the second.

She was dazed, still in his arms, not immediately processing his, "Where's the nurse?" He set her back a step.

That day nine months ago, he had let the kiss go on until she hadn't had a rational thought in her head. He'd broken it only to say in a smoky voice, *I'm going to my room for a cold shower. Or a condom, if you'd like to join me?*

She had hardly debated at all before she'd followed.

Today she wasn't so aroused she couldn't think straight, but she did cling to his arm as she tried to maintain her balance and catch up to his abrupt mood switch.

"I...um..." She glanced around, then remembered. "I sent her to buy some iron tablets if she's that concerned I bring my levels up."

"That's exactly the sort of thing she should be concerned about. Your doctor said you have to take it easy this week. And no lovemaking for six," he reminded her pointedly.

Oh, right. *That.*

"That wasn't—" She stopped to clear a huskiness from her throat only to discover she didn't know how to excuse their kiss. She decided not to try. "Well, there's no point in discussing marriage until we pass that six-week mark, then. Is there?" She spoke with false cheer and dug into the bags on the chair, ducking her head to hide her disconcerted blush.

"Having sex is not the reason I want to marry you, Scarlett. The physical attraction between us is simply nice to have."

"No kidding. If our lovemaking had meant anything more to you than 'nice to have,' you would have shown up to propose long before today."

"I asked you to stay that day," he reminded while her insides fell away. "If you had, we might have come to a proposal eventually. We'll never know, though, will we? You chose my father."

"Easy to claim that now," she muttered, certain their relationship would not have progressed beyond a brief affair. "Will you be going into work this week?"

She was trying to change the subject and he hesitated as if wanting to win their argument, but there was no winning.

"I was going to play it by ear." He frowned at the box she withdrew from the bag. "I thought your laptop was being shipped from the island." He glanced at the Bluetooth earpiece and high-speed, ultrasecure modem she'd ordered along with other gadgets.

"It will take at least a week before everything gets packed up and forwarded. I decided to start fresh. This way I can get back to work right away."

"Back to work? You gave birth three days ago. *No.* Go to bed." Javiero pointed toward the hallway to the bedrooms.

"Excuse me. I'm not five." She brought the box to the sofa, sat and swung her legs onto the cushions. "I just want to set it up so I can answer a few emails. I've spent the last three months building management teams, and they still need guidance."

Javiero moved to the chair and sat, hitching his pants and settling into a casual pose that was as lethally dangerous as any boxer or black belt who took up an agile stance, ready to both defend and attack.

"You mentioned you're supposed to manage my father's estate," he recalled.

"I am doing it, under a trustee arrangement, yes. Kiara is my co-trustee but prefers to be a silent one. She has voting and veto powers, but she doesn't want to be involved in the day-to-day decisions."

"But you do."

"Why wouldn't I?"

"Because you have a newborn who needs you?" he suggested.

"Will you be quitting work?" she shot back, but her bravado was caked in guilt. She knew babies required a lot of attention, and she wanted to be the best mother possible; nonetheless, she had additional responsibilities.

"I intend to be home more," he asserted firmly. "This isn't a debate on your right to work. It's about timing."

"And my time is now," she insisted. "This is exactly the sort of position I have always aspired to. Say what you will about Niko, but he knew what he was doing with money. I not only finished my business degree during my employment, I apprenticed under him. I worked my tail off to prove I was the best candidate to run his enterprises. Better than either of his estranged sons even, because I have been involved in every aspect for the last five years. I wouldn't be named as primary trustee if he hadn't believed I was qualified to do the job."

"That's the issue. He's dead, but you're still working for him."

"Actually, I work for your son." She picked a hole in the shrink film on the box.

"And Val's daughter, apparently. That's a mountain of responsibility to take on for someone else's child when you're still recovering from delivering your own. Are there provisions for alternates?"

"Like who? You?"

There were instructions to approach him and Val first if she was incapacitated, but all Scarlett could think was how smug Paloma would be if Javiero took control of the fortune she had always regarded as hers.

"I'm surprised you would even suggest taking over. You had your chance." She tore off the plastic and crinkled it into a ball. "I was here several times, asking if you wanted to. You declined."

"My interest in Dad's money is so remote, I want my future wife to treat it like the radioactive waste it is and distance herself completely," he bit out. "Set aside the fact my mother's obsession with keeping that money from going to Evelina broke something in her." His hand flicked angrily. "My aunties and uncles love to tell me what a sweet, kind, loving person she was before Niko. I never saw her like that. My whole life, she's been a cynical, angry *victim*."

"Then why didn't you go back and work for him? Take

control of your share?" She had never understood the incontrovertible rift between the men in this family. "He wanted you to." With strings, she recognized, but even so…

"That was later," he said tersely, his hand knotting into a fist on the armrest. "After he realized both Val and I were serious about disowning him. Then he sent you along like a good little recruitment officer to try conscripting us back. Don't pretend it was an engraved invitation on the bottom of an apology. It was an order. The only reason I ever did him the favor of hearing you out was for my mother's sake, in hopes he would relent in some way toward her. As we've seen, he did not. So as far as I'm concerned, he can rot in hell. I hope he's there now."

"But why did you reject him in the first place?"

He shook his head as though he pitied her. "You worked for him—lived with him—for *five years* and never saw what a manipulative and unforgiving person he was? Val gets his streak of malice from somewhere, Scarlett."

"And that's the other thing I don't understand! Why do you hate Val so much? Niko said you were competitive as children—siblings can be. I get that." Her own sister was a constant aggravation. "But he said your mothers were the ones who poisoned you against each other and him."

"He said that?"

"Yes." She could see she was riling him up, but she had always been baffled by these wide channels of animosity. "He said Val was a troublemaker and was expelled from the boarding school you attended. That after Val gave up any claim to his fortune, you did the same. That's never made sense to me. You cut off your nose to spite your face."

"What a liar," Javiero said through his teeth, his hand now clenching the arm of his chair as though to hold himself back from launching himself at her. "Val had the luxury of throwing Dad's money in his face. He was making six figures wearing a hoodie and a scowl. Where would I get that sort of income at thirteen? My mother's marriage was supposed to square off the debt my grandfather was in, but once she divorced him for his infidelity, Niko refused to pay her anything but child-support—in scrupulously equal amounts. Do you know what Niko said when my next semester came due and Val had dropped out?"

Oh, no.

"That he wanted to treat you equally," she surmised with dread. She wanted to bury her face in her hands, hiding from what she suddenly saw as the bitter truth.

"He said Val was showing initiative and independence. The sort of maturity and business acumen that would serve him well when he inherited *everything*—because why would he reward the *weaker* son?"

"No." Javiero was not weak in any way. He had had a steeper hill to climb and had lost his grandfather along the way. How could Niko dismiss him so cruelly? She had known him to have a ruthless streak, which she had thought of as the result of his sons' rejection, not the source of it.

She felt sick, genuinely sick.

"I had no choice but to renounce his magnanimous offers to reinstate me as his heir. I might have proven myself in his eyes by the time you came along, having recovered and surpassed what my grandfather had amassed. I might even have been driven by Niko's ridicule to achieve all that I did. But I have long ceased to care if he even remembered we shared DNA. I sure as hell didn't want his money. I especially didn't want to be beholden to him for anything. I still don't."

She couldn't even defend Niko. He had mellowed as his health declined and his granddaughter came on the scene. She had watched it happen, but none of that erased his heartlessness toward his own children.

"I'm so sorry, Javiero," she murmured.

"For what? For working for him? For showing up here and acting as though I was the one being hurtful and stubborn because I refused to go see him? Or for burdening our son with that tainted pile of cash? I don't want you touching it, Scarlett. It will ruin all our lives. It will ruin mine all over again."

CHAPTER FIVE

THE NURSE RETURNED from the shops, interrupting them. Her smile faltered, revealing she knew she had walked into a heavy discussion.

Javiero left her to badger Scarlett into a nap, going to the den to make some calls, mostly seeking privacy to regain his control. He didn't like that he'd slipped back into ancient rage that had no place in his life anymore. The source of it was dead and he had moved on, but it was difficult when Scarlett was hanging on so tightly to the role Niko had given her.

And what the hell had he been thinking by kissing her? His ego wasn't so fragile he needed proof a woman could still find him attractive! Rather, he had needed to know that the spark between them still existed. Not just to prove she could see past his disfigurement, but to prove to himself their passion hadn't been completely one-sided that day.

He didn't take much comfort from the confirmation. It only meant he had a weakness for her that she could exploit if he wasn't careful.

The next days—and nights—were consumed by the learning curve of new parenting. They hired a nanny who was cheerful and efficient—and unable to settle Locke. Even Javiero was at his wit's end with Locke's long bouts of crying. He didn't want to put the burden on Scarlett to walk him, but he was hideously relieved each time she turned up at his elbow and said, "I'll take him." Locke was happier when his mother held him. Javiero refused to torture his own child by separating them.

Scarlett didn't complain, either. Like any mother, she was anxious to soothe him, but the demands of a new baby took a toll. She refused to talk about wedding arrangements, and the one time he questioned whether she ought to be working, suggesting she nap, he stepped squarely on her frayed nerves. He managed to resist engaging with her temper. Although he was a man used to getting what he wanted with a single order, he couldn't fight a woman with dark circles under her eyes, especially when she was so sensitive that she teared up over a text.

"Was that Kiara? What did she say?" he asked as he noticed her glistening eyes. They were in the back of his car, headed to Casa del Cielo after nearly two weeks in Madrid.

"My sister. It doesn't matter." She leaned to check on Locke, fast asleep in his carrier.

Sister? She hadn't said much about her family, only that it was "complicated." The one time she had looked as though she was willing to open up, Locke had needed her and the moment had passed.

"What did she say to upset you?"

"Can we talk about it another time?" She flicked a glance at the nanny, who was staring out the window and trying to pretend she wasn't there.

Javiero bit back a curse of frustration. He couldn't fix problems she wouldn't identify.

"Things will calm down now we're home." He nodded as the villa came into view. He kept his attention on her as she took in Casa del Cielo atop a plateau draped in vineyards and orchards. From its vantage point, he had always felt as though he could see from the Atlantic Ocean to the Mediterranean. He loved his home with all his heart.

"Sky House," she murmured with awe. "Pictures don't do it justice."

Maybe he had expected covetousness to enter her expression, or judgment of its weathered age, both things he'd seen on other women's faces. Parts of the villa were three hundred years old. It definitely had its limitations, but his grandfather had added the "new" wing and the swimming pool sixty years ago, when he'd started his own family. The additional outbuildings for the vineyard had contributed to money troubles later, but were in good repair now.

Javiero had been picking away at further modernizations. Casa del Cielo was now a showpiece of old-world charm run on cutting-edge technologies of Wi-Fi, solar power and soil analysis sensors.

Wonder softened Scarlett's face as they drew closer, but the melancholy from her sister's missive lingered. His heart expanded when she touched Locke's curled fist and said, "Look. This is your *papi*'s home."

"His, too. And yours."

The tilt of her mouth said, *We'll see.*

It was a disturbing refutation that niggled at him. He'd achieved what he had through grit and drive, pushing past doubters with sheer force of will. In the past, he hadn't pulled back with Scarlett, either. She'd always been a formidable opponent, maintaining a serene expression no matter how biting he had become, doggedly looking for ways to get behind his defenses and tilt him toward Niko's bidding.

He had never softened toward her and didn't want to now. Still, even though her own shields were up, she had been visibly upset by what he'd told her of Niko's treatment of him. He was annoyed with himself that he'd revealed it. It was a sore spot that had never fully healed, but he was tired of her putting all the blame for his rift with his father on him.

He didn't want her dancing around it, though, *acknowledging* it. It was another reason he was keeping up his guard.

They wound past the wine-making sheds and around the old stables, now converted into a garage with staff housing on top.

Casa del Cielo was a small village unto itself with twenty staff members living on-site and another twenty coming and going daily from the nearby town. Then there were pickers and other seasonal workers as needed.

Maybe he was kidding himself, thinking they would have more peace and quiet here. He was always in high demand and family often dropped by unannounced, knowing they were always welcome. Today, though, only his mother knew of their intention to arrive

Paloma was waiting for them in the front parlor.

"Scarlett," she greeted in her frostiest tone, not offering her cheeks for a kiss, remaining seated, spine ramrod straight.

"It's nice to see you again, Señora Rodriguez." Scarlett stood with her hands clasped before her. "Thank you again for your assistance in Athens."

"Of course." She kept her gaze on Locke as Javiero released him from his infant seat.

Javiero expected his mother to tell Scarlett she needn't to be so formal, given the circumstances, but as the silence stretched, he realized he would have to do that himself.

"You can call her Paloma," he told Scarlett as he handed Locke to his mother.

His mother said nothing, only smiled at her grandson in

a way Javiero had never seen her gaze upon him. "He looks just like you," she said reverently. *"Bienvenido, querido."*

Locke clutched her finger and craned his neck, mouth opening the way he did when he was growing hungry.

"Oh," Scarlett said ruefully, moving forward. "He's still in that stage of nursing every hour or two. I should take him."

"Bottle-feed him. He'll go four hours." Paloma made no effort to give him up.

Scarlett's shoulders stiffened.

Paloma's chin set.

Javiero bit back a curse.

"He's two weeks old, Mother. There's time to introduce formula later." He took the baby and handed him to Scarlett. "The butler will show you to his room." He moved to touch the bell. "I'll find you once he's settled and show you around."

She nodded and Javiero waited until she was out of earshot before he turned on his mother. "Do not engage in a power struggle with her over our son. You'll lose. I'll side with her every time."

"By all means, tie your son to her nipple. What could possibly go wrong?" She picked up a cup of tea from near her elbow. "You're still allowing her to control Niko's fortune?" Those statements were not unrelated.

"Believe it or not, Mother, I have no control over who controls Dad's money. That's up to Scarlett and Kiara."

"And the lawyers we engage if we choose to. Who is Kiara? Oh, Val's broodmare. Excuse me. I should say, bride-to-be." She sipped as though to cleanse her palette. "They've posted banns in Milan. It came up in the links with your press release. Have you settled on a date for your own wedding? I noticed there was no mention of it."

"I'm waiting on my eye." He'd had a consultation yesterday and heard what he'd already known. He needed reconstruction. It would take months, possibly a year, before he was camera ready. He still wanted marriage, but he appreciated Scarlett's gesture of coming here and being willing to coparent.

"Squeamish, is she?" His mother set her cup in the saucer with a clink of disdain.

"Not as squeamish as Regina." He watched her mouth flatten, but gleaned no pleasure from his dig against his mother's poor choice in potential brides. "Look, I don't like that Scarlett worked for Dad either, but she's no longer his PA. She's the mother of my son."

"We're sure of that, are we?"

"You just said he looks like me. Would you like the test results?"

She pinched her mouth with annoyance.

"We'll talk more later," he muttered, and started from the room.

"Javiero."

He gathered his patience and turned.

"You'll find her in the guest wing, next to the room we prepared for Locke."

"Perdóneme?" He folded his arms. "What happened to finishing the dowager apartment and giving her your rooms?" That had been the plan when he'd been engaged to Regina. The work had been put on hold since the accident, but he had expected it to continue from the moment his mother had learned about Locke.

She sniffed. "I see no reason to move out of my room for anyone but your wife."

"I guess you'll have to listen through the wall while she shares mine, then." Fueled by angry disgust, he took the stairs two at a time.

* * *

Scarlett was struggling with more than moving a desk. She was trying not to feel the frostbite off Paloma when she already had freezer burn blisters from Javiero. Today in the car was the most she'd seen him since she'd come to Spain and he'd been on the phone for much of the drive.

How was it that she was missing a man she'd barely ever seen? He was sweet as pie to Locke and gave her all his attention when they spoke about their son, but the minute conversations turned to other topics, he grew reticent. There had been no more overtures or kisses, no interest in her at all beyond polite inquiries about her health.

Meanwhile, she felt like a fraying piece of yarn, stretched thin between her son and her job, strummed by Javiero's brief appearances, vibrating for hours afterward.

I can do this, she kept telling herself, refusing to give in to the sheer exhaustion that dogged her through each day.

"What are you doing? Stop that right now," Javiero said as he strode through the door.

"I can't reach the socket." She hadn't been sure what to make of the studio room she'd been given next to Locke's. She suspected it was intended for a nanny, given the kitchenette with a coffee press, microwave and shelf of mismatched dishes, but she was up in the night often enough that it seemed convenient.

"Am I the only one who remembers you had a baby two weeks ago? Ask the butler to bring in laborers if you want to move furniture. Ask *me*. Where's Locke?"

"Sleeping." She nodded at the baby monitor on her nightstand.

"And where's the nanny?" He took the monitor and followed her point to across the hall. She heard him say, "We'll be in my suite if he needs us. That's your room—

don't let the maid unpack Scarlett in there. She's sleeping with me."

"Since when?" Scarlett moved to the open door with a lurch in her chest.

"Since we're not having this conversation here." He motioned her to accompany him up the hall.

Scarlett didn't have much fight in her. Being a new mother left a woman feeling like a wet rag. She couldn't blame anyone, not even poor wee Locke and his upset tummy. She was avoiding coffee, worried caffeine was transferring and causing his fussiness so she didn't even have *that* in her system to counter her sleep deprivation.

"I'd like to be next to him," she mumbled. "Especially at night." This seemed like a long way away. Javiero was striding so fast she had to hurry to keep up with him. "I won't start him on a bottle, if that's what you're thinking. I don't care what your mother says."

"Say it louder so she'll hear you."

His gruff tone scraped the flesh from her bones, it really did. Was he going to punish her forever for not telling him about Locke? She wanted to cry, *Look at what I'm doing!* But it was no more than any new mother went through, she reminded herself.

It just felt awfully lonely.

They entered what appeared to be a newer wing of the house. He flung open a pair of double doors into a massive bedroom with a four-poster bed the size of a concert stage. Part of the exterior wall was made up of doors that slid open, stacking on one side so the room opened directly onto a wide terrace overlooking the vineyard and surrounding countryside.

It was a burst of sunshine and a glorious vista. A doorway into a new world that was grand and paradisiacal, yet masculine and intimate.

"This is beautiful." She was drawn outside to absorb the view. The terrace carried along, swelling in the middle where a small alfresco dining table stood, then narrowing again in front of another room on the far side. Below was a private garden and the pool.

Behind her, Javiero closed the entry doors with a snap. She came back inside to watch him cross to another pair of interior doors and lock those, as well.

"Where does that lead?"

"My mother has chosen not to relinquish her bedroom or the lounge that connects us. Not until you are my wife." His tone knocked that ball firmly into her court.

He hadn't mentioned marriage in over a week so she was a little surprised it was still on the agenda. She thought about it, a lot, but she couldn't see taking on the role of wife, especially an unloved one, on top of all the other changes she was dealing with. She'd crumple into a useless ball from the stress.

Not that she could reveal such a weakness when he was liable to see it as an opportunity to steamroll right over her.

She mustered some weak sarcasm. "Romantic as that proposal is, I respectfully decline to be the lever that pries your mother out of her rooms. Is that all? Because I'd like to make some calls while I don't have a crying baby in my arms."

"I'd like you to stop working."

Her heart stammered, and she had to dredge up further strength to elevate her chin.

"While we're throwing around things that won't happen, I want you and Val to reconcile so I can socialize with my friend and her daughter."

"Get another job in a few months. Running the estate is too much for you right now."

"Your concern is noted. I'm fine," she lied.

"I *am* concerned. You couldn't wait five minutes before setting up your desk?" He pointed in the direction of the room where he'd found her. "That sort of workaholic behavior isn't healthy when you only have yourself to worry about, never mind when you've recently delivered a baby. You should be resting more."

"First of all, the mansplaining of the effects of childbirth is very cute. Thank you. But speak to any new mother. They all look like this." She pointed at her face, very aware she was wan beneath the makeup she'd put on this morning. "What am I supposed to do if I don't work? Become a lady of leisure? Perhaps I could take over the running of the villa from your mother? We got off on such a good note, I'm sure she'd love *that*."

His jaw tightened.

She snorted. "Hit the nail on the head, did I?"

"She will step aside from her role once we're married. That was her intention when I was engaged to Regina. So yes, you can take control of the villa. I assure you there's enough to keep you busy."

"Keep me busy?" She tucked her chin. "Why don't you give me a box of crayons and a puzzle book if that's the goal?"

He sighed. "It's a real job, Scarlett. Did you oversee Dad's vineyards? You could do that here." He waved toward the terrace and the land beyond. "This villa is bigger than Dad's. We host parties. It's not a make-work project."

"Why would I supervise your vineyards when I'm already doing that for your son?"

"Why be reasonable when you can be obstinate?"

"*I'm* the one being unreasonable? You're upset that your mother won't come out of her room and you are taking it out on me. No, Javiero, I will not quit my job. I want to do it and I *have* to do it. As for marriage, I've given you my terms."

"Your terms are impossible. Even if you invited Kiara, do you think Val would allow her to come? I told you what he did to me, the corner he pushed me into. I don't want him here and I won't beg him to let Kiara and Aurelia come here. Did you know Kiara is marrying him? She's not demanding you attend *her* wedding."

"Because she knows I just had a baby and can't travel. We texted about it." She was trying not to let the tendrils of hope she detected in Kiara's texts fill her with envy. Her friend deserved to be happy. "Besides, her situation is different. She and Val are..." She cleared her throat, then stood tall, refusing to be coy about it. "They're sleeping together."

He pointed at the massive bed. "That's where you will be sleeping. With me."

Her heart leaped into her throat and thrummed there, making it difficult to talk around it.

"And why would I agree to that?"

"So you can tell me when it's my turn to get up with him."

That did sound nice, actually. They'd bumped into each other in the hall a few times in Madrid, but she'd always sent him back to bed and dealt with Locke herself.

"You don't have to," she dismissed wearily, too conditioned to do everything alone to seriously consider relying on him. "I'll manage."

"No, you won't. You'll be sitting at a desk half the night if I'm not there to berate you for it."

"That was one time! And it was a time zone thing!" She wanted to stamp her foot like a child. "I'm not giving up my job."

"You don't *have* to work. Do you realize how insulting

it is that you won't trust me to support you? You're acting just like him, hanging on to that rotting pile of gold because what *I* offer isn't enough. Exactly how high do your tastes run? Because I make a *lot* of money."

"Is that what you think?" She was still angry, but his comparison of her to Niko defeated her. "I'm not saying that *at all*. Fine. Support me." She threw out a hand. "In future, I'll put all my nursing bras and vitamin supplements on your credit card. But I can't ask you to support my family, Javiero." She withered into a chair, no longer strong enough to keep this from him. "And that's why I need to work."

CHAPTER SIX

HE DIDN'T MOVE, but the dark umbrage in his expression eased to a more concentrated consideration. He pushed his hands into his pockets. "You haven't said much about your family. Why are they dependent on you? How many are there? Tell me everything."

"How much time have you got?" she asked with grim humor, glancing at the door in hopes Locke would make his way down here on his own steam. No such luck, however.

"I have all day," Javiero assured her as he threw himself into the other wingback chair and stacked his feet on the footstool. His one eye packed a punch as he hit her with his intense stare.

She felt him willing her to spill her guts and her middle knotted up. She swallowed the rawness at the back of her throat, but it stayed as a scorched feeling behind her breastbone.

"I don't want to tell you." She stared toward the bright blue sky beyond the terrace, eyes stinging. "I don't want you to hate me more than you already do." She yearned for him to soften toward her, give her a chance, but this wasn't the way to do it.

The silence hung between them.

"I don't hate you," he finally said. His body was utterly

still, his voice quiet and level, yet it wrung her out even more than the silence that had preceded it. "My mother hated my father and he showed very little respect toward her and absolutely no affection. I refuse to raise my son in such a toxic atmosphere. I will never forget what you had to go through to birth him. I'll never slander you to him or force him to choose between us. But you can't expect me to trust you. Not until you've earned it."

"Ha." The sound was knocked out of her. "Such warm sentiments. I'll be sure to talk you up to him as well, tell him how understanding and generous you were during this difficult time."

"Don't test me, Scarlett," he warned.

She wanted to cry, but weeping was a useless waste of energy. No, she had developed skills and strengths and strategies to get herself through trying times. She just didn't remember where she'd put them.

Javiero's feet clapped back onto the floor and he leaned his elbows on his knees, pushing into her space. "You're the one who said we needed to get to know one another before we could discuss marriage. Talk."

She took a breath that hurt. It just *hurt*. It was effort and weight and guilt and shame.

"I'm the oldest, then there's my brother and our little sister. Marcus does his own thing these days. Went to America. Ellie catches up with him online sometimes, but I haven't heard from him in more than a year."

"Your sister upset you earlier. Why?"

She sighed, hurt all over again. "She saw the press release. Niko expected me to keep my pregnancy a secret so I only told Mum and that was just a few weeks before he was born. I didn't tell her who the father was, either. I just wanted her to know that I was expecting."

Her mother's reaction had been mostly about her job

and Scarlett's ability to send money. *There's a lawyer who thinks he can arrange an early release for your father.*

"Ellie was upset I didn't tell her, too. That I didn't trust her."

"Do you?"

She hated to say it aloud. "No."

"Where are they? London?"

"Near Leeds."

"And your father?"

Here she had to take another bracing breath.

"Dad's in prison. Drunk-driving accident. Thankfully only property damage, no one was hurt or killed, but he was a repeat offender and assaulted a police officer when he was arrested. He has another year." Her stomach turned to knots every time she thought about what would happen when he was released, so she tried not to.

"Is this why you don't want to marry? You think I can't handle a bit of bad press? That's why I have PR teams, Scarlett. His behavior isn't yours. People who judge you by association aren't the kind of people who matter."

She couldn't help her disparaging snort at that.

"It's not your association with my father that I judge. It's your loyalty to him."

It still stung. "You'll judge me even more harshly when I tell you why I was so loyal." She chewed the corner of her thumbnail, a bad habit she had kicked in adolescence. "It all ties to why I refused to stay that day and why I let Niko dictate when I would tell you about Locke."

He withdrew, physically, by leaning back into his chair.

That hurt, too. The way he had been reaching out with unconditional compassion had been nice. Now he was back to being absent of it.

"I presume he threatened to fire you, and you were afraid of being unable to support your family."

"Not exactly. It was complicated. I really did feel a duty to go back to him. He was very sick and couldn't run things without me. It was a job I'd devoted years to achieving. I didn't want to throw it away. Also, Kiara and I were the only family he had left. I'm not saying that to make you pity him or feel guilty for not being there. He made his choices and lived the consequences, but he was the grandfather of our children. Kiara and I felt it was the least we could do to nurse him through his final days. I won't apologize for that."

"Your heart was in the right place?" he asked with disdain. "I'll accept you had more sentiment than sense, and I still think he deserved to die alone."

She rolled her lips inward, aware it was futile to try to change his mind. Her mouth felt unsteady as she continued. She was coming to the part where she judged herself.

Her mother had been hurt by her silence, by her refusal to come home for a visit, then by learning she'd hidden her pregnancy. Scarlett felt horrible about all of it, but she had also embraced using Niko's wishes as a much-needed excuse to distance herself from her family.

Abusive relationships were very complex, she knew that, but her mother had had three years without her husband—enough time to attend the counseling Scarlett had arranged for her, to gain financial independence and form a healthy circle of friends. Yet she still talked about how soon her husband would be home.

Scarlett couldn't bear watching that slow-motion collision, couldn't withstand another fruitless argument. Mostly when she talked to her mother, she wanted to bawl her eyes out with frustration and helplessness, so she stood apart from it as much as she could.

Which soaked her in guilt. She felt in the wrong all the time, especially now that Locke was here and she didn't have Niko and Kiara as a distraction. She kept wondering what sort of mother her son actually had. A good one? She doubted that. Her view of herself was dark and contemptuous. Not healthy, but she didn't know how to improve it when she felt so guilty.

"Scarlett?" Javiero prompted.

"When I began working for Niko, I promised him I wouldn't turn my back on him. That my loyalty wouldn't falter."

"A pledge of fealty? How quaintly feudal. Or is the word *futile*? Because he never rewarded vows. My mother can attest to that."

"The reward came first. He did something for my family."

"It's starting to sound like a transaction, not a favor. He never did anything out of kindness."

"That's true." She frowned at her ragged nails. Niko had always ensured he benefitted as much or more from anything he did. "What he did for me—us—was quite big. My, um, father sold him our family home. Stonewood. It's an old farmhouse on a modest property, but it has a lovely view. It had been in my mother's family for generations. She didn't want to give it up, but it had fallen into disrepair and we couldn't afford to fix it." They'd barely been eating, mostly because her father drank all his income. "For Niko it was a place to park his money. He didn't even see it. His agent handled the transaction then came after us when he realized how bad the condition really was."

"Sounds like an incompetent agent."

"My father can be very persuasive." Manipulative. She found herself playing with the pendant Javiero had given her, fingering the key, which felt smooth and lovely on one side, like a worry stone. "Dad was in real estate and misrepresented the whole thing. Long story short, the agent knew Dad was cheating Niko and encouraged Niko to file a lawsuit. It ruined us. Mum had never had a job and Dad's agent license was suspended. The money he'd got for the sale of the house was put into a holding account while the suit was pending. We had no house, no money from the sale, and no income to pay rent on the place Mum and Dad had moved into. I had to drop out of university to go home and work. Help out. We all five wound up living in a tiny caravan. Things were very dire. Then Dad learned Niko was in London. He told me to go see if I could talk him into dropping the suit."

"Your *father* told *you* to do that." He knew where this was going. She could see the repulsion in his cold eye.

"You're judging," she pointed out with a fire of humiliation burning hot. "What choice did I have? My father wasn't going to save us. No one was."

"How old were you?"

"Twenty-one." She dropped the pendant to tangle her fingers in her lap. "Things were *bad*, Javiero. My brother was smoking drugs. My sister was shoplifting. Mum was… Dad was abusive when he was drinking and he drank when he was stressed."

"Violent? You should have let Niko send him to jail. Did he hurt you or your siblings?" His hands fisted, but when he caught her gaze flicking to them, he splayed his hands on his thighs. His tension remained palpable, though, coming off him in waves.

"Mum and my brother caught the worst of it," she mumbled. "Through most of my life, Dad would stay sober often enough and long enough we would convince ourselves it was behind us. Then something would happen and… After I went to work for Niko, things stabilized. They were back in Stonewood, but Dad was working a janitor job, resenting it and drinking because of it. It was a huge relief when he got picked up on that driving under the influence charge. He told Mum to tell me to hire a better lawyer. I refused, even though I could afford one."

"Good."

It hadn't felt good. It had felt cold-blooded. Cruel.

"Mum was beside herself. She's codependent, I guess. She keeps my sister very close, even though Ellie is like Dad, drinks and gets nasty. It's difficult for me to be around them. I support them, and keep an arm's length. Maybe I'm enabling. I don't know anymore."

"So you *did* sleep with my father." She'd never heard anyone sound so sickened. "To persuade him to go lenient on your family."

"No." Her voice rasped with anger. "I was prepared to. I told him I would do anything to help my family."

"Anything." His hands fisted up again.

"Anything," she confirmed, holding his gaze, holding it even as the tension pulled like a taut metal string between them, sharp enough to sever flesh.

"I have no way of proving it didn't come to sex. You'll have to believe me and I know you won't."

"How can I? Why else would he help you?"

Although she had braced herself, his ugly conclusion was still a slap in the face. She blinked and looked away, trying to clear the dampness that matted her lashes.

"Because he was impressed by how far I was willing to go for a man I hated. You and I have something in common," she added with a bitter smile. "My loathing toward my father is as deep as yours toward Niko." There was no humor in her, only despair as she added, "I used to think you and Val were such spoiled rich infants, throwing a tantrum at Niko when he had never hit you. Never sold your home out from under you or told you to throw yourself at a stranger and beg for mercy."

Javiero's nostrils flared right before he jumped to his feet and paced away. "When will your father be released? He's safer in prison. I hope he knows that."

"He's not your problem. He's mine," she said miserably. "And Niko was a dream by comparison. He said his sons hadn't shown him such fidelity and if I gave him that sort of allegiance, he would drop the charges and sell Stonewood back to me. He put the title in my name, then took the mortgage payments from the salary he paid me."

"So generous," he muttered.

"My mother got to live in her home and my father couldn't sell it out from under her. It was an absolute triumph as far as I'm concerned."

"It's indentured servitude, Scarlett, and it's illegal. What else did you have to do?"

"Nothing like you're implying." She rose, willing to suffer his disparagement over poor choices, but she wouldn't stand for being vilified over crimes she hadn't committed. "I had to work all hours crunching numbers and find rare Scotch at midnight in dry countries and face the scathing sarcasm of his recalcitrant sons."

He crossed his arms, tracking his one eye from the top of her head to her feet and back, much the way he had the first time she'd turned up in front of him on Niko's behalf.

"He must have been giddy when you said you were pregnant with my child."

"Not exactly. He insisted on tests, obviously. Then he was pleased, but…" She moved to the opening to the terrace, hugging herself, still miserable over the way Niko's hard-won regard for her had shifted. "He was disappointed in me."

"Disappointed? You made the ultimate sacrifice." Still so scathing he made her flinch.

"He didn't agree with me for making that final effort

to bring you and Val to see him. He had his heir in Aurelia and didn't care if that shut out you and your mother. I knew I would be on the hook to have to defend that after he was gone, though. We would all be sitting through litigation for a decade. I couldn't betray his plans to you, but I had to give you both an opportunity to discover what he intended. I had to give *you* that. Because what he was doing was wrong."

She didn't mention the part where she had been sure Javiero would never speak to her again after all of that shook out. That she had been driven to see him one more time while they had a small chance at civility.

"I didn't mean to sleep with you. I didn't plan to get pregnant. But he saw my behavior as similar to Evelina's when she allowed herself to get pregnant with Val, and he lost some respect for me."

"That's how it looks to everyone. Including me."

Her entire being flattened under that indictment, all shreds of hope lost. She conjured a distant smile to hide her despair. "You'd best not reward my underhanded behavior by marrying me, then."

He made a humorless noise. "You'd prefer a settlement without any promises or investment on your part? I've read that book. It's called *Val and Evelina Ruin Everything.*"

"And I've read the one where Mum made promises to a man who didn't love her. It's stacked in the horror shelves. Why would I marry a man who may not *hate* me but sure as hell doesn't care one little bit about me?"

He looked right past her then, eye narrow and flinty, mouth a flat line.

"I have a new baby, Javiero. I can hardly think straight from one moment to the next. What you see as overwork on my part is me trying to keep a grip on the one thing I can control. I'm trying to ensure my own security. I can't stop working and become reliant on you. My mother showed me what a mistake it is to put absolute trust in someone else. At least when I was beholden to Niko, he empowered me at the same time. He gave me an education and experience and a really good salary. I have authority and a job I already know how to do."

"You have a son."

"So do you! And you have a family relying on you, same as me." She flung her hand toward the open doors to the terrace and his small kingdom beyond. "Tell me, as someone who had to make hard choices in order to support his family, do you really expect me to give up my ability to help mine? To put that duty in *your* hands? You refused Niko's offer when he finally said he wanted to give you a piece of his fortune again. What's different about me refusing your offer to do the same thing?"

His shoulders bunched, and then he threw up his hands in frustration. "Fine. Work," he snarled. "But you'll set proper hours and you *will* sleep here." He pointed at the bed again.

"Why? Because you don't trust me?"

"No. I don't. And you don't trust *me*, obviously. Which annoys the hell out of me because the one thing I pride myself on is how well I take care of my family. So you and I will share a room and a bed along with a son, and we'll work on trusting each other."

Scarlett experienced a sudden, crushing insecurity that he would discover all the other little flaws that would make him truly hate her. She couldn't stand his doubts and cynicism as it was, but she didn't know how to break down the barriers between them.

Her fingertips found the grinding knot of tension between her brows and tried to smooth it away. It wasn't like her to have all this insecurity and angst. She used to feel confident in herself, but lately she felt like an awful fraud. She was blaming it on lack of sleep and all the changes around her. She doubted she would magically recover her confidence by sharing a bed with Javiero, but part of her wanted to believe that being around him in a more intimate setting would help them communicate better.

And maybe she was trying to orchestrate something that looked a lot like them going back to that torrid afternoon when they had conceived Locke. She wanted to see how far their relationship might have taken them if she'd allowed it to play out. Would they have fallen in love and married?

Oh, no, Scarlett. She closed her eyes. *Don't start dreaming about castles in the sky.*

The sound of a crying baby approached. It hadn't even been thirty minutes since she had put Locke down. That cry was starting to make her feel like such a failure.

Javiero moved to the door, but kept his hand on the latch without opening it.

"We both had parents who let us down, Scarlett. We have to at least *try* to do better than they did."

She couldn't argue that. She desperately wanted to feel like a good mum.

He opened the door and she moved to get Locke, bringing him into *their* room.

"I'm still awake," Javiero said as Scarlett slid carefully in beside him. His entire body was taut with futile anticipation.

"So is your mother," she said with a heavy sigh, sinking onto the mattress.

"She went in there?" He picked up his head and looked toward the connecting doors to the sitting room. Over dinner, he had announced that Locke would be using the small lounge as a night nursery and his mother had *not* been impressed. "I didn't hear her."

"She stayed in her room, but I heard her phone down for one of her headache pills and some tea to help her sleep. I should have stayed in the other wing. She already hates me. I don't want anything to impact her feelings toward Locke."

"How she reacts is up to her," he said with a stab of impatience. "If she wants to continue her war of passive aggression toward my dead father and resent our doing what's best for her grandson, that's her choice. I gave up trying to make her see reason years ago."

Did he hear the irony of his own years of stonewalling Scarlett and pulling dirty moves against Niko? Sure. He had even taken pleasure in sending Scarlett back to his father without so much as an inch of give on his part.

He was through with squeezing her in that power struggle, though. He might not agree with her methods, but he understood the bleak fear that had driven her. He was intimately familiar with the gnawing, intractable need to *know* that his family was secure.

He was still unsettled by the fact her father had been abusive, double-dealing his own wife and putting his entire family in an untenable position.

Niko had taken advantage of Scarlett's desperation, which was yet another reason Javiero would never forgive him, but he couldn't continue punishing Scarlett for her association with his father. He couldn't in good conscience become yet another hurdle she had to overcome in order to look after people she felt a duty toward.

She was still wriggling and rolling and pulling at the blankets.

While she had fed Locke, he had been lying there wondering who had come up with the brainless idea they should sleep together. Between taking turns brushing their teeth, he had put on pajama bottoms—something he'd started wearing so he could get up with the baby. She had put on a practical nightgown. With the way her figure was bouncing back from pregnancy, she could have worn a burlap sack and still looked like a fertility goddess. Her breasts were spectacular, and her hips and backside round and enticing beneath the soft drape of cotton. She'd always had amazing legs. All the pale skin he could see was smooth and—he recalled vividly—soft and warm and intoxicating.

Her shifting was further stimulating him, making him more aware of her weight pressing down that side of the mattress. She smelled like vanilla and pineapple, and her shaken sigh bore a resemblance to the hot breath she had released against his ear when they'd made love.

"What's wrong?" he asked with the gruffness of increasing sexual frustration. "Why can't you get comfortable?"

"I don't know. Colic? I've never slept with anyone. It's weird. I'm worried I'll kick you in my sleep. Or that you'll stretch out an arm and scare me in the night. Do you steal blankets? I don't know the protocol."

"You've never slept with *anyone*?"

"Just my sister when we were little." She rolled onto her stomach and pushed her arms under her pillow. Sighed again.

"But you've had relationships. Lovers." If she told him she'd been a virgin that day—

"I was a kid then, too," she grumbled, flipping her pillow. "Not underage. I was at university, but I was messing around just to feel like someone loved me. Childish reasons. I learned quickly that going all the way wasn't the beginning of a relationship. The boy in question invariably saw it as the end. Once I started working for your father..." Her pause seemed significant for a reason he couldn't identify, and he wished he could see her face. "There wasn't time for dating," she finished quietly. "I didn't miss it, so it was no real loss."

Her hair drew silver tracks against the dark pillowcase. He wanted to touch it. Fold it around his finger and rub his lips against it.

Unhelpful. The muscle between his thighs twitched with a strong pulse of desire.

"How many women have slept here?" she asked hesitantly, turning her head to peer at him through the dark.

"In this bed? None. As far as I know, the only woman who ever slept in this room was my grandmother. She died before I was born."

"Really?" She rolled onto her side, still facing him. "You and Regina didn't—"

"No."

"Why not?"

She wasn't you. "We were still getting to know one another."

"According to you, that happens here by sharing a bed." In the glow of the night-light, her pale face grew stiff with concentration. He felt her gaze like an infrared scanner heating his brow and cheekbones. "You don't wear your eye patch to bed."

Damn. He'd taken it off out of habit, not even thinking. His hand twitched as he debated reaching toward the nightstand for it. "It's more comfortable without."

"Then don't wear it. Listen, about surgery…" She came up on her elbow to hover over him. "Don't put yourself through that unless it's something you really want. Locke will never care how you look, not if we raise him right. And the only thing I feel about your injuries is upset that you were hurt."

She looked like an angel, hair in a loose golden halo,

voice laden with so much concern it disturbed him. His heart pounded an ancient drumbeat, calling to her. He wanted to pull her across him, *feel* whether she was telling the truth.

"I keep thinking how terrifying it must have been," she said in a solemn undertone. "You could have been killed. It would have been a horrific loss for Locke."

Only for Locke?

Where the hell had that thought come from?

"How did it even happen? Wasn't it caged—? Oh!" She gasped as he rolled her beneath him in one agile twist of his body.

"Exactly like that," he said, careful to hold himself off her while he trapped her, not squashing her flat the way the caveman in him wanted to. Desire had been soaking through him like gasoline when he'd been attacked. Desire for *Scarlett*, damn her, distracting him from the cat circling below. That hammer of need in his blood hadn't abated one bit. "I loosened my tie and it was flicking in the breeze. The animal shouldn't have been able to jump that high, but I guess it was my lucky day."

"Oh, my G— Ooh!"

Unable to resist, he opened his mouth against her soft neck, scraping his teeth before stealing one small taste of her skin with a damp swipe of his tongue against the pulse racing in the hollow at the base of her throat.

She quivered, her body taut beneath his.

"Scared?" He yanked a firm leash around his basest urges.

"N-no?" she squeaked.

"You don't sound sure." His breath on her sensitive nape made her flutter in his hold like a caught bird.

After a moment, she nervously settled as though she had decided to submit to her captor. "I'm sure." She still sounded tentative. "You won't hurt me. You wouldn't do that to Locke."

"I won't do that to *you*," he contradicted, shifting so they were nose to nose. "No matter how contentious things ever become between us, our conflicts will play out in words. Understand? You're always safe with me."

Another quake went through her, something so elemental and electric he could feel the individual hairs on his scalp standing up in response.

"Do you believe me?"

"Yes." It was barely above a whisper, but delivered without hesitation. Her hands against his chest weren't pushing him away. They shifted to offer the smallest of caresses.

"Good." Was it? Thoughts of her had stayed with him for months, nearly getting him killed. He needed as many walls as possible between them, but the idea of her fearing him made him sick.

He rolled her so she was spooned into his front, her warm butt snuggled firmly against his aching erection, her breasts a soft press beneath his forearm.

"Feel that?" he asked with a subtle thrust of his hips.

"Yes." A different type of tremble went through her, one that left her soft and pliant, and incited in him an urge to howl.

"I'm not going to do anything about it. Go to sleep. I'll get up with Locke next time and we'll hope he doesn't need the milkmaid."

"Is that what I am?" Her gurgled laugh was filled with discomfiture and a note of yearning that provoked as much satisfaction in him as it did sexual frustration.

"You're my future wife." Pure arrogance fueled his words.

"Fast asleep and dreaming already?"

He wasn't surprised by her swift reply. Or disappointed.

He rather liked her quick wit. She had always been a worthy adversary, but he nipped her earlobe in punishment, liking the sob of pleasure-pain that sounded in her throat.

"Go to sleep," he repeated.

She gave one retaliatory wiggle of her behind in his lap and exhaled, relaxing into slumber.

While he lay awake, aching.

CHAPTER SEVEN

SCARLETT STRUGGLED TO find a routine over the next while. Locke developed full-blown colic, which had her feeling incompetent as a mother. Paloma seemed to agree, making judgmental asides every chance she got. Scarlett rode that out, too tired to fight back and having enough trouble concentrating on work. When she did lie down for a nap, her mind raced with everything she ought to be doing and she couldn't sleep.

Her doctor thought she had a case of baby blues and recommended she let the nanny do more, but she couldn't bring herself to leave her son with anyone, not even Javiero. Locke sounded too distressed for her to do anything other than hold him, even though she felt helpless when she did.

She would have talked it out with Kiara, but her friend was in the throes of her Paris show. All Scarlett could do was send a hideously expensive gift, express her regret that she couldn't celebrate with her and wistfully read about Kiara's explosive success in the days afterward.

Scarlett was so proud of her she wound up crying over it, which flummoxed Javiero.

"You're still upset you couldn't attend?"

"I'm just really happy for her." She laughed off her overreaction, but melancholy had taken hold of her lately, swamping her at different times. She didn't understand how she could feel as though a rain cloud hung over her when things with Javiero had improved. She ought to feel happier, but she was so afraid that this tentative truce between them could end at the least wrong word, she was filtering everything she said.

Her tension was off the scale and when a package turned up a week after Kiara's show, she had no choice but to talk about her friend.

She clasped her hot cheeks when Javiero called her to his study, and she recognized the shape. "I completely forgot about that."

"What is it?" Javiero asked.

"A painting. Of me."

"By Kiara?" The light went out of his eye and even though he didn't move, he retreated.

"Yes." She shrugged self-consciously and would have opened it in private, but he used his pocketknife to release the bands of tape, starting the process.

She carefully worked the rest of the packaging off the framed oil, revealing herself in a summer dress, pregnant, reading a book.

"It's one of the last ones she finished before Niko passed. She promised it to me, but wanted to display it at her show. It turned out well, don't you think?"

She peered up at him, anxious for approval on her friend's behalf. *Don't hate me for loving her.*

"It's beautiful," Javiero said with surprised appreciation as he studied the expression of concentration Kiara had caught on her face, one that conveyed both the excitement and angst of becoming a new mother. The fact the book was a self-help on motherhood injected a poignant irony to the composition, but Kiara's deep affection toward her and the affinity all mothers felt toward one another imbued the image as well.

"She's very talented," Javiero said after a long minute.

"*So* talented." Scarlett hid her gush of fresh tears by plucking the envelope from where it was attached to the back of the frame and swiping her sleeve under her eyes to read it. "Oh, gosh." She blushed again. "I wouldn't think anyone would want a pregnant stranger on their wall, but she had several offers. This is a list of collectors to contact if I ever want to sell it." She showed him the extremely healthy bids.

Javiero gave a low whistle. "That's a very generous gift. I'll arrange to have it insured."

"She is generous. So warm and funny. I miss her a lot," she said before she thought better of it.

Just as she feared, Javiero seemed to take that as a nudge for him to mend fences with Val. His mood slid into the tundra of the subarctic. He offered her a tissue, but his compassion stopped there. "You're texting and calling her, aren't you?"

She tried not to, knowing he barely tolerated their friendship. "We're both busy." She blew her nose, embarrassed. "I don't mean to cry. I think I'm grieving a little."

"For Dad?" He withdrew even more.

"For the way things were. Life wasn't perfect in Greece, but those problems were familiar. I knew how to surmount them. I…" She hesitated, not sure how he would take this. "I feel lonely here. Which isn't rational," she rushed to add. "I was lonely on the island, too. At first. Working for Niko didn't leave time for any sort of personal life. The staff kept a polite distance because I gave them orders on his behalf. If I accompanied him anywhere, I was there to work. Then Kiara joined us and she was caught in this strange middle ground, too. She wasn't family, but she wasn't an employee. We became very close."

His cheek ticked. After a moment, he said, "My cousin invited us for dinner. I put her off because you're spread so thin, but maybe an evening out would be welcome?"

A few members of Javiero's extended family had dropped by to meet Locke. They had offered Scarlett a variety of cool, curious and cautious welcomes. That particular cousin had a baby a few months older than Locke and had seemed genuine in her offer to make tea if Scarlett wanted to visit and swap war stories, but Scarlett wasn't anxious to admit to a stranger that she was struggling.

She could tell Javiero was trying to help, though. She forced a smile. "That sounds nice."

Accepting that dinner seemed to open a floodgate. Invitations poured in and they were out every other night for the next while, throwing off what little routine Scarlett had established. Most were intimate soirees, but that still meant she was tied up in the evening and had to make time midday for trying on dresses and finding a hostess gift.

It was awkward in other ways, too, especially when they returned to Madrid for higher-profile events. Scarlett was used to wearing a pretty dress and making small talk, but with Niko she'd been relegated to the background. He would introduce her, and then she would largely be ignored.

With Javiero, she was his *date*. He brought in stylists to up her wardrobe game, and there was no retreating to the sidelines after twenty minutes. He wasn't the focus of attention because of his attack or his new baby or his mysterious affair with his father's PA, either. He was Javiero Rodriguez, a marquis guest for any hostess or gala.

Which put Scarlett in the spotlight alongside him.

Thankfully, her Spanish was decent, and she had her

position as trustee of Niko's fortune to mention whenever someone tried to dismiss her with, "I suppose the baby keeps you busy." The fact she held such a prestigious position always earned her a reevaluation.

It didn't quash the oblique inquiries as to her exact role in Javiero's life, however, and apparently he had grown tired of it.

She came back into their room one evening having just fed Locke. She wore only her silk robe and was about to shower and finish getting ready for the charity ball they were due to attend.

Javiero had just come out of the shower. His hair was damp and he wore only a towel, comfortable now in letting her see the scars down his chest. They no longer alarmed her. They were merely a part of him—the same way his nipples were that light shade of brown—but her mouth went dry as she took in his burnished shoulders, muscled chest and abs that went on for days. Especially when he assumed that commanding air and gave her a thousand percent of his focus.

"We're engaged," he informed her.

"We are?" He caught her off guard completely with that pronouncement.

"We are." He produced a velvet box and opened it.

She was further dumbfounded.

"It's beautiful," she said of the gold setting that held a round white diamond and at least a dozen smaller stones. The blue-green gems made it truly eye-catching, though. "Sapphires?"

"Blue emeralds. Trilliant cut, or so I was told by the jeweler."

"It's not a family ring? It looks like an heirloom."

"It probably was," he said drily. "And like my grandfather, whoever owned it must have had to sell his wife's jewelry to hang on to his house. I was looking for something like what my grandmother wore in our old family photos, and this jumped out at me." He held it near her cheekbone. "It reminded me of your blue eyes and golden hair."

His smile quirked with self-deprecation before he picked up her hand. He glanced at her as he began to thread the ring onto her finger, challenging her to refuse it.

Her fingers flexed lightly in his grip, the feel of the ring sliding into place more impactful than she expected.

Perhaps he felt her instinctive tension. His own grip tightened.

"'Fiancée' is a lot nicer than some of the euphemisms I've been trying to find for 'mother of my illegitimate child.' I want to call you my wife, Scarlett."

"I know." Guilt had her pursing her lips, but marriage was such a big decision. "I do think about it every day, you know." She stared at the sparkling ring until her eyes went hot. "What our life would look like."

"It would look exactly like what we have right now." He let their joined hands relax into the space between them. His other hand rose to touch her chin, nudging her gaze to come up to meet his. "With the addition of physical intimacy. Which *I* think about daily."

Her cheeks went hot and little tugs and pulls accosted her insides.

"Do you?" she asked with a measure of doubt. "You're very…" She shrugged, trying to turn her spasm of insecurity into a diffident smile. Aside from innocuous touches to her lower back or a brush of his hands against her as they transferred Locke, he only made physical contact with her in bed and that was—at most—a bit of spooning in the middle of the night when one of them came back from tending their son. "You've been very hands-off since that first night."

"Because we have seven more nights to get through. If you think I'm not counting them down, you're not nearly as smart as I've always believed."

She wrinkled her nose, humor breaking through a veil of worry she hadn't realized was thick enough to weigh on her until she caught this glimmer of light. "I thought you were…"

His brow went up, prompting her to continue.

"I don't know." She drew her hand from his and tangled her fingers. Sharing a bed and a bedroom meant there had been a few wardrobe slips that had revealed a stretch mark here and a plump thigh there. She hadn't run on a treadmill in months, unable to find the energy.

"I don't look like I did before."

"No, you don't," he agreed gruffly. His touch on her chin tightened slightly. He gently turned her face so he could examine each side of her profile. "You look fragile with these hollow cheeks and dark circles under your eyes. Your skin is translucent and even your lips are pale. I heard the doctor telling you to take your iron and get more rest. I want you to eat more and quit worrying about losing weight, but that's the only demand I feel comfortable making when you well up over a kitten crying in a tree. That doesn't mean I think there's anything wrong with this new figure of yours."

He raked his gaze down the blue silk of her robe, eyeing where her lapel lay against the inner swell of her breast. He bit his own lip.

The air changed. Her scalp prickled and she curled her toes in her slippers.

"Make no mistake," he said in a throaty voice. "I'm obsessed with seeing more of it."

She swallowed, accosted by a flush of wry pleasure

and sexy twinges she hadn't experienced in what felt like ages. And she was tearing up, but they were happy tears.

"Really?"

"Deeply. But I'm afraid if I start touching you..." He allowed his fingertip to draw light patterns on her breastbone. The back of his knuckle caressed the swell of her breast, making both her nipples peak against the light layer of silk. "I may not stop."

She looked at his mouth. *I don't want you to stop*, she wanted to say, but his mouth was already coming down on hers.

They both moaned with satisfaction as the kiss dragged them into passion like an undertow pulling them into a heavy sea. She crashed herself into his big frame, knocking her own breath from her lungs.

His hands caught her and roamed, greedy, his touch everything she needed and not nearly enough. She folded her arms behind his neck and tried to drag him down closer. Into a harder kiss. Something that could appease this ache that had been simmering below the surface, ignored and quilted over with exhaustion and worry, but now rose up as a conflagration that engulfed her.

It was like that day in this apartment. Once the fuse was lit, it ran from one to the other, setting barrels of gunpowder alight so they exploded again and again until there was only this. Fire and flame and heat and light.

His big hands slid down her backside and caught under her cheeks, and he pulled her up. Her legs parted and she hugged his waist with her thighs as a wall pressed against her back.

He felt so good! Heavy and strong. So much warm satiny skin beneath her splaying fingers, muscles shifting and straining. She couldn't get enough. His mouth devoured hers and she loved that, too. The soft abrasion of his beard, the scent of his soap and the faint taste of mint in his mouth as he raked rough kisses across her lips. Their tongues tangled as the kiss grew flagrant and unmistakably sexual. He plunged his tongue between her lips, letting her know what he really wanted.

The erotic signal made her blood run like warm honey, sweet and thick. Her body dampened with slick heat and she moaned her capitulation. To passion. To *him*.

He dragged his head up. They panted, breaths mingling.

"My towel is falling off."

"I know." She could feel the shape of him against the gusset of her knickers, so hard and hot the silk should have singed away. She wanted him so badly she could have wept.

The belt on her robe had loosened. Her soft belly was pressed to his firm one. Her breasts were exposed.

"We can't," he growled in a voice that rang with agony. "I know we can't. But I want to." He gave a thrust of his hips to punctuate his need.

He hit such a magic spot that she let out a strangled groan of pleasure.

"Oh," he said in a tone of pleased discovery. "You like that." He did it again.

Her whole body shimmered with pleasure.

"More?"

"Yes," she sobbed. Her fingernails clawed into his shoulder.

"It doesn't hurt?" He licked at her dry, parted lips.

"*No.* It feels so good," she gasped helplessly, catching at his mouth with her teeth. "Keep doing it."

He did, sawing his hard shape against the thin layer of damp silk. It barely shielded her aching folds and her swollen, neglected button of nerve endings. His mouth smothered hers again, swallowing her moans of pleasure in a brazen kiss as he kept stimulating her, naked and powerful and deliberate.

She consumed his mouth and gave him her tongue. She thought she would die when he pinned her stiffly to the wall with the weight of his hips, not moving anymore, just holding her on that pinnacle of acute pleasure, the pressure of him *there* sending her eyes rolling into the back of her head. It was too much and not enough, being held in this vise between everything and nothing.

He let go of her bottom with his one hand and yanked her robe aside, fully exposing her breast to his hot palm while his mouth trailed into her throat.

She groaned again, arching her back to increase his touch. Her thighs stayed clamped around him, but her movement sent a pulse of joy up from between her legs. Her hips began rocking in an abbreviated grind, feeding the excitement still gripping her. He shook with strain, holding her pinned and suspended while she found the sensations she needed.

She stroked her fingers through his hair, pleading, "Don't stop, please don't stop." She clung to him and writhed in the tight space between his hard body and the hard wall, nipped at his stubbled jaw and bared her throat to the rough suction of his love bite. And when the striving tension turned to tingling shivers of climax, she nearly screamed, she needed it so badly.

As an achingly splendid release washed over her, he grabbed her butt in both hands again. All of him went taut as he thrust his erection across wet silk. He tipped back his head and made the sexiest, most animalistic noises of pleasure she'd ever heard. It was earthy and primal, and time stopped while throbbing ecstasy fused them together, melting and hot and indelible.

When she came back to awareness, her forehead was lax

on his shoulder. He was still trembling with exertion. They were both quaking with aftermath. Javiero still leaned on her, heavy and damp. His weight made it hard for her to catch her breath, but he seemed as wrung out and weak as she felt. The slam of his heart was still hitting her breast and her own pulse felt as though it would remain unsteady and panicked forever—because that had been every bit as intense as their only other time together, and it had happened after only a bit of groping and necking. Surely that terrified him as much as it did her?

She lifted her head off his shoulder and thunked her head against the wall.

He made an admonishing, concerned noise and eased his hold on her until she found her feet. He stayed pressed tight to her and caged her with his forearms on either side of her head. He kissed her again, lazy and thorough, until she nearly sank into a puddle on the floor. Only the unrelenting press of his body held her up.

"That," he said in a feral rasp beneath her ear, "is what our marriage will be like."

"We might not survive," she said in a shaky attempt at humor. "Dare we risk orphaning our son?"

"Heh." His cloud of warm breath pooled against her cheek, causing a final pleasurable shiver down her spine.

He drew back enough to swipe the edge of her gaping robe across her stomach and his own, then he pushed the garment off her shoulders.

"Laundry," he said with a quirk of his mouth as he let the robe dangle from his hand. He ate up her naked breasts with his gaze. "I'd join you in the shower, but..." His growl was hungry and possessive. The kiss he touched to her mouth, however, was surprisingly tender.

Her lips clung to his, begging him to linger. He drew back long before she'd had her fill.

"Thank you. That was every bit as incredible as I remember," he said throatily.

For some reason, she wanted to cry. She wasn't sad. That *had* been incredible. She had loved every second of it and wished they could fall into bed and do intimate things to each other all night long. She wanted to build on this connection until she didn't feel things were so tenuous between them.

She was also aware that he could have dragged an officiate into the room right now and she would have spoken any vows he told her to repeat through these buzzing lips. She didn't have an excuse to leave or a promise to someone he hated. She had no guardrails at all against slipping straight over the edge into falling for him completely.

Which was terrifyingly dangerous because she couldn't imagine him ever feeling the same toward her.

Javiero entered the gala without any self-consciousness over his appearance. Most people had at least seen pictures of him by now and he'd caught a bit of sun the last few weeks. The claw marks had faded, no longer standing out nearly as horrifically as they had in the early days.

Besides, nothing could bother him while he was riding this smug, endorphin high after his fervid tussle with Scarlett.

He had only meant to kiss her, but they'd both lost control. He ought to be scared out of his skin by that, but it was amazing how omnipotent he felt when he made her come. If he thought too long about the way she had clung to him and sucked his lip and fairly dissolved the silk between them with her wet response, he would embarrass himself with a fresh bulge behind his fly.

Crazed as the experience had been, he'd needed it. Sexual frustration had been approaching lethal concentration in his bloodstream. Her too, he suspected. They were both tossing and turning every night.

Not that deprivation had fueled that madness. That was how they reacted to each other and he *liked* it.

Thankfully, they were proving to be compatible in other ways, as well. Scarlett was fitting nicely into his life. The cool English cucumber she'd always been made a perfect foil for his more passionate, forceful personality at events such as these.

A deeply primal and gratifying *mine* rang in his head as he wove their fingers together and felt the warm gold of her engagement ring dig into his skin.

She caught him looking at her and must have read his thoughts because a pretty, shy blush hit her cheeks.

A strange thing happened in that moment. One of those odd musical pauses occurred, leaving space for a familiar voice to carry.

"...had to come see Beauty and the Beast myself, but which one is which?"

It was a savagely cheap shot that elicited a few titters from the group where Regina was holding court a short distance away.

Scarlett stiffened and would have pulled her hand from his if he hadn't tightened his grip on reflex. The people they'd been speaking with widened their eyes in appalled horror.

Javiero turned his head and saw Regina comprehend she'd been overheard. She didn't waste time looking remorseful. She slapped a wide smile over her gaffe and braved it out.

"*Querido*, it's so good to see you again." She wove toward them through the pockets of people who fell into a watchful silence.

The music rose again, sounding overloud now that everyone had closed their mouths to blatantly eavesdrop.

"Introduce me to your frien—"

"Fiancée," he corrected sharply. "We won't keep you. I'm sure you're on your way to the door." He was not the host of this gala, but it *was* a banishment.

Regina paled as she realized she had lost social cache that would never be recovered.

"You must be Regina? I'm Scarlett." She shot out her free hand. "Javiero and I were about to dance, but I'd love to chat properly after. I hope you'll stay a little longer?"

"I would love to," Regina said with a wary glance at him and a weak shake of Scarlett's hand.

"Excellent. *Querido?*" Only he heard the facetiousness in Scarlett's use of the endearment Regina had used. She squeezed his arm and brushed against his stiff body, trying to draw him onto the dance floor.

He resisted, watching Regina until she swallowed and looked down. Then he followed Scarlett and whirled her into his hard arms.

"Why did you do that?" He demanded through his teeth. He wanted to *crush* Regina.

"Oh, I wanted to spit in her face, believe me." She didn't look it. She wore an unbothered smile. "But I won't start the sort of grudge match with your old flame that your mother and Evelina still cling to. Who has the time or energy?"

He did. Animosity and resentment drove him pell-mell through this endurance event called life. He had axes aplenty to grind and regarded setting them aside as quitting.

Recognizing that vengeful side of himself was a disturbing moment of self-reflection, one that made him glance down at the glimmer of despondency beneath Scarlett's outwardly serene expression.

Concern rushed through him. "Are you tired? Do you want to go home?"

"No," she said after the briefest hesitation. She found a fresh smile. "People would say she put me on the run, and they're gossiping enough about me as it is."

"Are they? I never even notice anymore." Of course he and Scarlett would be the subject of askance looks and talking behind hands. It was inevitable. But between Niko's perfidy and the money troubles Javiero had inherited from his grandfather, his family had always been a bottomless well for chinwags. Scarlett—his estranged father's PA, who had birthed his son—provided a fresh buffet of speculation, but he hadn't given it any notice.

He had assumed she was impervious as well, handling their notoriety like the stalwart soldier she'd always been.

He could feel tension in her, however, even as she kept it from her face. The silver gown she wore was stunning and draped her figure lovingly, but he suddenly saw it as the armor it was. Delicate chain mail with a protective ruffle at her neck.

Was she feeling attacked? Had she been struggling with these appearances all along?

A wave of protectiveness had him closing his arm across her back and drawing her closer. "I don't care what people think. If you're tired, we'll go home."

"I'm fine," she insisted, fingers cool in his as she smiled a deflection. "Did you hear someone ask her if you had called me your fiancée? She gets to be the source of *that* fresh gossip and will be forced to admit that, yes, she had the chance to marry you and blew it. You couldn't have devised a more diabolical revenge if you had tried."

Another time he might have appreciated the irony, but he was infuriated that she hadn't been forthright with him about her troubles. She would share her body, but not the bruises his world was leaving under her skin?

"If you're struggling with something, I expect you to tell me," he said. Demanded.

"I fight my own battles." Her chin came up in the unbothered way it always had when she had crossed swords with him. Exactly the way it had all those times she had driven him crazy, acting tough and unwavering against any pressure he had put on her. "This isn't even a skirmish. Don't worry about it."

He didn't want to worry. Deep in the back of his head, he was still thinking of her as his enemy. It was a slippery label to hang on to, though. She was also his son's mother. His lover. Soon he would make her his wife.

As he whirled her on the dance floor, he tracked his one eye around the room, letting the feral beast inside him signal a deadly warning to any coyotes and wolves who thought they could nip at his woman and get away with it.

Beauty and the Beast. *Which one is which?*

That remark continued to grind against Scarlett's self-worth because, beneath the anger was hurt and—she winced as she acknowledged it—shame. *She* was the beast. That's what she kept thinking. She wasn't a good person. She had left her mother and siblings to their father's anger, first escaping to university and later to Greece.

She could rationalize all she wanted that by working for Niko she had "saved" them, but Niko hadn't been a pillar of the community. He'd been horrible to Javiero. Selfish and demanding and cutthroat. *Entitled.* No wonder Javiero hated her for working for him.

Now she was a terrible mother who couldn't seem to comfort their child. The doctor assured her Locke was healthy, that it was "just colic," but she had tried every tip she could find online and nothing seemed to help.

Javiero knew on some level. He must. He began curtailing their socializing, something that should have been a relief and, instead, made her feel as though he didn't want to be seen with her.

At least he still wanted to kiss and touch her. He did every night, until they were sighing with bliss.

She needed that. She craved his touch because his kisses and caresses drowned out the blaring, berating voices in her head and, for a brief time, she felt beautiful and cherished and *good*.

But she wasn't. Even when it came to the work she had fought so hard to continue she was dropping balls and making stupid mistakes. She managed to clean up her own messes, but it took extra time and she was so embarrassed she didn't tell anyone, not even Kiara, afraid her friend would insist on replacing her.

She put her mental state down to stress over Javiero's suggestion they go to London. He had business there and suggested she accompany him as a mini honeymoon of sorts, once she had her final checkup. He even arranged for her mother to come down to London and meet her grandson.

Scarlett appreciated all of that, but she couldn't shake a sense of impending doom at the prospect of going back to England. She didn't have energy to come up with reasons to put it off, however.

She saw her doctor the morning they were leaving, mostly as a formality. Locke was hitting all his milestones, and Scarlett needed only a proper prescription for the mini-pill. She'd started a sample pack after her last visit to see how she reacted.

When the doctor asked whether the baby blues were still

troubling her, she brushed off mentioning the weepiness and fatigue she continued to experience. She was still adjusting to her new life. Anxiety and impatience were to be expected. Nothing could be done except wait it out. Eventually things would settle down and she wouldn't feel so overwhelmed, she reasoned.

Besides, she was afraid the doctor wouldn't give her the all clear to use the bed for other purposes if she mentioned she wasn't sleeping well. The physical closeness she had with Javiero was so reassuring that she wanted to continue it. She hoped taking it to the next level would draw them even closer.

She filled her prescription on her way back to the flat and smiled shyly when she found him in his den.

"Cleared to travel?" he asked as he ended a call and rose to come around his desk.

Dear Lord, the man was sexy as hell. His shirt shifted across his bulky shoulders and chest. He had the natural grace of a predator lazily coming across to its mate, brimming with confidence in his right to push into her space.

She swallowed and nodded, blushing deeply. "And to resume all other activities."

"Well, that is good news. I've been anxious to go ice-skating." He tilted up her chin and set a teasing kiss on her laughing mouth. "Unfortunately, I have some news that's less so. I'll stay with you in London long enough to meet your mother, but I have to leave for New York by tomorrow afternoon."

"Should Locke and I come to America with you?"

"I'll be tied up every day," he dismissed. "You'll be more comfortable making your way back to Casa del Cielo at your own pace. Spend as much time as you like with your family."

Counteroffer, she wanted to say, but he was turning her toward the door.

"I've made dinner reservations. Let's get to London before I become distracted with 'other activities.'"

Scarlett had traveled extensively with Niko and had always stayed in five-star hotels or luxury properties that he owned. She'd overseen enough of his real estate deals that she immediately understood what a gem Javiero had obtained with this penthouse atop a newly built glass skyscraper in Mayfair.

The views were stupendous, of course, and the terrace was to die for, but the interior was equally beautiful. It was furnished in ultramodern clean lines, the color scheme a neutral bone with pops of silver and blue gray. There were five bedrooms, each with a bath—the master had two, a his and a hers.

Javiero nipped out briefly while she was getting settled and returned with a pair of drop earrings, fanned white diamonds that draped a string of dangling pale blue ones.

"Please tell me that's a loan," she said on a gasp.

"It's a gift. This is our first proper date."

"Flowers would have sufficed," she said, but the sweetest pleasure bathed her. He was trying to make this evening special and she found that incredibly endearing. Promising, even. "Thank you. They're beautiful."

She put them on. She had already done her hair and makeup, and was in her robe, about to dress. She picked up her loose hair so he could see the earrings.

"That's very pretty," he said, touching her elbow in a way that acted like a spell, freezing her with her hands in her hair while he tracked the view all the way down the front of her robe to where her raised arms lifted her breasts against silk. "Perhaps you should stay exactly like that while I push our reservation."

"I *just* put Locke down. We probably have at least…ten minutes," she joked.

His brutish face softened into something like tenderness as he hooked his hand behind her neck and drew her close.

"I can work with that. Can you?"

"Try me." She played her touch over his buttons. His particular scent, spicy and elemental, lingered in the air around her and called her to step even closer.

It struck her that no man had ever made her feel this way—soaked in yearning. She doubted any other man ever would, and that was both a relief and an unbearable loss. Her eyes grew hot as a strange, clamoring desperation gripped her. What if he rejected her? What would happen *when* he rejected her?

That wasn't happening now. He drew her closer and covered her mouth in a languorous kiss that had nowhere to be except right here. It was dreamy and reassuring and made a moan of sheer luxury climb from her chest into her throat. She leaned into him and he cupped her head, and they stood like that, kissing and kissing. He drew on her bottom lip and returned to capture her open mouth. She greeted his tongue with her own and her knees nearly disappeared from under her, but she didn't care so long as they kept doing this.

He was hard behind his fly. She shifted to press herself into his shape and ran her hands over his back. She wanted to do everything—tear off his clothes and feel his skin and stroke him past his control and feel his lips mapping her every curve. But as he lifted his head and revealed the heat in his gaze, giving her a slow, wicked smile, she knew they had time. Her heart could race, but they didn't have to.

She was so happy in that moment. Deliriously happy.

She ran her hand up to the back of his head, urging him to return for another kiss.

When her fingers grazed the strap of his eye patch, he flicked it off and tossed it toward the night table, then scooped her off her feet and into his arms.

A knock sounded on the bedroom door.

His face blanked with outrage.

"Busy," he bit out.

"Shall I dismiss the woman downstairs?" the butler asked. "Ms. Walker?"

"Mum?" Scarlett asked with concern. "Tell them to send her up," she called while Javiero set her onto her feet. "I'm so sorry. I texted her when we were leaving Spain, telling her we would be here this evening. I thought she was coming on the morning train. Maybe she misunderstood."

"Nothing a cold shower can't fix," he said with rueful frustration. "Invite her to join us for dinner."

"I'm really sorry."

"I've waited this long." He caught her chin and kissed her once. Hard. "Make it up to me later," he suggested, and disappeared into his bathroom.

She heard the ding of the elevator and hurried out of the bedroom, not worrying about the fact she was in her robe. It was only Mum.

Except it wasn't. It was her sister, Ellie.

CHAPTER EIGHT

ELLIE WORE FULL makeup. Her hair was bumped and curled and teased into flyaway wisps. She was dressed for clubbing in a short, tight skirt. Her leopard-print top was scooped low to show a lot of her breasts.

She took a pull off her vaping pen and released a cloud of moisture while she looked Scarlett up and down, gaze sticking at her chest. "Are those real?"

"What?" Scarlett touched the pendant of the diamond-encrusted lock that Javiero had given her. "This?"

"Your boobs. They used to be a lot smaller."

"I just had a baby."

"Oh. Right. Where is he?" Ellie glanced around.

"With the nanny. Sleeping." Scarlett glanced at the butler with a strained smile. "This is my sister, Ellie."

"Shall I prepare a room?"

Scarlett realized Ellie had brought an overnight bag. "Arrange something with a nearby hotel. My treat," she assured Ellie with a smile that hid the way she was freaking out. "So the baby doesn't keep you up."

Ellie made a choking noise as the butler melted away. "You have a nanny *and* a butler?"

And a housekeeper who also cooked, but Scarlett didn't bother to mention it.

"It's nice to see you. How are you?"

Ellie released a fresh cloud of cherry-scented vapor through a pursed smile that derided Scarlett's manners.

And Scarlett gave them up as she waved to dispel the sickly sweet aroma from the air, already feeling a head-ache coming on.

"Can you not do that in here? Where's Mum?" She glanced toward the elevator.

"Didn't want to come." Ellie turned off her pen and dropped it into her overstuffed bag. "Dad asked her to visit him tomorrow. She'd rather do that."

"But..." Scarlett's heart plummeted with disappoint-ment while part of her had to wonder if she deserved that disregard. "So she's not coming at all? Did you try to talk her into it?"

"What's the point?"

It was a careless dismissal of Scarlett's feelings, but not deliberately cruel. Ellie had been as affected as all of them by their twisted upbringing. Her way of coping had been to act out and run around with boys, all of them terrible. Ellie's pain was the same as Scarlett's and Scarlett's was so acute her chest was tight.

"Mum sounded so excited to meet Locke," she mur-mured.

Actually, Mum had tried to talk Scarlett into staying with them at the house and going to the prison with her, but Scarlett had made excuses about Javiero's demanding schedule and her colicky son.

Maybe she shouldn't complain about her mother's pri-orities when her own were deeply self-interested, but her reasons for refusing were about protecting herself and her son while trying to help her mother. She had hoped her mother agreeing to a day trip had meant she was mov-ing past allowing her husband to control her every move.

So much for that. Why was Mum still pinned under his

thumb? Scarlett had done so much to try to pull her out of that pattern—supported her, invited her a million times to come to Greece, offered to pay any bills that would get her a divorce.

Mum stayed grimly tied to her husband. Why? Dad wasn't using his time in prison for self-reflection and meetings to overcome his alcoholism. He wasn't seeking counseling over the abuse he'd inflicted. Anytime Scarlett brought up his behavior, her mother defended him. *Your father loves all of us very much.*

"This place is unreal." Ellie was wandering the flat, goggling at the cut crystals dangling off the lampshades and smelling the enormous fresh-cut floral arrangement. She trailed her fingers along the back of the overstuffed leather sofa. "'Luxury must be comfortable, otherwise it is not luxury.' Coco Chanel," she informed in an aside, one that held the canny calculation of a fox. A survivor by any means. "You're living really well these days."

"This belongs to Javiero," Scarlett dismissed.

"You're marrying him," Ellie said in a harder voice, her sharp gaze hitting Scarlett's ring, then her necklace, then her earrings.

"We haven't set a date." Scarlett pinched her lips together.

"I guess that's why I haven't received an invitation. But, oh, that's right. We never get invited anywhere. Except London. For a sandwich."

"I've been working." *Paying for where you live.* "I didn't get vacation except for a few days here and there. Then Niko was sick—"

"Whatever." Ellie dismissed her words with boredom.

It was the same stale argument they'd been having for years.

"Mum could have called to say she couldn't make it."

You didn't have to come. She bit back the words. "We were expecting her tomorrow and were about to go to dinner."

Ellie snorted and gave her a side-eye. "I can tell what you were about to do. I guess that's what you *have* to do, isn't it? To get all this?"

"Don't be gross."

"I'm gross? You're the one who slept with an old man to get your hands on his money. Then got yourself knocked up by his son to seal the deal. I have to give it to you— you're platinum level at this game. I'm just wondering when you'll start sharing the— Oh, hello." Ellie batted her thick lashes.

The bottom of Scarlett's stomach dropped out before she turned to see Javiero had silently come from the bedroom. He wore a fresh white shirt and crisp black trousers. His hair was damp, his expression stiff and unreadable. He offered a distant nod.

"My sister, Ellie," Scarlett said, mortified at what he must have overheard. "Mum couldn't make it. Ellie, this is Javiero."

"I didn't want the train ticket to go to waste." Ellie swanned across to shake his hand. "And I fancied a taste of London's nightlife. Sounds like you two were about to enjoy some yourselves. Mind if I tag along? I haven't caught up with Scarlett in ages."

"Of course," Javiero said as Scarlett opened her mouth.

"I've booked Ellie into a hotel," she hurried to assure him. "Our tame, early dinner isn't what she had in mind for nightlife."

"Oh, it's definitely a start," Ellie said. "Get dressed while I chat up your fiancé?"

Scarlett had never zipped herself into a dress faster.

When they got to the restaurant, she could have cried. It was exclusive and intimate and obviously a careful choice by Javiero for its air of romance. There was a small dance floor and a live trio playing swoony tunes. If they had come here alone, it would have been a perfect evening.

Instead, it was an uncomfortable meal, with her sister asking pointed questions about Javiero's properties while making not-really-kidding suggestions that he introduce her to his rich friends. All the while she swallowed back one fancy cocktail after another.

Scarlett was dying to end the night, but didn't want a scene.

"Have you had many bites on doing hair and makeup for the movies? I thought you were planning a trip to California?" Scarlett tried to keep Ellie talking so she wouldn't swill her drinks.

"Oh, yes. So generous of you to pay for my cosmetology courses. Not sure why I have to work at all when you're rolling in dough the way you are. She always plays it like she made such a great sacrifice," Ellie said to Javiero. "Getting a cushy job working for your old man, traveling all over the world with him, talking him into giving us our own house. Where are you in Spain? Do you have a beach house I could visit?"

"Ellie," Scarlett muttered.

"What? This sort of life is only for you? Not the rest of us lowlifes?"

"I told you, things have been difficult. I'll see what I can arrange for you in way of a holiday *if* you behave yourself," she said through her teeth.

"Ooh, sounds like someone will be getting lucky tonight," Ellie said with a smirk at Javiero.

He had barely said a word all evening, and Scarlett was so appalled she couldn't meet his gaze. She cut things short before dessert, insisting she had to get back to Locke.

"I've tried to pull off your innocent act, but never

had the success you have," Ellie said in a slur as Scarlett poured her into a cab to her hotel. "Trading up from a Sugar Daddy to a Baby Daddy and being all like, *What? I got pregnant by* accident." Ellie clutched her hands beneath her chin and blinked her eyes, then saluted her. "My hat is *off.*"

"I am *so* sorry," Scarlett said when she and Javiero were in his car. "Ellie was thirteen when I left for uni. It was only a few years later that I went to Greece. I've never spoken frankly to her about how that came about. To her mind, I've made a habit of running away from our problems and had everything easy while she struggled in school and felt saddled with Mum."

"Are you going to see your mother tomorrow?" he asked stiffly, making it clear he didn't want to listen to her defend Ellie.

"She has an appointment." The despondency ringing through her made it impossible to admit where her mother was going. "We could come to New York with you?"

"Unnecessary." His flat refusal dashed any glimmer of hope that he wasn't thoroughly repulsed by her family.

I tried to warn you, she wanted to say as she twisted her engagement ring.

"I'll join the London team leaving on the charter in the morning. You can have my jet to fly back to Madrid when it suits you."

"Thank you," she murmured, because what else could she say? *Don't go?*

The thick silence stayed fixed between them when they returned to the flat. She said she would check on Locke and Javiero said, "I have an early start. I'm going to bed."

He was still awake when she crawled in beside him, though.

"Javiero, I'm really sorry. I wanted tonight to be..." She

hesitated to say *special*, afraid it would be too revelatory. She didn't want to come off as insecure and needy, even though she definitely was. "Are we okay?"

"Of course." He sounded brisk, though.

She searched the dark, trying to read his expression. They had been so attuned a few hours ago, but that accord had been snuffed as quickly as blowing out a candle.

"I was..." She swallowed, certain she would have to make the moves here if she wanted to bridge the divide. "I was looking forward to making love with you," she confessed in a whisper. She wanted him to *love* her, but she knew that wasn't something she could force. She didn't even know how to inspire it.

His silence made her shrink into herself.

"We don't have to rush it," he finally said in a strained voice.

"You don't want to?" She dared to slide her hand across the mattress and find his arm. She went farther, to his bare chest, where the fine hairs prickled and his beaded nipple poked her palm.

"I'm sure you could persuade me, if you set your mind to it." She couldn't read his expression, but his voice sounded faintly bitter. Self-deprecating, perhaps?

Her hand jerked, but she left it on his chest, where his heart was thumping steadily. She knew all the filthy things that Ellie had said must be ringing in his head, but they weren't true! She wanted him for him, not his money or his father's.

"Are you saying I should, um, seduce you?" Her voice thinned on the last words.

"If you want to."

She didn't know how. She lost herself every time he touched her, but it wasn't a conscious thing. It was pure response and uncouched greed for the feel of him. For the pleasure of being stroked and petted, kissed and caressed. She loved how loved she felt when they were close like that.

She didn't know how to bring him to that sort of pitch, though. She was thinking, *This is it. This is where I lose him*, but as she started to withdraw her touch from his chest, she felt the twitch in his arm, as though he wanted to stop her drawing back and only kept himself from it by freezing at the last second.

She could feel the strain in his tense muscles, suggesting his control was being tested.

In a bold move, she circled his nipple with the edge of her thumb and heard his faint inhale. It was incredibly encouraging.

She slid closer, but he stayed on his back, only moving his arm to curl it beneath his head so she could align herself alongside him. When she kissed his jaw, he turned his head, but let her take the lead on teasing him into parting his lips. Although she kept waiting for evidence of his natural inclination to dominate, he stayed almost passive, as though testing her resolve.

Or was his interest that tepid?

Anguished by the thought, she drew back a little, but her hand had shifted to his flat belly and it was rock hard. She smoothed the rippling muscles across his abdomen, traced the line of hair down the center, circled his navel and let her hand slide lower.

He was *very* hard.

It was the reassurance she had needed. She kissed him again as she stroked him, her own body growing languid and excited. She crooked her knee and rested her thigh across his, lying against him as she kissed and caressed him.

She dipped her head to press her mouth to his chest and the raised line of one of his scars met her lips. Stark fear of loss echoed through her. So close… He had been so close to being out of her reach forever.

She rubbed her lips with more purpose against the scar, trying to kiss it better. Heal it. Trying to tell him how grateful she was that he was here.

His hand came up to her hair as though to pull her away—something that might kill her when she had such an aching emptiness in her chest. Such an unbearable need to be close to him.

She moved to his nipple and pressed an openmouthed kiss there, teased the bead with her tongue and enjoyed a rush of confidence as he sucked in a breath that swelled his chest.

His response stayed stubbornly muted, however. It was frustrating. She wanted the wildness. She needed to know he wanted her the way she wanted him. She ached for the tenuous connection between them to be forged into steel by white-hot fire.

Had his desire for her been killed tonight? She couldn't bear the thought.

She slid herself fully atop him, lips tracing from shoulder to shoulder across the smooth skin against his collarbone and over the muscles of his chest.

His hand left her hair and she thought he was going to embrace her; instead, both his arms went up to the headboard, catching under the edge of it so he was one long, straining beast beneath her. Her heart leaped with excitement.

She was having an effect on him. Whatever he was trying to prove to her or himself wasn't easy for him. With a secretive smile, she danced her open mouth down his torso, following where her touch had strayed, dislodging the sheet as she went.

His musky scent filled her nostrils as she took a blatant taste of his salty length.

His whole body jerked and she pushed at his thighs, making room for herself to explore with her touch and her tongue. Filled with helpless craving, she did everything she could to give him pleasure. She wanted him to fall apart, to feel as vulnerable to her as she was to him.

Just when she thought he couldn't grow harder or thicker, couldn't possibly hold on to his control, he said in a rasp, "I need a condom."

She rose to kneel between his legs. "I'm on the pill."

"Let's not take chances." He rolled and reached into the side table drawer, withdrew one and handed it to her.

Shakily she tried to apply it, but she'd never done that before. He finally brushed her touch away and said, "I'll do it. Take off your nightgown."

He sounded distant and implacable. Not nearly as moved and aroused as she was. Her eyes grew damp with helplessness as she threw her nightgown off the bed and stayed kneeling where she was.

"Come." He finally touched her, guiding her to straddle him. "This is what you want, isn't it?"

"Is it what you want?"

"I just put on a condom. What does that tell you?"

His hands were on her now and he ran them over her, greedily filling his palms with her breasts and hips and the round cheeks of her butt, as if he couldn't get enough. One hand rode up the front of her thigh, and his thumb slid inward to part her damp folds. When he found the slick center of her, he made a rumbling noise of satisfaction in his chest.

Here, finally, was the lover who had been generously teasing her past the point of no return each night. She wanted to give that back to him and shifted, rising to guide him to her entrance, then slowly taking him in.

Oh, dear.

"Hurt?" he asked gruffly, making her aware she'd caught her breath.

Had that been the source of his reticence? Worry? Tenderness filled her as she folded herself onto him.

"It feels really good," she sighed. His penetration wasn't so much painful as painfully intense. Profound. She hadn't had a lot of sex and he'd been her only lover in years. Now they had so much between them—not just a son, but history and a tangle of emotions that still remained knotted. They had a very tentative trust that needed protecting, but in this moment, she felt incredibly close to him.

She kissed him with abandon, long and deep, letting the joy of being entwined with him spin her into that depthless space of pure, luxurious passion they always found. The eddies of arousal within her became a deeper imperative. Her hands roamed over every inch of him that she could reach while his own hands molded her back and hips and thighs.

When she began to move, he guided her. Moved with her. Let her sit tall while she touched where they were joined. Moments later she was crying out with exaltation, shaken by her powerful orgasm. Breathless, she sank bonelessly onto him.

With her skin damp and her heart still pounding, he rolled her beneath him and said, "My turn."

"Mmm," she agreed, and wrapped her arms around his shoulders. She locked her ankles behind his lower back and groaned with abandon as he began to thrust and withdraw in slow, powerful strokes.

When the tension wound tight in her again, however, and she hovered on the brink, he settled his weight on her, no longer thrusting, and soothed her down from the peak.

"What are you doing?" she panted, confused.

"You don't like it?"

"No, it feels really good, but…" She made a restive noise and moved beneath him.

"I'm in charge now, Scarlett," he said, and she felt his will like a force that took hold of her very soul.

He drew her back up to the peak and let it recede again, making her so crazy she wound up scraping her nails down his back and biting into his shoulder.

He laughed and nipped at her jaw. "What's wrong, *querida*?"

"Don't make me beg, Javiero." She turned her face to the side and one tear leaked out her closed eyes and ran down her temple.

He made a noise of pity and gathered her in. When his lips found the dampness at her temple, he used his thumb to rub the tear into her skin.

"What do you want from me?" he asked.

"This. You." More. She had wanted to return to what they had had eleven months ago. She had wanted their lovemaking to be a reset. A fresh start.

That had been the fantasy of a fool, but she couldn't let him go, either.

She held him in a clasp so intimate she could feel the pulse of his heartbeat between her legs, but too much had happened to allow them to go back to that moment of profound pleasure and an unstained history. If she had stayed with him that day, she might have had a chance.

Now here she was, trying to recreate magic that had been an illusion in the first place.

Her heart beat outside her chest, trying to reach his, but his was closed off. How else could he hold her like this, on the brink of ecstasy, and deny them both?

When his mouth touched hers, she poured everything into the kiss, her heart and soul and all the love within her. All of this, what little she had of him, was going to disappear. She knew it. But she quit fighting his agonizing pace and savored it with him, wanting the moment to last forever. She held him deep as they drew out each caress and kiss. It imbued the act with something emotive and profound, until she was shaking under the intensity of this exquisitely powerful joining. A single press of his lips to the point of her shoulder became her world. She traced his crooked lips with her fingertip and it was the most exquisite kiss of her life.

When a frantic desperation closed her fist in his hair, trying to hang on to something she couldn't grasp, he caught that hand and pressed it to the mattress, linking his fingers through hers.

Then he began to move. For real.

By that time, she was pure, liquid desire, steeped in arousal. The impact of his hips became something so beautiful and pure that the burn of tears hit her eyes again, these ones of veneration. Jubilation.

She loved him, she acknowledged, as the last vestiges of self-possession left her. She loved him with every fiber of her being.

But as the little death of climax overtook her and she faced the fact that nothing was eternal, most especially this brief paradise she had found with him, she felt something break inside her, and her tears squeezed between her lashes to track her cheeks.

CHAPTER NINE

JAVIERO EXTRICATED HIMSELF carefully from Scarlett's sleeping form.

Waking her to say goodbye would be the decent thing, but she had been up in the night and had come back to make love with him again, wordless and so intense he still felt like she'd stolen a piece of him.

He wouldn't have touched her again if she hadn't reached for him. He was still disturbed by the way she'd wept after their first lovemaking, which had followed that atrocity of a dinner with her sister. Given his turmoil after *that*, he wouldn't have touched her at all. He'd been feeling riled and newly suspicious.

Was she a master gold digger and he the ultimate fool?

Whether she had set him up or not didn't change the fact they had a son. But did they have a future?

If he could keep her at arm's length, he would have done that by now, but she exerted this damned *pull* on him. He'd resisted it as long as he could, and then she'd taken apart his control piece by piece—which added to the grate of discontent in him.

Then she had cried afterward.

He'd hated himself, feeling like an animal even though she swore he hadn't been too rough. She had mumbled something about hormones and fallen asleep, then reached for him again a few hours ago.

She hadn't cried that time. She hadn't said anything but his name, and that had been a cry of ecstasy while her body had quaked in climax beneath him.

Why had she wanted to make love again? Because they were a potent combination? Or because she wanted to keep him in a sexual stupor so he wouldn't ask too many questions about her situation with her family?

He didn't want to deconstruct their lovemaking or her motives and, most of all, wanted to avoid considering how powerfully their lovemaking had impacted him. He was left feeling knocked off his foundation. The entire night, from the first touch of her lips against the scar on his chest to the tender joining an hour ago, had been conducted behind his firewalls. He'd run the gamut of emotions from anger at her and himself, to suspicion and disgust, with impatience and hurt ego following. They all terminated in a greedy desire he hadn't been able to resist.

Then pleasure. Such intense, prolonged pleasure laced with concern and possessiveness and a strange bleakness afterward because he still didn't think he could trust her.

Which meant these doors inside him that she'd blasted open had to be sealed shut, with her on the outside.

Sitting on the edge of the bed, he held his head in his hands, trying to pinpoint how and where his defenses had been breached so he could repair them. He wasn't one of those throwbacks who refused to feel anything at all, believing tears made a man weak and love was a lie. He respected the power of emotions, though, especially their ability to devastate and manipulate. Between his parents' backstabbing intrigues and his bitter rivalry with Val and the loss of his grandfather, he had learned to be judicious about allowing anyone near his heart.

His son had slid right in, of course, and he didn't regret that at all, except that Locke had created a massive vulnerability in him, and now he was much more cautious about letting Scarlett in. It would be years before his son was old enough to betray him, but she could turn on him at any moment. He didn't want to believe she would, but nor did he want to trust her completely and find out the hard way he'd been imprudent to do so.

He dressed and went through to say goodbye to his son. Locke was sleeping and Javiero told the nanny to let Scarlett sleep as long as possible. She would be annoyed with him for it. She pumped so Locke could take a bottle when they went out, but thought it fostered better attachment if she fed him herself as much as possible.

She was a devoted mother. He couldn't dispute that. He also couldn't shake the "Sugar Daddy to Baby Daddy" accusation her sister had dropped.

As he left, he experienced the same tug in his heart at leaving her that he felt at leaving his son, which told him how necessary this small separation was. He needed time to put his defenses firmly back in place.

Three days later, Scarlett braced herself, then started down the stairs to the small office Javiero had arranged for her there at Casa del Cielo. It shouldn't feel like a gauntlet— or a green mile to an execution room—but Paloma was invariably in the main lounge or otherwise taking note of her every move.

Scarlett didn't have the energy to bear up bravely in front of her. Not today. Depression and exhaustion had her feeling like the walking dead, but she couldn't blame all her sleep deprivation on Locke. A gnawing insecurity had been keeping her awake since London. A harrowing sadness she couldn't seem to shake.

Javiero had left while she'd been sleeping and they'd barely spoken since. She had texted him to let him know she'd arrived back in Spain safely. They'd managed an abbreviated call yesterday, with Locke fussing throughout. She hadn't had much to say anyway. She was still very sensitive over the awkward dinner with her sister, and their torrid lovemaking and her newly identified feelings.

Should she have told him she loved him? In the moment, being physically close with him had been an expression of everything in her heart. Since then she hadn't been able to read his mood, and her own had descended into despondency.

It didn't help that Ellie hadn't answered any of her texts. She'd had to hear from her mother that Ellie had arrived home safely. For some reason Scarlett was the one feeling horribly guilty and ashamed over the way things had gone with her sister. And then there was the brief call from her mother that had ended in a plea for money. Her mother had to pay some legal bills for her father to work toward his early release.

Scarlett's stress level was already through the roof, which was affecting her work. Now she was worrying about her mother, and being here with Paloma without Javiero's buffering presence was awful. She felt like a guest who had long overstayed her welcome.

All of it made every footstep feel as though she had anchors tied to them and was walking through freshly poured cement.

"Here she is now," she heard Paloma say.

"Pardon?" She jerked out of her fog as she passed the archway into the lounge.

"Javiero would like to speak to you." He was on a video call on his mother's tablet.

"Oh. Hello." Her heart gave a dip and roll, but her

shy smile died before it formed as she took in his distracted frown.

"I was telling Mother that things have gone sideways." He gave a terse nod toward someone off camera. "I'll be here the rest of the week."

"Oh." And this was how she was being informed? Second to his mother, called onto the carpet so Paloma could look down on her from her seated position, her expression a mix of superiority and boredom?

"That's unfortunate." Scarlett met his gaze in the tablet, trying to hide her disquiet with an unbothered smile. Words like *I miss you* tangled on her tongue and she bit them back. Her love was too new to reveal for the first time like this, in front of his mother.

Given Javiero's seeming indifference, she wasn't sure there would be a good time. He didn't look receptive at all. The skinless feeling she'd been suffering made her feel positively translucent. Tumescent. Tender and sensitive and throbbing painfully.

"Perhaps try me later and we'll chat properly," she suggested.

"With the time difference, you'll be in bed. No, not that one," he said impatiently to someone off-screen. "I have to go."

"Of course," she murmured as Paloma took back the tablet and ended the call with, *"Cuídate bien."*

Scarlett hovered a moment, turning her ring, not sure she could endure more of this tension with Paloma. Maybe this was the opportunity she'd been looking for to defuse it?

"May I have a seat and speak with you about something?" she asked.

Paloma lifted her gaze from the tablet as she set it aside, regarded her a moment, then assented with a tiny nod at the chair.

Scarlett lowered into it, trying to find the woman she used to be when she had been Niko's emissary. That had been such a different dynamic, though. Her only priority then had been to advance Niko's interests. It had been easy not to care too deeply whether Paloma *liked* her. Now, however, every action she took had to be bounced off a mirror to see how it reflected on Javiero. Paloma had asked her yesterday how long she intended Locke to remain illegitimate, and loved to report on how much sleep she had lost due to Locke's fussy nights.

Scarlett couldn't go on like this, not with so many other concerns drowning her. This animosity with Paloma was choking her. If she was going to seriously consider Javiero's proposal, she needed to lift some of the pall off her relationship with her future mother-in-law. She had to find a way to make this villa feel more like her own home, as well as her husband's and son's.

"Yes?" Paloma was exactly as frosty as she'd always been, making sure Scarlett knew her patience was razor thin.

"In the past," Scarlett began carefully. "It was always important to Niko that he be seen as treating his sons and their mothers equally."

"Yes, I know," Paloma cut in icily. "*I* was his wife, yet I received as little consideration as his mistress. It was galling."

And thirty-three years later, she still clung tightly to her grudge.

"Well, in the spirit of Niko's wishes, I thought it fair to inform you…" Scarlett licked her lips. "I'm not sure if you were aware of all the details in the will. For instance, Kiara and I are each entitled to an allowance."

"I'm sure, as trustee, that was something that was very important to you."

"It was something Niko stipulated so we could raise his grandchildren in the standard of living he enjoyed." Scarlett's own patience was eroding.

Paloma's brows went up at Scarlett's impertinence.

Scarlett scraped herself back under control. "Since Val is supporting Kiara, she doesn't need her allowance. She made an arrangement with Evelina to use her allowance to purchase an estate Evelina may use for her lifetime and which will ultimately benefit Aurelia."

Paloma's sour expression didn't change. "I don't understand why you think I have an interest in those people and how they conduct their financial affairs."

"Well, I thought it was a sensible compromise. I know you feel what Niko bequeathed to you is inadequate."

"You think I 'feel' it was inadequate? It was insult after years of injury."

"Yes, well, that's why I wanted to offer you the same thing."

"Are you suggesting you will pay me to leave my home so you can live here on Javiero's good graces? How dare you? Really." Paloma leaned forward to emphasize it. "I genuinely want to know where you find the nerve to make such an offer to me."

Scarlett was slack-jawed, frantically trying to see how she'd failed to say this respectfully. Her stomach turned. She should have waited until Javiero was back and run it by him first, but the damage was done now.

"I suggest you keep that allowance for yourself. You'll need it when you and Javiero divorce."

"We're not even married!"

"And why is that? Because you were hoping to get rid of me first? You lived off Niko, you control his fortune, you have a generous allowance, your son will inherit from Javiero, yet you want *more*. You want to push me out and take the home my ancestors built! I have never in my life met a more avaricious opportunist, and I am acquainted with Evelina Casale!"

"That is not what I'm trying to do," Scarlett cried on a flash point of heat, then forced her indignation back into its box, trying to see this from Paloma's side. "I know you still harbor rancor, because I worked for Niko. That was my job, Paloma."

Using her name got her a stiffened spine for the over-step.

"I would hope you would give me a fair chance to prove who I am outside of being Niko's PA," she persevered.

"I know exactly who you are," Paloma hissed. "I have a full report on your entire family. Your father is a drunk who went to prison for nearly killing people. Your mother runs some type of brothel—"

"*Excuse me?* She takes in students from time to time."

"Your sister has light fingers and a light skirt."

"Hey!"

"She's a freeloader who can't hold a job *cutting hair*. Your brother escaped drug charges by fleeing the country."

"That's not the way it is at all!" It was a lot like that.

"And *everyone* knows what type of work you were really doing for Niko. It makes me sick that my son has to attach himself to you. Do you think Javiero *wants* to be tarred with that brush? No. He'll do it for his son, but your marriage won't last. Dragging your feet won't change anything. Move this cart along."

"You didn't even love him." Scarlett found herself shooting to her feet.

All the taut strings that had been pulling her in a dozen directions for weeks snapped, and she stepped out of her own body while a fiery demon took over, spewing venom she hadn't known was inside her.

"You have spent three decades crying 'Poor me!' because Niko hurt your *pride*. You want to know how I dare suggest you live somewhere else? Because I don't know how anyone lives with you, especially *yourself*. You let Niko and your father throw adult responsibilities onto a child. You turned your son against his own father so he wouldn't even see Niko when he was *dying*. You are the vile human being here, Paloma. Not me."

Paloma's eyes were wide. Appalled. "Yes," she bit out in a glacial tone. "I can see that *I'm* the one whose behavior deserves to be criticized. Your roots are showing."

The monster inside her ghosted away as quickly as it had taken her over. Scarlett sagged where she stood, her rage gone, leaving a swell of reactionary tears and a massive sense of mortification that she'd utterly lost control of herself.

Humiliation as much as anger prompted her words. "I'm taking Locke to Madrid."

"What the *hell*, Scarlett?"

She had ignored his texts and calls while traveling into the city, but now that she was behind the closed door of their bedroom in Madrid, she had returned his call—without video because she was a coward—and that was his searing greeting.

"I shouldn't have lost my temper."

She had had time to absorb how terribly she'd behaved. Yes, she'd been provoked, but she felt sick at not keeping control of herself. The fact that she didn't know what had come over her was sitting like a nest of snakes in her belly. She already felt so miserable, so unloved and wrong, she could hardly bear it. Now she'd made it all worse.

The dark clouds that seemed to follow her around closed

in and jabbed lightning bolts of admonition and insecurity through her, wearing her down even more.

"Is it *true*?" he cut in. "You suggested she move out?"

"It wasn't like that. I know I should have talked to you first. Your mother and I have been on the wrong foot from the beginning. I thought she would like having options."

"You thought calling her a vile human being was an option? You don't know what she's been through! You don't know what treatment we had to suffer from Niko all those years. All you know is the last few years when he'd lost all power to hurt us any longer. You were totally offside."

"Do you want to hear my side of it at all?" Tears were cracking her voice, filling her eyes and seeping like fiery poison into the cracks of her fractured composure.

"Your side is always Niko's," he said coldly. "So, no. I don't."

"That's not fair! She… She—" She had to swallow back a choke of anguish. "She said you just wanted to marry me so you can divorce me. That you'll never want me because of my family. Is that true?"

"It wasn't. Now that I've met them, I definitely have reservations."

Wow. She stood there stunned, breath punched from her body.

After a moment, he swore and asked, "Is it true? What your sister said? Has this been your master plan all along, get Dad's money, then get mine?"

The pain kept rolling over her in waves. "You really believe that?"

"I want to hear you deny it."

"You're the one who has been pushing for marriage, not me."

"Marriage. Not a coup. You waited until my back was turned to try to evict my mother."

The world around her seemed to expand while she shrank until she was nearly nothing at all. She felt very, very alone then. Bereft and unwanted. Useless. Off in the bedroom, she heard Locke begin to cry and despair engulfed her.

"If that's what you think of me, then it's a good thing we're not married."

"Oh, we're still marrying, Scarlett," he ground out. "I want my son."

His son. Not her.

Something broke in her. Drips of mascara were falling off her cheeks onto her blouse.

"I can't do this anymore." She ended the call and made another one.

Javiero wrapped up in New York as quickly as he could, irritated that Scarlett didn't call or text after hanging up on him—although he didn't reach out, either. He was too furious.

Too conflicted. Did he want to marry her? Yes. They had a child. And after he had cooled down, he recognized that his mother wouldn't have been as blameless in their argument as she cast herself. She had transferred her grudge against Niko over to Scarlett, and that needed addressing.

London was supposed to have gone very differently. Javiero had been waiting for Scarlett to be cleared by the doctor before pushing for a wedding date. With a special night and a seduction, he had expected to secure her commitment. He then would have had a conversation with his mother himself. Paloma had had enough time to lick her wounds over Niko's abysmal last act. She may not like her son's choice in bride, but she would have to respect that he had one.

It had all gone off the rails with the arrival of Scarlett's sister. She'd been quite the piece of work, and he'd questioned the wisdom in tying his name to Scarlett's.

He'd been trying to convince himself that Scarlett wasn't anything like the people she'd come from, and then she'd thrown a tantrum, suggesting Paloma leave the only home she'd ever known.

That overstep had left him so incensed he had reciprocated her silence, giving them both time to cool off.

When he walked into the Madrid flat, he was prepared to address the whole thing with civility, but she wasn't here. She wasn't in Spain, he learned from the housekeeper. She had taken their son to Niko's island villa.

All Javiero's intentions to stay rational were incinerated in a bonfire of fresh wrath.

This was why he couldn't trust her! His mother had warned him this would happen—that Scarlett would use their son as a hostage to get whatever she wanted from him. Damn her!

He called her, but it went to voice mail. She continued to ignore his calls and texts for two days. He grew more livid by the second. Finally, he tracked down the number for the landline and blistered the ear of a maid until she put him through.

"Hello?" a fresh female voice greeted warily.

"Get me Scarlett," he said through his teeth. *"Now."*

"Javiero? This is Kiara. How are you?"

"Devoid of patience. Put Scarlett on."

"She's asleep." Her tone held rebuke. "Is this an emergency?"

He looked at the phone. No one said no to him. No one except—

"Is Val there?" he asked through gritted teeth.

"No." She sounded defensive, though. "I'm here to pack up my studio."

"And what is Scarlett doing there? Also packing?"

Kiara left a silence that made a howl lodge in his chest.

"Put her on the phone, Kiara. *Now.*"

"I'll tell her you called, but I can't make her talk to you. I'm not going to try. She—"

"She can talk to me in the morning. I'm leaving now," he cut in with a snap. He had begun making preparations the minute he'd learned where she was, hoping it wouldn't come to this, but apparently it had.

"You're coming *here*?"

"Don't bother preparing a room," he said with distaste. "I have a yacht on standby in Athens. I swore I'd never sleep another night in that house and I refuse to start now."

Besides, he wasn't staying. And neither were they.

"I looked up postpartum symptoms," Scarlett told Kiara the next morning. "I think you're right." Her eyes welled, but when had they not been soggy lately? Her inability to control her emotions added to everything else that made her feel like a giant failure. "But making an appointment with the doctor feels like one more thing to deal with." She hated herself for sounding so miserable and weak.

Kiara, bless her, crinkled her brow in empathy and said, "I called already. I'll take you this afternoon."

"Your being here means the world to me, you know. *Thank you.*"

"Of course. There's nowhere else I want to be."

A slight shadow flickered across Kiara's warm smile. She wasn't being completely truthful. She wanted to be with Val. Scarlett had watched Kiara's face soften and glow each time she spoke of him—which baffled her because Scarlett had always found Val to be very challenging. Sarcastic and superior and devoid of kindness. There was even less tenderness in him than Javiero, as far as Scarlett could discern.

Val had won the heart of his daughter, though. Aurelia had had a meltdown last night, missing her *papà*. Kiara was making a family with the father of her baby and Scarlett was envious as hell.

Kiara hadn't heard from Val since yesterday, though. She had been talking to him on her mobile when Javiero's call had come through on the line into the studio. Val had mistaken it to mean Javiero was there and had hung up on Kiara, furious. Kiara had been trying to get hold of him to explain, but he wasn't responding.

"Oh," Scarlett moaned as she saw the boat appear on the horizon. "That's him." She didn't know how she knew it was Javiero, but she did.

"I'll take Locke." Kiara reached out her hands. "You can shower and dress."

"I can manage," Scarlett insisted, even though a simple shower felt like a marathon through quicksand.

"I want to hold him." Kiara was the gentlest bully, taking the baby and enfolding him to her bosom as though he was her very own. "I'll put him down when he falls asleep."

And here came the tears again, these ones stemming from gratitude. Scarlett left for the shower if only to hide that she was such a complete wreck.

Twenty minutes later, as she stepped from the shower, she heard a helicopter approaching. She glanced out the window and saw Javiero coming off the yacht into shore, piloting a launch himself. So who was landing in the back—?

Oh, no. *Val*.

In all her years working for Niko, Scarlett had never seen the two men together, but Kiara had relayed the scene at the hospital as a narrowly averted clash of the titans.

Scarlett met Kiara on the stairs. They could already hear raised voices outside and hurried onto the terrace.

Val had indeed arrived. Rather than come into the house, he was confronting Javiero in the middle of the lower lawn.

"Javiero," she called, but they didn't hear her.

Harsh words were being slung between them. Blows were seconds away. They were a pair of territorial wolves thirsty for a taste of blood, neither likely to come away unscathed.

Kiara ran down to them as Scarlett stood paralyzed, fingernails scraping against the stone balustrade. A bleak blanket of despair, heavy as lead, pinned her in place.

She was so tired of the anger and blame. She couldn't hear them, but she could see the bitterness and antipathy that permeated every cell of their beings.

Javiero hated this place. He hated being here, hated his brother and hated the man she had worked for. He could say he didn't hate her, but given that endless well of bitterness in him, he could never look past her connection to Niko, never look past her family.

He could never love her.

That filled her with such despair she could hardly stand it.

Below her, the energy between the three changed. Whatever Val had said had shocked Javiero into stepping back.

Val turned to walk away, rejecting them. Kiara caught at his arm, but he rebuffed her and walked around the house toward the helicopter pad while Kiara stood there, fingers curled against her mouth, devastated.

Her expression of anguish matched exactly the shattered hopes in Scarlett's heart. She was so unutterably sad then, so defeated by this terrible, tangled history, she couldn't bear it.

There was no hope for any of them. Her heart gave up and shattered into pieces.

Javiero had had one purpose in coming here—retrieve Scarlett and his son.

As he approached the island, his anger and resentment had climbed to levels he hadn't experienced since his adolescence. This villa was a place he'd been forced to visit as a child, and being dropped here had always felt like being thrown into a dogfight.

First his mother would fill his ears with Val's inferiority, warning him against trusting his half brother while stressing, "Be nice to your father." In those early days, she had been certain there was a path to having her son recognized as Niko's rightful heir if they could only flatter Niko enough and expunge the imposter.

Evelina had done the same to Val. They would glare at each other with suspicion, equally miserable to be left with a man whose idea of parenting was to "toughen them up." Chores in the vineyard had been the easy part, all things considered. It had been hot and hard, and it had forced them into each other's company, often requiring cooperation to get a task done. That had led to power struggles, but they'd also wanted to finish as quickly as possible. They had managed.

No, the truly hellish part had been Niko's constant desire to test which one of them was stronger, faster, smarter. He would demand they count the number of cases and barrels they had moved, review their grades, and send them swimming to a buoy and back. He'd judged them on everything, including their looks.

"Val is the good-looking one. The other one is Javiero."

Javiero didn't care. *He didn't care.* But who the hell treated any child that way, let alone one's own?

His gut was churning as though he was still seven or nine or eleven. The fact Scarlett was forcing him to come to a place that held not one single decent memory did nothing to soften his mood.

Then, the cherry on top. Val was here.

As Javiero's feet found the lawn, he ran straight into his tempestuous past.

Everything and nothing had changed. Val glowered and came at him like a feral dog, spitting warnings that Javiero should stay the hell away from his wife and child—as if Javiero had any damned interest in either of them.

Javiero was in a mood to rip his half brother's throat out once and for all when Kiara thrust herself between them.

"For the sake of your children, bury the hatchet," she cried.

Maybe it was childish to say Val had started it, but it was the *truth*. Javiero found himself churning up Val's crimes, compelled to make one final effort at forcing Val to take responsibility for what he'd done.

"You set me up," Javiero snarled. "You knew Dad would yank his support when you left, but you did it anyway." Val had sentenced Javiero and his family to years of hardship. He wanted to kill him for that—he really did.

"I *had* to get away," Val spit back, so bitter it was palpable. "If you had backed me up when you had the chance, I might have made other choices. You didn't."

This was supposed to be his fault? Javiero wanted to

knock him into next week for having the temerity to suggest such a thing.

Then some flicker of a memory glinted in the recesses of his mind. A brief conversation that had seemed so insignificant he had buried it beneath a thousand others.

But that ring of blame in Val's hostility made Javiero recall Niko's question. *What do you know about your brother and this teacher?*

Javiero hadn't *wanted* to know. Val had been a rival who existed to be derided. Javiero had been young enough that he hadn't fully grasped what was being asked. Or what it meant.

He was a man now, though, hearing it and seeing it as an adult. Val had been a child. A rebellious pain-in-the-ass adolescent, but a child all the same.

The look in Val's eyes today was one of infinite betrayal. Revilement.

As comprehension dawned, Javiero's face nearly melted off his head. The ancient rumor that he'd dismissed as salacious and unimportant had had truth behind it. His vision of Val and their shared past broke open, leaving him reeling.

Val's rejection of Niko's fortune came into focus under a fresh light. Val hadn't done it as a deliberate effort to harm Javiero. Val had escaped an untenable situation, plain and simple.

Niko was the one who had used Val's quest for independence as a benchmark against which he had compared Javiero. *Niko* had used it as an excuse to yank his support and leave Javiero flailing. Javiero could blame Niko for his struggles and his grandfather's early death, but he couldn't blame Val. Not anymore.

Struck dumb, he watched Val and Kiara hold a sharp exchange that resulted in Val walking away from her.

A movement in his periphery dragged his attention to the terrace.

He couldn't tell if Scarlett had heard, but she was so pale her lips had disappeared. Tears tracked her cheeks. Her hopelessness was so visceral, her heartbreak so tangible, he nearly buckled under the agony of it.

She turned into the house and he felt it as an indictment. Reflexively, he started to go after her.

Kiara stopped him with a distraught hand clenching his sleeve. "Javiero, you have to tell me."

He splintered, longing to go after Scarlett. Not ready to face the shame wedging into him, cleaving a line through him, splitting Val off the block of hatred he'd nursed all these years.

He told her what he knew, which was only a whisper of gossip about Val and one of their female teachers. He still couldn't fathom it, but it had to be true.

"Did you tell Niko?" she asked, eyes wide with horror.

"He asked me what I knew and I told him the truth, that I hadn't seen anything, only heard other boys tease him because she flirted with him."

Val had been thirteen. Tall and mature looking and, yes, selling a glossy image of sex for stupid amounts of money. That didn't mean an adult woman having sex with him was okay. That didn't mean it had been his choice.

"What did Niko do? Anything?" Kiara asked desperately.

Javiero drew a deep, pained breath, appalled as he recalled with a harsh, humorless laugh, "He said, 'I guess your brother is a man now. When will *you* become one?'"

Javiero had pushed that out of his head the way he'd pushed away all his father's disparaging comparisons.

What Val had suffered had been abuse, though. He could see that now and was filled with self-loathing at not having done more. No wonder Val had walked away without a backward glance.

"I have to go after him," Kiara said, tears in her eyes. "But Javiero, we have to talk about Scarlett. She needs to see her doctor."

CHAPTER TEN

SCARLETT WAS SHAKING as she paced the upstairs sitting room. She knew there was no avoiding Javiero, but he didn't follow her right away, which only set her nerves more on edge.

When he did appear, Kiara was with him. They both looked shell-shocked.

"I have to go after Val," Kiara said in a plea for understanding. "I've requested the corporate helicopter and will leave as soon as it gets here. I'm so sorry to abandon you like this. Javiero will explain."

As Kiara disappeared, Scarlett looked to Javiero, whose profile was stony and unreadable. He stepped onto the small terrace that overlooked the pool. Waves of emotion rolled off him., but they were strapped down beneath layers of acute tension.

He wasn't railing at her or demanding she come back to Spain, and she realized with deep chagrin that that was what she had been hoping for. She wanted him to want her. Needed him to demand she remain a part of his life.

He was damningly silent.

Nausea cramped her stomach.

"What happened with Val?" she asked in a voice that creaked with the strain she was under.

"I let him down." His voice was brutally unforgiving.

"I can blame Niko and our mothers and the fact I was a child, but—" He raked his hand across his stubbled beard, making a noise of self-disgust. "Kiara tells me I let you down, too."

He turned, and his one eye was so empty of light it was a depthless sea of futility.

That bleak look cut through what was left of her nervous energy, reaching the parts of herself she kept hidden and protected from everyone.

"You didn't." She sank into a chair, exhaustion falling over her the way it did lately. "I didn't see it. Didn't tell the doctor how bad my symptoms were. I thought it was hormones or grief or the stress of being fully in charge of Niko's money. I used to get blue sometimes, during my cycle, if things were particularly difficult. It always passed. I was sure this would, too..." These stupid tears. She was so tired of feeling weak! "I don't want to be this unhappy, Javiero."

He blew out a breath as if she had punched him.

"It's not your fault," she murmured.

"No?" He studied her as though she was a puzzle he couldn't work out, his mouth tight with frustration. "You ran away."

"I couldn't stay with your mother after blowing up at her like that." She didn't know how she would ever face her again.

"You could have stayed in Madrid."

"I wanted to see Kiara. I knew you wouldn't forgive me if I went to her in Italy."

"You could have met her anywhere. Anywhere but here, Scarlett." His voice was grim. "This was the one place you could come that you believed I wouldn't follow."

Anger reared above her emotional exhaustion. "In case you haven't noticed, this is the closest thing to a home I have. That's what every creature does when they're feeling run to ground. They hide where they feel safe."

"You feel safe here?" He gave a ragged laugh of astonishment.

Not with him here. Maybe she *had* hoped his revulsion with Niko would act as a moat and drawbridge. There was so much wrong with them and so much wrong in every other aspect. She didn't know how to deal with everything.

"At least I feel like I'm *allowed* to be here," she murmured. "And having Kiara here—I don't feel right handing Locke to a nanny." She shrugged at the way it made her heart hurt to do so. "But Kiara feels like family. She's the one person I can actually rely on."

"You don't think you can rely on *me*?"

"There's not much room for error, is there? Explain to me how crying for help would elevate me in your eyes." Hers were welling again with tears.

Javiero's cheeks hollowed.

Into their charged silence, little feet came running toward them.

Aurelia appeared with a plush koala toy she'd taken a shine to. It had been a shower gift to Scarlett months ago. It had big glossy eyes and a button in its ear that made it say, *G'day, mate.*

"Auntie Scarlett, is this Locke's?" Aurelia asked from the archway into the sitting room. Her little head tilted with entreaty as she hugged it.

"It is."

A rush of love filled her. Not all the emotions that overwhelmed her were dark. Some were so intense she could hardly breathe through them, and love for this little imp filled her up to bursting. She was going to miss her *so* much.

"Would you like to take him home and look after him until we see you again?"

Aurelia nodded her head of riotous curls.

"Tell your mama I said you can take him, but can I have a goodbye cuddle?" She held out her arms.

Aurelia ran to her and climbed into her lap. Her little arms squeezed Scarlett's neck while her soft mouth pressed a damp kiss to her cheek. "I lub you."

"I love you, too."

Aurelia started to slide off her lap, but she noticed Javiero on the terrace and froze.

He seemed equally arrested by the sight of her.

Aurelia leaned deeper into Scarlett's lap.

"It's okay," Scarlett murmured, her heart lurching at Aurelia's instinctive wariness. She gave her a reassuring hug. "This is Javiero. He's Locke's *papi* and your *papà*'s brother. You can call him Tio."

Aurelia tilted her head back to look at Scarlett. "Why is his face like that?"

"He was hurt. The doctors helped him and he's still getting better."

Javiero stood stiffly under Aurelia's open stare, and said in a surprisingly gentle voice, "You have your father's eyes."

"Why is that thing on your eye?" Aurelia pointed.

"It's called a patch. My eye was hurt, too," he said simply.

"Mama should kiss it."

And there was why Scarlett adored her. Life was so simple and pure for Aurelia. No injury was too big it couldn't be healed by a kiss and a cuddle.

"Mama is probably looking for you." Scarlett noted the sound of an approaching helicopter and helped the girl slide to her feet. "I'll talk to you on the tablet soon, okay?"

Aurelia ran back down the hall, calling loudly, "Auntie Scarlett said I can take him."

"Tio?" Javiero repeated on an exhale of disbelief.

"She's your niece, whether you want to acknowledge that or not," Scarlett chided.

"Exactly what I need, more family I can fail to protect."

"Javiero, you can't protect me from depression. I'm probably going to need medication." She sagged into her chair, not understanding why the idea of taking something felt like defeat, but it did.

He nodded with decision. "Let's get you to a doctor, then. See what we can learn."

Javiero sat through Scarlett's appointment with the doctor who had seen her through her pregnancy. It was difficult. Scarlett mercilessly berated herself for not managing better.

"We have staff. I'm not raising this baby alone without resources. This should be easy. I should be happy and I'm *not*. I keep crying." She was welling up as she spoke.

When she admitted she had been having spells of tears since before they'd left for London, Javiero was beside himself. "Why didn't you tell me?"

"I told you I was struggling when I got Kiara's painting, but you thought I needed to get out more."

It seemed to be the last straw. She burst into tears and cried like he hadn't seen anyone cry in his lifetime.

"Scarlett." He reached across while looking to the doctor, consumed by guilt that he hadn't seen what was happening to her. "What do I do? How do I help her?" He was at such a loss he couldn't bear it.

"A hug?" the doctor suggested gently. "Would you like him to hold you, Scarlett?"

Still inconsolable, with her face buried in her hands, she nodded.

Javiero drew her from her chair. He picked her up like

a child and carried her to the sofa, where he sat and cradled her in his lap, his heart breaking at the way she had completely shattered.

The doctor rose and said, "I'll check on your son."

Scarlett gulped back sobs and raised her tear-ravaged face, alarmed.

"Not for medical reasons. I was disappointed when you delivered in Athens. I want to see him. You take a moment to gather yourself, then I'll come back and we'll discuss treatment."

"I'm sorry," Scarlett said as the doctor left. "I hate myself for being like this."

"Don't apologize. This isn't something you've done." It felt like something *he* had done. He hadn't *seen*.

He soothed her and a short while later they left the clinic with a prescription for an antidepressant and one for a different type of birth control since the one she'd been using had a possible side effect of depression. The doctor had also endorsed Javiero's suggestion that, rather than fly back to Spain, they take a week to sail among the islands.

They boarded his yacht, where Scarlett remained tense and jumpy. She checked her phone several times while they sailed toward a cove on a neighboring island that was reputed to offer excellent sunsets.

"Kiara is home safe," she murmured, phone in hand yet again as they ate a light snack in the stern. "I hope she and Val can work things out."

"Scarlett." He gently took her phone. "Worry about *you*, not other people."

Kiara had told him that Scarlett always put herself last and he saw it clearly now. The facade of infinite dependability he'd seen her wear all these years was not infinite, yet it was something she clung to as a means of reassuring herself she had value.

If I don't look after Locke, how will he know that I love him? she had sobbed while Javiero had held her in the doctor's office.

And if he wanted to look after her, if she cut him to his very soul when she refused to rely on him, what did that say about his feelings for her?

That thought was a land mine he walked back from, not ready to contemplate it yet. He had arrived in a temper this morning. His entire world had been flipped on edge by his own failings with his half brother. By the fact Scarlett was drowning and he hadn't noticed.

They both needed a breathing space to assimilate things.

They needed what they had never had—courtship. Time.

He called to a steward and handed over Scarlett's phone, along with his own.

"Put these in a drawer until morning. If one of us tries to pry them from you before then, drop both of them over-board."

"He's joking," Scarlett said with a panicked look.

"I'm not," Javiero assured the young man. "The world will not end if we take a few hours off." He was as guilty as she was of burying himself in work to avoid stickier problems.

She looked at her empty hands as though she didn't know what to do with them.

He realized she wasn't wearing his ring. Everything in him screeched to a stop.

He took her hands. Maybe he just wanted to touch her. Hell, yes, he did. He had been aching to lie with her as he'd left the bed they'd shared in London. His heart was racing, hackles up over her removing his ring, but her cheeks were hollow, her hands tense in his grip. He felt her brace herself against whatever he might say.

He ground his molars, defeated by her fragility.

"You're going to relax if I have to force you." He was joking, mostly.

Her mouth twitched, then quickly went down at the corners. "How can I?"

She pulled her hands from his and stood to move to the rail in the stern. The breeze dragged tendrils of hair from her ponytail, whipping them around her face.

When he moved to stand beside her, her profile remained pale and strained.

"There's so much that needs to be sorted. Look, I'm sorry about what happened with your mother—"

"Scarlett. Stop." He squeezed her shoulder, then set his forearms on the rail, hands linked, and watched the wake of the yacht trail in a widening V behind them. "I've talked to Mother. She admitted what you really proposed. I said it sounded like a damned good offer and advised her to take it."

"But—" Her eyes became big pools of blue, wide and depthless as the Aegean surrounding them. "I can't. Not now. I need that allowance for myself."

The possessive beast in him roared, wanting to lunge and grab and drag her back into his lair. He suppressed it, clinging to what shreds of civility he still possessed.

"If that's your way of telling me we're not getting married, don't. We're going to spend the next week *not* talking about that. We're just going to be."

They took a dip in the sea before dinner, then ate while indigo and fuchsia bled across the horizon. They talked about inconsequential matters and took turns holding their son. When Javiero rose to put Locke down for the night, she protested, "I can do it. Please don't treat me like an invalid."

"Maybe I should," he said with concern. "If you had broken your leg, you wouldn't try so hard to do everything yourself. You would expect me to help. I don't think less of you for needing me, Scarlett. I wish you would quit berating yourself for it."

Fine to say when *he* didn't need any help and she would be the last place he'd look if he did.

He offered the baby for her to kiss.

She did, and when he cradled Locke against his shoulder, she died at the picture he made, this brutish hulk of a man securing Locke's tiny form so tenderly with his wide hands.

Nervous about what would happen when they went to bed, she searched out a romance novel from the small library of books in the saloon and fell asleep reading it.

She woke much later in their stateroom, still in her summer dress, spooned into his body with the weight of his arm across her waist. Through the baby monitor, she heard Locke stirring.

"I'll get him," Javiero said before her foot reached the edge of the mattress.

He brought Locke for feeding and took him back to bed after. She was asleep again before he rejoined her.

Perhaps it was the medication or the lull of the boat or maybe straight up boredom, but she seemed to sleep constantly for the next few days. In between, they swam and snorkeled and used the paddleboards. They read and ate the chef's eclectic mixes of French pastries, Spanish tapas, Greek delicacies and freshly caught fish.

As for work, they allowed themselves one hour in the morning and one hour in the afternoon, just enough to answer a few pressing emails.

As Scarlett handed off her phone to the steward one afternoon, she said to Javiero, "Can I ask your advice? I completely respect that you want nothing to do with managing Niko's money. I *want* to do it. I want to do it *well*. However, I don't want to burn out and obviously that was starting to happen. How could I manage myself better? How do you do it?"

"Can I ask a very obvious question?" He paused in opening the spy thriller he'd been reading whenever she picked up her own book.

"Of course."

"What did Niko have that you don't?"

She tried to ignore the voice in her head that suggested Niko had been smarter than she was. She didn't really believe that. By the end, he had often gone along with her suggestions even when she contradicted his first instincts. Still, she had to shrug.

"More experience?" she hazarded.

"For God's sake, Scarlett. He had *you*. Hire yourself a PA as good as you were. Hire two. You went above and beyond far too often."

"But I *have* me. I can do all the mindless things Niko couldn't. I can type my own emails and summarize my own reports— Okay, I hear it." She rolled her eyes at herself. The transition had been so gradual she had wound up over her head without realizing it.

Hiring an assistant wasn't a silver bullet, but she felt she was doing something savvy and constructive when she put in a hiring request with a headhunter the next morning. The weight that had been suffocating her had eased a little, leaving her feeling more buoyant than she had in a long while.

They gave up their phones and took the Jet Skis with a picnic lunch into a small cove where an old ruin was reported to be hiding among the trees.

"I'm always astonished when a structure this big is reduced to almost nothing," Scarlett said as they walked idly from one ancient room to another, stepping over walls that had disintegrated to knee height. The villa had been roofless long enough for the floor to have become only sand and patches of wildflowers. Sheep grazed the green hillocks beyond. "Even if people took the stones to build other things, it's so much work to dismantle it."

"Less work than cutting and carving new ones."

"I guess, but what made them give up on what they had?" She found a spot where overarching trees framed the water and a view of their yacht. She paused to admire it. "It looks as though they had everything they could want right here."

"Is that a rhetorical question or something more profoundly related to our situation?"

She cocked her head. "I suppose that is the nature of our conflict, isn't it? Where to live. Whether we have anything worth salvaging." She sent him a cheeky grin. "I'd love to say I'm clever enough to talk in metaphor, but I'm really not."

"There it is," he said with a tone of relieved discovery exactly as if he'd found something he'd spent months hunting for.

"What?"

"Your smile." His big hands cupped her face. "You haven't smiled at me since London."

"Have I been that sour? I didn't mean to be."

"I know." His thumb skimmed a light caress across her mouth. "And that's why we haven't talked about where we'll live or any other heavy topics. We do, though." His thumb traced her lips again, this time slower, bringing her nerve endings alive.

"We do what?" she asked dumbly, leaving her mouth parted against the pad of his thumb.

"Have something worth salvaging."

She shook her head, unsure, as he continued to cradle her face. He lowered his head and let his mouth brush hers, redoubling the tingle in her lips. Gently—very, very gently—he stole one kiss, then another. Kisses that were light and lovely and sweet. Tears pressed behind her eyes.

They hadn't made love since London. He hadn't made a move and she had been convinced that if she did, he would read it as acquiescence to fully resuming their relationship.

"I want to believe we do," she said as he drew back. "But I'm afraid."

"Don't be afraid of me," he commanded. Maybe it was a plea. "Never be afraid of me."

Something deeply emotional lifted her hand to cradle his cheek. Her hand flexed subtly, inviting him to return.

This kiss was not so chaste. She tasted the hunger in him and it fed her own.

She moved her hand to the back of his head and returned the kiss, moaning with a mix of pleasure and happiness as he drew her up against him. She wore a bikini and sarong; he was in board shorts. They had nothing else between them except a layer of sunscreen and a dwindling sense of decorum.

He lifted his head and glanced to the handful of sheep in the distance, the trees providing a shady bower, the yacht barely visible through the leaves, bobbing on the water.

"Are you sure you want to do this here?" He was rueful as he looked at her with tender indulgence, and she saw something more serious behind his gaze.

She understood what she would be signaling in resuming intimacy with him, but the very fact they had come this far—able to read each other's thoughts—made the moment too precious to turn her back on.

She stepped away and untied her sarong, then let the

filmy cotton of abstract patterns drift down to form a thin bed on the grassy sand next to the low wall.

He sank down with her, kissed and covered her. Drew her along the path of passion with a sensitivity she hadn't felt from him before. It was beautiful. Cleansing and healing. The way they came together was ancient, there against rocks carved hundreds of years before by hands as strong as his own. It was renewal in the same way Mother Nature had begun to reclaim the space with wildflowers and blades of grass stealing into the cracks in the stones.

It was exulting, making love with the clouded heavens above, the pagan gods witnessing their earthly act.

It was enduring and eternal and left them in glorious, sated ruin.

They made love again that night and at breakfast Scarlett was still blissed out when Javiero said, "I've made arrangements for our return to Madrid. I'd like to set a wedding date as soon as possible once we're there."

Scarlett supposed this was what she got for letting him make all the decisions while they'd been aboard the yacht. It had been enormously freeing to let him tell her when to eat and when to swim. Now it was time to start thinking for herself again.

Her doctor had warned her that the medication wasn't an overnight cure-all, but sleeping and eating properly felt like one. It went a long way to clearing her head and lifting the cloud of despair that had weighed on her. Whether Locke sensed her relaxation or was simply growing out of his colic, she didn't know. He was sleeping for longer stretches and smiling more. She was beginning to feel as though she might be a pretty good mother after all.

That didn't mean she was confident in becoming Javiero's wife.

"It won't be the way it was, Scarlett." He read her like his spy thriller now. "Mother has used this week wisely. Her things have gone into storage. She's leaving for New York in the morning and will stay with friends until her new suite at Casa del Cielo is finished. She'll come back for the wedding, of course."

Scarlett's engagement ring had come with her from Niko's villa, but she'd asked the steward to put it in the safe while they were in and out of the sea a dozen times a day. Now Javiero held it out to her.

She tucked her hands in her lap and looked out to where the mainland was growing larger as they neared Athens. Real life was closing in.

"Why can't we go back to the way things were," she pleaded softly. "Talk about marriage later, when we're sure."

He waited a beat before he pocketed the ring, his voice cooling. "Why aren't you sure now?"

Because he didn't love her. For the first time in days, hot tears pressed behind her eyes, but they stemmed from legitimate hurt, not depression.

"How are *you* sure? Two weeks ago, you were accusing me of plotting my takeover of your empire."

A steward tried to approach with fresh coffee. He shooed the man away with a flick of his hand, a signal that would keep all staff at bay until they were finished this discussion.

"I wouldn't want you to judge me by Val's actions. I shouldn't have let your sister's words color my view of you."

"Ellie is the tip of the Titanic-sinking iceberg, Javiero. My mother is asking me to pay for a lawyer to secure my father's early release." She had to laugh at that outrageous request or she'd cry.

"Why didn't you tell me?"

"Because I don't want to think about it, let alone fight with you about the actions I decide to take. Not when I don't even know what they will be." The desolation that threatened to cloak her was an old one. Heavy and suffocating.

"We're not going to fight about it," he said firmly. "I'm asking you why you haven't brought this up sooner so I can help you find solutions."

"There are none! Every single option is lousy. What am I supposed to do? Refuse to hire someone so she uses her living allowance and goes hungry? Because she will. Do I kick her out of the house I own if she brings him into it? Do I pay for a lawyer who will help him leave prison so he can move in with her, take advantage of her again and probably start throwing his fists? He'll try to blackmail me, you know. Not in so many words, but he'll work on my fears for her to bleed me dry. You don't want to be married to this, Javiero."

She dropped her head into her hands, exhausted just imagining it.

"Scarlett, I have very good lawyers who can attach conditions to any assistance we offer."

"I've tried that," she said miserably. "I get called selfish or heartless or something else that implies I'm a terrible daughter. Protecting my mother means I'm hurting her at the same time. It's *impossible*."

"Well, you're not the one insisting on his good behavior, are you?" he said in the ruthless tone she hadn't heard from him since they'd reunited. "Your tyrant of a husband is. And I *will* press charges if he so much as glances out of line. There will be risks, I understand that, but we'll make sure they're as minimal as possible, and there will be very firm and dire consequences for him if things go wrong."

"Good cop, bad cop?" She blinked in astonishment at the idea this might not all be on her for a change. It would be such a relief to let someone else be the villain. "Would you really do that for me?"

He shook his head, snorting with bafflement.

"Of course I would do that for you." He leaned forward, a frown of impatience on his face as he cupped the side of her neck. "All you have to do is ask me for what you need. I will give it to you every time. I don't know how to make that more clear to you."

It was the most beautifully tragic thing he had ever said to her, because the one thing she needed above all else, he would never give her.

Give me your heart. Love me.

The words were right there, trembling on her lips, and she didn't say them. Helplessness overwhelmed her.

His hand dropped away and fell on the table hard enough to rattle the dishes.

"*Why* don't you trust me? Because your mother can't trust your father? We are entirely different people, Scarlett."

"Do you trust me? Do you trust *this*?" She pointed between them, where a very fragile thread, delicate as spider silk, had formed between them.

"I trust that we have what it takes to make a future together." His cheek ticked, though. That tell of doubt broke her heart.

"How can you when…?" Her entire being ached with yearning. With a longing she had suppressed successfully for most of her life. "I don't know how to be with you and keep myself from being destroyed," she admitted.

He inhaled as though she'd sunk a knife into his belly.

"I love you, Javiero. That is the problem. Because love is *never* a solution." Her lashes dampened. "I love you and

I want to give you everything. My heart, my independence, my *son*. I want to live in your house and wear your ring, and I'll even be nice to your mother. But what do I get in return?" she asked with anguish. "Are you going to give me every last ounce of pride *you* possess? Do you even know *how* to love when all you've ever been taught is hate?"

"This is how you tell me you love me?" The pupil in his eye obliterated all the color in his iris. "You say it in the same breath as you accuse me of lacking the capacity to love you as completely as you love me?"

"Do you?"

"Yes, damn you, not that you'll believe it. Do you?"

She clasped her arms across her middle, trying to make sense of words he'd thrown at her like the scattered shards of something broken.

"Do you?" he demanded.

She searched his expression, wanting to believe him—

At her hesitation, he shot to his feet, overturning his chair with a clatter. His face was transformed with fury. He looked around. For one stark moment, she expected him to sweep the deck clean of furniture, throwing everything into the sea with a roar.

She pressed into her chair, frozen with apprehension and holding her breath.

"Every last ounce of pride? That's the price? Damn you, Scarlett. *Damn you*." He walked away.

CHAPTER ELEVEN

SCARLETT DIDN'T KNOW what to say. She sat there for the longest time, clenched fists against her cheeks, heart pounding at the worst confrontation ever between them. She closed her eyes, trying to convince herself to simply *believe*. Maybe the fault was in her. Maybe her tattered self-esteem wasn't capable of seeing herself as lovable.

When the nanny turned up, she took Locke gratefully. Holding him brought her comfort for a few minutes. She continued to hold him after he nursed, pointing out a seaplane that was landing not far away.

He probably didn't take in more than its movement and sound, but when she smiled at him, he smiled back and that brightened her spirits.

Their game was interrupted by the buzz of the seaplane's propeller approaching. She looked up to see it taxiing right up to their yacht.

Javiero appeared. Stewards trailed him with their luggage.

"Get in," he said.

She hesitated, astonished.

"For God's sake, Scarlett, trust me this much."

She did, unquestioning because she didn't want to damage things between them any more than she had.

They flew over water, heading north as far as she could

tell and went over some mountains. They descended far too soon to be in Spanish airspace. The plane skimmed down onto a jewel of a lake surrounded by green hillsides dotted with elegant villas and mansions.

"Where are we?" she asked, her stomach filling with butterflies. She had a good idea, she just didn't believe it.

Javiero remained grimly silent.

Her suspicion was confirmed when they taxied toward Kiara, standing on the end of a private dock. She held Aurelia's hand and used the other to shade her eyes. Val stood next to them dressed in his usual black. He wore aviator sunglasses and not one hint of welcome.

Every last ounce of pride.

"Javiero, you don't have to do this," she said in a strained voice.

"Who do you want at our wedding, Scarlett? Who is the *one person* you want there?"

"You," she insisted.

"When? If I don't do this, *when* are you going to marry me? When are you going to trust in what we have?"

She didn't get a chance to answer. They were close enough that Val caught at one of the uprights on the wing. He used his weight to lever the plane into the dock, then helped the pilot tie off.

Seconds later, Scarlett disembarked into Kiara's open arms.

"Is everything okay?" Kiara asked anxiously into her hair. She drew back to study her with concern. Her expression softened and she smiled. "You look better. A lot better."

"You, too."

Kiara was glowing, her dark eyes full of adoration for the husband who came to stand next to her.

"When Kiara said you wanted to drop in, I didn't realize she meant it so literally," Val said.

Scarlett didn't look at him, unable to bear what was bound to become a smirk or worse. This was her fault. He was going to flay Javiero to pieces. She half wished they could turn around and leave, but there was Aurelia, holding up her arms, wanting to be lifted and hugged.

"You darling. You smell like cookies. I might have to eat you." Scarlett made chomping noises at her neck so the little girl shrieked with giggles.

Javiero emerged with Locke in his infant seat.

"And you're still bringing good news and sunshine with every visit," Val said in a scathing undertone.

Scarlett searched for something to say that might encourage Val to be merciful, but she'd never once conjured that particular magic spell successfully.

"I have to talk to you," Javiero said bluntly to Val.

"I don't have to listen," Val retorted in the annoyingly droll tone he liked to use when he stonewalled. "There's this thing in modern society called consent."

Just like that, hackles went up and their stares locked.

"Javiero, I appreciate what you're trying to do," Scarlett began, touching his arm.

At the same time, Kiara moved to stand in front of Val. She touched his jaw to force him to look at her.

"Right now would be an excellent time to set a good example for a sugar bowl with big handles."

Val's gaze flicked from Kiara to Aurelia, who was reacquainting herself with Scarlett's lock pendant, something she'd found infinitely fascinating while they'd been in Greece.

"This is my very best behavior, *bella*. I allowed them to tie up, didn't I?"

Scarlett bit back a sigh. "Val, I only want to ask if Kiara—"

Javiero cut her off. "I want to talk to Val about more

than that. Kiara, would you please take Scarlett and the children to the house? Give us a moment?"

Scarlett hesitated, rife with misgiving. Javiero and Val were holding another staring contest that drew lines in the sand.

"Of course," Kiara said quickly. "I'm not going to stand here wasting time that I could fill with holding a baby." She leaped toward Locke, taking him from Javiero. "Come see our home," she said to Scarlett. As Kiara passed Val, she added ominously, "We'll wait for you on the terrace."

The women walked up a line of stepping stones that formed a path toward a modern split-level villa with expansive windows and abundant outdoor living space. There was likely a pool behind the hedgerow. The terraced grounds were blooming. Stretches of lawn were littered with climbing gyms, a playhouse and other outdoor toys.

It was very Val. Lavish and tasteful with a disheveled projection of indolence, yet compelling and appealing at the same time.

"This is nice," Javiero said.

"I know."

Javiero bit back a curse of impatience and walked away from the pilot, who was checking oil levels. He turned onto the stretch of pebbled beach and glanced at what he suspected was Kiara's studio.

"Scarlett is inviting Kiara to our wedding." Javiero angled himself so Val wasn't in his blind spot.

"Where?" His voice was crisp. "When?"

"Tomorrow. In Gibraltar, likely, since that's where I can accomplish it fastest. Do you have other plans?"

"No, but I'd rather fill my pockets full of rocks and walk into that lake than spend a minute with your mother."

Same, Javiero resisted saying. "She won't be there. Just you and Kiara and the children."

"You're not seriously asking me to be your best man? There are so many things wrong with that, I don't even know where to start."

"Give it a rest, Val. This has to stop. Our kids won't have a chance if it doesn't."

Javiero had walked away from Scarlett a few hours ago so furious he hadn't known how to contain it. Oddly, he had known immediately that this was the price she was asking, even though she hadn't said it in so many words. He'd balked out of reflex, but there was no cost that was too high, not if he finally won the woman he loved.

Once he had recognized that, making a few calls—one of them to Kiara—had been easy.

Which didn't make this conversation with Val easy, but it had to happen for the exact reason he'd just given.

Val didn't say anything, only bent to pick up a handful of rocks. He picked through them, discarding all except a flat one that he moodily sent skipping a dozen times across the water. His infamous, million-dollar brooding pout was firmly on display.

"It didn't even occur to me," Javiero began carefully. "That someone as confident and contrary as you are could be taken advantage of."

"We're not talking about that. Ever." His voice was as flat as the next rock he found. It was a stone-cold warning, but after Val sent another pebble across the water's surface, he said darkly, "It wasn't up to you to save me."

No, Val had saved himself because their father hadn't.

Weary disgust washed over Javiero. So much time and energy and emotion wasted. So much damage. For what?

"I've tried to tell Scarlett what a sociopathic nightmare he was. She never saw the full scope of his ugliness, though," Javiero said.

"Kiara's the same. It's probably a good thing they never saw him at his worst. He always did like women, though."

"He liked them to like him," Javiero corrected. "To want things from him."

"True fact." Val sent another stone spinning.

It struck Javiero that Val was the only person on this earth who understood his loathing of their father without his having to explain any of it. They were two sides of the same bent coin.

"How is Scarlett?" Val asked. "Kiara said she has postpartum depression. I don't know much about it, but Kiara's been worried about her."

"Therefore you are?" Javiero asked skeptically.

Val shrugged. "Scarlett's the little sister I never wanted. I felt sorry for her, working for Dad all those years because we wouldn't."

"Yeah. About that." Javiero squeezed the back of his neck. "She's improving, but I don't want to jeopardize her recovery. She's as bad as you or I when it comes to burning the candle at both ends."

"Me?" Val splayed a hand on his chest. "I'm lazy as hell."

"And you work harder than anyone imagines at projecting that image."

"You know me so well." Val shot another rock into the water, this one hitting a ripple and sinking after two skips. "And I know you. You're going to charge in on your white horse to take over Dad's fortune. This is a courtesy call so I don't kick up a fuss. Have fun with that. I could care less."

"Actually, it's more than I can handle on top of my present responsibilities. I'm going to propose she let the two of us help her. She won't trust anyone else to have our children's best interests at heart. It would be temporary. As much or as little as she wants to delegate. She can fire us and take over whenever it suits her."

"You want me to work for Scarlett. Help her manage Dad's money." Val showed the rocks in his palms. "These really are going in my pockets while I take a long walk off that short pier. *You* have a bigger pair of rocks than I ever gave you credit for."

"You love irony," Javiero cajoled. "What better revenge could we possibly dream up?"

"He would roll over in his grave, wouldn't he?" Val let the rocks fall away and dusted his palms. "Hell, it would put both our mothers into an early one. There's a selling feature."

"Mine's halfway there. When I tell her I'm married and she wasn't invited but you were…?" Javiero blew out a breath. "I'm stepping on your brand."

Val snorted, then said without heat, "Scarlett doesn't want me at her wedding. Why do you?"

"Scarlett needs to know I can put all of this behind me."

"Wow." Val scratched under his chin. "You've got it bad, haven't you?"

"Oh, you don't?" Javiero chided, prickling at having his deepest vulnerability poked at. Still, he wouldn't flinch from showing his heart. Not now. Not ever again. Scarlett was too important to him.

Which didn't mean he was above some old-fashioned fraternal ribbing when he saw the same in Val.

"I knew you were sunk that day at the hospital, when you backed down for Kiara's sake. She'll feel better if we agree to a truce. Especially if it means Scarlett will have the support she needs."

"You can't snow the snowman." Val's eyes narrowed.

"I was raised on emotional manipulation. I can smell it a mile away."

"This isn't a snow job. It's past time we put our swords down," Javiero insisted. "For the women we love. For our kids. For *ourselves*."

Val's disobliging profile turned to focus on the far side of the lake.

At least Javiero could tell Scarlett he'd tried, he thought grimly.

Behind them, a high voice called, "Papà? Do you and Tio want lunch?"

They turned to see Aurelia loping toward them. She let go of her nanny's hand and ran the rest of the way across the sand.

"Kiara must be worried we're not playing nice." Val scooped up his daughter as she reached them. He threw Aurelia high into the air, making her scream with laughter, then caught her and hugged her close.

She curled her arms trustingly around his neck, then lifted her sweet, happy, innocent face and pointed at Javiero. "Tio got hurted."

After a surprised beat, Val said, "He did." His tone was somber enough to resonate like a cold bell inside Javiero's chest. Val turned a flinty look on Javiero, saying cryptically to his daughter, "He's what we call collateral damage. He wasn't supposed to be hurt. It just happened."

It wasn't an apology, but it was an acknowledgment that Val's actions had had repercussions he hadn't intended. They'd both suffered, but neither had deliberately caused what the other had endured.

"Tio is Locke's *papi*." Aurelia disregarded the big words she didn't understand.

"You're full of important information, aren't you?"

She nodded, probably not fully getting that, either.

"But do you know that *you*...?" Val tickled his fingers into her chest, making her squirm and giggle and catch at his hand. "*You* are the reason Tio and I will eat our lunch with our spoons?"

Not knives. No more swords.

A strange whoosh rushed through Javiero. He had told himself he didn't care whether he won Val over, that trying would be enough. If anything, he had expected a sense of triumph if he did. There was no satisfaction, though, only relief. As though he had put down something inordinately heavy. As though the rocks in his pockets fell away and he was able to kick to the surface and breathe.

"It's not soup," Aurelia was telling Val, holding his face in her hands, earnest and completely oblivious to what was going on between the men. "It's *capelli d'angelo*."

"Your favorite."

"And yours."

"And mine," he agreed, then sent Javiero a look of mild disgust before jerking his head toward the house. "*Mi casa* and all that. Let's eat some angel hair."

They walked up to the house with Aurelia between them, holding their fingers while she leaped and swung, feet barely touching the ground.

"Do you know what a flower girl is, Aurelia?" Javiero asked her. "It means Auntie Scarlett and I want to buy you a *very* pretty dress and that you get to hold some flowers for us at our wedding."

Her little feet hit the ground and she stopped moving. Pale blue eyes blinked up at him as she said importantly, "I have a dress for when Papà and Mama had a wedding. I *am* a flower girl."

God help him, he might fall in love with her. "I came to the right place then."

They were close enough to the terrace that Kiara came

to the rail and looked down at them. She held Locke, and Scarlett appeared beside her.

"Did I hear that we're going to a wedding?"

"*Sì*. And you have a decision to make, *bella*. Are we going overnight or are we bringing your paints and staying the week? He's paying either way." Val motioned toward Javiero.

Kiara shook her head in affectionate exasperation. "You're incorrigible. He's teasing."

"I'm not," Val assured him.

Javiero shrugged it off, not even looking at his brother. He was too entranced by the glow of sheer happiness in Scarlett's face. He didn't care what the wedding cost him. No price was too high if it meant he would be with her every day for the rest of his life.

They landed late in Gibraltar and everyone went straight to bed.

Scarlett didn't properly absorb what was happening until she woke at dawn, fed Locke and put him back to bed, then stood watching the sunrise off their private balcony. Through the haze across the water, she thought she glimpsed Morocco.

"What are you thinking?" Javiero asked in a rough morning voice. His arms came around her from behind.

"That one day, when Locke is old enough, we should take him on safari."

He shifted, releasing her so he could turn his back on the view. He leaned his hip on the rail and regarded her with his one eye. He wasn't wearing a stitch, not even his eye patch, but his mutilated eye socket and scars were something she saw only in the way she noted that he hadn't shaved or had forgotten his watch. All these battle marks were simply him. The man she loved.

"I'm thinking…" She stroked a caressing hand down the center of his naked chest and grew emotional. Her eyes welled. "That I can see a future for us. It's beautiful. It's vast and solid and the memories it might contain are like Christmas gifts. They're exciting surprises that already make me happy, before I even know what they are. I'm thinking I love you beyond measure and I am awed by how much you love me." Her hand was shaking now. "I'm sorry I made you prove yourself. I should have taken you at your word."

He caught her hand and kissed her knuckles.

"My past was still damaging my life. All you did was point that out to me." He drew her into his front. "I'm grateful, Scarlett. I feel…lighter. When Locke was born, I swore to him that I would be a better father to him than I had. I'm following through on that. It feels good."

She couldn't help the tears wetting her lashes. At least they were happy ones. Ecstatic ones. "Can I ask you something?"

"Put on some clothes?" he guessed.

"That seems like a waste of time when we only have a short while before our busy day. No, I was wondering if you, Javiero Rodriguez, would consent to marry me?"

His mouth twitched and the harsh lines in his face softened. His brutish, marred features were handsome and brimming with love, and she grew light-headed.

"Yes, Scarlett Walker," he said in a voice that sounded deeply moved. "I love you with all my heart. I would be honored to join with you in matrimony. Later." His smoldering smile widened. "Right now, go back to the part about the time we don't want to waste…"

EPILOGUE

Two years later...

"WHAT'S WRONG?" ASKED JAVIERO.

Scarlett paused in removing her earring, dragging her gaze from the view of the Eiffel Tower. "Hmm? Nothing."

"You've been quiet all evening. Was it something your mum said?"

"No, things are okay there." Not fantastic, but not terrible. Ellie had gone to America and Scarlett's father was ordered by the court to attend addiction classes as part of his release agreement. Her mother went to meetings for families of alcoholics at the same time. At least it gave her a network of people who understood her situation and kept an eye out for early signs of trouble.

"Val, then? Did you fire him?"

She grinned. "No, I said he could take maternity leave."

"Ruthless." He smiled, too.

She turned so he could unclasp her necklace. "And I said we'd talk more tomorrow. It was Kiara's night. I didn't want to get into it at the gallery."

"That was quite a crush, wasn't it? I knew Kiara was talented, but when you see her body of work assembled like that, it's astonishing. I'm really annoyed I didn't win more bids. How is she managing with a new baby and all the work that went into preparing, though? Is that why Val wants time off?"

Scarlett turned to take the necklace and saw he was genuinely concerned. She nearly melted into a puddle of liquid sugar at his feet, he was so sweet. She set aside the necklace.

"She's good. Really good. Val admitted he's motivated by pure selfishness, wanting to spend more time with Rafael, which is understandable." Val had missed his daughter's first two years. "But I didn't want to let him go permanently."

"No? I told him I didn't think you'd have a problem with firing both of us." He snapped off his cuff links.

"He ran it by you first?"

"Of course. He didn't want to leave you in the lurch if you weren't ready."

"Men," she tsked, secretly thrilled at the working relationship they'd developed, one that had spilled into a social one. A familial one.

"We weren't conspiring. He brought it up because you're sticking your nose in more than usual, checking up on us." He tilted his head in what would have been a stern look, but held a little too much indulgence to be taken seriously. "We would both rather pull back and let you take the wheel than be micromanaged."

"But I like bossing you two around." She tugged at his bow tie to unravel it. "It's delicious payback after all those years when you obstructed me at every turn."

"The heady drug of a power trip has hit her veins, ladies and gentlemen. We're not above mutiny, you know."

"You're going to take Val's side against me?" She splayed an appalled hand on her chest.

"You've got me there. I couldn't do it." He sighed in mock despair.

She grinned as she worked her way down his buttons, revealing a strip of tawny skin sprinkled lightly with hair.

"Really," he said with hands coming to rest heavily on her hips. "Before we get distracted, are you sure you're not ready to fire both of us? I thought you only wanted to wean off the pills and see if you still had symptoms."

That had been three months ago and she had been feeling really good ever since.

"I thought I was ready, too." She tugged his tuxedo shirt from his waistband and exposed more of his wide, powerful chest, then smoothed her hands over his sides, loving the warm silk of his skin against her palms. "The five-year plan we've made has me very excited for all the new challenges. I was ready to go full steam ahead at work, but earlier today..."

He tilted up her chin so he could see her expression.

"A setback?" His real eye was troubled, the matching false one pretty to look at, though not the place she sent her attention when they were having a serious discussion. "What happened?"

She clasped her hands around the open edges of his shirt and sheepishly admitted, "I held Rafael."

His frown held for a second longer before comprehension dawned. He grew infinitely more tender. His heavy hands drew her closer.

"You were bitten by the baby bug."

As her head came to rest on his chest, she heard the hard, uneven thump of his heart.

"It feels like I fell into a hill of them and I'm itching all over. And I know it took me a long time to find an even keel after Locke. And I know Val ought to have a lighter load while they have a new baby in the house so Kiara doesn't risk becoming overwrought like I was. And I know my chances of suffering postpartum depression again are high if I have another baby, and still… I really want one," she confessed in a whisper, afraid to look at him. "What do you think?"

"I think our son is the most amazing little person I could have imagined." His arms cradled her as though she was precious. "I would make a dozen more children with you if you were up for it. But it has to be your decision, my love, given what you might go through again."

"I was thinking just *one* more. For Locke. To keep him company." She looked up at him, letting him see the yearning in her eyes.

"For Locke." His mouth twitched.

"And me. And you," she allowed, giving a little tug on his collar to entice him to come down for a kiss. "We know the signs to look for. You wouldn't let me lose myself again."

"I would not. I refuse to lose you to anyone or anything. I love you far too much."

"So maybe that's a yes?"

"That's definitely a passionate yes."

She smiled as they got started.

* * * * *

CLAIMED IN THE ITALIAN'S CASTLE

CAITLIN CREWS

To the fairy tale heroines who didn't get to be princesses.

CHAPTER ONE

This door you might not open, and you did;
So enter now, and see for what slight thing
You are betrayed... Here is no treasure hid,
No cauldron, no clear crystal mirroring
The sought-for Truth, no heads of women slain
For greed like yours, no writhings of distress;
But only what you see... Look yet again:
An empty room, cobwebbed and comfortless.
Yet this alone out of my life I kept
Unto myself, lest any know me quite;
And you did so profane me when you crept
Unto the threshold of this room tonight
That I must never more behold your face.
This now is yours. I seek another place.
　　　　　—Edna St. Vincent Millay, *Bluebeard*

HER SISTERS WERE in a dither.

This was not an unusual state of affairs. Petronella and Dorothea Charteris had never met a molehill they couldn't make into the Alps. Angelina, the younger sister they preferred to exclude from anything and everything, usually ignored them.

But as Angelina slipped through the servants' passageway this evening, racing to change for dinner after another long day of hiding from her family in this petri dish they called their home, she paused. Because she could hear the rise and fall of her sisters' voices a little too well, and they weren't discussing one of their usual topics—like why they were cruelly sequestered away in the family mausoleum as their youth and vitality slipped away...

Because it never occurred to them to leave and make their own way, as Angelina planned to do, when they could sit at home and complain instead.

"We shall be slaughtered in our sleep!" Petronella screeched.

Angelina paused, there on the other side of the paper-thin wall of the drawing room, because that sounded extreme. Even for the notably dramatic Petronella.

"It will be me, I am sure of it," Dorothea pronounced in the trembling tones of an Early Christian Martyr. Her happy place, in other words. "He will spirit me away, and no. No, Petronella. Do not attempt to make this better." Angelina could hear nothing that suggested Petronella had attempted anything of the kind. "It will be a sacrifice—but one I am prepared to make for the sake of our family!"

Angelina blinked. Dorothea preferred to talk about sacrifices rather than make any, in her experience. What on earth was going on?

Petronella wailed, then. Like a banshee—a sound she had spent a whole summer some years back perfecting, waking everyone round the clock with what their mother had icily called *that caterwauling*. That had been the summer Petronella had wanted to go on a Pilates retreat to Bali with the loose group of pointless women of indiscernible means she called friends—when she wasn't posting competing selfies on social media. Petronella had claimed the screams had nothing at all to do with Papa's refusal to fund her trip.

"Everything is blood and pain, Dorothea!" she howled now. "We are *doomed*!"

That sounded like the usual drama, so Angelina rolled her eyes. Then, conscious that time was passing and her happiness was directly related to remaining invisible to her stern mother, she hurried along the passage. She took the back stairs two at a time until she reached the family wing. Though it was less a wing and more the far side of the once great house that everyone pretended had not fallen into ruin.

Charming, her mother liked to say stoutly whether or not anyone had asked. *Historic.*

Angelina was well aware that in the village, they used other words. More appropriate words. *Rundown,* for example. She had once pretended not to hear the grocer's wife refer to the once-proud Charteris family estate, nestled in what bits of the French countryside her father hadn't sold off to pay his debts, as *"that crumbling old heap."*

Though it had never been made clear to her whether the woman referred to the house or Angelina's father.

Either way, while her sisters flounced about screaming and carrying on about everything from the lukewarm temperature of their thin soup at lunch to the lack of funds for the adventures they wished to take with their far flashier friends—because they wished to perform it on social media, not because they had an adventurous bone in either one of their bodies—Angelina had spent another pleasant afternoon practicing piano in the conservatory. A room not a single member of her family had been inside in the last decade, as far as she knew. Mostly because there was nothing there any longer. Just the old piano and Angelina, who far preferred the company of Bach, Mozart, and Beethoven to her sisters.

She had nurtured grand dreams of leaving the family entirely and going off to Paris when she hit eighteen. Or anywhere at all, as long as it was elsewhere. But there had been no money for what her father had sniffed and called her "vanity project."

There had been money for Petronella's Year of Yoga, as Angelina recalled. And for Dorothea's "art," which had been two years in Milan with nothing to show for it but some paint smudged on canvases, a fortune spent on wine and cafes, and a period of dressing in deeply dramatic scarves.

But that was a long time ago. That was when Papa had still pretended he had money.

"Of course there's no money for you to *play piano*," Dorothea had scoffed. "When Petronella and I have scrimped and saved these past years in the vain hope that Papa might throw us a decent debutante ball. Ironically, of course, *but still*."

Angelina had learned early on that it was better not to argue with her older sisters. That was a quick descent into quicksand and there was no getting out of it on one piece. So she had not pointed out the many problems with her eldest sister's statement. First, that Dorothea was thirty and Petronella twenty-six—a bit long in the tooth for debutante balls, ironic or otherwise. And second, that there was no point in pronouncing oneself a debutante of any description when one was a member of a rather shabby family clinging desperately to the very outskirts of European high society, such as it was.

Her sisters did not like to think of themselves as shabby. Or clingy, come to that.

Even if it was obvious that the house and family were not *in* a decline. The decline had already happened and they were living in the bitter ashes that remained.

She slipped into her bedchamber, staring as she always did at the water damage on her bare walls. Her ceiling. All the evidence of winters past, burst pipes, and no money to fix it. Her mother claimed that the family's reliance on the old ways was a virtue, not a necessity. She waxed rhapsodic about fires in all the fireplaces to heat the house, no matter how cold it got in this part of France. She called it atmospheric. *It is our preference,* she would tell anyone who even looked as if they might ask. *A family custom.*

But the truth was in the cold that never lifted in this place of stone and despair, not even in the summertime. The house was too old, too drafty. It was June now and still chilly, and the picked-bare rooms and stripped walls didn't help. Slowly, ever so slowly, priceless rugs disappeared from the floors and paintings from their hooks. Family heirlooms no longer took pride of place in the echoing rooms.

When asked, Mother would laugh gaily, and claim that it was high time for a little spring cleaning—even when it was not spring.

The more time Papa spent locked up his office, or off on another one of those business trips he returned from looking grim and drawn, the more the house became a crumbling patchwork of what had once been a certain glory.

Not that Angelina cared. She had her piano. She had music. And unlike her sisters, she had no interest at all in scaling the heights of society—whether that was bright young things who called themselves influencers, who Petronella desperately emulated, or the dizzy heights of the European once-nobles who turned Dorothea's head.

All she wanted to do was play her piano.

It had been her escape as a child and it still was now. Though more and more she dreamed that it might also be her ticket out of this house. And away from these people she knew only through an accident of birth.

She hurried into the bath attached to her chamber, listening for the comforting symphony of the leaking pipes. She wanted a bath, but the hot water was iffy and she'd spent too much time in the servants' passage, so she settled instead for a brisk, cold wash in the sink.

Because evening was coming on fast, and that meant it was time for the nightly charade.

Mother insisted. The Charteris family might be disappearing where they stood, but Mother intended they should go out holding fast to some remnant of their former grandeur. That was why they maintained what tiny staff they could when surely the salaries should have gone toward Papa's debts. And it was why, without fail, they were all forced to parade down to a formal dinner every evening.

And Margrete Charteris, who in her youth had been one of the fabled Laurent sisters, did not take kindly to the sight of her youngest in jeans and a sweater with holes in it. Not to mention, Angelina thought as she stared in the mirror, her silvery blond hair wild and unruly around her and that expression on her face that the piano always brought out. The one Mother referred to as *offensively intense*.

Rome could be burning in the drawing room and still Angelina would be expected to smile politely, wear something appropriate, and tame her hair into a lady-like chignon.

She looked at herself critically in the mirror as she headed for the door again, because it was too easy to draw her mother's fire. And far better if she took a little extra time now to avoid it.

The dress she'd chosen from her dwindling wardrobe was a trusty one. A modest shift in a jacquard fabric that made her look like something out of a forties film. And because she knew it would irritate her sisters, she pulled out the pearls her late grandmother had given her on her sixteenth birthday and fastened them around her neck. They were moody, freshwater pearls, in jagged shapes and dark, changeable colors and sat heavily around her neck, like the press of hands.

Angelina had to keep them hidden where none of her sisters, her mother, or Matrice, the sly and sullen housemaid, could find them. Or they would have long since been switched out, sold off, and replaced with paste.

She smoothed down the front of her dress and stepped back out into the hallway as the clock began to strike the hour. Seven o'clock.

This time, she walked sedately down the main hall and took the moldering grand stair to the main floor. She only glanced at the paintings that still hung there in the front hall—the ones that could not be sold, for they had so little value outside the Charteris family. There were all her scowling ancestors lined up in ornate frames that had perhaps once been real gold. And were now more likely spray painted gold, not even gilt.

Angelina had to bite back laughter at the sudden image of her mother sneaking about in the middle of the night, spray painting hastily-thrown-together old frames and slapping them up over all these paintings of her austere in-laws. Margrete was a woman who liked to make sweeping pronouncements about her own consequence and made up for her loss of her status with a commensurate amount of offended dignity. She would no more *spray paint* something than she would scale the side of the old house and dance naked around the chimneys.

Another image that struck Angelina as hilarious.

She was stifling her laughter behind her hand as she walked into the drawing room, just before the old clock stopped chiming.

"Are you *snickering*?" Mother demanded coolly the moment Angelina's body cleared the doorway. She looked up from the needlepoint she never finished, drawing the thread this way and that without ever completing a project. Because it was what gently bred women did, she'd told them when they were small. It wasn't about *completion,* it was about succumbing to one's duty—which, now she thought about it, had been the sum total of her version of "the talk" when Angelina left girlhood. "What a ghastly, unladylike sight. Stop it at once."

Angelina did her best to wipe her face clean of the offending laughter. She bowed her head because it was easier and dutifully went to take her place on the lesser of the settees. Her sisters were flung on the larger one opposite. Dorothea wore her trademark teal, though the dress she wore made her look, to Angelina's way of thinking, like an overstuffed hen. Petronella, by contrast, always wore smoky charcoal shades, the better to emphasize her sloe-eyed, pouty-lipped beauty. None of which was apparent tonight, as her face looked red and mottled.

That was Angelina's first inkling that something might actually be truly wrong.

"Have you told her?" Petronella demanded. It took Angelina a moment to realize she was speaking to their mother, in a wild and accusing tone that Angelina, personally, would not have used on Margrete. "Have you told her of her grisly fate?"

Dorothea glared at Angelina, then turned that glare back on Petronella. "Don't be silly, Pet. He's hardly going to choose *Angelina*. Why would he? She's a teenager."

Petronella made an aggrieved noise. "You know what men are like. The younger the better. Men like him can afford to indulge themselves as they please."

"I've no idea what you're talking about," Angelina said coolly. She did not add, *as usual*. "But for the sake of argument, I should point out that I am not, in fact, a teenager. I turned twenty a few months ago."

"Why would he choose Angelina?" Dorothea asked again, shrilly. Her dirty-blond hair was cut into a sleek bob that shook when she spoke. "It will be me, of course. As eldest daughter, it is my duty to prostrate myself before this threat. *For all of us.*"

"Do come off it," Petronella snapped right back. "You're gagging for it to be you. He's slaughtered six wives and will no doubt chop your head off on your wedding night, but by all means. At least you'll die a rich man's widow." She shifted, brushing out her long, silky, golden blond hair. "Besides. It's obvious he'll choose me."

"Why is that obvious?" Dorothea asked icily.

Angelina knew where this was going immediately. She settled into her seat, crossing her ankles demurely, because Mother was always watching. Even when she appeared to be concentrating on her needlepoint.

Petronella cast her eyes down toward her lap, but couldn't quite keep the smug look off of her face. "I have certain attributes that men find attractive. That's all I'm saying."

"Too many men, Pet," Dorothea retorted, smirking. "He's looking for a wife, not used goods."

And when they began screeching at each other, Angelina turned toward her mother. "Am I meant to know what they're talking about?"

Margrete gazed at her elder two daughters as if she wasn't entirely certain who they were or where they'd come from. She stabbed her sharp needle into her canvas, repeatedly. Then she shifted her cold gaze to Angelina.

"Your father has presented us with a marvelous opportunity, dear," she said.

The *dear* was concerning. Angelina found herself sitting a bit straighter. And playing closer attention than she might have otherwise. Margrete was not the sort who tossed out endearments willy-nilly. Or at all. For her to use one now, while Dorothea and Petronella bickered, made a cold premonition prickle at the back of Angelina's neck.

"An opportunity?" she asked.

Angelina thought she'd kept her voice perfectly clear of any inflection, but her mother's cold glare told her otherwise.

"I'll thank you to keep a civil tongue in your head, young lady," Margrete snipped at her. "Your father's been at his wit's end, running himself ragged attempting to care for this family. Are these the thanks he gets?"

Angelina knew better than to answer that question.

Margrete carried on in the same tone. "I lie awake at night, asking myself how a man as pure of intention as your poor father could be cursed with three daughters so ungrateful that all they do is complain about the bounty before them."

Angelina rather thought her mother lay awake at night wondering how it was she'd come to marry so far beneath her station, which seemed remarkably unlike the woman Angelina knew. Margrete, as she liked to tell anyone who would listen, and especially when she'd had too much wine, had had her choice of young men. Angelina couldn't understand how she'd settled on Anthony Charteris, the last in a long line once littered with titles, all of which they'd lost in this or that revolution. Not to mention a robust hereditary fortune, very little of which remained. And almost all of which, if Angelina had overheard the right conversations correctly, her father had gambled and lost in one of his numerous ill-considered business deals.

She didn't say any of that either.

"He's marrying us off," Petronella announced. She cultivated a sulky look, preferring to pout prettily in pictures, but tonight it looked real. That was alarming enough. But worse was Dorothea's sage nod from beside her, as if the two of them hadn't been at each other's throats moments before. And as if Dorothea, who liked to claim she was a bastion of rational thought despite all evidence to the contrary, actually *agreed* with Petronella's theatrical take.

"We are but chattel," Dorothea intoned. "Bartered away like a cow or a handful of seeds."

"He will not be marrying off all three of you to the same man," Mother said reprovingly. "Such imaginations! If only this level of commitment to storytelling could be applied to helping dig the family out of the hole we find ourselves in. Perhaps then your father would not have to lower himself to this grubby bartering. Your ancestors would spin their graves if they knew."

"Bartering would be one thing," Dorothea retorted in a huff. "This is not *bartering*, Mother. This is nothing less than a guillotine."

Angelina waited for her mother to sigh and recommend her daughters take to the stage, as she did with regularity—something that would have caused instant, shame-induced cardiac arrest should they ever have followed her advice. But when Mother only stared back at her older daughters, stone-faced, that prickle at the back of Angelina's neck started to intensify. She sat straighter.

"Surely we all knew that the expectation was that we would find rich husbands, someday," Angelina said, carefully. Because that was one of the topics she avoided, having always assumed that long before she did as expected and married well enough to suit her mother's aspirations, if not her father's wallet, she would make her escape. "Assuming any such men exist who wished to take on charity cases such as ours."

"Charity cases!" Margrete looked affronted. "I hope your father never hears you utter such a phrase, Angelina. Such an ungrateful, vicious thing to say. That the

Charteris name should be treated with such contempt by one who bears it! If I had not been present at your birth I would doubt you were my daughter."

Given that Margrete expressed such doubts in a near constant refrain, Angelina did not find that notion as hurtful she might have otherwise.

"This isn't about marrying," Petronella said, the hint of tears in her voice, though there was no trace of moisture in her eyes. "I've always wanted to marry, personally."

Dorothea sniffed. "Just last week you claimed it was positively medieval to expect you to pay attention to men simply because they met Father's requirements."

Petronella waved an impatient hand. The fact she didn't snap at Dorothea for saying such a thing—or attempting to say such a thing—made the prickle at Angelina's nape bloom into something far colder. And sharper, as it began to slide down her spine.

"This isn't about men or marriage. It's about *murder*." Petronella actually sat up straight to say that part, a surprise indeed, given that her spine better resembled melted candle wax most of the time. "We're talking about the Butcher of Castello Nero."

Invoking one of the most infamous villains in Europe—maybe in the whole of the world—took Angelina's breath away. "Is someone going to tell me what we're talking about?"

"I invite you to call our guest that vile nickname to his face, Petronella," Margrete suggested, her voice a quiet fury as she glared at the larger settee. "If he really is what you say he is, how do you imagine he will react?"

And to Angelina's astonishment, her selfish, spoiled

rotten sister—who very rarely bothered to lift her face from a contemplation of the many self-portraits she took with her mobile phone—paled.

"Benedetto Franceschi," Dorothea intoned. "The richest man in all of Europe." She was in such a state that her bob actually trembled against her jawline. "And the most murderous."

"Stop this right now." Margrete cast her needlepoint aside and rose in an outraged rustle of skirts and fury. Then she gazed down at all of them over her magnificent, affronted bosom. "I will tolerate this self-centered spitefulness no longer."

"I still don't know what's going on," Angelina pointed out.

"Because you prefer to live in your little world of piano playing and secret excursions up and down the servants' stairs, Angelina," Margrete snapped. "This is reality, I'm afraid."

And that, at last, made Angelina feel real fear.

It was not that she thought she'd actually managed to pull something over on her mother. It was that she'd lived in this pleasant fiction they'd all created for the whole of her life. That they were not on the brink of destitution. That her father would turn it all around tomorrow. That they were ladies of leisure, lounging about the ruined old house because they chose it, not because there were no funds to do much of anything else.

Angelina hadn't had the slightest notion that her mother paid such close attention to her movements. She preferred to imagine herself the ignored daughter.

Here, now, what could she do but lower her gaze?

"And you two." Margrete turned her cold glare to the other settee. "Petronella, forever whoring about as if giving away for free what we might have sold does anything but make you undesirable and useless. Wealthy heiresses can do as they like, because the money makes up for it. What is it you intend to bring to the table?"

When Petronella said nothing, Mother's frosty gaze moved to her oldest daughter. "And you, Dorothea. You turned up your nose at a perfectly acceptable marriage offer, and for what? To traipse about the Continent, trailing after the heirs to lesser houses as if half of France doesn't claim they're related to some other dauphin?"

Dorothea gasped. "He was Papa's age! He made my skin crawl!"

"The more practical woman he made his wife is younger than you and can afford to buy herself a new skin." Margrete adjusted her dress, though it was perfect already. Even fabric dared not challenge her. "The three of you have done nothing to help this family. All you do is take. That ends tonight."

Angelina found herself sitting straighter. She was used to drama, but this was on a different level. For one thing, she had never seen her sisters ashen-faced before tonight.

"Your sisters know this already, but let me repeat it for everyone's edification." Margrete looked at each of them in turn, but then settled her cold glare on Angelina. "Benedetto Franceschi will be at dinner tonight. He is looking for a new wife and your father has told him that he can choose amongst the three of you. I am not interested in your thoughts or feelings on this matter. If he chooses you, you will say yes. Do you understand me?"

"He has had six wives so far," Petronella hissed.

"All have died or disappeared under mysterious circumstances. *All*, Mother!"

Angelina felt cold on the outside. Her hands, normally quick and nimble, were like blocks of ice.

But deep inside her, a dark thing pulsed.

Because she knew about Benedetto Franceschi. *"The Butcher of Castello Nero,"* Petronella had said. Everyone alive knew of the man so wealthy he lived in his own castle on his own private island—when the tide was high. When the tide was low, it was possible to reach the *castello* over a road that was little more than a sandbar, but, they whispered, those who made that trek did not always come back.

He had married six times. All of his wives had died or disappeared without a trace, declared dead in absentia. And despite public outcry, there had never been so much as an inquest.

All of those things were true.

What was also true was that when Angelina had been younger and there had still been money enough for things like tuition, she and her friends had sighed over pictures of Benedetto Franceschi in the press. That dark hair, like ink. Those flashing dark eyes that were like fire. And that mouth of his that made girls in convent schools like the one Angelina had attended feel the need to make a detailed confession. Or three.

If he chooses you, came a voice inside her, as clear as a bell, *you can leave this place forever.*

"He will choose one of us," Petronella said, still pale, but not backing down from her mother's ferocious glare. "He will pick one of us, carry her off, and then kill her. That is what our father has agreed to. Because he thinks that the loss of a daughter is worth it if he gets to keep this house and cancel out his debts. Which man is worse? The one who butchers women or the man who supplies him?"

Angelina bit back a gasp. Her mother only glared.

Out in the cavernous hallways, empty of so much of their former splendor, the clock rang out the half hour.

Margrete stiffened. "It is time. Come now, girls. We must not keep destiny waiting, no matter how you feel about it."

And there was no mutiny. No revolt.

They all lived in what remained of this sad place, after all. This pile of stone and regret.

Angelina rose obediently, falling into place behind her sisters as they headed out.

"To the death," Petronella kept whispering to Dorothea, who was uncharacteristically silent.

But it would be worth the risk, Angelina couldn't help but think—a sense of giddy defiance sweeping over her—if it meant she got to live, even briefly.

Somewhere other than here.

CHAPTER TWO

WHEN A MAN was a known monster, there was no need for posturing.

Benedetto Franceschi did not hide his reputation.

On the contrary, he indulged it. He leaned into it.

He knew the truth of it, after all.

He dressed all in black, the better to highlight the dark, sensual features he'd been told many times were sin personified. Evil, even. He lounged where others sat, waved languid fingers where others offered detailed explanations, and most of the time, allowed his great wealth and the power that came with it—not to mention his fearsome, unsavory reputation—to do his talking for him.

But here he was again, parading out like *l'uomo nero*, the boogeyman, in a crumbling old house in France that had once been the seat of its own kind of greatness. He could see the bones of it, everywhere he looked. The house itself was a shambles. And what was left of the grounds were tangled and overgrown, gardeners and landscapers long since let go as the family fortune slipped away thanks to Anthony Charteris's bad gambles and failed business deals.

Benedetto had even had what was, for him, an unusual moment of something like shame as he'd faced once more the charade he was reduced to performing, seemingly preying on the desperation of fools—

But all men were fools, in one form or another. Why not entertain himself while living out what so many called the Franceschi Curse?

The curse is not supposed to mean you, a voice inside him reminded him. *But rather your so-called victims.*

He shrugged that away, as ever, and attempted to focus on the task at hand. He had little to no interest in Anthony Charteris himself, or the portly little man's near slavering devotion to him tonight. He had suffered through a spate of twittering on that he had only half listened to, and could not therefore swear had been a kind of "business" presentation. Whatever that meant. Benedetto had any number of fortunes and could certainly afford to waste one on a man like this. Such was his lot in life, and Charteris could do with it what he liked. Benedetto already failed to care in the slightest, and maybe this time, Benedetto would get what he wanted out of the bargain.

Surely number seven will be the charm, he assured himself.

Darkly.

His men had already gathered all the necessary background information on the once proud Charteris family and their precipitous slide into dire straits. Anthony's lack of business acumen did not interest him. Benedetto was focused on the man's daughters.

One of them was to be his future wife, whether he liked it or not.

But what he liked or disliked was one more thing he'd surrendered a long time ago.

Benedetto knew that the eldest Charteris daughter had been considered something of a catch for all of five minutes in what must seem to her now like another lifetime. She could have spent the last eight years as the wife of a very wealthy banker whose current life expectancy rivaled that of a fragile flower, meaning she could have looked forward to a very well-upholstered widowhood. Instead, she had refused the offer in the flush of Anthony's brief success as a hotelier only to watch her father's fortunes—and her appeal—decline rapidly thereafter.

The possibilities of further offers from wealthy men were scant indeed, which meant Dorothea would likely jump at the chance to marry him, his reputation notwithstanding.

Unlike her sister, the middle daughter had shared her favors freely on as many continents as she could access by private jet, as long as one of the far wealthier friends she cozied up to were game to foot the bill for her travels. She had been documenting her lovers and her lifestyle online for years. And Benedetto was no Puritan. What was it to him if a single woman wished to indulge in indiscriminate sex? He had always enjoyed the same himself. Nor was he particularly averse to a woman whose avariciousness trumped her shame.

Of them all, Petronella seemed the most perfect for him on paper, save the part of her life she insisted on living in public. He could not allow that and he suspected that she would not give it up. Which would not matter if she possessed the sort of curiosity that would lead her to stick her nose into his secrets and make a choice she couldn't take back—but he doubted very much that she was curious about much outside her mobile.

The third daughter was ten years younger than the eldest, six years younger than the next, and had proved the hardest to dig into. There were very few pictures of her, as the family had already been neck deep in ruin by the time she might have followed in her sisters' footsteps and begun to frequent the tiresome charity ball circuit of Europe's elite families. What photographs existed dated back to her school days, where she had been a rosy-cheeked thing in a plaid skirt and plaits. Since graduating from the convent, Angelina had disappeared into the grim maw of what remained of the family estate, never to be heard from again.

Benedetto had already dismissed her. He expected her to be callow and dull, having been cloistered her whole life. What else could she be?

He had met the inimitable Madame Charteris upon arrival tonight. The woman had desperately wanted him to know that, once upon a time, she had been a woman of great fortune and beauty herself.

"My father was Sebastian Laurent," she had informed him, then paused. Portentously. Indicating that Benedetto was meant to react to that. Flutter, perhaps. Bend a knee.

As he did neither of those things, ever, he had merely stared at the woman until she had colored in some confusion, then swept away.

Someday, Benedetto would no longer have to subject himself to these situations. Someday, he would be free…

But he realized, as the room grew silent around him, that his host was peering at him quizzically.

Someday, sadly, was not today.

Benedetto took his time rising, and not only because

he was so much bigger than Charteris that the act of rising was likely to be perceived as an assault. He did not know if regret and self-recrimination had shrunk the man opposite him, as it should have if there was any justice, but the result was the same. And Benedetto was not above using every weapon available to him without him having to do anything but smile.

Anyone who saw that smile claimed they could see his evil, murderous intent in it. It was as good as prancing about with a sign above his head that said *LEAVE ME ALONE OR DIE*, which he had also considered in his time.

He smiled now, placing his drink down on the desk before him with a click that sounded as loud as a bullet in the quiet room.

Charteris gulped. Benedetto's smile deepened, because he knew his role.

Had come to enjoy it, in parts, if he was honest.

"Better not to do something than to do it ill," his grandfather had often told him.

"If you'll c-come with me," Charteris said, stuttering as he remembered, no doubt, every fanciful tale he'd ever heard about the devil he'd invited into his home, "we can go through to the dining room. Where all of my daughters await you."

"With joy at their prospects, one assumes."

"N-naturally. Tremendous joy."

"And do you love them all equally?" Benedetto asked silkily.

The other man frowned. "Of course."

But Benedetto rather thought that a man like this loved nothing at all.

After all, he'd been fathered, however indifferently, by a man just like this.

He inclined his head to his host, then followed the small man out of what he'd defiantly announced was his "office" when it looked more like one of those dreadful cubicles Benedetto had seen in films of lowbrow places, out into the dark, dimly lit halls of this cold, crumbling house.

Once upon a time, the Charteris home had been a manor. *A château,* he corrected himself, as they were in France. Benedetto could fix the house first and easily. That way, no matter what happened with his newest acquisition, her father would not raise any alarms. He would be too happy to be restored to a sense of himself to bother questioning the story he received.

Benedetto had played this game before. He liked to believe that someday there would be no games at all.

But he needed to stop torturing himself with *someday,* because it was unlikely that tonight would be any different. Wasn't that what he'd learned? No matter how much penance he paid, nothing changed.

Really, he should have been used to it. He was. It was this part that he could have done without, layered as it was with those faint shreds of hope. All the rest of it was an extended, baroque reconfirmation that he was, if not precisely the monster the world imagined him, a monster all the same.

It was the hope that made him imagine otherwise, however briefly.

This was not the first time he'd wished he could excise it with his own hands, then cast it aside at last.

The house was not overly large, especially with so much of it unusable in its current state, so it took no time at all before they reached the dining room on the main floor. His host offered an unctuous half bow, then waved his arm as if he was an emcee at a cabaret. A horrifying notion.

Benedetto prowled into the room, pleased to find that this part of the house, unlike the rest with its drafts and cold walls despite the season, was appropriately warm.

Perhaps too warm, he thought in the next moment. Because as he swept his gaze across the room, finding the oldest and middle daughter to be exactly as he'd expected, it was as if someone had thrown gas on a fire he could not see. But could feel inside of him, cranked up to high.

The flames rose higher.

He felt scalded. But what he saw was an angel.

Angelina, something in him whispered.

For it could be no other.

Her sisters were attractive enough, but he had already forgotten them. Because the third, least known Charteris daughter stood next to her mother along one side of a formally set table, wearing a simple dress in a muted hue and a necklace of complicated pearls that seemed to sing out her beauty.

But then, she required no embellishment for that. She was luminous.

Her hair was so blond it shone silver beneath the flickering flames of a chandelier set with real candles. Economy, not atmosphere, he was certain, but it made Angelina all the more lovely. She'd caught the silvery mass back at the nape of her neck in a graceful chignon that he longed to pick apart with his hands. Her features should have been set in marble or used to launch ships into wars. They made him long to paint, though he had never wielded a brush in all his days.

But he thought he might learn the art of oils against canvas for the express purpose of capturing her. Or trying. Her high cheekbones, her soft lips, her elegant neck.

He felt his heart, that traitorous beast, beat too hard.

"Here we all are," said Anthony Charteris, all but chortling with glee.

And in that moment, Benedetto wanted to do him damage. He wanted to grab the man around his portly neck and shake him the way a cat shook its prey. He wanted to make the man think about what it was he was doing here. Selling off a daughter to a would-be groom with a reputation such as Benedetto's? Selling off an angel to a devil, and for what?

But almost as soon as those thoughts caught at him, he let them go.

Each man made his own prison. His own had contained him for the whole of his adult life and he had walked inside, turned the key, and fashioned his own steel bars. Who was he to cast stones?

"This is Benedetto Franceschi," Charteris announced, and then frowned officiously at his daughters. "He is a very important friend and business partner. *Very* important."

Some sort of look passed between the man and his wife. Margrete, once a Laurent, drew herself up—no doubt so she could present her bosom to Benedetto once more. Then again, perhaps that was how she communicated.

He remained as he had been before: vaguely impressed, yet unmoved.

"May I present to you, sir, my daughters." Margrete

gestured across the table. "My eldest, Dorothea." Her hand moved to indicate the sulky, too self-aware creature beside the eldest, who smirked a bit at him as if he had already proposed to her. "My middle daughter, Petronella."

And at last, she indicated his angel. The most beautiful creature Benedetto had ever beheld. His seventh and last wife, God willing. "And this is my youngest, Angelina."

Benedetto declared himself suitably enchanted, waited for the ladies to seat themselves, and then dropped into his chair with relief. Because he wanted to concentrate on Angelina, not her sisters.

He wanted to dispense with this performance. Announce that he had made his choice and avoid having to sit through an awkward meal like this one, where everyone involved was pretending that they'd never heard of the many things he was supposed to have done. Just as he was pretending he didn't notice that the family house was falling down around them as they sat here.

"Tell me." Benedetto interrupted the meaningless prattle from Charteris at the head of the table about his ancestors or the Napoleonic Wars or some such twaddle. "What is it you do?"

His eyes were on the youngest daughter, though she had not once looked up from her plate.

But it was the eldest who answered, after clearing her throat self-importantly. "It is a tremendous honor and privilege that I get to dedicate my life to charity," she proclaimed, a hint of self-righteousness flirting with the corners of her mouth.

Benedetto had many appetites, but none of them were likely to be served by the indifferent food served in a place like this, where any gesture toward the celebrated national cuisine had clearly declined along with the house and grounds. He sat back, shifting his attention from the silver-haired vision to her sister.

"And what charity is it that you offer, exactly?" he asked coolly. "As I was rather under the impression that your interest in charity ball attendance had more to do with the potential of fetching yourself a husband of noble blood than any particular interest in the charities themselves."

Then he watched, hugely entertained, as Dorothea flushed. Her mouth opened, then closed, and then she sank back against her seat without saying a word. As if he'd taken the wind out of her sails.

He did tend to have that effect.

The middle daughter was staring at him, so Benedetto merely lifted a brow. And waited for her to leap into the fray.

Petronella did not disappoint. Though she had the good sense to look at him with a measure of apprehension in her eyes, she also propped her elbows on the table and sat forward in such a way that her breasts pressed against the bodice of the dress she wore. An invitation he did not think was the least bit unconscious.

"I consider myself an influencer," she told him, her voice a husky, throaty rasp that was itself another invitation. All of her, from head to toe, was a carefully constructed beckoning. She did not smile at him. She kept her lips in what appeared to be a natural pout while gazing at him with a directness that he could tell she'd practiced in the mirror. Extensively.

"Indeed." His brow remained where was, arched

high. "What influence do you have? And over what—or whom?"

"My personal brand is really a complicated mix of—"

"I am not interested in brands," Benedetto said, cutting her off. "Brands are things that I own and use at will according to my wishes. The purpose of a brand is to sell things. Influence, on the other hand, suggests power. Not the peddling of products for profit. So. What power do you have?"

She shifted in her chair, a strange expression on her face. It took him a moment to recognize it as false humility. "I couldn't possibly say why some people think I'm worth listening to," she murmured.

Benedetto smiled back, and enjoyed watching the unease wash over her as he studied her, because he was more the monster they thought he was than he liked to admit.

Especially in polite company.

"Pretty is not power," he said softly. "Do you know how you can tell? Because men wish to possess it, not wield it. It is no different from any other product, and like them, happily discarded when it outgrows its usefulness or fades in intensity. Surely you must know this."

Petronella, too, dropped her gaze. And looked uncertain for the first time since Benedetto had walked in to the dining room.

He was not the least bit surprised that neither of the Charteris parents intervened. Parents such as these never did. They were too wrapped up in what they had to gain from him to quibble over his harshness.

But he hardly cared because, finally, he was able to focus on the third daughter. The aptly named Angelina.

"And you?" he asked, feeling a coiling inside of him, as if he was some kind of serpent about to strike. As if he was every bit the monster the world believed he was. "What is it you do?"

"Nothing of consequence," she replied.

Unlike her sisters, Angelina did not look up from her plate, where she was matter-of-factly cutting into a piece of meat he could see even from where he sat was tough. They had given the choice cuts to him and to themselves, of course. Letting their children chew on the gristle. That alone told him more than he needed to know about the Charteris family. About their priorities.

Perhaps the truth no one liked to face was that some people deserved to meet a monster at the dinner table.

"Angelina," bit out Margrete, in an iron voice from behind a pasted-on smile and that magnificent chest like the prow of a ship.

"I spoke the truth," Angelina protested.

But she placed her cutlery down, very precisely. She folded her hands in her lap. Then she raised her gaze to Benedetto's at last. He felt the kick of it, her eyes blue and innocent and dreamy, like the first flush of a sweet spring.

"I play the piano. Whenever I can, for as long as I can. My other interests include listening to other people play the piano on the radio, taking long walks while thinking about how to play Liszt's *La Campenella* seamlessly, and reading novels."

Her voice was not quite insolent. Not *quite*. Next to her, her mother drew herself up again, as if prepared to mete out justice—possibly in the form of a sharp slap, if Benedetto was reading the situation correctly—but he lifted a hand.

"Both of your sisters attempt to interact with the outside world. But not you. There's no trace of you on the internet, for example, which is surpassingly strange in this day and age."

There was heat on her cheeks. A certain glitter in her gaze that made his body tighten.

"There are enough ways to hide in a piece of music," she said after a moment stretched thin and filled with the sounds of tarnished silver against cracked china. "Or a good book. Or even on a walk, I suppose. I have no need to surrender myself to still more ways to hide myself away, by curating myself into something unrecognizable."

Petronella let out an affronted sniff, but Angelina did not look apologetic.

"Some would say that it is only in solitude that one is ever able to stop hiding and find one's true self," Benedetto said.

And did not realize until the words were out there, squatting in the center of the silent table, how deeply felt that sentiment was. Or was that merely what he told himself?

"I suppose that depends." And when Angelina looked at him directly then, he felt it like an electric charge. And more, he doubted very much that she'd spent any time at all practicing her expression in reflective glass. "Are you speaking of solitude? Or solitary confinement? Because I don't think they're the same thing."

"No one is speaking about solitary confinement, Angelina," Margrete snapped, and Benedetto had the sudden, unnerving sensation that he'd actually forgotten where he was. That for a moment, he had seen nothing but Angelina. As if the rest of the world had ceased to exist entirely, and along with it his reality, his responsibilities, his fearsome reputation, and the reason he was here...

Pull yourself together, he ordered himself.

The dinner wore on, course after insipid course. Anthony and Margrete filled the silence, chattering aimlessly, while Benedetto seethed. And the three daughters who were clearly meant to vie for his favor stayed quiet, though he suspected that the younger one kept a still tongue for very different reasons than her sisters.

"Well," said Anthony with hearty and patently false bonhomie, when the last course had been taken away untouched by a surly maid. "Ladies, why don't you repair to the library while Signor Franceschi and I discuss a few things over our port."

So chummy. So pleased with himself.

"I think not," Benedetto said, decisively, even as the older daughters started to push back their chairs.

At the head of the table, Anthony froze.

Benedetto turned toward Angelina, who tensed—almost as if she knew what he was about to say. "I wish to hear you play the piano," he said.

And when no one moved, when they all gazed back at him in varying degrees of astonishment, outright panic, and pure dislike, he smiled.

In the way he knew made those around him...shudder.

Angelina stared back at him in something that was not quite horror. "I beg your pardon?"

Benedetto smiled wider. "Now, please."

CHAPTER THREE

"Alone," added the terrible, notorious man when Angelina's whole family made as if to rise.

He smiled all the while, in a manner that reminded Angelina of nothing so much as the legends she'd heard all her life about men who turned into wolves when the moon was high. She was tempted to run to the windows and see what shape the moon took tonight, though she did not dare.

And more, could not quite bring herself to look away from him.

Angelina had not been prepared for this. For him.

It was one thing to look at photographs. But there was only so much raw magnetism a person could see on the screen.

Because in person, Benedetto Franceschi was not merely beautiful or sinful, though he was both.

In person, he was volcanic.

Danger simmered around him, charging the air, making Angelina's body react in ways she'd thought only extremes of temperatures could cause. Her chest felt tight, hollow and too full at once, and she found it almost impossible to take a full breath.

When he'd singled her out for conversation she'd responded from her gut, not her head. And knew she'd handled it all wrong, but only because of her mother's reaction. The truth was, her head had gone liquid and light and she'd had no earthly idea what had come out of her mouth.

Nothing good, if the pinched expression on Margrete's face was any guide.

Still, disobedience now did not occur to her. Not because she feared her parents, though she supposed that on some level, she must. Or why would she subject herself to this? Why would she still be here? But she wasn't thinking of them now.

Angelina wasn't thinking at all, because Benedetto's dark, devil's gaze was upon her, wicked and insinuating. A dare and an invitation and her own body seemed to have turned against her.

He wanted to hear her play.

But a darker, less palatable truth was that she wanted to play for him.

She told herself it was only that she wanted an audience. Any audience. Yet the dark fire of his gaze worked its way through her and she knew she wasn't being entirely honest. The yearning for an audience, instead of the family members who ignored her, wasn't why her pulse was making such a racket, and it certainly wasn't why she could feel sensation hum deep within her.

She could hardly breathe and yet she stood. Worse, she knew that she *wanted* to stand. Then she turned, leading him out of the dining chamber, careful not to catch her sisters' eyes or sneak a glance at her worryingly, thunderously quiet father on her way out.

Angelina tried to steel herself against him as she moved through the murky depths of the house, certain that he would try to speak to her the moment they were alone. Charm her into unwariness or attempt to disarm her with casual conversation.

But instead, he walked in silence.

And that was much, much worse.

She was so aware of him it made her bones ache. And it took only a few steps to understand that her awareness of him was not based on fear. Her breasts and her belly were tight, and grew tighter the farther away they moved from the dining room. Deep between her legs she felt swollen, pulsing in time with her heart as it beat and beat.

Helpless. Hopeless.

Red hot and needy.

The house brought it all into sharp relief. It was dimly lit and echoing, so that their footsteps became another pulse, following them. Chasing them on. Angelina was certain that if she looked at the shadow he cast behind them, she would see not a man, but a wolf.

Fangs at the ready, prepared to attack.

She could not have said why that notion made her whole body seem to boil over, liquid and hot.

She walked on and on through a house that seemed suddenly cavernous, her mind racing and spinning. Yet she couldn't seem to grasp on to a single thought, because she was entirely too focused on the man beside her and slightly behind her, matching his stride to hers in a way that made her feel dirty, somehow.

It felt like a harbinger. A warning.

She was relieved when they reached the conservatory at last, and for once didn't care that it was more properly an abandoned sunroom. She rushed inside, shocked to see that her hands trembled in the light from the hall as she picked up the matches from the piano bench, then set about lighting the candles on the candelabra that sat atop her piano.

Because her parents only lit a portion of the house, and this room only Angelina used did not qualify.

But then it was only the two of them in the candlelight, and that made the pulse in her quicken. Then drum deep.

Especially when, overhead through the old glass, she could see the moon behind the clouds—a press of light that did not distinguish itself enough for her to determine its shape. Or fullness.

Angelina settled herself on the piano bench. And it took her a moment to understand that it wasn't her pulse that she could hear, seeming to fill the room, but her own breathing.

Meanwhile, Benedetto stood half in shadow, half out. She found herself desperately trying to see where the edges of his body ended and the shadows began, because it seemed to her for a panicked moment there that there was no difference between the two. That he was made of shadows and inky dark spaces, and only partly of flesh and bone.

"We have electricity," she felt compelled to say, though her voice felt like a lie on her tongue. Too loud, too strange, when his eyes were black as sin and lush with invitation. Everything in her quivered, but she pushed on. "My parents encourage us to keep things more…atmospheric."

"If you say so."

His voice was another dark, depthless shadow. It moved in her, swirling around and around, making all the places where she pulsed seem brighter and darker at once.

She sat, breathing too heavily, her hands curved above the smooth, worn keys of this instrument that— some years—had been her only friend.

"What do you want me to play?"

"Whatever you like."

She did not understand how he could say something so innocuous and leave her feeling as if that mouth of his was moving against her skin, leaving trails all over her body, finding those places where she already glowed with a need she hardly recognized.

You recognize it, something in her chided her. *You only wish you didn't.*

Angelina felt misshapen. Powerful sensations washed over her, beating into her until she felt as if she might explode.

Or perhaps the truth was that she wanted to explode.

She spread her hands over the keys, waiting for that usual feeling of rightness. Of coming home again. Usually this was the moment where everything felt right again. Where she found her hope, believed in her future, and could put her dreary life aside. But tonight, even the feel of the ivory beneath her fingers was a sensual act.

And somehow his doing.

"Are you afraid of me, little one?" Benedetto asked, and his voice seemed to come from everywhere at once. From inside her. From deep between her legs. From that aching hunger that grew more and more intense with every second.

She shifted on the bench. Then she stared at him, lost almost instantly in his fathomless gaze. In the dark of the room with the night pressing down outside. In the flickering candlelight that exposed and concealed them both in turn.

Angelina felt as if she was free falling, tumbling from some great height, fully aware that when she hit the ground it would break her—but she couldn't look away.

She didn't *want* to look away.

He was the most marvelous thing that had ever happened to her, even if he really was a murderer.

She didn't know where to put that.

And again, she could hear her own breath. He leaned against the side of the piano, stretching a hand out across the folded back lid, and her eyes followed the movement. Compulsively. As if she had no choice in the matter.

She would have expected a man so wealthy and arrogant to have hands soft and tender like the belly of a small dog. She wouldn't have been surprised to see a careful manicure. Or a set of garish rings.

But his hand was bare of any accoutrement. And it was no tender, soft thing. It looked tough, which struck her as incongruous even as the notion moved in her like heat. His fingers were long, his palms broad.

And she could not seem to keep herself from imagining them touching her skin, cupping her breasts, gripping her bottom as he pulled her beneath him and made her his.

When a different sound filled the room, she understood that she'd made it. She'd gasped. Out loud. And that darkness he wore too easily seemed to light up with a new kind of fire she couldn't read.

"I'm accustomed to having my questions answered," he said in a quiet tone, but all she heard was menace.

And she had already forgotten the question, and possibly herself. So she did the only thing she could under the circumstances.

Angelina began to play.

She played and she played. She played him melodies that spoke of her dreams, her hopes, and then the crushing storm of her father's losses. She played him stories of her confinement here and the bitter drip of years in this ruined, forgotten place. Then she played him songs that felt like he did, impossible and terrifying and thrilling all the same.

She felt caught in the grip of his unwavering, relentless gaze. And the notes that crashed all around them, holding them tight even as they sang out the darkest, most hidden parts of her.

And while she played, Angelina found she couldn't lose herself the way she usually did.

Instead, it was as if she was found. As if he had found her here, trapping her and exalting her at once.

So she played that, too.

She played and played, until he stepped out of the shadows and his face was fully in the candlelight.

Fierce. Haunted. Sensual.

And suffused with the same rich, layered hunger she could feel crashing around inside of her.

For a long time, while the music danced from her fingers into the keys and then filled the room, it was as if she couldn't tell which one of them was which. His hands did not touch her body, and yet somehow they were all over her. She could feel the scrape of his palm, the stirring abrasion of his calloused fingers.

And she explored him, too, with every note she coaxed from her piano. They were tossed together in the melody, tangled, while the music tied them in knots and made them one glorious note, held long and pure—

When she stopped playing, for a moment she couldn't tell the difference.

And then the next, his hands were on her.

His beautiful, terrible hands, for real this time.

He sank his fingers into her hair, pulling it from her chignon—and not gently. And her whole body seemed to bloom. His face was over hers, his mouth as grim as his eyes were hot. And then he bent her back at an angle that should have alarmed her, but instead sent a thick delight storming through her in every direction.

He feasted on her neck like the wolf she half imagined he was, teasing his way around those sullen, moody pearls she wore.

I need, she thought, though she could not speak.

The more he tasted her flesh, the more she felt certain that he stole her words. That as his mouth moved over her skin, he was altering her.

Taking her away from here. From herself. From everything she knew.

He shifted then, spreading her out on the piano bench. She lay down where he put her, grateful to have the bench at her back. Then he lowered himself over her, the dark bespoke suit he wore seeming blacker than pitch in the candlelight. He skimmed his wicked hands down the length of her body, moving his way down until he wrenched the skirt of her shift dress up to her waist.

It didn't occur to her to object.

Not when every part of her wanted to sing out instead, glory and hope alike, and no matter that this man was not safe. There was no safety in staying where she was, either. There was only disappointment and the slow march of tedious years, and Benedetto felt like an antidote to that.

He touched her and she felt as if she was the piano, and he was making her a melody.

She threw her arms over her head and arched into him.

Then she felt his mouth, again. She heard his dark laugh, desire and delight. He tasted the tender flesh of her inner thigh and she could not have described the sounds she made. She could only *feel* them, coming out of her like an echo of those same songs she'd played for him.

When she could feel the harsh beauty of them in her fingers, she realized that she was gripping his strong shoulders instead.

"Angelina," he said, there against her thigh where she could feel her own name like a brand against her skin. In the candlelight that danced and flickered, she lifted her head and found herself lost in his gaze with only her own body between them. "Are you afraid of me?"

"Yes," she lied.

He laughed, a rich, dark sound that crashed over her like a new symphony, louder and more tumultuous by far.

Then he shifted, pulled her panties to one side, and licked deep into the center of her need.

And then Benedetto Franceschi, the Butcher of Castello Nero, ate her alive.

He made her scream.

She bucked against him, crying out for deliverance but receiving nothing but the slide of his tongue, the faint scrape of his teeth. A benediction by any measure.

And when she died from the pleasure of it—only to

find she lived somehow after all, shuddering and ruined and shot through with some kind of hectic glee—he pulled her to her feet, letting her shift dress do what it would. He sank his hands into her hair again, and then this time, he took her mouth with his.

Sensation exploded in her all over again, hotter and wilder this time.

The madness of these melodies. The glorious terror of his possession.

The dark marvel of it all.

His mouth had been between her legs, and the knowledge of that made her shake all over again. She pulsed and shook, and she was too inexperienced to know what part of the rough, intoxicating taste was him, and which part her.

So she angled her head and met him as he devoured her.

Angelina felt debauched and destroyed. As ruined as this house they stood in.

And why had she never understood that the real price of a ruin like this was the sheer joy in it?

The dark, secret joy that coursed through her veins, pooled between her legs, and made her arch against him as if all this time, all these years, her body had been asleep. Only now had it woken up to its true purpose.

Here. With him.

Like this.

He kissed her and he kissed her.

When he finally lifted his mouth from hers, his grin was a ferocious thing. Angelina felt it inside her, as if she was made fierce, too, because of him.

And she had never known, until this moment, how deeply she wanted to be fierce.

"If you marry me," he told her, in that dark, intense voice of his, "you can never return here. You will no more be a part of your family. You will belong to me and I am a jealous, possessive creature at the best of times. I do not share what is mine."

Angelina hardly felt like herself. There was too much sensation coursing in her and around her, she couldn't tell if it was the music she'd played or the way he'd played her body in turn, but she couldn't seem to worry about that the way she should.

The way a wiser woman would have, with a man like him.

"Is that a warning or promise?" she asked instead.

"It is a fact."

And her skirt was still rucked up. She felt uncomfortably full in the bodice of her dress. She could not tell which was more ravaged and alight, the aching center of her need between her legs or her mouth.

But the candlelight made all of that seem unimportant.

Or perhaps, whispered a voice inside her, *it is not the light that seduces you, but the dark that makes it shine.*

"If I marry you," she said, because she was already ruined, and she wanted things she was afraid to name, "I want to live. I don't want to die."

And then, for the first time since they'd walked away from her family and into this chilly, barren room, it occurred to her to worry about the fact that he was a man with six dead wives. She was all alone with him and everyone believed he was a murderer.

Why did something in her want to believe otherwise?

His mouth was a bitter slash. His eyes were much too dark.

For the first time, Angelina wanted to cover herself. She felt cold straight through.

If she could have taken the words back, she would have. If she could have kept him from touching her, she—

But no. Whatever happened next, his mouth on her had been worth it.

"Every one of us must die, little one," Benedetto said, his voice a mere thread of sound. It wound through her and then flowered into something far richer and more textured than fear, making Angelina shudder as if he was licking into her molten core again. "But we will do so in the way we live, like it or not. That I can promise you."

CHAPTER FOUR

A MONTH LATER, Angelina woke up to the sound of hammering, the way she had almost every morning since that first night.

The only difference was that today was her wedding day, like it or not.

Construction on the old house had begun immediately. Benedetto had made good on his promise with crews arriving by truckload at first light. Since then, day after day, the hammering fused with that pulse inside her, until she couldn't tell whether her heart beat inside or outside of her body.

It had been the longest and shortest month of her life.

Her sisters veered between something like outrage and a more simple, open astonishment. And sometimes, when they remembered themselves, a surprising show of concern.

"You must be careful," Petronella had said very seriously, one evening. She'd come and interrupted Angelina in the conservatory, where Angelina played piece after piece as if the piano was telling stories to keep her alive. And as long as she played she would be safe. Night after night, she played until her fingers cramped, but nothing eased that ravaged, misshapen feeling inside of her. "Whatever happens, and whatever he does to you in that castle of his, you must not react."

"I didn't think you knew where the conservatory was." Angelina blinked at her sister in the flickering candlelight. Outside, a bloated summer moon rose over the trees. "Are you lost?"

"I'm serious, Angelina," Petronella snapped, scowling, which felt more like her sister than this strange appearance and stab at worry. "One dead wife could be an accident. The second could be a terrible tragedy. I could even *maybe* think that a third might be a stroke of very bad luck indeed. But six?"

Angelina slammed her hands on the keys, the discordant jangle of noise sounding a great deal like she felt inside. As if her ribs were piano keys she'd forgotten how to play.

Maybe that was what getting married was supposed to feel like.

"I don't need you to remind me who he is," she said.

Another slap of noise.

Petronella looked different in the candlelight. Younger. Softer. She lifted her hand, almost as if she intended to reach over and stroke Angelina with it. But she thought better of it, or the urge passed, and she dropped it to her side.

"I really did think he would choose me," she said, softly.

And when Angelina looked up again, Petronella had gone.

Dorothea was far less gracious. If she was worried about her younger sister, the only way she showed it was in an officious need to micromanage the trousseau that

Benedetto was funding for his new bride along with everything else.

"If he's a murderer," Angelina had said tightly one afternoon, after Dorothea made her try on armful after armful of concoctions she'd ordered straight from atelier in Paris on Angelina's behalf, "do you really think that choosing the right selection of negligees will save me?"

"Don't be ridiculous," Dorothea tutted, bustling about Angelina's bedchamber as if she'd never sat on a settee wailing about her impending death. "You know how people like to talk. That's all it is, I'm certain. A series of tragic events and too many rumors and innuendos."

"I hope you're right," Angelina had said.

But Dorothea's only response had been to lay out more soft, frilly things for Angelina to try on.

And it was a strange thing indeed to know that her life had changed completely—to understand that nothing she knew would be hers any longer, and soon—when for thirty days, only the trappings of her life changed. The manor house slowly returned to its former glory. Her father laughed again. Margrete looked less stiff and tense around the eyes.

But Angelina still woke in her same old bed. She still timed her breakfast to avoid the rest of the family, and then set off for her long morning walk, no matter the weather. She still played the piano for hours, alone in the conservatory.

If it weren't for the endless hammering, she might have been tempted to imagine that she'd made the whole thing up.

Then again, every time that Benedetto visited—a

stolen evening here, a day or two there—the balance in Angelina's family…shifted.

Because she was shifting, she thought as she lay in her bed at night with her hands between her legs, not sure if she wanted to sob or scream out all the wildfires he'd lit inside her. With that dark gaze. With the things he did to her when they were alone. His mouth, his fingers. And always that dark, seductive laugh.

She had always thought of a seduction as something…quicker. The mistake of an evening. Something hasty and ill-considered that would take time and space to repent.

But Benedetto taught her many lessons about time. And patience.

And the exquisite torture of anticipation.

The only thing Angelina had ever wanted was her piano and a place to play it. She had been certain she knew herself inside and out. But this man taught her—over and over—that there were banked fires in her she hardly understood.

Dark, greedy claws that dug in, deep, whenever he touched her and when he did not. Red and terrible longings that made her toss and turn when she wanted to sleep.

This hunger that made her run to him when she knew full well she should have run the other way.

"Such a pretty, needy little thing you are," he murmured one evening.

Like all the nights he came here, there had first been the awkward family dinner where he'd demonstrated his mastery over her father, then cowed her sisters and mother into uncharacteristic silence—usually with little more than a lift of one dangerous brow. When her mother and sisters repaired to the drawing room, leaving her father to his solitary port, Benedetto would usher Angelina to the conservatory.

It was the same every time.

That long, *fraught* walk through a house only half-alive. The sound of his footsteps mingled with hers. The humming, overfull silence stretched out between them and echoing back from the walls. Her breath would change as they moved, and she was certain he could hear it, though he always remained behind her. And he never spoke.

She told herself she marched toward her own, slow execution. She walked herself off the plank.

But the truth she never wished to face was that the closer they got to the conservatory, the quicker her steps. The quicker her breath.

And oh, how molten and hot her blood ran in her, pooling between her legs with a desperate intent.

Because inside that room, who knew what might happen?

He always made her play.

And then he played her, always making her scream and arch and shake. Always his wicked fingers, his clever mouth, tasting her, tempting her.

Training her, something in her whispered.

"Is this how you murder them all?" she asked one evening, a scant week away from their wedding.

Benedetto had laid her out on the chaise that had appeared one morning, along with all kinds of furniture throughout the *château*. It was as if the house was a visual representation of her own femininity, and she could see it grow its own pleasure. Lush and deep.

Paintings reappeared. Priceless antiques took their

places once again. There were updates everywhere, light where there had been darkness, the cobwebs swept away and cracks plastered over.

She'd forgotten herself, with her skirts tossed up and his head so dark between her thighs.

She'd forgotten herself, but she remembered with a jolt when she shifted and caught a glimpse of them in the fogged-up windows that surrounded them on all sides.

Benedetto was so big, tall and strong, and she was laid out before him, splayed wide like an offering. He was eating her alive and she was letting him, but she should never have let herself forget that the pleasure he visited upon her untried body was a weapon.

Everything about this man was a weapon only he knew how to use.

"I didn't mean that," she managed to gasp out while her heart galloped inside her, lust and fear and that same dark ache fusing into one.

She tried to pull her legs closed but his broad shoulders were between them, and he did not move. He lifted his head and his night-black eyes bored into her. He pressed his palm, roughened and huge, against the faint swell of her abdomen.

And something about the pressure made a new, dangerous heat uncurl inside her.

"What do you know of marriage?" he asked, and his voice was as dark as the rest of him, insinuating and dangerous.

She could feel that prickle that was as much longing as it was fear sweep over her body, leaving goose bumps in its wake.

"I have never been married before."

Angelina didn't know why she was answering him so prosaically. When she was as he liked her, still dressed for dinner but with her skirts around her waist, so she was bared only to him. Bared and wet and aching again.

Sometimes she thought the aching might actually kill her, here in this house before she had the chance to leave it, and that notion made her want to sob out loud.

Other times, she hoped it would.

Benedetto shifted his weight so that he held himself up on one crooked elbow. He let his hand drift from her abdomen to her secret, greedy flesh.

"Put your hands above your head," he told her, and she knew it was an order. A command she should have ignored while she still could, but her arms were already moving of their own accord. Lifting over her head so that her back arched and her breasts pressed wantonly against the bodice of the old dress she wore.

She knew he liked that. She knew a lot of the things he liked, by now. He liked her hair free and unconfined, tangled about wherever he lay her. He liked to get his fingers in it so he could guide her head where he wanted it. Particularly when he kissed her, tongue and teeth and a sheer mastery that made her shiver.

"Tell me what you know of men, Angelina," he said now, stroking the bright need between her legs, though he had already had her sweating, shaking, crying out his name.

This time, when her hips began to move, he found her opening. And he began to work one of those blunt, surprisingly tough fingers into her depths of her body.

She felt the stretching. The ache in her intensified.

Her nipples were delirious points, and every time she

breathed, the way her breasts jarred against the fabric of her bra made her want to jerk away. Or move closer.

"I have never spent much time with men," she managed to pant out. "I had a piano tutor, a boy from the village, but I learned all he had to teach me long ago."

"Did you play for him as you play for me?" Benedetto asked, his voice something like a croon—but much, much darker. "Did you open your legs like this? Did you let him slip between your thighs and taste your heat?"

And even as he asked those questions, he added a second finger to the first. He began to stroke his way deep inside her, and the sensation made it impossible to think. Impossible to do anything but lift her hips to meet him, then try to get away, or both at once.

His hand found a rhythm, but her hips took convincing.

"N-No…" She wasn't sure what, precisely, she was saying *no* to. His fingers plunged, withdrew. Then again. And again. A driving, relentless taking. "No one has ever touched me."

"Not even you?" he asked. "Late at night, tucked up beneath your covers in this tomb of a house? Do you not reach down, slip your fingers into all this molten greed, and make yourself shudder into life?"

Angelina was bright red already. But the flash of heat that he kindled within her swept over her until she was making a keening, high-pitched cry. Her hips finally found their rhythm, thrusting against him wildly as her head fell back.

And she thrashed there, not sure how anyone could survive these little deaths, much less the bigger one that waited for her.

Not sure anyone should.

"Look at me," Benedetto ordered her.

She realized she didn't know how much time had passed. How long she had shaken like that, open and exposed. It took her a long while to crack open her eyes. She struggled to sit up because he was sitting too, regarding her in his typically sinful and wicked way.

Angelina couldn't tell if it was shame or desire that worked inside of her, then.

Especially when he held her gaze, lifted the fingers he'd had inside her, and slowly licked them clean.

She heard herself gasping for breath as if she was running. If she was running to escape him, the way she knew she should. She could crash through the windows into the gardens that her parents had let go to seed, and were now manicured and pruned. She could race into the summer night, leaving all this behind her.

She could save herself and let her family do as they would.

But she only gazed back at him, breathing too heavily, and did not move an inch to extricate from this man who held her tight in his grip—though he was not touching her at all.

"I want you desperate, always," he told her, his voice that same, serious command. "I want you wet and needy, Angelina. When I look at you, I want to know that while you look like an angel, here, where you are naked and only ever mine, you are nothing but heat and hunger."

"Do you mean…?"

"I mean you should touch yourself. Taste yourself, if you wish. I insist. As long as you are always ready for me."

She understood what he meant by *ready* in a different way, now. Because it was one thing to read about sex. To read about that strange, inevitable joining. She understood the mechanics, but was not until now, so close to her wedding night, that she understood that it would be far more than merely *mechanical*.

Benedetto's head tilted slightly to one side. "Do you understand me?"

"I do," she said, and his smile was dark.

"Then I do not think, little one, that you need to worry overmuch about murder."

That was the last time she'd seen him.

She pushed herself upright in her bed this morning, her head as fuzzy as if she'd helped herself to the liquor in the drawing room when she didn't dare. Not when she had Benedetto to contend with and needed all her wits about her.

And it shocked her, as she looked around her room, that there was a lump in her throat as she accepted the reality that this room would no longer be hers by the time the sun set.

Her bedchamber had already undergone renovations, like so much of the house had in the past month. It already looked like someone else's. Plush, quietly elegant rugs were strewn about the floors, taking the chill away. She'd forgotten entirely that once, long ago, there had been curtains and drapes and a canopy over her bed, but they were all back now.

He'd given her back her childhood so she would know exactly what she was leaving behind her when she left here today.

She got up and headed to her bathroom, walking gingerly because she could feel the neediest, greediest part of her ripe and ready—just the way he wanted her. But she paused in the doorway. Because she could no longer hear the symphony of the old pipes.

And when she turned on the water in her sink, it ran hot.

Angelina ran herself a bath and climbed in, running her hands over her slick, soapy skin. Her breasts felt larger. Her belly was so sensitive she sucked in a breath through her teeth when she touched it.

And when she ran her hands between her legs, to do as he'd commanded her, she was hotter than the water around her.

Then hotter still as she imagined his face, dark and knowing, and made the water splash over the sides of her tub onto the floor.

But too soon, then it was time to dress.

Margrete bustled in, her sisters in her wake like sulky attendants. And for a long while, the three of them worked in silence. Petronella piled Angelina's hair on top of her head and pinned in sparkling hints of stones that looked like diamonds. Dorothea fussed with her dress, fastening each of the parade of buttons that marched down her spine. Margrete called in Matrice, the notably less surly housemaid now that there was money, and the two of them packed Angelina's things.

Petronella did Angelina's makeup. She made her younger sister's face almost otherworldly, and did something with her battery of brushes and sponges that made Angelina's eyes seemed bluer than the summer sky.

Matrice left first, wheeling out Angelina's paltry belongings with her.

And there was no need to keep her hiding place a secret now, so Angelina let her mother and sisters watch as she walked over to the four posts of her bed, unscrewed one tall taper, and pulled out her grandmother's pearls.

Her sisters passed a dark look between them while Angelina fastened the dark, moody pearls around her neck and let the weight of them settle there, against her collarbone.

And then her mother led her to the cheval glass.

The dress had arrived without warning two weeks before the wedding. Angelina had tried it on and let the seamstress who'd arrived with it take her measurements and make her alterations. The dress had seemed simple. Pretty. Not too much, somehow.

But now there was no escaping the dress or what it meant or what would become of her. She stared into the mirror, and a bride stared back.

The dark pearls she'd looped around her neck looked like a bruise, but everything else was white. Flowing, frothy white, while her hair seemed silvery and gleaming and impossible on top of her head.

She looked like what she was.

A virgin sacrifice to a dark king.

"You must ask him for what you want," Margrete told her, her voice matter-of-fact, but her eyes dark. "A piano, for example."

"He has already promised me a Steinway."

Margrete moved the skirt of the wedding gown this way, then that. "You must not be afraid to make demands, but you must also submit to his." Again, a touch of her dark gaze in the mirror. "No matter what, Angelina. Do you understand me? With a smile, if possible."

Angelina expected her sisters to chime in then, making arch comments about sex and their experiences, but they were silent. She looked in the glass and found them sitting on the end of her bed, looking…she would have said lost, if they had been anyone else.

"I'm not afraid of his demands," she said.

It wasn't until her mother's gaze snapped to hers again that she realized perhaps she ought to have been.

"You must remember that no matter what, you need only call and I will come to you," Margrete said then, as if she was making her own vows.

Angelina could not have been more shocked if her mother had shared sordid details of her own sexual exploits. "I… Really?"

Margrete turned Angelina then, taking her by the shoulders so she could look into her face.

"You're not the first girl to be ransomed off for the benefit of her family," Margrete said in a low, direct voice. "My father lost me in a card game."

There was a muffled sound of surprise from the bed. But their mother did not wait for that astonishing remark to sink in. Margrete lifted her chin, her fingers gripping Angelina's shoulders so hard she was half worried they would leave a mark.

"Life is what you make of it. Some parts are unpleasant, others regretful—but those are things you cannot control. You can always control yourself. You can school your reactions. You can master your own heart. And no one can ever take that from you, Angelina. No one."

"But Papa…" Angelina was turning over the idea of a card game and her severe grandfather in her head. "Papa was not a murderer."

"All men are murderers." Margrete's dark eyes flashed. "They take a daughter and make her a woman whether she wants it or not. They kill a girl to create a wife, then a mother. It's all a question of degrees, child."

And with those words, Margrete took her youngest daughter by the hand and led her down the grand, restored stair to the ballroom, where she handed Angelina off to her father.

The father who had *won* her mother, not wooed her, as Angelina had always found so hard to imagine.

The father who did not look at the daughter he was sacrificing to line his pockets even once as he marched her down the aisle, then married her off to a monster.

CHAPTER FIVE

BENEDETTO TOLERATED THE CEREMONY.

Barely.

God knew, he was tired of weddings.

His angel walked toward him, spurred on to unseemly haste by her portly father, who was practically salivating at the opportunity to hand her over to Benedetto's keeping. Or to her death. That Anthony Charteris had not required Benedetto to make any statements or promises about Angelina's well-being showed exactly what kind of man he was.

Tiny. Puny. Greedy and selfish to his core.

But then, Benedetto already knew that. If Anthony hadn't been precisely that kind of man, he wouldn't have come to Benedetto's notice.

As weddings went, this one was painless enough. There was no spectacle, no grand cathedral, no pageant. The words were said, and quickly, and the only ones he cared about came from Angelina's mouth.

"I do," she said, her voice quiet, but not weak. "I will."

He slid a ring onto her hand and felt his own greed kick hard enough inside that he could hardly set himself apart from Charteris. What moral high ground did he think *he* inhabited?

Soon, he told himself. *Soon enough.*

The priest intoned the words that bound them, and then it was done.

He was married for the seventh time. The last time, he dared to hope, though there was no reason to imagine he could make it so.

There was no reason to imagine this would be anything but the same old grind. The lies, the distrust. In his head he saw a key in a lock, and a bare white room with nothing but the sea outside it.

Oh, yes. He knew how this would end.

But despite everything, something in him wished it could be otherwise. Her music sang in him, and though he knew better, it felt like hope.

Once the ceremony was over and Angelina was his wife, he saw no reason to subject himself to Charteris or his family any longer. With any luck, neither he nor Angelina would ever see any of them again—for one reason or another.

He left Angelina to the tender mercies of her mother and sisters for the last time. He cut through the small gathering, ignoring the guests that Charteris had invited purely to boast about his sudden reversal of fortune, something that was easy to do when they all shrank from him in fear. And when he reached the place where Anthony was holding court, he scared off the cluster around him with a single freezing stare.

"My man of business will contact you," he told his seventh father-in-law with as little inflection as possible. "He will be your point person from now on for anything involving the house or the settlement I've arranged. Personal communications from you will not be necessary. And will no longer be accepted."

"Yes, yes," Charteris brayed pompously, already florid of cheek and glassy of eye, which told Benedetto all he needed to know about how this man had lost the fortune he'd been born with and the one he'd married into, as well. "I was thinking we might well have a ball—"

"You may have whatever you wish," Benedetto said with a soft menace that might as well have been a growl. "You may throw a ball every weekend. You may build a *château* in every corner of France, for all I care. The money is yours to do with as you wish. But what you will not have is any familiarity with me. Or any access to your daughter without my permission. Do you understand?"

He could see the older man process the rebuke like the slap it was, and then, just as quickly, understand that it would not affect his wallet. He did not actually shrug. But it was implied.

"I wish you and my daughter every happiness," Charteris replied.

He raised his glass. Benedetto inclined his head, disgusted.

And then he went to retrieve his seventh wife.

As he drew closer to the little knot she stood in with her mother and sisters, he felt something pierce his chest at the sight of her. Gleaming. Angelic.

All that, and the way she played the piano made him hard.

And that was nothing next to her taste.

Something in him growled like the sort of monster he tried so hard to keep hidden in public. Because people so readily saw all kinds of fiends when they looked at him—why should he confirm their worst suspicions?

"Come," he said, when his very appearance set them all to wide-eyed silence. "It is time to take you to my castle, wife."

He watched the ripple of that sentence move through the four of them. He could see the words *Butcher of Castello Nero* hanging in the air around them.

And whatever he thought of Anthony Charteris, whatever impressions he'd gleaned of these women over the past month, they all paled in unison now.

Because everyone knew, after all, what happened to a Franceschi bride. Everyone knew the fate that awaited her.

For the first time, the things others thought about him actually…got to him.

Benedetto held out his hand.

The Charteris sisters remained white-faced. Their mother was made of stouter stuff, however, and the look she fixed on him might have been loathing, for all the good it would do her.

But it was Angelina who mattered. Angelina whose cheeks did not pale, but flushed instead with a brighter color he knew well by now.

Angelina, his seventh bride, who murmured something soothing in the direction of her mother and sisters and then slid her delicate hand into his.

Then she let him lead her from her father's house, never to return.

Not if he had anything to say about it.

He assisted her into the back of the gleaming black car that waited for them, joining her in the back seat. He lounged there, as the voluminous skirts of her soft white wedding gown flowed in every direction, like seafoam.

Benedetto found he liked thinking of her that way,

like a mermaid rising from the deep. A creature of story and fable.

"Why have you waited to…seal our bargain until our wedding night?" she asked as the car pulled away from the front of the old house that was already starting to look like itself again. Its old glory restored for the small price of Angelina's life.

What a bargain, he thought darkly.

Of course, neither Angelina nor her noxious father had any idea of the bargain he intended to pose to her directly—but he was getting ahead of himself.

And if this time was different—if he had found himself captivated by this woman in ways he did not fully understand and had never experienced before—well. He was sure he would pay a great penance for that, too, before long.

But she was gazing at him, waiting for him to answer her.

"It is customary to wait, is it not?" Because he was happy to have her think him deeply traditional. For now. He watched her, but she did not turn around to watch her life disappear behind her. So she did not see her sisters, clutching each other's hands as they stood at the top of the stairs, staring after her. She did not see her mother in the window, her face twisting. She did not note the absence of her father from these scenes of despair. "Some things have fallen out of favor in these dark times, I have no doubt, but I hope a white wedding will always be in fashion." He allowed his mouth to curve. "Or a slightly off-white wedding, in this case. It is your piano playing, I fear. It undoes all my good intentions."

Angelina looked at him, her blue eyes searching his

face though her own looked hot. "You have had many lovers, if the tabloids are to be believed."

"First, you must never believe the tabloids. They are paid to write fiction, not fact. But second, I have always kept my affairs and my wives separate."

She cleared her throat. "And now? Will you continue in the same vein?"

He picked up her hand, and toyed with the ring he'd put there, that great, gleaming red ruby that shone like blood in the summer light that fell in through the car windows. "What is it you are asking me?"

"Do you conduct your affairs while you're married?" She sat straighter, though she didn't snatch her hand back from him. "Will one of my duties be to look the other way?"

"Are you asking me if I plan to be faithful? Less than an hour after we said our vows before God, man, and your father's creditors?"

"I am. Do you?"

Again, he was struck by how different she was from the rest of his brides—none of whom had seemed to care who he touched, or when. It was as if Angelina had cast a spell on him. Enchanted him, despite everything.

"As faithful as you are to me, Angelina." His voice was darker than it should have been, but it was one more thing he couldn't seem to control around her. "That is how faithful I will be to you in return."

This time he was certain he could see those words, like another set of vows, fill up the car like the voluminous skirts she wore.

"That's easy enough then," she replied with that tartness that surprised and delighted him every time she dared show it. "I have only ever loved one thing in my life. My piano. As long as you provide me with one to play as I wish, as you promised, why shouldn't I keep the promises I made to you?"

He lifted her hand to his mouth, and then, idly, sucked one of her fingers into the heat of his mouth.

"I've never understood cheating," she continued, her voice prim, though he could see the way she trembled. He could taste it. "Surely it cannot be that difficult to keep a vow. And if it is, why make it in the first place?"

"Ah, yes. The certainty of youth." He applied more suction, and she shuddered beautifully. "You know very little of passion, I think. It has a habit of making a mockery of those who think in terms of black and white."

Her eyes were much too blue. "Have you cheated on your wives before?"

And he had expected silence. That was typical. Or if there were questions, this being Angelina who seemed so shockingly unafraid of him, perhaps more pointed questions about murderers or mysterious deaths. Or euphemisms that didn't quite mention either. But not this. Not what he was tempted to imagine was actual possessiveness on her part. He noted that the hand he was not holding was balled into a fist.

Benedetto would have sworn that he was far too jaded for passion to make a mockery of him, and yet here he was. Hoping for things that could never be.

"I have never had the opportunity to grow bored," he replied, deliberately. With no little edge to his voice. "They were all gone too soon."

He watched her swallow hard. He watched the column of her neck move.

He wished he could watch himself and this dance of his as closely.

"You have not told me your expectations," she said, shifting her gaze away from him and aiming it somewhere in front of her. He found he missed the weight of her regard. "You're obviously a very wealthy man. Many wealthy men have staff to take on the position normally held by a wife."

"I assure you that I do not intend to take my staff to my bed."

He saw the lovely red color on her cheeks brighten further but she pushed on, and her carefully even voice did not change. "I'm not referring to your bed. I'm referring to the duties involved in running a great house. Or in your case, a castle."

"You are welcome to engage my housekeeper in battle for supremacy, Angelina. But I warn you, Signora Malandra is a fearsome creature indeed. And jealously guards what she sees as hers."

His bride looked at him then, narrowly. "Does that include you?"

Benedetto shrugged, keeping his face impassive though he was once again pleased with her possessiveness. "She's been with my family for a very long time. You could argue that in many ways, she raised me. So yes, I suppose she does see me as hers. But she is not my lover, if that is what you are asking."

He didn't actually laugh at that. Or the very notion of suggesting such a thing where his housekeeper could hear it.

Angelina managed to give the impression of bristling without actually doing so. "It had not occurred to me that you might install your lovers under the same roof as your wife. Though perhaps, given your infamy, I should anticipate such things."

"I will not do anything of the kind," he drawled, trying to sound lazy enough that the car would not reverberate with the truth in his words. "But whether you believe that or not will be up to you."

"You expect me to be jealous?"

"I'm not afraid of jealousy, Angelina. On the contrary. I do not understand why it is considered a virtue to pretend the heart is not a greedy organ when we can all feel it pump and clench in our chests. Lust starts there. And where there is lust, where there is need and want and longing, there will always be jealousy." He shrugged. "This is the curse of humanity, no? It is better to embrace the darkness than to pretend it does not or cannot exist."

"Jealousy is destructive," she said, again in that matter-of-fact tone he suspected was a product of her youth.

"That depends what you are building," he replied. "And whether or not you find beauty in the breaking of it."

And then he laughed, darkly and too knowingly, as she reddened yet again.

It was not a long drive to the private airfield where his plane waited for them. Once there, he escorted her up the stairs and then into the jet's luxurious cabin.

Angelina looked around at the ostentatious display of his wealth and power and swallowed, hard. "Are my things here? I can change—"

"I think not," he said, with a quiet relish. "You will remain in that gown until I remove it myself, little one."

Again, that glorious flush that made her glow. Her lips fell open while her pulse went wild in her throat. "But… But how long…?"

"We will have a wedding night," he assured her, though wedding nights with him were rarely what his brides imagined. "Were you worried?"

"Of course not," she said.

But she was lying. He could hear the music she played in his head. He could remember all too well those steamy evenings in that barren room that she'd filled with art and longing and her own sweet cries of need and release.

He was entirely too tempted to indulge himself—because he couldn't recall the last time he'd been tempted at all.

Benedetto tilted his head slightly as he regarded her, not surprised when that bright glow crept down her neck. "You have my permission to please yourself as you wish if you find you cannot wait. No need to lock yourself away." He indicated one of the plush leather seats in the cabin. "Pull up your skirts, bare yourself to me, and show me your pleasure, Angelina."

He could hear her ragged breath as she took that in. "I… I can't."

Her voice was barely a whisper.

"Then you must suffer, wife. And you must wait."

And he watched her almost idly as he handled matters of business on the short flight. She sat in her seat as if it was made of nails, shifting this way, and that. Clearly squirming with anticipation, though he supposed she might lie to them both about that. Too bad it was stamped all over her.

He couldn't wait to indulge himself. He, who usually preferred his wedding nights be more theater than anything else.

Why couldn't he stick to the script with this woman?

They landed in Italy on another private airfield not far from the coast where the Franceschis had lived for centuries. He ushered her into another car that waited for them, gleaming in the afternoon sun, but this time he drove it himself.

"We must hurry if we wish to make the tide," he told her.

And the dress she wore barely fit into the bucket seats of the low-slung sports car. But the helpless, needy sound he heard her make when he put the car into gear could only be a harbinger of things to come.

If he let it.

And oh, how he wanted to let it. He had already tasted her—and he couldn't seem to get past that. He couldn't seem to keep his head together when he was near her. He couldn't remember his duties, and that spelled disaster.

He knew all that, and still, all he could focus on was her reaction to his car.

He could imagine the way the low, throaty growl of the engine worked its way through her where she sat. But even if he couldn't, the way she began to breathe— too heavily—told him what he needed to know.

She might not like him. She might want him for the concert piano he'd had made especially for her. She might choose to leave him like all the rest, and soon.

But she wanted him.

Desperately.

There was an honesty in that. And it was new. Completely different from the six who'd come before her.

Benedetto found he was less interested in her sensual suffering than he probably should have been.

"I cannot wait, Angelina," he told her now. "I want

you to lift your wedding gown to your waist, as if we were back in your stark conservatory."

And he could tell the state she was in when she didn't argue. Or stammer. Or even blush again.

He shifted the car into second gear as he raced down the old roads toward the coastline his grandparents had kept undeveloped, even when that had required they fight off "progress" with their own hands, and watched as she obeyed him.

So quickly her hands were shaking.

"Good girl," he murmured when she'd bared all the soft, silken flesh of her thighs to his gaze. He could only glance at all that warm lushness as he drove, faster and faster, but it was enough. It made him so hard he ached with it. "Touch yourself. I want you to do whatever you need to do to come, Angelina. Fast and hard. Now."

She let out a sound that could have been a sob. A moan.

But he knew when she'd found her own heat, because she made a sound that was as full of relief as it was greed.

It made his sex pulse.

And he drove too fast down the coastal road he knew by heart. Then he sped up as he hit the treacherous drive that stretched out into the water that rose higher and higher by the moment as the tide came in and began to swallow it whole.

"Come," he ordered her.

She rocked her hips, making mindless, glorious little sounds. He could hear the greediness of her flesh, and a quick glance beside him found her with her head thrown back and her hands buried between her legs. The summer afternoon light streamed into the sports car, bouncing off the water and making her so bright, she nearly burned.

So beautiful, it cut at him.

So perfectly innocent, it should have shamed him, but it didn't. Not when he wanted her this much.

If he hadn't been a monster already, this would have made him one, he was sure of it.

Benedetto heard her breath catch. Her head rocked back, and he was sure that he could feel her heat as if it was his hands on her, clutched deep in her molten core. That hot rush of sweet, wet fire as she took herself over the edge.

She shook and she sobbed, and he drove faster. There was light and water and his seventh bride, coming on command. And when her sobs had settled into a harsh panting, he reached over. He took one of her hands, and sucked her fingers into his mouth because that heat was all for him. It was his.

She was his, and no matter if that damned them both, he didn't have it in him to stop this madness. He couldn't.

"Open your eyes, Angelina," he told her then, another soft order. "We are here."

That was how he drove her into Castello Nero, the ancestral home of his cursed and terrible clan. Flushed and wanton, wet and greedy, the taste of her in his mouth and that wild, ravaged look on her face.

Welcome home, little one, Benedetto thought darkly.

And then he delivered them both into their doom.

CHAPTER SIX

ANGELINA BARELY HAD the presence of mind to shove her skirts back down, letting the yards and yards of soft white fabric flow back into place. To preserve whatever was left of her modesty.

Though she almost laughed at the thought of modesty after…that. After the past month, after this drive—what was left for him to take?

But, of course, she knew the answer to that.

And imagining what she had to lose here in this place made it difficult to breathe.

The castle keep rose on all sides, the stone gleaming in the summer afternoon light. The sunshine made it seem magical instead of malevolent, and she tried her best to cling to that impression.

But her body felt like his, not hers. Even her breath seemed to saw in and out of her in an alien rhythm.

His, she thought again. Not hers.

Benedetto swung out of the car but Angelina stayed where she was. The drive from the airfield had been a blur of heat, need, and the endless explosion that was still reverberating through her bones, her flesh. Still, she could picture the car eating up the narrow road that flirted with the edge of the incoming tide on what was little more than a raised sandbar. Some of the waves had already been tipping over the edge of the bar to sneak across the road as Benedetto had floored his engine. It was only a matter of time before water covered the causeway completely.

And all the molten heat in the world, all of which was surely pooled between her legs even now, couldn't keep her from recognizing the salient point here in a very different way than she had when she was merely thinking about Castello Nero instead of experiencing it herself.

Which was that once the tide rose, she would be stuck here on the island that was his castle.

Stranded here, in fact.

"How long is it between tides?" she had asked at the family dinner table one night while Benedetto was there, oozing superiority and brooding masculinity from where he lounged there at the foot of the table, his hot gaze on her.

Because she might have already betrayed herself where this man was concerned, but that didn't mean she hadn't read up on him.

"Six hours," Dorothea had said stoutly.

"Or a lifetime," Benedetto had replied, sounding darkly entertained.

She could feel her heart race again, the way it had when she'd been back in the relative safety of her father's house. But it was much different here, surrounded by the stone walls and ramparts. Now that this was where she was expected to stay. High tide or low.

Come what may.

The door beside her opened, and he was there. Her forbiddingly beautiful husband, who was looking down at her with his mouth slightly curved in one corner and that knowing look in his too-dark eyes.

And his hand was no less rough or insinuating when he helped her from the sports car. No matter where he touched her, it seemed, she shuddered.

"Welcome home, wife," he said.

The ancient castle loomed behind him, a gleaming stone facade that seemed to throb with portent and foreboding. It had been built to be a fortress. But to Angelina's mind, that only meant it could make a good prison.

The summer sky was deceptively bright up above. The castle's many towers and turrets would surely have punctured any clouds that happened by. Her heart still beat at her, a rushing, rhythm—

But in the next moment, Angelina understood that what she was hearing was the sea. The lap of tide against the rocks and the stone walls.

She didn't know if that odd giddiness she felt then was terror or relief.

When she looked back at her husband, that same devil that had worked in her the first night he'd come to her father's house brushed itself off. And sat up.

"Why do you call me 'wife' instead of my name?" she asked.

"Did you not marry me?" he asked lazily, giving the impression of lounging about when he was standing there before her, his hands thrust into the pockets of the dark bespoke suit he wore that made him look urbane and untamed at once. "Are you not my wife?"

"I rather thought it was because all the names run together," Angelina said dryly. "There have been so many."

She didn't know what possessed her to say such a

thing to the man who had rendered Margrete Charteris silent. Or how she dared.

But to her surprise, he laughed.

It was a rich, sensuous sound she knew too well from back in her father's conservatory. Here, it seemed to echo back from the ancient stone walls, then wrapped as tightly around her as the bodice of the wedding dress she wore.

"I never forget a name." He inclined his head to her. "Angelina."

Hearing her name in his mouth made the echo of his dark laughter inside her seem to hum.

Benedetto took his time shifting his gaze from her then. He focused on something behind her, then nodded.

That was when Angelina realized they were not, as she'd imagined, alone out here in this medieval keep. She turned, her neck suddenly prickling, and saw an older woman standing there, dressed entirely in black as if in perpetual mourning. The housekeeper, if she had to guess, with a long, drawn face and a sharp, unfriendly gaze.

"This is your new mistress," Benedetto told the woman, who only sniffed. "Angelina, may I present Signora Malandra, keeper of my castle."

"Enchanté," the older woman said in crisp, cut-glass French that did not match her Italian name.

"I'm so pleased to make your acquaintance," Angelina murmured, and even smiled prettily, because Signora Malandra might have been off-putting, but she was no match for Margrete Charteris.

"Come," said Angelina's brand-new husband, once again fixing that dark gaze of his on her. "I will show you to the bedchamber."

The bedchamber, Angelina noted. Not *her* bedchamber.

Her heart, having only just calmed itself, kicked into high gear again.

He did not release her hand. He pulled her with him as he moved, towing her through an archway cut into the heavy stone wall. Then he drew her into the interior of one of the oldest castles in Italy.

She still felt off balance from what had happened in his car, but she tried to take note of her surroundings. *Should you have to run for your life,* something dark inside her whispered. She tried her best to shove it aside—at least while she was in her husband's presence.

Unlike the house where she'd grown up, Castello Nero was flush with wealth and luxury. Benedetto took her down corridors filled with marble, from the floors to the statues in the carved alcoves, to benches set here and there as if the expectation was that one might need to rest while taking in all the art and magnificence.

He laughed at her expression. "Did you expect a crumbling Gothic ruin?"

She blinked, disquieted at the notion he could read her so easily. "I keep imagining kings and queens around every tapestry, that's all."

"My family have held many titles over time," he told her as they walked. Down long hallways that must have stretched the length of the tidal island. "A count here, a duke there, but nobility is much like the tide, is it not? In favor one century, forbidden the next."

Angelina's family considered itself old money rather than new, but they did not speak in terms of *centuries.* They were still focused on a smattering of generations. The difference struck her as staggering, suddenly.

"The castle has remained in the family no matter the revolutions, exiles, or abdications that have plagued Europe," Benedetto said. "Titles were stripped, ancestors were beheaded, but in one form or another this island has been in my family since the fall of the Roman Empire. Or thereabouts."

Angelina tried to imagine what it must feel like to be personally connected to the long march of so much history—and to have a family castle to mark the passage of all that time.

"Did you grow up here?" she asked.

Because it was impossible to imagine. She couldn't conceive of children running around in this shining museum, laughing or shrieking in the silent halls. And more, she couldn't picture Benedetto ever having been a child himself. Much less engaging in anything like an ungainly adolescence. And certainly not here, in a swirl of ancient armor and sumptuous tapestries, depicting historical scenes that as far as Angelina knew, might have been the medieval version of photo albums and scrapbooks.

"In a sense," he replied.

He had led her into a gallery, the sort she recognized all too well. It was covered with formal, painted portraits, she didn't have to lean in to read the embossed nameplates to understand that she was looking at centuries of his ancestors. The sweep of history as represented by various Franceschis across time. From monks to noblemen to what looked entirely too much like a vampire in one dark painting.

Benedetto gazed at the pictures on the wall, not at her. "My parents preferred their own company and my grandfather thought children were useless until properly educated. When my parents died my grandfather—and Signora Malandra—were forced to take over what parenting was required at that point. I was a teenager then and luckily for us all, I was usually at boarding school. It felt like home. I was first sent there at five."

Angelina had never given a single thought to the parenting choices she might make one day, yet she knew, somehow, that she did not have it in her to send such a tiny child away like that. Off to the tender mercies of strangers. Something in her chilled at the thought.

"Did you like boarding school?" she asked.

Benedetto stopped before a portrait that she guessed, based on the more modern clothing alone, might have been his parents. She studied the picture as if she was looking for clues. The woman had dark glossy hair and a heart-stoppingly beautiful face. She sat demurely in a grand chair, dressed in a gown of royal blue. Behind her chair stood a man who looked remarkably like Benedetto, though he had wings of white in his dark hair. And if possible, his mouth looked crueler. His nose more like a Roman coin.

"There was no question of liking it or not liking it," Benedetto said, gazing at the portrait. Then he turned that gaze on her, and she found the way his eyes glittered made her chest feel constricted. "It was simply the reality of my youth. My mother always felt that her duties were in the providing of the heir. Never in the raising of him."

"And did… Did your parents…?"

Angelina didn't even know what she was asking. She'd done what due diligence she could over the past month. Meaning she had Googled her husband-to-be and his family to see what she could find. Mostly, as this castle seemed to advertise, it seemed the Franceschi family was renowned for wealth and periodic cruelty stretching back to the dawn of time. In that, however, she had to admit that they were no different from any other storied European family. It was only Benedetto—in modern times, at any rate—who had a reputation worse than that of any other pedigreed aristocrat.

His mother had been considered one of the most beautiful women in the world. She and Benedetto's father had run in a glittering, hard-edged crowd, chasing and throwing parties in the gleaming waters of the Côte d'Azur or the non-touristy parts of the Caribbean. Or in sprawling villas in places like Amalfi, Manhattan, or wherever else the sparkling people were.

"Did my parents regret their choices in some way?" Benedetto laughed, as if the very idea was a great joke. "How refreshingly earnest. The only thing my parents ever agreed upon was a necessity of securing the Franceschi line. Once I was born, their duties were discharged and they happily returned to the things they did best. My father preferred pain to pleasure. And as my mother was a martyr, if only to causes that suited her self-importance, they were in many ways a match made in heaven."

Angelina's mouth was too dry. "P-Pain to pleasure?"

Benedetto's eyes gleamed. "He was a celebrated sadist. And not only in the bedroom."

Angelina didn't know what expression she must have had on her face, but it made Benedetto laugh again. Then he drew her behind him once more, leading her out of this gallery filled with black Franceschi eyes and dark secrets, and deeper into the castle.

"Why is that something you know about your own

father?" she managed to ask, fighting to keep her voice from whispering off into nothingness. "Surely a son should be protected from such knowledge."

Benedetto's laugh, then, was more implied than actual. But Angelina could feel it shiver through her all the same.

"Even if my parents had exhibited a modicum of modesty, which they did not, the paparazzi were only too happy to fill in the details before and after their deaths. Barring that, I can't tell you the number of times one or other of their friends—and by friends, I mean rivals, enemies, former lovers, and compatriots—thought they might as well sidle up to me with some ball or other and share. In excruciating detail." He glanced down at her, his mouth curved. "They are little better than jackals, these highborn creatures who spend their lives throwing fortunes down this or that drain. Every last one of them."

"Including you?" She dared to ask.

That curve in the corner of his mouth took on a bitter cast. "Especially me."

Together they climbed a series of stairs until they finally made it to a hall made of windows. Modern windows in place of a wall on one side, all of them looking out over the sea. Angelina could see that the wind had picked up, capping the waves in white, which should have added to the anxiety frothing inside her. Instead, the sight soothed her.

The sea carried on, no matter what happened within these walls.

It made her imagine that she might, too.

Despite everything she knew to the contrary.

"This is the private wing of the castle," Benedetto

told her as they walked beside the windows. "The nursery is at one end and the master suite far on the other end, behind many walls and doors, so the master of the house need never disturb his sleep unless he wishes it."

"Your parents did not come to you?" Angelina asked, trying and failing to keep that scandalized note from her voice.

"My provincial little bride." He sounded almost fond, though his dark gaze glittered. "That is what nannies are for, of course. My parents held regular audiences with the staff to keep apprised of my progress, I am told. But Castello Nero is no place for sticky hands and toddler meltdowns. I would be shocked to discover that your parents' shoddy little *château* was any different."

That was a reasonable description of the house, and still she frowned. "My parents were not naturally nurturing, certainly," Angelina said, choosing her words carefully. "But they were present and in our lives."

"No matter what, you need only call and I will come to you," Margrete had said fiercely before the wedding ceremony today. It had shocked her.

But Margrete had always been there. She might have been disapproving and stern, but she'd always been involved in her daughters' lives. Some of Angelina's earliest memories involved reading quietly at her mother's feet, or laboriously attempting to work a needle the way Margrete could with such seeming effortlessness.

It had never occurred to her that she would ever look back on her childhood fondly.

Of all the dark magic Benedetto had worked in the last month, that struck Angelina as the most disconcerting. Even as he towed her down yet another hall festooned with frescoes, priceless art, and gloriously thick rugs.

"You will find a variety of salons, an extensive private library, and an entertainment center along this hall." Benedetto nodded to doors as he passed them. "Any comfort you can imagine, you will find it here."

"Am I to be confined to this hall?"

"The castle is yours to explore," her husband said. "But you must be aware that at times, the castle and grounds are open to the public. Signora Malandra leads occasional tours. Because of course, there is no shortage of interest in both this castle and its occupant."

"But…"

Once more, she didn't know what on earth she meant to say.

Benedetto's dark eyes gleamed as if he did. "Foolish, I know. But far be it from me not to profit off my own notoriety."

He paused in the direct center of the long hall that stretched down the whole side of the castle. There was a door there that looked like something straight out of the middle ages. A stout wooden door with great steel bars hammered across it.

"This door opens into a stairwell," Benedetto told her. He did not open the door. "The stairwell goes from this floor to the tower above. And it is the only part of the castle that is strictly forbidden to you."

"Forbidden?" Angelina blinked, and shifted so she could study the door even more closely. "Why? Is the tower unsafe?"

His fingers were on her chin, pulling her face around to his before she even managed to process his touch.

"You must never go into this tower," he said, and there was no trace of mockery on his face. No curve to that grim mouth. Only that blazing heat in his dark eyes. "No matter what, Angelina, you must never open this door."

His fingers on her chin felt like a fist around her throat.

"What will happen if I do?" she asked, her voice little more than a whisper.

"Nothing good, Angelina." The darkness that emanated from him seemed to take over the light pouring in from outside. Until she could have sworn they stood in shadows. At night. "Nothing good at all."

She felt chastened and significantly breathless as Benedetto pulled her along again. Hurrying her down the long corridor until they reached the far end. He led her inside, into a master suite that was larger than the whole of the family wing of her parents' house, put together. It boasted a private dining room, several more salons and studies, its own sauna, its own gym, a room entirely devoted to an enormous bathtub, extensive dressing rooms, and then, finally, the bedchamber.

Inside, there was another wall of windows. Angelina had seen many terraces and balconies throughout the suite, looking out over the sea in all directions. But not here. There was only the glass and a steep drop outside, straight down into the sea far below.

There was a large fireplace on the far wall, with a seating area arranged in front of it that Angelina tried desperately to tell herself was cozy. But she couldn't quite get there. The fireplace was too austere, the stone too grim.

And the only other thing in the room was that vast, elevated bed.

It was draped in dark linens, gleaming a deep red that matched the ring she wore on her finger. *Like blood,* a voice inside her intoned.

Unhelpfully.

Four dark posts rose toward the high stone ceiling, and she had the sudden sensation that she needed to cling to one of them to keep herself from falling. That being in that bed, with nothing but the bloodred bedding and the sky and sea pressing down upon her, would make her feel as if she was catapulting through space.

As if she could be tossed from this chamber at any moment to her death far below.

Angelina couldn't breathe. But then, she suspected that was the point.

She only dimly realized that Benedetto had let go of her hand when she'd walked inside the room. Now he stood in the doorway that led out to the rest of the suite and its more modern, less stark conveniences.

Perhaps that was the point, too. That inside this chamber, there was nothing but her marriage bed, a fire that would not be lit this time of year, and the constant reminder of the precariousness of her situation.

And between her and the world, him.

"Is this where it happens, then?" She turned to look at him, and thought she saw a muscle tense in his jaw. Or perhaps she only wished she did, as that would make him human. Accessible. Possessed of emotions, even if she couldn't read them. "Is this where you bring your wives, one after the next? Is this where you make them all scream?"

"Every woman I have ever met screams at one point or another, Angelina," he said, and there was a kind of challenge in his gaze. A dark heat in his voice. "A better question is why."

But that impossible heat pulsed inside her, and Angelina didn't ask. She moved over to the bed and as she moved, remembered with a jolt that she was still dressed in her wedding gown. And between her legs, that pulsing desire he had cultivated in her thought it had all the answers already. She ran her hand over the coverlet when she reached it, not at all surprised to find that what she'd seen gleaming there in the dark red linens were precious stones. Rubies. Hard to the touch.

She pressed her palm down flat so that the nearest precious stone could imprint itself there. She gave it all her weight, as if this was a dream, and this was a kind of pinch that might jolt her awake.

Did she want to wake up? Or would it be better still to dream this away?

You keep thinking something can save you, something in her mocked her. *When you should know better by now.*

Angelina's palm ached, there where the hard stone dug into her flesh. And the man who watched her too intently from across the room was no dream.

She already knew too well the kind of magic he could work on her when she was wide awake.

Outside, she could hear the thunder of the sea. The disconcerting summer sky stretched off into the horizon.

But here in this castle filled with the plunder and fragments of long-ago lives, she was suspended in her white dress. Between the bloodred bed and the husband who stood like a wall between her and what remained of her girlhood. Of her innocence.

Whatever was left of it.

And suddenly, she wanted to tear it all off. She wanted to pile all the girlish things that remained inside her into that fireplace, then light a match.

Angelina was tired of being played with. She was tired of that dark, mocking gleam in his eye and that sardonic curve to his mouth. Of being led through a castle cut off from the mainland by a man who trafficked in nightmares.

She'd married him in a veil, but he had peeled it back when he claimed her mouth with his, there in front of witnesses.

She wanted to burn that down, too. No more veils of lace or ignorance.

If this was her life, or what remained of it, she would claim it as best she could.

She pressed her palm down harder on the coverlet, until it ached as much as she did between her legs.

Then Angelina faced the husband she couldn't quite believe was going to kill her like the rest. But she had to know if that was the real dream. Or a false sense of security six other women had already felt, standing right where she was now.

"I don't want to talk about screaming," she said.

He looked amused. "That is your loss."

"I have a question, Benedetto."

She thought he knew what she wanted to ask him. There was that tightening in his jaw. And for a moment, his black eyes seemed even darker than usual.

"You can ask me anything you like," he said.

She noticed he did not promise to answer her.

But Angelina focused on the question that was burning a hole inside her. "Don't you think it's time you told me what happened to the six who came before me?"

CHAPTER SEVEN

"As you wish," Benedetto said. His own voice was a rumbling thing in the bedchamber of stone, like thunder. Though outside it was a mild summer afternoon inching its way towards evening. "If you feel the shade of the marital bed is the place for such conversations."

He did not wish. He would prefer not to do this part of the dance—and he would particularly prefer not to do it with her.

The things he wanted to do with her deserved better than a castle made of unbreakable vows to dead men. She deserved light, not darkness. She deserved a whole man, not the part he played.

His still-innocent angel, who came apart so beautifully while the sea closed in around them. His curious Angelina, who would open doors she shouldn't and doom them both—it was only a matter of time.

His brand-new wife, who thought he was a killer, and still faced him like this.

Benedetto had expected her to be lovely to look at and reasonably entertaining, because she'd showed both at her dinner table the night they'd met. He had developed a deep yearning for her body over the course of the past month.

But he didn't understand how she'd wedged herself beneath his skin like this.

It wasn't going to end well. That he knew.

It never did.

And he had a feeling she was going to leave her mark in a way the others never had.

"Do you do the same thing every time?" she asked, as if she knew what he was thinking.

Benedetto couldn't quite read her, then. It only made him want her more. There was a hint of defiance in the way she stood and in the directness of her blue gaze. The hand on the wide bed shook slightly, but she didn't move it. Or hide it.

And he could see fear and arousal all over her body, perhaps more entwined than she imagined. He didn't share his father's proclivities. But that didn't mean he couldn't admire the things trembling uncertainty mixed with lust could do to a pretty face.

She tipped up her chin, and kept going. "Did you marry them all in bright white dresses, then bring them here to this room of salt and blood?"

It was a poetic description of the chamber, and he despised poetry. But it was also the most apt description he'd ever heard of what he'd done to this room after his grandfather had died. Benedetto had gutted it and removed every personal item, every hint of the man who'd lived and died here, every scrap that a ghost might cling to.

Because that was what he and his grandfather had done together after his grandmother had died, and it seemed only right to continue in the same vein.

And because he was haunted enough already.

"Where else would I bring them?" he asked softly.

"Tell me." Her gaze was too bright, her voice too urgent. "Tell me who they were."

"But surely you already know. Their names are in every paper, in every language spoken in Europe and beyond."

"I want to hear you say them."

And Benedetto wanted things he knew he could never have.

He wanted those nights in that stark conservatory in her father's ruined house, the wild tangle of music like a cloud all around them, and her sweetness in his mouth. He had wished more than once over this past month that he could stop time and stay there forever, but of all the mad powers people whispered he possessed, that had never been one of them.

And innocence was too easily tarnished, he knew. Besides, Benedetto had long since resigned himself to the role he must play in this game. Monster of monsters. Despoiler of the unblemished.

He had long since stopped caring what the outside world thought of him. He had made an art out of shrugging off the names they called him. His wealth and power was its own fortress, and better still, he knew the truth. What did it matter what lesser men believed?

What mattered was the promise he'd made. The road he'd agreed to follow, not only to honor his grandfather's wishes, but to pay a kind of penance along the way.

"And who knows?" his grandfather had said in his canny way. With a shrug. *"Perhaps you will break your chains in no time at all."*

Benedetto had chosen his chains and had worn them proudly ever since. But today they felt more like a death sentence.

"My first wife was Carlota di Rossi," he said now, glad that he had grown calloused to the sound of her name as it had been so long ago now. It no longer made him wince. "Her parents arranged the match with my grandfather when Carlota and I were children. We grew up together, always aware of our purpose on this planet. That being that we were destined to marry and carry on the dynastic dreams of our prominent families."

"Did you love her?"

Benedetto smiled thinly. "That was never part of the plan. But we were friendly. Then they found her on what was meant to be our honeymoon. It was believed she had taken her own life, possibly by accident, with too many sleeping pills and wine."

"Carlota," Angelina murmured, as if the name was a prayer.

And Benedetto did not tell her the things he could have. The things he told no one, because what would be the point? No one wanted his memories of the girl with the big, wide smile. Her wild curls and the dirty jokes she'd liked to tell, just under her breath, at the desperately boring functions they'd been forced to attend together as teenagers. No one wanted a story about two only children who'd been raised in close proximity, always knowing they would end up married. And were therefore a kind of family to each other, in their way. The truth was Carlota was the best friend he'd ever had.

But no one wanted truth when there was a story to tell and sell.

Benedetto should have learned that by watching his parents—and their sensationalized deaths. Instead, he'd had to figure it out the hard way.

"Everyone agrees that my second wife was a re-bound," he said as if he was narrating a documentary of his own life. "Or possibly she was the mistress I'd kept before, during, and after my first marriage."

He waited for Angelina to ask him which it was, but she didn't. Maybe she didn't want to know. And he doubted she would want to know the truth about the understanding he and Carlota had always had. Or how his second marriage had been fueled by guilt and rage because of it.

Benedetto knew his own story backward and forward and still he got stuck in the darkest part of it. In the man he'd allowed himself to become. A man much more like his detestable father than he'd ever imagined he could become.

When Angelina did not ask, he pushed on, his voice gritty. "Her name was Sylvia Toluca. She was an actress of some renown, at least in this country, and a disgrace to the Franceschi bloodline. But then, as most have speculated, that was likely her primary appeal. Alas, she went overboard on a stormy night in the Aegean after a well-documented row with yours truly and her body was never found."

"Sylvia," his new wife said. She cleared her throat. "And I find I cannot quite imagine you actually…rowing. With anyone."

Benedetto detached himself from the wall and began to prowl toward her. His Angelina in that enormous white gown that bloomed around her like a cloud, with those dark pearls around her neck and eyes so blue they made the Italian sky seem dull by comparison.

"I was much younger then," he told her, his voice a low growl. "I had very little control."

He watched her swallow as if her throat hurt. "Not like now."

"Nothing like now," he agreed.

She swayed slightly on her feet, but straightened, still meeting his gaze. "I believe we're up to number three."

"Monique LeClair, Catherine DeWitt, Laura Seymour." Angelina whispered an echo of each of their names as he closed the distance between them. "All heiresses in one degree or another, like you. There were varying lengths of courtship, but yes, I brought each of them here once we married. All lasted less than three months. All disappeared, presumed dead, though no charges were ever brought against me."

"All of them."

He nodded sagely. "You would be surprised how many accidents occur in a place like this, where we are forever pitted against the demands of the sea. Its relentless encroachment." He stopped only scant inches from where she stood, reaching over to trace her hand where it still pressed hard against the bejeweled coverlet. "The tide waits for no man. That is true everywhere, though it is perhaps more starkly illustrated here."

"Surely, after losing so many wives to the sea, a wise man would consider moving inland," Angelina said in that surprising dry way of hers that was far more dangerous than the allure of her body or even her music. Those only meant he wanted her. But this… This made him like her. "Or better still, teach them to swim."

"Do you know how to swim?" he asked, almost idly, his finger moving next to hers on the bed.

"I'm an excellent swimmer," she replied, though her color was high and her voice a mere whisper. "I could swim all the way to Rio de Janeiro and back if I wished."

He watched the way her chest rose and fell, and the deepening flush that he could see as easily on her cheeks as on the upper slopes of her breasts.

"I applaud your proficiency," he said. "But I am only a man. I can control very few things in this life. And certainly not an ocean or a woman."

She did not look convinced.

"And your last wife?" she asked, her breath sounding ragged as he began to trace a pattern from the hand on his bed up her arm, lazy and insinuating. "The sixth?"

"Veronica Fitzgibbon." Benedetto made a faint tsk-ing sort of sound. "Perhaps the best-known of all my wives, before marrying me. You might even call her famous."

"More than famous," Angelina corrected him softly as his hand made it to the fine, delicate bridge of her collarbone and traced it, purely to make her shiver. "I doubt there's a person alive who cannot sing at least one of her father's songs. And then she dated his drummer."

"Indeed. Scandalous." He concentrated on that neck-lace of hers, then. The brooding pearls against the soft-ness of her skin. The heat of her body, warming the stones.

"She lasted the longest. Three months and two days," Angelina whispered.

He made himself smile. "See that? You do know. I thought you might."

"She crashed her car into a tree," Angelina told him, though he already knew. He'd spent two days in a po-lice station staring at the pictures of the wreckage as the authorities from at least three countries accused him of all manner of crimes. "On a mountain road in the Alps, though no one has ever been able to explain what she was doing there."

"There are any number of explanations," Benedetto corrected her. "Most assume she was fleeing me. And that I was hot in pursuit, which makes for a delicious tale, I think you'll agree." He lifted his gaze to hers. "Alas, I was giving a very boring lecture at a deeply tedious conference in Toronto at the time."

"And how will I go, do you think?" she asked, a different sort of light in her blue eyes, then.

He hated this. He had disliked it from the start, though a truth he'd had to face was that he'd found a certain joy in the details. The game of it. The end justifying the means. But here, now, with her and that bruised look on her face and his own heretofore frozen emotions unaccountably involved this time—he loathed it all.

"I have already told you," he said quietly. "We all die how we live. It is inevitable."

"But—"

"A better question to ask," he said quietly, cutting her off, "is why any woman would marry me, knowing these things. These assumptions and allegations that must be true, because they are repeated so often. There must be a fire after all this smoke, no? Why did you say yes, Angelina?"

He watched, fascinated, as goose bumps shivered to life all over her skin. And she shifted, there where she stood. "I had no choice."

"Will we be starting this marriage off with lies?" Benedetto shook his head. "Of course you had a choice. Your father promised me a daughter. Not you in particular. Had you refused to marry me I had two others to choose from."

"My mother made it very clear that none of us were permitted to say no, no matter what."

"That must be it, then." He didn't quite smile. It was too hard, too furious a thing. "But tell me, Angelina, how do you rationalize away the many times you came apart in my hands?"

"I don't rationalize it." Her blue eyes flashed. "I deplore it."

"I don't think you do," he told her, and he moved his hand to her jaw, tilting her head so that her mouth was where he wanted it. "I think you're confusing hunger for something else. But then, you did spend all that time in the convent, did you not? I'm surprised you feel anything at all save shame."

"I have a full complement of emotions, thank you. Chief among them, revulsion. Fury. Disgust."

"I want you too, little one," he said, there against her mouth. "I hear the seventh time is the charm."

She made a tiny little noise, protest and surrender at once, and then Benedetto took her mouth with his.

Because a kiss did not lie. A kiss was not a story told around the world, losing more and more truth each time it was sold to the highest bidder.

There was only truth here in the tangle of tongues. In the way her body shuddered beneath his hands. In the way she pressed herself against him, as if she would climb him if she could.

He could taste her fear and her longing, her need and her hope.

Benedetto tasted innocence and possibility, and beneath that, the sheer punch that was all Angelina.

He anchored her with an arm around her back, and bent her over, deepening the kiss. Taking more and more, until he couldn't be sure any longer which one of them was more likely to break.

She was intoxicating.

Despite all the times he'd done this, there had never been a time that he had wanted a wife like this. Or at all. But then, in all the ways that mattered, she was his first.

That thought made a kind of bitterness well in him, and he pulled away. And then took his time looking at her. Her lips parted. Her eyes dark with passion.

This from the woman who claimed she didn't want him at all. That she had been forced into this.

He rather thought not.

He liked to think he had been, though that wasn't quite true either. He'd had his choices, too.

"Not yet," he murmured, as much to himself as to her.

Because one choice he did have was to treat her the way he'd treated the others. He had already tasted her more than the rest of them, save Sylvia. He had already betrayed himself a thousand times over while in the thrall of her piano.

But she didn't have to know that. And he didn't have to succumb to it here.

And now that they were married, he could get this back on track.

Benedetto let go of her, pleased despite himself when she had to grip the bed beside her to stay on her feet. He picked up the hand she'd been pressing against the bed and could see the indentation of the coverlet's stone on her palm.

He was savage enough to like it.

"What do you mean, *not yet*?" she demanded. "I thought that once we were married—"

"So impatient," he taunted her. "Especially for one forced to the altar as you have been."

If she dared, he could tell, she would have cursed him to his face.

Instead, she glared at him.

"Don't you worry about consummating our marriage." He laughed, though the lie of it caught a little in his chest. "I will take you in hand, never fear. But first, I wish to show you something."

Benedetto turned and headed for the door without taking her hand to bring her with him. And he smiled when he heard her follow him.

He didn't have to turn around and study her face to understand her reluctance. It was entirely possible she didn't know why she was following him. That she was simply as compelled as he was. He hoped so.

It was a good match for this mad yearning he felt inside, when he knew better. A yearning that he was terribly afraid would be the end of him. This innocent, untrained girl could bring him to his knees.

But then, that was a power he had no intention of handing over to her. If she didn't know, she couldn't use it.

He led her out into the master suite, then through a door that led to a separate tower from one of the salons.

Angelina balked at the door, looking around a little bit wildly.

"This is your tower," he told her, sounding almost formal. "You can enter whenever you wish."

"That seems like a lot of towers to remember," she

said, a little solemnly, from behind him. "I wouldn't want to make a mistake."

He looked over his shoulder as they climbed the stairs.

"Don't," he warned her, and meant it more than he usually did. More than he wanted to mean it. "Whatever else you do here, do not imagine that the warning I gave you was a joke, Angelina."

He saw her swallow, hard, but then they were at the top of the stairs. He threw open the door, then waited for her to follow him inside.

And then Benedetto watched as she tried to contain her gasp of joy.

"A piano," she whispered, as if she couldn't believe it. "You really did get me a piano. A Steinway."

"I am assured it is the finest piano on the Continent," he told her, feeling...uncertain, for once. Unlike himself. Did he crave her approval so badly? When he didn't care in the least if the entire world thought him a monster? It should have shamed him, but all he could do was drink in the wonder all over her. "It is yours. You can play it whenever you wish, night or day. And I will give instructions to my staff that you are to be left to it."

There was a look of hushed awe on her face. She aimed it his way, for a moment, then looked back at the piano that sat in the center of the room. When he inclined his head, she let out a breath. Then she ran to the piano to put her hands on it. To slide back the cover, and touch the keys.

Soft, easy, reverent. Like a lover might.

And for a deeply disturbing moment, Benedetto found himself actually questioning whether he was, in fact, jealous of an inanimate object.

Surely not.

He shoved that aside, because he'd been called a monster most of his life and he could live with the consequences of that. He had. It was smallness and pettiness he could not abide, in himself or anyone else. Benedetto hated it in the men who auctioned off their daughters to pay their debts; he despised even the faintest hint of it in himself.

"Play, Angelina," he urged her. And if his voice was darker than it should have been, rougher and wilder, he told himself it was no more than to be expected. "Play for me."

He was married. Again. Every time he imagined he might be finished at last. That it would be the end of this long, strange road. That finally, this curse would be lifted and he would be freed.

Finally, he could bury his grandfather's dark prophecies in the grave where the old man lay.

And every time, Benedetto was proved wrong. He'd almost become inured to it, he thought as Angelina spread her fingers, smiled in that inward, mysterious manner that he found intoxicating, and began to coax something stormy and dark from the keys.

As the music filled the tower he admitted to himself that this time he wanted, desperately, to be right.

He wanted to be done.

He wanted *her*.

It was the way she played, as if she was not the one producing the notes, the melodies, the whole songs and symphonies. Instead, it was as if she was a conduit, standing fast somewhere between the music in her head and what poured out of her fingers.

Benedetto had never seen or heard anything so beautiful.

And he couldn't help but imagine that she could do the same for him and the dark destiny he had chosen to make his own.

Outside, the afternoon wore on, easing its way into another perfect Italian evening.

And his bride played as if she was enchanted, her fingers like liquid magic over the keys. Half-bent, eyes half-closed, as if she was caught in the grip of the same madness that roared in him.

Or perhaps Benedetto only wished it so.

When *wishing* was another thing he had given up long ago.

Or should have.

But everything had changed when he'd walked into that dining room in her father's house and seen an angel where he'd expected nothing more than a collection of wan socialites. He stood against the wall in the tower room, his back against the stones that had defined him as long as he'd drawn breath.

It was easy to pretend that he had been disconnected from this place, shuttled off to boarding school the way he had been, but Castello Nero lived inside him and always had. As a child he'd loved coming home to this place. Endless halls, secret passages, and his beloved grandmother. His parents had always been away, but what did that matter when he could play mad siege games on the rocks or race the tide?

There was a part of him that would always long for those untroubled times. That wished he could somehow recreate them, if not for himself, for a child like the one he'd been too briefly. Maybe that was nothing more than a fantasy. Then again, maybe it was all he had.

He had to take his fantasies where he could.

Because it wasn't long after those dreamy days that he'd understood different truths about this place. These ancient walls and the terrible price those who lived here had paid, and would pay. Some would call it a privilege. Some would see only the trappings, the art and the antiques, the marble gleaming in all directions. Some would assume it was the shine of such things that made the difference.

They never saw any blood on their hands. They never heard the screams from the now defunct dungeons. They walked the halls and thought only of glory, never noticing the ghosts that lurked around every corner.

Or the ghosts that lived in him.

But as Angelina played, Benedetto imagined that she could see him.

The real him.

The music crashed and soared, whispered then shouted. The hardest part of him stood at attention, aching for her touch—and yet feeling it, all the same, in the music she played, here in the tower he had made a music room, just for her.

She played and played, while outside the tide rose, the waves swelled, and the moon began to rise before the sun was down.

That, too, felt like a sign.

And when she stopped playing, it took Benedetto too long to realize it. Because the storm was inside him, then. *She* was. Her music filled every part of him, making him imagine for a moment that he was free.

That he could ever be free.

That this little slip of a woman, sheltered and sold off, held the key that could unlock the chains that had held him all his life.

It was a farce. He knew it was a farce.

And still, when she turned to look at him, her blue eyes dark with passion and need and all that same madness he felt inside him, he…forgot.

He forgot everything but her.

"Benedetto…" she began, her voice a harsh croak against the sudden, bruised silence.

"I know," he heard himself say, as if from a distance. As if he was the man he'd imagined he'd become, so many years ago, instead of the man he became instead. The man he doubted his grandmother would recognize. "I know, little one."

He pushed himself off from the wall and had the same sensation he always did, that the *castello* itself tried to hold on to him. Tried to tug him back, grip him hard, smother him, until he became one more stone statue.

Some years he felt more like stone than others, but not today.

But Angelina sat on the piano bench, her wedding gown flowing in all directions, and her chest heaving with the force of all the emotions she'd let sing through her fingers.

And she was so obviously, inarguably *alive* that he could not be stone. She was so vibrant, so filled with color and heat, that he could not possibly look down and find himself made into marble, no matter how the walls seemed to cling to him.

Benedetto crossed the floor, his gaze on hers as if the heat between them was a lifeline. As if she was saving him, here in this tower where no one was safe. And then he was touching her, his hands against her flushed cheeks, his fingers finding their way into the heavy, silvery mass of her blond hair.

At last, something in him cried.

"What are you doing?" she asked, though there was heat in her gaze.

"Surely you know," Benedetto said as he swept her up into his arms. "Surely your mother—or the internet—should have prepared you."

"Neither are as useful as advertised," she said, her head against his shoulder. And that dry note in her voice gone husky.

He had not planned to take her, as he had not taken the rest. They were offerings to fate, not to him. They were meant to worry over the bed that made his chamber look blooded, like so much stage dressing. They were never meant to share it with him. Not like this, dressed like a bride and at the beginning of this bizarre journey.

But Angelina was nothing like the others.

She never had been.

She was music, and she was light. She was every dream he'd told himself wasn't for him, could never be for him.

And every time he tasted her, he felt the chains that bound him weaken, somehow.

So Benedetto carried her, not down the tower stairs to the master suite, but to the chaise he'd set beneath the windows in this tower room. Because it had amused him to make this tower look as much like the conservatory in her father's shambles of the house as possible, he'd assured himself.

Or perhaps he'd done it because he wanted her to feel at home here, however unlikely that was—but he shied away from admitting that, even to himself. Even now.

He laid her down before him, admiring the way her hair tangled all about her. Like it, too, was a part of the same magic spell that held him in its thrall.

The same spell that made this feel like a real marriage after all.

"Welcome to your wedding night," Benedetto said as he lowered himself over her, and then he took her mouth with his.

Claiming Angelina, here in this castle that took more than it gave.

At last.

CHAPTER EIGHT

ANGELINA FELT TORN apart in the most glorious way and all he was doing was kissing her.

It was the music. The sheer excellence of the piano he'd found for her, and had set up in perfect tune.

She had only meant to play for a moment, but the keys had felt so alive beneath her fingers, as if each note was an embrace, that too soon, she'd lost herself completely.

She still felt lost.

And yet, somehow, she'd been aware of Benedetto the whole time. Her husband and perhaps her killer—though she couldn't quite believe that, not from a man who could give a piano like this as a gift—standing in the corner of the room with his gaze fixed on her.

She would not say that she was used to him, because how could anyone become used to a hurricane?

But she craved that electric charge. The darkness in his gaze, the sensual promise etched over his beautiful face, his clever mouth.

She'd played and played. And she could not have explained it if her life depended on it, as she supposed it might, but the longer she played, the more it was as if her own hands moved over her body. As if she was making love to herself, there before him, the way she had in the car.

Exposed and needy and at his command.

Right where she'd wanted to be since that very first night.

Angelina could hardly contain herself. All she could think of were the many times in this last, red-hot month of waiting and worrying and wondering, when her legs had been spread wide and he had been between them. His mouth. His fingers.

She'd played because her body felt like his already and there was no part of her that disliked that sensation.

She'd played because playing for him felt like his possession. Irrevocable. Glorious. And as immovable as the stone walls of the tower that sang the notes she played back to her, no matter the piece, as sweet and sensual songs.

Benedetto lowered himself over her on the chaise, and she forgot about playing, because he kissed her like a starving man.

Angelina kissed him back, because his shoulders were as wide as mountains and behind him she could see only the darkening sky. And her ears were filled with the rushing sound of the sea waiting and whispering far below.

He was hard and heavy, and this time, he did not crawl his way down her body to bury his head between her legs. This time he let her feel the weight of him, pressing her down like a sweet, hot stone.

And all the while he kissed her, again and again, rough and deep and filled with the same madness that clamored inside her.

Angelina could no longer tell if she was still playing the piano, or if he was playing her, and either way, the notes rose and fell, sang and wept, and she could do nothing about it.

She didn't want to do anything about it but savor it.

Because whatever song this was, it made her burn.

Again and again, she burned.

Only for him, something in her whispered. And that made her burn all the more.

Benedetto tore his mouth from hers and began to move down her body, then, but only far enough to tug on the bodice of her dress. Hard.

He glanced at her, his dark eyes bright and gleaming, and tugged on her dress until it tore. Then he tore it even more, baring her breasts to his view.

And when she gasped at the ferocity, or at the surge of liquid heat that bloomed in her because of it, he laughed.

Benedetto looked at her, his face dark with passion and set fierce like a wolf's, as he shaped her breasts with those calloused palms of his and then took one aching nipple into his mouth.

And then she was a crescendo.

Angelina arched up, not sure if she was fighting him or finding him, or both at the same time. His mouth was a torture and treat, and she pressed herself even more firmly into his mouth. Whatever he wanted to give her, she wanted to take. As much as possible.

His hands moved south, continuing their destruction. He tore her white dress to ribbons, baring her to him. And she thrilled to every last bit of sensation that charged through her from the air on her flesh, or better still, his wicked mouth.

And when he thrust his heavy thigh between hers

even as he continued to hold her down and take his fill of her, she found that gave her something to rock the center of her need against.

Over and over again, because it felt like soaring high into the night.

And when she shattered, tossed over a steep edge as if from the window of this tower to the brooding sea far below, he laughed that same dark, delighted laugh that had thrilled her from the first.

Angelina could feel the laugh inside her, and it only made her shudder more.

When she came back to herself, rising from the depths somehow, he had rolled off of her. Her wedding dress was torn to pieces, baring her to his view completely. That he could see all of her was new, and faintly terrifying. No one had seen Angelina fully naked since she was a small child.

But far more overwhelming was the fact that as Benedetto stood beside her, looking down at the chaise from his great height, he was shrugging out of his own wedding clothes.

In all this time, all throughout this longest month, he had never dislodged his clothing or allowed her to do so.

"Are you horribly scarred?" she'd asked him once, feeling peevish with lust and longing and that prickling fear beneath. She'd been stretched out on her piano bench in the conservatory back home, after he'd buried his face between her thighs and made her scream.

As usual.

Benedetto had only smiled, drawing her attention back to that mouth of his and the things it could do. *"None of my scars are external."*

And now the first stars were appearing in the sky

outside. He blocked them all out and somehow made them brighter at the same time, because he was perfect. He was everything.

She had never seen a naked man in real life. She had never imagined that all the various parts that she'd seen in pictures could seem so different in person. Because she knew what it felt like to be in his arms and she knew what it felt like to taste him in her mouth.

But Benedetto naked was something else. Something better. He looked as if he'd been fashioned by a sculptor obsessed with male beauty, but she knew that he would be hot to the touch. And more, unlike all the marble statues she'd ever seen—many of them here— there was dark hair on his chest. A fascinatingly male trail that led to a part of him she'd felt against her leg, but had never seen.

"What big eyes you have," he said, sounding dark and mocking.

Angelina jerked her gaze up over the acres and acres of his fine male chest, all those ridges and planes that made her fingers itch. To touch. To taste. To make hers, in some way, the way he had already taken such fierce possession of her.

"I understand the mechanics," she confessed. "But still…"

"Your body knows what to do." He came down over her again, and she hissed out a breath because it was so much different, now. Bare flesh against bare flesh. Her softness against all the places where he was so impossibly hard. Everything in her hummed. "And so do I."

And then, once again, she felt as if she was the piano.

Because he played her like one, wringing symphonies out of her with every touch, every brush of his mouth over parts of her body she would have said were better ignored.

He flipped her over onto her stomach, right when she thought that she might simply explode out of her own skin—

And he laughed in that dark, stirring way of his, there against the nape of her neck. Then he started all over again.

Angelina…lost track.

Of herself. Of him. Of what, exactly, he was doing.

All she could seem to do was feel.

He slipped his fingers between her legs and stroked her until she shattered and fell apart, but he didn't stop. There was no ending, no beginning. There was only the rise and fall. The fire that burned in both of them and between them, flickering one moment, then roaring to life the next.

And all the while Angelina couldn't seem to get past the feeling that all of this was exactly how it was supposed to be. All of this was *right*.

It was full dark outside when Benedetto turned her over again. He stretched her arms up over her head and finally, finally, settled himself between her thighs. She could *feel* him, a hard ridge of perfect male arousal where she was nothing but a soft melting.

She was shuddering. She thought maybe there was moisture on her face. But all Angelina could care about was the blunt head of his masculinity that she could feel pressing into her.

Not exactly gently. And yet not roughly, either.

It was a pinch she forgot about almost as soon as it happened followed by a relentless, masterful thrust, and then Benedetto was seated fully inside her.

And that time, when Angelina burst into flame and shattered into a million new pieces, each more ragged than the last, she screamed herself hoarse.

Benedetto was laughing again, dark and delirious and too beautiful to bear, as he finally began to move.

And all her notions about piano music and symphonies shattered.

Because this was far more *physical* than she could possibly have imagined. Her body gripped him. He worked himself into her, then out. His chest was a delicious abrasion against hers, she could feel the press of his hipbones with every thrust, and there was heat and breath and so much *more* than the things she'd read in books.

He dropped his hard, huge body against hers and Angelina thought that should smother her, surely. But instead she bloomed.

As if her body was made to be a cradle, to hold him between her thighs. Just like this.

He bent his head to hers and took her mouth again, so that she was being taken with the same sheer mastery in two places at once.

And she understood that there was no place he did not claim her.

Inside and out, she was his.

She could feel that ring of his on her finger and that hard male part of him thrust deep inside her body.

And it seemed to her that her pulse became a chant. *His. His.*

His.

And then, finally, Angelina tore her mouth from his. She gripped the fierce cords of his neck with her hands, and found herself staring deep into his dark, ferocious gaze.

Into eternity, she was sure of it.

His.

And when she exploded into fire and fury, claimed and reborn, he cried out a word that could have been her name, and followed.

Angelina was hardly aware of it when he moved. She came back to herself, disoriented and gloriously replete, as he lifted her up into his arms.

She was aware of it as he carried her down the tower's narrow stair, high against his chest with only her hair trailing behind them. As naked as the day they were born.

Maybe she should have been embarrassed, she thought idly. For she knew full well that just because a staff was unseen did not mean they were not witnessing the goings-on of the house.

But how could she care if there were eyes on them when she felt like this? More beautiful than she ever had been. Perfect in his arms.

Right, straight through.

And so she looped her arms around his neck, rested her head against his shoulder, and said nothing as he took her back to that master suite. She did nothing but *feel* as he carried her into that room she'd seen before that contained only a massive, luxurious tub with a view straight on to forever.

Benedetto put her down carefully beside it so she could hold on if her knees gave way. They did, and he smiled, and then he set about drawing the bath himself. Soon enough, the water was steaming. And the salts he threw in it give the water a silky feel when she dipped her fingers in.

He said nothing. He only indicated with his chin that she should climb into the hot water, so she did.

Then she sat there, relaxing against the sloping side, the warm water like an embrace. The heat holding her the way he had. She thought he would climb in with her, but instead, with a long, dark look she had no hope of reading, Benedetto left her there to soak.

Something curled around inside her, low and deep, so she stayed where she was to indulge it. The water felt too good. She was too warm, and outside the sea danced beneath the stars, and flirted with her. She could not bring herself to climb out.

Angelina didn't think she slept, there in a bathtub where she could so easily slip beneath the water to her death—in a place that hinted at death around every corner. But she was still startled when there were hands on her again, and she was suddenly being lifted up and out of the warm water.

But in the next moment, she knew it was him. And the knowledge soothed her.

It felt like a dream, so she didn't really react as Benedetto wrapped her in a towel and set about drying her himself. She had tied her hair in a knot on top of her head and she could feel the curls from the heat, framing her face, in a way she had never liked—but she did not have the energy to do anything about it.

She blinked, realizing that he had showered. She could smell the soap on him. And all he wore now were a pair of low-slung trousers. Somehow that felt more intimate than his nakedness.

For the first time, Angelina actually felt shy in this man's presence.

The absurdity did not escape her, after the things he'd done to her in her father's house. The things he'd done to her tonight. She should have been immune to him by now. Instead, he toweled her dry and then wrapped her in the softest, most airy robe she had ever felt in her life, and she suddenly felt awkward. Exposed.

She thought he would say something then. The way he looked at her seemed to take her apart, his dark eyes so unreadable and his mouth in that serious, somber line. But he didn't. He ushered her from the room, with a certain hint of something very nearly ceremonial that made her heart thud inside her chest.

"Where we going?" she asked.

And it was times like these, when she was walking next to him—close enough that they could have been hand in hand if they were different people—that she was more aware of him than was wise. How tall he was. How beautiful and relentlessly male.

How dark and mysterious, even though he wore so little.

And she was forced to confront the fact that it wasn't the things he wore that made him seem so dangerous. So outrageously powerful. It was just him.

The master of Castello Nero. The boogeyman of Europe.

Her husband. Benedetto.

"You did not think that was the sum total of your wedding night, I hope." There was the faintest hint of a smile on his hard face. "We have miles to go, indeed."

That didn't make her heart thud any less.

Angelina followed him down the hall inside the

grand suite and noticed that all the doors stood ajar. All the doors in the castle were wide open, now that she thought of it, save the one he'd showed her out in the hallway.

She thought of reinforced steel and heavy oak. Hidden stairs to a secret tower.

And she didn't know why it made her pulse pick up.

"Do you live here now?" she asked. His brow arched, as if to say, *We are here, are we not?* She could almost hear the words and felt herself flush, ridiculously. But she pushed on. "I mean to say, after spending all that time in boarding school. And knowing that your own parents did not spend much time here, from what you said. When did you move back yourself?"

"After my grandfather died," he replied. Not in the sort of tone that invited further comments.

"Were these his rooms?"

But she already knew the answer. She eyed a portrait on the wall of an old man gripping a cane with a serpent's head as its handle, while staring down from his great height with imperious eyes that look just like Benedetto's.

"When I was young," Benedetto said, his voice sounding something slightly less than frozen through, "my grandfather entertained me for at least one hour every Sunday in his drawing room here. He asked me fierce and probing questions about my studies, my life, my hopes and goals, and then explained to me why each and every one of them was wrong. Or needed work."

He stopped at a different door, and beckoned for Angelina to precede him.

"He was a terrifying, judgmental, prickly old man who would have been a king in a simpler time. He was never kind when he could be cutting, never smiled when he could scowl, and I miss him to this day."

Angelina was so startled by the indication that Benedetto had emotions or feelings of any kind that she almost stumbled on her way into the room. And it took her a moment to realize that the reason she didn't recognize it outright as the private dining room she'd seen when she'd first walked into the suite was because it was transformed.

There were candles lighting up the table, and clearly not, as in her parents' house, because of worries about an impending electric bill. Because out in the hallway, lights were blazing. The candles were here to set a mood.

The table was filled with platters of food. And not, she thought she drew closer, just any food. A feast. There were only two table settings, straddling the corner of the highly polished, deep mahogany table, but there was food enough for an army.

"This looks like…"

But she couldn't finish the sentence.

"It looks like a celebration, I hope," Benedetto said stiffly. He pulled out the chair that was clearly meant to be hers, and she almost thought she saw a hint of something like apprehension on his face. Could it be…uncertainty? Her heart stuttered. "I stole you away from your wedding reception. I offer this instead."

And suddenly, Angelina found the world around her little bit blurry. She sat in the chair he indicated, jolting slightly when her bottom found the chair beneath her because she was tender. Gloriously, marvelously tender between her legs.

He had given her a perfect piano and let her play, so

that her introduction to her new life—her new home, her new status, her possible dark fate—was draped in a veil of music.

He had taken her down on that chaise and made a woman of her.

Her chest felt tight because he had made her wedding feast, and her *heart*. Her traitorous, treacherous, giddily hopeful heart beat out a rhythm that was much too close to joy for the seventh wife of the Butcher of Castello Nero.

Angelina could only hope it wouldn't be the death of her.

Literally.

CHAPTER NINE

SHE DID NOT ask him directly if he'd killed his wives.

How they'd died, yes. Not whether or not he was guilty of killing them. Not whether he'd done the dark deeds with his own two hands.

And Benedetto couldn't decide, as they sat and ate the wedding feast he'd had his staff prepare for them, if he thought that was evidence that she was perfect for him or the opposite.

All he knew was that he was in trouble.

That he had already treated her differently than any other woman, and all other wives.

He kept expecting something—anything—involving this woman to be *regular*. Ordinary. But instead, she was incomparable to anyone or anything, and he had no idea what to do with that.

Even now, when she was scrubbed clean, bathed so that all her makeup was gone and her hair was merely in a haphazard knot on the top of her head, she was more radiant than she had been at their wedding ceremony.

And he didn't think he could bear it.

"You look quite angry with your crab cakes," she pointed out in that faintly dry tone of hers. "Or is it the company that does not suit?"

"Tell me about the piano," he said, instead of answering her question. "You are quite talented. Why did you never think to leave that ruin of a *château* and do something with it?"

"I thought of nothing else." And she actually grinned at him. At *him*. "There was no money for necessities, much less ambition."

"I do not understand," Benedetto said, with perhaps more ill-temper than necessary. "Surely your father could have avoided most of the unpleasantness in his life if he had made money from you and your piano. Rather than, say, trying his hand at high stakes card games he was doomed to lose before he walked in the room."

And this woman, this unexpected angel who should never have agreed to become his wife, grinned even wider.

"But to do so, you understand, he would first have to believe that that infernal racket I was forever making could benefit him in some way. Instead, he often asked me why it was I could not entertain myself more quietly while sucking off the family teat, quote unquote. The way my sisters did."

Benedetto couldn't keep his eyes off of her. She was grinning as she waved away her father's indifference to her talent. And while she did, she applied herself to each course of the feast he had ordered with equal abandon.

He liked her hunger. He wanted to feed it.

All her hungers.

"It sounds as if you were kept in a prison," he told her, his voice in a growl. "But you do not seem the least bit concerned by this."

"Because you freed me."

And there was laughter in her voice as she said it. In her eyes, too, making the blue into a sparkle that was brighter than the candles.

A sparkle that faded the longer she gazed at him.

"It is a long, long time indeed since I have been viewed as the better of two options," he said darkly.

"People always tell you the devil you know is better," Angelina said, a wisdom beyond her years where that sparkle had been, then. "But I have never thought so. There's more scope for growth in the unknown. There has to be."

"How would you know such a thing? Did they teach it in the convent?"

Again, her lips moved into something wry. "Ask me in three months and two days or so."

And despite himself, Benedetto laughed.

What was the harm in pretending, just for a little while, that this was real? That it could be precisely what it seemed. No more, no less. Would that really be the worst thing that ever happened?

He suspected he knew the answer. But he ignored it.

When they finished eating, he led her out onto one of the balconies, this one equipped with a fire pit built into the stone, benches all around, and a hot tub on one end with nothing before it but the sea. He could imagine winter nights in that tub, the two of them wound around each other—

But he stopped himself, because she wouldn't be here when winter came.

He watched as she stood at the rail, the sea breeze playing with her hair, making it seem more like spun silver than before.

Or making him feel like spun silver himself, which should have appalled him.

"You look remarkably happy." The words felt like a kind of curse as they came out of his mouth. As if he was asking for trouble. Or tempting fate too directly, standing there beside her. It was as if his heart seized up in his chest, then beat too hard, beating out a warning. "Particularly for a woman who married a monster today."

She turned her dreamy face to his and then his fingers were there, helping the breeze at its work, teasing her hair into curls and lifting them seemingly at random.

"If you think about it," she said softly, "we are all of us monsters. In our hearts, most of all."

"Are you already forgiving me?" Benedetto asked, though it seemed to him that the world had gone still. The tide had stopped turning, the planet had stopped spinning, and there was only Angelina. His last, best wife and her gaze upon him, direct and true, like his own north star. "Don't you think that might be premature?"

"Do you need forgiveness?"

Something inside him crumbled at that. It was a question no one had ever asked him. Because everyone thought they already knew all the answers to the mystery that was Benedetto Franceschi. Everyone believed they were privy to the whole story.

Or they preferred to make up their own.

Over and over again.

"Carlota," he heard himself say. And though he was horrified, he couldn't seem to stop himself. "I should never have married her."

Angelina's gaze moved over his face, but he didn't see the revulsion he expected. Or anything like an accusation. It made him…hurt.

"I thought you had to marry her." She tilted her head slightly. "Isn't that what you said?"

"That was the understanding, but I doubt very much we would have been marched down the aisle with shotguns in our backs if we'd refused." He let go of her hair and straightened from the rail. And no matter how many times he asked himself what he thought he was doing, he couldn't seem to stop. "Still, we were both aware of our duty. I thought she was like me—resigned to our reality, but happy enough to play whatever games we needed to along the way. Because as soon as the line was secure, we could do as we liked. And even before, for that matter. All that needed to happen was that we set aside a certain period of time of strict fidelity to ensure paternity."

"That sounds very dry and matter-of-fact. We are talking about sex and marriage and relationships, are we not?"

"We are talking about ancient bloodlines," Benedetto replied. "Ancient bloodlines require ancient solutions to problems like heirs. And once the deed was done, we could carry on as we pleased. Another grand old tradition."

Angelina blinked. "You do know that science exists, don't you? No need to do the deed at all."

He should have stopped talking. He shouldn't have started. But he didn't stop.

"You must understand, Angelina. Carlota and I knew we were to be married before either one of us had any idea what that meant. We were intended for each other, and everything we learned about the opposite sex we learned in the shadow of that reality. And when it finally came time to do our duty, she suggested we jump right in and get the heir taken care of, rather than messing about with invasive medical procedures we would inevitably have to discuss in the press. We were friends. We were in it together. She rather thought we should handle things the old-fashioned way because it was quicker and easier. Theoretically."

"What did you think?"

There was a certain gleam in her gaze then that reminded him that this was a woman he'd not only married, but had enjoyed for the past month. And just today, had made sob out his name like another one of her symphonies.

Benedetto smiled. "I was young and brash and foolish. I thought that as long as Carlota and I had agreed on all the important things—like the fact neither one of us was interested in fidelity once our duties were handled, hale, and hardy—we might as well."

He could remember Carlota's bawdy laugh. The way she'd smoked cigarettes with dramatic, theatrical flourish. The way she rolled her eyes, speaking volumes without having to speak a word.

I can't cope with having it all hanging there over my head, she'd declared a few months before their wedding. It will be just be too tedious. Let's get in, get out. Get it done.

Are we a sports team? Benedetto had asked dryly.

In his memory, he was as he was now. Cynical. Self-aware and sardonic. But the reality was that he'd been twenty-two. Just like her. And he'd had no idea how quickly things could change. Or how brutally life could kick the unwary, especially people like them who thought their wealth protected them from unpleasant realities.

They'd both learned.

"I was so arrogant," he said now, shaking his head. "I was so certain that life would go as planned. Looking back, there were any number of warning signs. But I saw none of them."

"Was she very depressed?" Angelina asked, her eyes troubled.

"Carlota? Depressed? Never." Benedetto laughed. "She was in love."

"With you." Those blue eyes widened. "So you did break her heart when you refused to give up your mistress."

"That is a very boring tabloid story." Benedetto sighed. "Sylvia was my mistress, though I think you will find that when a man is twenty-two years old and dating an actress of roughly the same age, they're just… dating. But no matter, that does not make for splashy, timeless headlines."

"Mistress is certainly catchier," Angelina said quietly.

"Carlota was in love, but not with me," he said, because he couldn't seem to stop doing this. Why was he doing this? Nothing good could come of unburdening himself to her. "He was not of our social class, of course. Her parents would not have cared much if she carried on with him, because everyone could boast about sleeping with the odd pool boy—which is something her mother actually said to me at her funeral. But you see, Carlota wasn't simply sexually involved with this man of hers. She was head over heels in love with him, and he with her. Something I knew nothing about."

And then he hissed in a breath, because Angelina lifted a hand and slid it over his heart.

"It works, Benedetto," she said quietly. "I can feel it."

He felt something surge in him, huge and vivid. Something he could hardly bear, and couldn't name, though he had the terrible notion that it had been frozen there inside him all this time. That it was melting at last.

And the only thing this was going to do was make this worse. He knew that all too well.

"We spent the first few days of our honeymoon as friends, because that was what we'd always been," he gritted out, because he'd started this. And he would finish it, no matter the cost. "But then she decided that we might as well start making that heir as quickly as possible, so we could move on. She went off to prepare herself. Which, because she was in love with another man and had never had the slightest interest in me, involved getting drunk and then supplementing it with a handful of pills."

"You don't think she killed herself," Angelina breathed.

"On the contrary," Benedetto said grimly. "I know she did. It was an accident, I have no doubt, but what does that matter? It happened because she needed to deaden herself completely before she suffered a night with me."

He had never said anything like that out loud before in his life. And he hated himself for doing it now. He wanted to snatch the words back and shove them down his throat. He wanted to insist that Angelina rip them out of her ears.

"Was she truly your friend?" Angelina asked, and he couldn't understand why she wasn't looking at him with horror, as he deserved.

Or with the same resigned bleakness his grandfather had.

"She was," he said, another thing he never spoke about. To anyone. "She really was."

"Then, Benedetto." And Angelina's voice was soft. "You must know that she would never want you to suffer like this. Not for her. Don't you think she would have wanted at least one of you to be free?"

That landed in his gut like a punch.

He wasn't sure he could breathe.

"You have no idea what you're talking about, Angelina. You have no idea the kinds of chains—"

But he cut himself off, because that wasn't a conversation he could have, with her or anyone else. He'd promised. He'd chosen. He gathered her to him instead, then crushed his mouth to hers, pouring it all into another life-altering kiss.

For a moment, he imagined that it really could alter his life instead of merely *feeling* that way. That he could change something. Anything.

He kissed her and he kissed her.

And Benedetto realized with a surge of light-headedness that the taste he hadn't been able to get enough of over the past month, that impossible glory that was all Angelina, was hope.

Damn her, she was giving him *hope*.

He sensed movement in his peripheral vision, so he lifted his head, holding Angelina close to him so he could see who moved around in the dining room on the other side of the windowed doors.

It was Signora Malandra, and he felt himself grow cold as the older woman stared out at him.

She didn't say a word. But then, she didn't need to. Because if this castle was a prison, then Signora Malandra was the jailer, and it was no use complaining about a simple fact.

Angelina didn't see the silent, chilly exchange. Benedetto checked to make sure, and when he looked up again the housekeeper had disappeared.

Taking his fledgling hope with her.

"You don't have to tell me anything further," Angelina told him then. "You don't have to tell me anything at all, Benedetto."

Her face was still so perfect. Her expression still so dreamy. And he knew that she had forgiven him for acts she knew nothing about, even if that was something he could never do himself.

He swept her up into his arms again. And he didn't head for that bloodred bed in the room of stone that might as well have been a stage.

Benedetto shouldn't have done any of the things he'd done with Angelina, but he had. And he wasn't going to stop until he had to. But that only meant he needed to make sure what stolen moments they had were real.

She was the only thing in his life that had ever been real, as far as he could tell, for a long, long time.

He carried her into one of the salons, this one with a fireplace and a thick, soft rug before it. He lay her down and then busied himself preparing the fire.

"I would have sworn that there was no way a man of your consequence would know how to light a fire," Angelina said, laughing again.

And what was he supposed to do with her when she

kept laughing where any other woman would have been crying? Shivering with fear? Barring herself in a bathroom? All things other wives of his had done after Sylvia had died, and with far less provocation.

But then, he hadn't touched any of them.

He looked over his shoulder at her, incredulously, but she didn't seem to take the hint.

"The only reason I know how to do it is because we relied on fires for light and heat in my father's house," she confided. Merrily, even. "Necessity makes you strong or it kills you, I suppose. Either way, not something the great Benedetto Franceschi would ever have to worry about, I would have thought."

He busied himself with the logs. "It was not always in my best interests to alert members of this household as to my whereabouts. I can fend for myself. Inside the walls of the castle, anyway."

"But surely—"

But Benedetto was done talking.

"Quiet, little one," he growled, and then he crawled toward her, bearing her back down beneath him.

And he taught her everything he knew.

How to take him in her mouth. How to indulge herself as if he was her dessert. How to ride him and how to drive him wild by looking over her shoulder with that little smile of hers while he took her from behind.

He was a man possessed, falling asleep with her there before the fire, only to wake up and start all over again.

He could not taste her enough. He could not touch her enough.

As if, if he only applied himself, he could take all

that hope and beauty, all that magic and music, and infuse it directly into his veins.

As if there was more than one way to eat her alive.

As if he could keep her.

And in the morning, dawn crept through the windows, pink and bright. It woke him where he lay stretched out before that fire still.

He had done everything wrong. He knew that.

But that didn't change what had to happen now. It didn't alter in the slightest the promises he'd made. The choices he'd walked into with his eyes wide open, never expecting this. Never expecting Angelina.

Benedetto lifted her up. He tried to steel himself against the way she murmured his name, then turned to bury her face against his shoulder, not quite waking up.

He carried her through the suite, everything in him rebelling as he walked into the bedchamber at last. Outside the windows, he could see the light of the new day streaking over the sea.

It should have been uplifting, but all he wanted to do was rage. Hit things. Make it stop.

He took her to that bloodred bed and laid her in it. He drew the coverlet up, but left her hand exposed, that bloodred ruby marking her as his. And a fortune or two of them surrounding her.

Blood on blood.

He didn't want to leave, but he knew he had no choice if he was to keep his old vow. He handled the hateful practicalities and then he tore himself away. He forced himself out of the bedchamber and refused to allow himself to look back.

But the sight of her was burned into his brain anyway. Blond hair spread out over the pillows like silver filigree, somehow making all that dark red seem less ominous. Cheerful, almost.

As if she really was an angel.

Benedetto took a long shower, but that didn't make it any better. He dressed in a fury, then had another fight on his hands to keep himself from walking back into the bedchamber and starting all over again.

Instead, he stepped out into the hall. He wasn't the least bit surprised to see the figure of his housekeeper waiting there, halfway down. Right in front of the door he'd told Angelina she was never to open.

Inside him, he was nothing but an anguished howl. But the only sound he made was that of his feet against the floor.

Walking toward his duty and his destiny, as ever.

When he reached Signora Malandra, they stared at each other for a quiet eternity or two.

"It is done," Benedetto said, the way he always did.

The older woman nodded, her canny gaze reminding him of his grandfather.

Or maybe that was his same old guilt talking too loudly once again, trying to drown out that tiny shimmer of hope.

"Very well then, sir," she said. She smiled at the door, locked tight, then at him. "So the game begins. Again."

CHAPTER TEN

ANGELINA WOKE UP on the first morning of her married life with a buoyancy inside her chest that she would have said was impossible—because she'd certainly never felt anything like it before.

At first, she was a bit surprised to find herself in that great, blood colored bed. More than surprised—she was taken aback that she had no memory of getting into it. The memories she did have were white hot, stretched out in front of a fire her forbiddingly grand husband built himself. A delicious shiver worked its way over her body, inside and out.

She sat up slowly, holding the bejeweled coverlet to her chest as she looked around. But nothing had changed. The room was still a stark aerie, nothing but stone before her and above her, and the sea outside. Waiting.

But for some reason, what she'd expected would feel like a fall to her death felt like flying instead. Exhilarating. She shoved her hair back from her face, and spent a good long while staring out at the sea in the distance. Blue. Beautiful.

Only as brooding as she made it.

When she swung her legs over the side of the high

bed and found the cool stones beneath her feet, she felt almost soothed. Not at all the reaction she would have expected to have in this room that had scared her silly yesterday.

She took a long, hot shower, reveling in such a modern installation only yards from that medieval bedchamber. And as she soaped herself up, reveling in how new her own skin felt, she thought that Benedetto was much the same as this castle of his. Stretched there between the old and the new and somehow both at once.

Benedetto.

Her heart seem to cartwheel in her chest, and she couldn't help the wide, foolish smile that took over her face at the thought of him. He had taken her virginity— or more accurately, she'd given it to him. First while she played, offering him everything she was, everything she had, everything she hoped and dreamed.

The physical manifestation of the music she'd played for him had been appropriately epic.

She could still feel his hands, all over her flesh. She could feel the tug and rip of her gown as he'd torn it from her, then buried himself inside her for the first time. She still shuddered as images of the darkly marvelous things he'd taught her washed through her, over and over.

And she couldn't wait to do all of it again.

Maybe, just maybe, she could be the wife who stuck.

She was turning that over in her head, thinking about stories that lost more truth in each telling, as she dressed herself in the sprawling dressing room that was filled with clothes that she knew, somehow, would fit her perfectly. Even if they bore no resemblance to the meager selection she'd brought herself. And she remembered, against her will, what Petronella had said. That two or three lost wives could be a tragedy, but add another three on top of that and there had to be intention behind it.

That, or Benedetto Franceschi, the least hapless man she had ever met, was just...profoundly unlucky.

A notion that made her laugh a little as she found her way out of the dressing room, following her nose. Coffee, if she wasn't mistaken. And she could feel excitement and anticipation bubbling inside of her, as if she was fizzy from the inside out, because she couldn't wait to see him again. His dark, forbidding face that she knew so much better now. That she'd kissed, touched. That she'd felt on every inch of her skin.

Between her legs, she felt the deep pulse of that hunger she would have said should surely have been sated by everything they'd done the night before.

But it seemed her husband left her bottomless.

Her husband, she repeated to herself. Giddily, she could admit.

She pushed the door open to one of the pretty little salons, expecting to see Benedetto there, waiting for her in all his formidable state. But instead, the dour housekeeper waited there with a blank expression on her dolorous face.

Or an *almost* blank expression. Because if Angelina wasn't mistaken, there was a glitter in Signora Malandra's too-dark eyes. It looked a little too much like triumph.

Angelina didn't like the trickle of uneasiness that slipped down her back.

"Good morning," Angelina said, sounding as frosty as her own mother. She pulled the long, flowing sweater she'd found more tightly around her, because it might be the height of summer out there, but old castles were cold. All that stone and bloody history, no doubt.

"I trust you slept well," the older woman said, lifting an accusing eyebrow in a manner Angelina was all too familiar with. "If...deeply."

This woman could not possibly be attempting to shame her master's brand-new wife because she'd slept half the morning away. After her *wedding night*. Surely not.

"Have you seen my husband?" Angelina asked instead of any number of other things she might have said. Because if Margrete had taught her anything, it was that a chilly composure was always the right answer. It made others wonder. And that was far better than showing them how she actually felt.

Signora Malandra indicated the small table near a set of French doors that stood closed, no doubt to control the sea air. And then waited there, gazing back at her, until Angelina realized the woman had no intention of answering her until she obeyed.

Luckily, Angelina had spent her entire life under the thumb of overly controlling women. What was one surly housekeeper next to her mother and sisters? So she only smiled, attempted to look meek and biddable, and went to take her seat. As ordered.

Her act of rebellion was to crack open one of the doors, and then she smiled as the breeze swept inside, fresh and bright.

"Coffee?" the older woman asked. It sounded like an accusation.

Angelina channeled her mother and smiled wider, if more icily. "Thank you for asking. The truth is, I don't care for much in the way of breakfast. I like my coffee strong and very dark, and sometimes with a bit of cream. But only sometimes. I don't like anything to interfere with my walk."

"And where will we be walking?" the housekeeper asked as she poured Angelina a cup of coffee. "Perhaps we have forgotten that this is an island. The castle covers the whole of it, save a few rocks."

It took everything Angelina had not to respond to that. Not to point out that *we* were not invited.

The other woman sniffed as if she'd spoken aloud. "Though I suppose if you are feeling enterprising, you could walk the causeway. It's quite a pretty walk, though I'm not sure I would attempt it until I became more conversant with the tides."

"What a wonderful idea," Angelina said with a sweetness she did not feel. And when she took a sip of the coffee, it was suitably bitter. Which matched her mood.

"I was born and raised in this castle," Signora Malandra said, and again, Angelina could see something she didn't quite like in the older woman's gaze. "It sounds like foolishness, to warn every person who visits here about the inevitability of the tide when the ocean is all around us. But I warn you, mistress." And there was an inflection on that word that made Angelina's stomach tighten. "This is not a sea to turn your back on."

Angelina felt chilled straight through, and it had nothing to do with the breeze coming in from the water. She was glad she'd thought to wrap the sweater around her when all she wore beneath was a light, summerweight dress that she'd chosen because the color—a bright pop of yellow—made her happy.

She did not feel quite so happy now.

And she did not appreciate having dour old women try to scare her, either.

"My husband?" she asked again, as Signora Malandra looked as if she was headed for the door.

"Your husband is gone," the old woman said coolly. And again, with that hint of triumph in her gaze. "Did you not get what he left you?"

"What he left me?" Angelina repeated, not comprehending. How could Benedetto be *gone*? Did she mean…into town, wherever that was? She tried to conceal her shock. "Has he gone out for the day?"

And this time, there was no mistaking the look on the other woman's face. It was far worse than *triumphant*. It was pitying.

"Not for the day, mistress. Two months, I would say. At the very least."

And by the time Angelina had processed that, Signora Malandra was gone.

This time, when she found her way back into the bedchamber, it seemed ominous again. Altered, somehow. Almost obscene.

Someone had made up the bed in Angelina's absence, and that felt as sickening as the rest, as if some unseen evil was swirling around her, even now—

A sound that could have been a sob came out of her then, and she hated herself for it.

She remembered his face, out there on the balcony last night. That had been real. She was sure of it. Angelina had to believe that what she felt was real, not the rest of this. Not the stories that people had told, when the one he'd told her made more sense. Not because she wanted to believe him, though she did.

But because real life was complicated. It had layers and

tragedies. It was never as simple as *a bad man*. It was never black and white, no matter how people wanted it to be.

There was nothing in the room, not even bedside tables, and she thought the housekeeper must have been playing with her.

Even as she breathed a little easier, however, she realized with a start that the mantel over the fire didn't look the way it should. She drifted closer to the fireplace, her heart in her throat, because there was a bit of paper there with an object weighting it down.

She could have sworn it hadn't been there when she woke up. Then again, her attention had been on that happiness within her that now felt curdled, and the watching, waiting sea.

Her whole body felt heavy, as if her feet were encased in concrete as she moved across the floor. But then, at the last moment—almost as if she feared that someone would come up behind her and shove her into the enormous hearth if she wasn't careful—she reached out and swiped the paper and its paperweight up. Then moved away from the fireplace.

The object was a key. Big and ornate and attached to a long chain.

She stared at it, the weight of it feeling malevolent, somehow. Only when she jerked her gaze from it did she look at the thick sheaf of paper with a few bold lines scrawled across it.

This is the key to the door you must not open.

Benedetto had written that. Because of course, this was his handwriting. She had no doubt. It looked like him—dark and black and unreasonably self-assured.

You must wear the key around your neck, but never use it. Can I trust you, little one?

And for a long time after that, weeks that turned to fortnights and more, Angelina careened between disbelief and fury.

On the days that she was certain it was no more than a test, and one she could handily win, she achieved a kind of serenity. She woke in the morning, entertained herself by sparring with the always unpleasant housekeeper, and then tended to her walk. When the weather was fine, and the tide agreeable, she did in fact walk the causeway. Out there on that tiny strip of not quite land, she felt the way she did when she was playing the piano. As if she was simultaneously the most important life in the universe, and nothing at all—a speck in the vastness. The sea surged around her, birds cried overhead, and in the distance, Italy waited. Wholly unaware of the loneliness of a brand-new bride on a notorious island where a killer was said to live. When the man she'd married had been a dark and stirring lover instead.

Her husband did not call. He did not send her email. She might have thought she'd dreamed him altogether, but she could track his movements online. She could see that he was at meetings. The odd charity ball. She could almost convince herself that he was sending her coded messages through these photographs that appeared in the society pages of various international cities.

Silly girl, she sometimes chided herself. *He is sending you nothing. You don't know this man at all.*

But that was the trouble. She felt as if she did.

She didn't need him to tell her any more of his story.

She knew—she just *knew*—that her heart was right about him, no matter what the world said.

Those were the good days.

On the bad days, she brooded. She walked the lonely halls of the hushed castle, learning her way around a building that time had made haphazard. Stone piled upon stone, this wing doubling back over that. She walked the galleries as if she was having conversations with the art. Particularly the hall of Franceschis past. All those dark, mysterious eyes. All those grim, forbidding mouths.

How many of them had locked their women away? Leaving them behind as they marched off to this crusade or that very important business negotiation, or whatever it was men did across time to convince themselves their lives were greater than what they left behind.

On those days, the portraits she found online of the stranger she'd married felt like an assault. As if he was taunting her from London, Paris, Milan.

And all the while, she played.

Her tower was an escape. The safest place in the castle. She played and she played, and sometimes, she would stagger to the chaise, exhausted, so she could sleep a bit, then start to play all over again.

And if she didn't know better, if food didn't appear at regular intervals, hot tea and hard rolls, or sometimes cakes and coffee, she might have imagined that she was all alone in this lonely place. Like some kind of enchanted princess in a half-forgotten fairy tale.

She played and she played.

And the weeks inched by.

One month. Another.

"Sweet God," said Petronella, when Angelina was finally stir crazy enough to call her parents' home. "I convinced myself he'd killed you already and was merely hiding the evidence."

"Don't be melodramatic," Angelina replied primly, because that was easier. And so familiar, it actually felt good. "He's done nothing of the kind."

Or not in the way that Petronella meant it, anyway. They put her on speaker, and she regaled her mother and sisters with tales of the castle. She'd tagged along on enough of Signora Malandra's tours by then that she could have given them herself, and so spared no flourish or aside as she shared the details of the notorious Castello Nero with her family.

Because she knew they would think wealth meant happiness.

Because to them, it did.

"Everywhere I look there's another fortune or two," she assured her mother. "It's really spectacular."

"I should hope so," Margrete said, in her chilliest voice. "That was the bargain we made, was it not?"

And when she hung up, Angelina was shocked to find herself…sentimental. Nostalgic, even, for those pointless nights huddled together in the drawing room of the dilapidated old *château*, waiting to be sniped at and about. Night after night after night.

Who could have imagined she would miss that?

She would have sworn she could never possibly feel that way. But then again, she thought as she moved from one well-stocked library to the next—because the castle boasted three separate, proper libraries that would take a lifetime or two to explore—she was more emotional these days than she'd ever been in her life.

She'd woken up the other morning crying, though she couldn't have said why. She slept in that absurd bed every night, almost as if it was an act of defiance. But she couldn't say her dreams were pleasant. They were dark and red, and she woke with strange sensations in her body, especially in her belly.

Angelina was glad she couldn't remember the one that had rendered her tearful. Though the truth was, everything seemed to make her cry lately. Even her own music.

That night, she followed her usual routine. She played until her fingers hurt, then she staggered down the stairs from her tower to find a cold dinner waiting for her. She ate curled up on a chilly chair out on the balcony while the sea and wind engaged in a dramatic sort of dance in front of her. There was a storm in the air, she could sense it. Smell it, even.

When she could take the slap of the wind no longer, she moved inside. She was barefoot, her hair a mess, and frozen straight through when she left the master suite and walked down that hallway. The key he'd left her hung around her neck as ordered, the chain cool against her skin and the key itself heavy and warm between her breasts.

And she stood there, on the other side of that door, and stared at it.

Some nights she touched it. Other nights she pounded on it with her fists. Once she'd even gone so far as to stick the key into the lock, though she hadn't turned it.

Not yet.

"I am not Pandora," she muttered to herself.

As always, her voice sounded too loud, too strange in the empty hallway.

She had no idea how long she stood there, only that the world grew darker and darker on the other side of the windows, and she'd neglected to put on any lights.

When lightning flashed outside, it lit everything up. It seemed to sizzle inside of her like a dare.

A challenge.

It had been two months and three days. It was nearly September. And she was beginning to think that she had already gone crazy. That she was a madwoman locked away in a castle, which was an upgrade from the proverbial attic, but it ended up the same.

Alone and unhinged. Matted hair and too much emotion. And an almost insatiable need to do the things she knew she shouldn't.

There was another flash of lightning, and then a low, ominous rumble of thunder following it.

She heard a harsh, rhythmic kind of noise, and realized with some shock that she was panting. As if she'd been running.

And then, when another roll of thunder seemed to shake that wall of windows behind her, she found herself sobbing.

Angelina sank to her knees, there in that solitary hall.

She had waited and waited, but it was nights like this that were killing her. Was this how he'd rid himself of all those wives?

And as soon as she had that thought, she had to ask herself—what kind of death was worse?

This had to be a test. But how long could she do it? She'd had a month of play, and then one impossibly beautiful night with a man everyone insisted was evil incarnate. Her heart had rejected that definition of him.

Could she set that against these months of neglect? She was slowly turning into one of the antiques that cluttered this place. Soon she would be nothing more than a story the dour old woman told, shuffling groups of tourists from room to room.

"I have been a prisoner my whole life," she sobbed, into her hands.

Her piano made her feel free, but she wasn't.

At the end of the day, she was just a girl in a tower, playing and playing, in the hopes that someone might hear her.

All Benedetto had done was trap her. Her family had never wished to listen to her play, but they'd heard her all the same. Now the only thing that heard her was the sea, relentless and uncaring. Waiting.

She lifted her head, shoving the mass of her hair back. Her heart was kicking at her, harder and harder.

She already knew what her mother would tell her. What her sisters would advise.

You've got it made, Petronella would say with a sniff. *You're left to your own devices in a glorious castle to call your own. What's to complain about?*

Angelina understood that she would fail this test. That she already had, and all of this had been so much pretending otherwise. The key suspended between her breasts seemed to pulse, in time with that hunger that she still couldn't do anything to cure.

Before she knew what she meant to do, the key was in her hand. She stared at it, as another flash of lightning lit up the hall, and she could have sworn that she saw the key flash too. As if everything was lightning and portent, dread and desire.

The ring Benedetto had put on her other hand seemed

heavy, suddenly. And all she could think about was six dead women. And a bedchamber made bloodred with dark rubies.

And was she really to blame if she couldn't stay here any longer without looking behind the one door that was always kept closed?

What if he was in there? Hurt?

What if something far more horrible was in there?

Like all the women who had disappeared, never to be heard from again.

Even as she thought it, something in her denied it. Her heart would not accept him as a villain.

But either way, she found herself on her feet.

And then she was at the door, one palm flat against the metal. She blew out a breath that was more like a sob. She thrust the key into the lock, the way she'd done one time before, amazed how easily it went in. Smooth and simple and *right*.

She held her breath. Then she threw the dead bolt.

Alarms didn't sound. The castle didn't crumble to ash all around her.

Emboldened, Angelina blew out the breath she was holding. She took another one, deeper than before, and pushed the heavy door open. She expected it to creak ominously, as if she was in a horror film.

But it opened soundlessly on a stair, very much like the one she climbed every day to her own tower.

Thunder rumbled outside, the storm coming closer. She couldn't see a thing, so she inched inside, then reached out her hand into the darkness, sliding it along the stone, her whole body prickling with a kind of premonition. Or fear. Panic that she would thrust her hand into something terrible—

But she found a light switch where she expected to, in the same place it was in her stairwell. She flicked it on and then began to climb.

Each step felt like a marathon. So she went faster and faster, climbing high, until she reached another door at the top. And her heart was beating too hard for her to stop now. There was too much thunder outside and in her, too.

She threw open the second door and stepped inside, reaching and finding another light and switching it on.

And then she blinked. Once, then again, unable to believe her eyes. Angelina dropped her hand to her side, drifted in a few more steps, and looked around as if she expected something to change…

But nothing changed.

It was an empty room with windows over the sea, just like the tower room she spent her days in. There were stone walls, a bare floor, and a high ceiling where a light fixture hung, illuminating the fact that there was nothing here.

Benedetto had demanded she stay out of an empty room.

That sparked something in her, half a laugh, half a sob.

Angelina thought she heard a noise and she jumped, expecting *something*… But that was the trouble. She didn't know what she wanted. And the room was empty. No monsters. No dead wives. No words scrawled on a paper, or carved into the stone. Just…nothing.

The same nothing these last two months had been.

That made something in her begin to throb, painfully.

She was disgusted with herself. She didn't know if

she wanted to go play her piano until she felt either settled or too wound up to breathe, or if she should crawl beneath that heavy coverlet again to dream her unsettling dreams.

But when she turned around to go, she stopped dead.

Because Benedetto stood in the doorway to the empty chamber, the expression on his face a far more terrible thunder than the storm outside.

CHAPTER ELEVEN

BENEDETTO HAD STAYED away for six weeks. It was easy enough to do, touring his various business concerns. Such a tour would normally have claimed all of his attention, but this time he had found himself distracted. Unable to focus on what was in front of him because he was far more concerned with what he'd left behind.

That hadn't happened in as long as he could remember.

He wasn't sure it had ever happened. But that was Angelina. She was singular even when she wasn't with him.

And since his return to this castle he'd forgotten how to love the way he had as a child, he had become a ghost.

The irony wasn't lost on him. That he should be the one to haunt these old halls, staying in the servants' quarters and wandering in the shadows, both part of the castle and apart from it... Perhaps it was a preview of what awaited him.

Because the other option was that it was a memory of his time here when he was young and had seen the *castello* as his personal playground, magical and inviting in every respect, and that was worse, somehow.

But Angelina had cracked, as he'd known she would. He'd hoped her singularity would extend to this and she might be the one to resist temptation, but she didn't. None of them managed it. Sooner or later, they ended up right here in this empty room above the sea, staring at him as if they truly expected him to come in wielding an ax.

He had come to enjoy, on some level, that they believed all the stories they heard about him and married him anyway. The triumph of his wealth over their fear.

It wasn't as if any of them had touched him the way Angelina had. None of them had seen him, listened to him, or made love to him. None of them had played him music or treated him as if he was a man instead of a monster.

They had married his money. And they all came into this empty room, sooner or later, despite his request they stay away, expecting to come face-to-face with the monster they believed he was. The monster they *knew* he was.

Benedetto had long since stopped minding the way they looked at him when they saw him in the door, as if they could *see* the machete he did not carry with him.

This time, it hurt.

This time, it was a body blow.

"What are you doing here?" Angelina demanded. Her face was pale, her beautiful blond hair whipping around her with the force of her reaction. One hand was at her throat, and he could see the panic in her eyes.

If he was a better man, the fact that *her* fear pierced his soul would drop him, surely. And he would not stand here, wondering why it was that heightened emotion made her even more beautiful.

Or why it reminded him of the look on her face when she'd shuddered all around him, again and again.

Or why nothing about her was like the others—and he *hated* that they were here in this room anyway. Playing out this same old scene. This curse of his he had chosen when he'd never imagined he would want to see the end of it, much less meet someone who'd made it— and him—feel broken from the start.

"Why should I not be here?" he asked, aware as he spoke that he was…not quite as in control of himself as he might wish. Not as in control as he usually was for this scene. "Perhaps you have forgotten that I'm the master of this castle."

"Now that you mention it, you do look vaguely familiar," she threw at him, any hint of fear on her face gone as if it had never been. Instead, she looked fierce. "You almost resemble a man I married, who abandoned me after one night."

"I did not abandon you." He spread his hands open before him. "For here I am, Angelina. Returned to you. And what do I discover but betrayal?"

"You ordered me to stay out of an empty room," she said, as if she couldn't believe it. The hand at her throat dropped to her side, and she took a step toward him, her blue eyes as stormy as the sea and sky outside. "Why would you do that? Do you know what I thought…?"

"But this is a room of terror, clearly," he taunted her, his voice dark, and it was less an act than it usually was. "Look closely, little one. Surely you can hear the screams of the women I've murdered. Surely if you squint, you can see their bodies, splayed out like some horrific art installation."

He watched her emotions move over her face, too

quickly to read. And wished—not for the first time—
that it was different.

Lord help him, but he had wished that she would
be different.

"That is what you came for, is it not?" he demanded,
his words an accusation.

"Are you trying to tell me that is not exactly what
you wish me to think?" She waved one hand, the ring
he'd put on her finger gleaming like the only blood in
this room. "Is that what makes you happy?"

"I gave up on happiness a long time ago," Benedetto
growled. "Now I content myself with living down to
people's worst nightmares? Why shouldn't I? Everyone
needs a villain, do they not?"

Angelina moved toward him, staggering slightly, her
bare feet against the cold stone. "I do not want a villain,
Benedetto. I want a husband."

"If that were true, you'd be asleep even now, tucked
up in the marital bed. It would not have occurred to
you to disobey me."

"What you are describing is a dog, not a wife," she
snapped at him. "I never promised you obedience."

"Surely that was understood," he shot back. "When
I bought you."

And again, he knew that he was far less in control
of himself than he ought to have been. He had played
this scene out before, after all. He usually preferred an
iciness. A cool aloofness that wasn't an act, because it
was his usual, normal state.

Nothing about Angelina had been normal or usual.
Nothing about this was ordinary.

Even now he wanted to bundle her up into his arms
and carry her off. And never, ever put her down again.

"Are you going to tell me what all of this is about?" she asked after a moment, when he'd found himself entirely too entranced by the way her jagged breaths made her body move.

He could see her cheeks were tearstained. She was the one who had disobeyed, the way they all disobeyed, and yet he felt as if *he* had betrayed *her*.

For moment he couldn't understand why.

And then it hit him.

For the first time since he'd met her, Angelina was looking at him as if he really might be a monster, after all.

Of all the things he'd lost, of all the indignities the choices he'd willingly made long ago required that he endure, it was this he thought might take him to his knees.

"Or are these just the kinds of games you like to play?" Angelina asked when he only stared at her. She shook her head, swallowing hard, as if she was holding words back. Or a sob. Or, if that hectic look in her eyes was any guide, a scream. "I am so deeply sick and tired of being nothing more to anyone but a game piece to be moved around a board that is never of my choosing. Is this how you do it, Benedetto? Do you set up every woman you marry in the same way? Do you plot out the terms of your own betrayal, give them the key, and then congratulate yourself on having weeded out yet another deceitful bride? When all along it is you who creates an unwinnable situation?"

He eyed her, amazed that he felt stung by the accusation when he knew it was perfectly true—and more, deliberate. Yet no matter the sting, he was entranced by the magnificence of her temper that reminded him of nothing so much as the way she played that piano. In his weeks here as the resident ghost of his own lost childhood, he'd found himself listening to her play more than he should. He'd found himself sitting behind the stairs, losing himself on the notes she coaxed from the keys.

As if she'd still been playing for him.

Focus, he ordered himself.

"Am I the only one you made sure would fail?" Angelina demanded. "Or is this how you do it? And what do you gain from this? Do you toss us out a tower window, one by one?"

Benedetto laughed, though nothing was funny. "Would that suit your sense of martyrdom, wife?"

She stiffened. "I am no martyr."

"Are you not? Tell me, how else would you describe a young woman who was presented to a known murderer and allowed him a taste of her on that very first night? Do you also write to mass murderers in prison, offering your love and support? There are many who do. I'm sure the attendant psychological problems are in no way a factor."

She looked at him for what felt like a very long time, a kind of resolve on her face. "I didn't believe you were a murderer. I still don't."

And something in him rocked a bit at that. "Because you had made such an in-depth study of my character over the course of that one dinner?" He didn't like the emotion on her face then. He didn't like *emotion.* He growled. "Perhaps, as we are standing here together, stripped down to honesty in this empty room, we can finally admit that what you truly wanted was to escape. And all the better if you could do it while hammered to the family cross."

"Surely a martyr is what you wanted," she replied, displaying that strength he'd heard in her music time and time again. And quietly. "Or why would you go to such trouble to present yourself as a savior, willing to haul a family like mine out of financial ruin—but only for a price."

"I know exactly why it is I do what I do," Benedetto growled with a soft menace. "A better question is why you imagined you could marry a man like me, surrender yourself to my dark demands, and have things end differently for you than the rest. Do you truly imagine yourself that special, Angelina?"

"I don't know," she said, and there was something in her gaze then. A kind of knowing on her lovely face that clawed at him like the storm outside, thunder and flashes of light. "But there were times you looked at me and it seemed clear that you thought so, Benedetto."

She could not have pierced him more deeply had she pulled out a knife and plunged it into his heart. Then twisted it.

Benedetto actually laughed, because he hadn't seen it coming. And he should have. Of course he should have.

Because there was nothing meek about his Angelina. His angel. She was all flaming swords and descents from on high in a blaze of glory, and if he hadn't understood that when he had first seen her—well. When she'd played for him that first night, it had all been clear.

Then he'd tasted all that flame himself.

And there was no coming back from that.

She had introduced music into his life. Now it would live in him, deep in his bones no matter where in the world he went, and he had no idea how he was going to survive without it.

Or without her.

Because these last two months had been torture. If they had been a preview of what awaited him, he might as well chain himself up in his own dungeon and allow himself to go truly mad at last.

It almost sounded like a holiday to him.

"Are you going to kill me?" she asked, and despite the question, she stood tall. She didn't try to hide from him. After a beat he realized there was no fear on her face. "Is that the truth of you, after all?"

And this was the life he had chosen. He had made a promise to his grandfather years ago, and time after time he had kept it.

He had considered it a penance. He had taken a kind of pride in being so reviled and whispered about on the one hand, yet courted and feted all the same because no matter what else he was, he was a man of a great and historic fortune.

Benedetto had considered it a game. For what did he care what names he was called? Why should it matter to him what others said? He had yet to meet anyone who wouldn't risk themselves in his supposedly murderous presence if it meant they would get paid for their trouble.

He had cynically imagined he understood everything there was to know about the world. He had been certain he had nothing left to learn—that nothing could surprise him.

He understood, now it was too late, that the point of it all had been a woman like Angelina.

It was possible his grandfather had expected someone like her to come along sooner, so that Benedetto would learn his lesson. It had never been a game or a curse. It had been about love all along.

Love.

That word.

Franceschis do not love, his mother had told him with one of her bitter trills of laughter. *They destroy.*

Love yourself, his father had said as if in agreement, his tone mocking in response to his wife. He'd cast a narrow sort of look at his only son and heir. *No one else will. Not because Franceschis destroy, or any such superstition. But because the only thing anyone will ever see is your fortune.*

He loves me, Carlota had told him on the day of their wedding. *He knows me. And so he also knows that my duty to you must come first.*

She was joy and she was love, his grandfather had said stiffly on the morning of his grandmother's funeral, staring out at the sea. *And none of each can possibly remain without her.*

I love you, Benedetto, his grandmother had told him long, long ago, when she'd found him hiding in one of the *castello*'s secret passageways. *I will always love you.*

But always had not lasted long.

As far as he had ever been able to tell, love had died along with her, just as his grandfather had said.

Something he'd been perfectly happy with all these years.

Until now.

When it was too late.

Because he knew how this scene between them was about to go. He played the monster and his wives believed it, and he'd been satisfied with that system since the start. There was only ever one way this could go.

He had always liked it. Before.

He raked his hair back from his face, and wished that he could do something about the way his heart kicked at him. Or better yet, about the fact he had a heart in the first place, despite everything.

Surely if he could rid himself of the thing the way he thought he had a lifetime ago, all of this would be easier.

"I am not going to kill you," he told her, his voice severe as he tried to draw the cloak of his usual remoteness around him. But he couldn't quite get there. "Nonetheless, you have a choice of deaths before you. You can consider this chamber a passageway, of sorts. A bridge between the life you knew until today, and one in which you can be anyone you choose. Assuming you meet the criteria, that is."

She swayed slightly on her feet. "The criteria?"

And he had done this so many times. It should have come as easily to him as breath.

But his chest was too tight. That damned heart of his was too big. "The criteria for escape is simple, Angelina. If you meet it, we will create a new identity for you. You can go anywhere you wish in the world under this new name. You will not have to worry about supporting yourself, because I will take care of your financial arrangements in perpetuity."

"Wait…" Angelina shook her head slightly. "Does that mean…?"

He nodded. "My third wife runs a scuba diving business on an island you would never have heard of, off the coast of Venezuela. My fourth wife lives a nomadic lifestyle, currently traveling about mainland Europe in a converted van. It looks modest from the outside but is, I am assured, the very height of technology within.

My fifth wife prefers the frenetic pace of Hong Kong, where she runs a spa. And Veronica, my most famous wife, never able to have a moment to herself in all her days, has settled down on a farm in a temperate valley on the west coast of America. Where she tends to grapes on the vine, raises goats, and makes her own cheese." His smile was a grim and terrible thing. He could taste it. "You can have any life you wish, Angelina. At my expense. All you need to do is disappear forever."

"But if they're not… If you didn't…" She pulled in a visible breath with a ragged sound. "Are you married to all these women at the same time?"

He actually laughed at that. "That is not usually the first question. No, I'm not a bigamist, though I commend you for adding yet another sin to my collection. Murderer and bigamist, imagine! I'm almost sorry to tell you that my marriages have all been quietly and privately annulled. Save the first."

Angelina shifted, hugging herself she stared back at him. "I don't understand. Why would you set yourself up to be some sort of…one-man smuggling operation for women in search of better lives? When you know that the whole world thinks the worst of you?"

"Who better?" Benedetto shrugged. "I don't care in the slightest what the world thinks of me. And you've spent two months acquainting yourself with this castle. It is the tip of the iceberg of the kind of money I have. I could marry a hundred women, support them all, and never feel a pinch in my own pocket."

"So it's altruism then?" She looked dubious, and if he wasn't mistaken, something like…affronted. "If that was true, why not give all that money to charity?

Shouldn't there be a way to do it that doesn't brand you the monster beneath every bed in Europe?"

"What would be the fun in that?"

This was the part where normally, the women he'd married—despite their cynicism or inability to trust a word he said because they feared him so deeply, yet not quite deeply enough to refuse to marry him—began to waver. Hope began to creep in. He would watch them imagine, as they stood there before him, that he might be telling them the truth. And if he was, if he could really give them what he was offering, did that mean that they could really, truly be free?

Of him—and of everything else that had brought them here?

But Angelina was staring at him as if what he was telling her was a far worse betrayal than games with his fearsome housekeeper and a key to a locked tower door.

"What do I have to do to qualify for this extraordinary death?" she asked.

He wanted to go to her. He wanted his hands on her. But the point of this, all this, was that Benedetto wasn't supposed to want such things.

He never had before.

"I already told you that the primary purpose of my existence is to produce an heir," he told her stiffly. "It was why I married Carlota and why we planned to consummate a union that was never passionate."

"I remember the story. But that hardly sounds like reason enough to inflict your unhappy childhood on another baby."

"My childhood wasn't unhappy." He heard the outrage in his voice and tried to rein it in. "My grandmother—" But he stopped himself. Because Angelina already knew too much about him. He had already given her too much. Benedetto gritted his teeth and pushed on. "Ordinarily, this is when I offer my wives the opportunity to produce the Franceschi heir themselves."

"Surely they signed up for that when they said, 'I do'?"

He ignored that, and the flash of temper in her blue gaze. "Should you choose that route, life here will continue as is. At the end of a year, if no heir is forthcoming, the same offer for a new life will be made to you. If you're pregnant, however, the expectation would be that you remain until the child is five. At which point, a final offer will be made. If you choose to go, you can do so, with one stipulation. That being, obviously, that you cannot take the child with you. If you choose to stay, we will have contracts drawn up to indicate that you may remain as much a stranger to the marriage as you wish."

He cleared his throat, because this was all standard. This was the labyrinthine game he and his grandfather had crafted and it had served him well for years. But Angelina was staring at him as if he'd turned into an apparition before her very eyes. When this was usually when that sort of gaze faded and a new one took its place. The sweet, bright gleam of *what if.*

"Of course, in your case, everything is different," he said, forcing himself to keep going. "I always leave after the wedding. Usually while they are locked in the bathroom, pretending not to be terrified that I might claim a wedding night. Then I wait to see how long it takes each wife to open the door to this tower. Once she does, we have this discussion."

Again, the way she looked at him was…different.

He cleared his throat. "But your choices might be more limited, regrettably, because you could already be pregnant. I'll confess this has never happened before."

Her lips parted then, and she made a sound that he couldn't quite define. "Are you telling me...? Are you...? Did you not sleep with all your wives on your wedding night? On all your wedding nights?"

"Of course not." He belted that out without thinking. "Nor do I touch them beforehand. I may be considered a monster far and wide, Angelina, but I do *try* not to act like one."

She let out a laugh, a harsh sound against the storm that battered at the windows outside. "Except with me."

Benedetto ran a hand over his face, finding he was only more unsettled as this conversation wore on. Instead of less, as was customary—because he always knew what his wives would choose. He always knew none of them had married *him*. They'd married his money and hoped for the best, and this was him giving it to them.

"The truth is that you were different from the start," he told Angelina, grudgingly. "I had no trouble whatsoever keeping my hands to myself with the rest. It was all so much more...civilized."

He found himself closing the distance between them, when he shouldn't. And he expected her to flinch, but she didn't. She stood her ground, even tilting up her chin, as if she wanted him to do exactly this. As if she wanted him to make it all worse.

Benedetto slid his hand along her cheek, finding it hot and soft, and that didn't solve a single one of his problems. "But you played for me, Angelina. And you wrecked me. And I have been reeling ever since."

Her mouth moved into something far too stark to be a smile. Far too sad to be hers. "That would sound more romantic if you weren't threatening to kill me, one way or another."

"No," he gritted out. "As it happens, you are the only wife I have slept with on a wedding night."

Her eyes seemed remarkably blue then. "What about your second wife? Your mistress? Surely she—"

"She was paralytically drunk after our reception," he said, not sure if that darkness in him was fury, anticipation, or something else he'd never felt before. Something as overwhelming and electric as the storm outside. "And I was little better. I am afraid, Angelina, that you are unique."

"I feel so special," she whispered in that same rough tone, but she didn't jerk her cheek away.

Even so, Benedetto dropped his hand. And for a moment, they stood there, gazing at each other with all these secrets and lies exposed and laid out between them.

He could feel the walls all around him, claiming him anew. For good this time.

When she left him, as he knew she would because they always did, perhaps he would give up the fight altogether. In another year he could be nothing more than another statue, right here in this room. Another stop along the tour.

There was a part of him that longed for the oblivion of stone.

There was a part of him that always would.

"Why?" she asked, her voice a quiet scrape of roughness that reminded him, forcefully, that there was no part of him that was stone. That there never had been, especially where she was concerned. "Why would anyone go to all this trouble?"

"I will answer any and all questions you might have," he told her, sounding more formal than he intended. Perhaps that was his last refuge. The closest he could get to becoming a statue after all. "But first you must choose."

"As you pointed out, I might already be pregnant," she replied, her arms crossed and even the wildness of her long blond hair a kind of resistance, silver and bright against the bare walls.

Why did he want nothing more than to lose himself in her—forever? How had he let this happen?

"It is true. You might be. I used nothing to prevent it."

"Neither did I. There seemed little need when my life expectancy was all of three months."

And she stared at him, the rebuke like a slap.

He felt it more like a kick to the gut.

"What if I'm pregnant and still choose to disappear tonight?" she asked after a moment, sounding unnervingly calm. "What then? Will you surrender your own child? Or will you force me to stay here despite the choice I make?"

He shook his head, everything in him going cold. "I told you, you are unique. This has never happened before. That doesn't mean that the possibility is unforeseen. Your choice will hold, no matter your condition."

"You would give up your own child," she murmured. Her eyes widened. "But I thought I was the martyr here."

Benedetto realized his hands were in fists. He didn't know which was worse, that he would have to live without her, which he should have figured out how to handle already, or that it was distinctly possible that she would go off into whatever new life she wished and raise his child without him.

But the rules to this game had been always been perfectly clear.

He and his grandfather had laid them out together.

Half in penance, half for protection. He had already lost two wives. Why not more?

Benedetto had never imagined his heart would be involved. He'd been certain he'd buried that along with his grandmother.

"You must choose," he gritted out, little as he wanted to.

And for moment, he thought maybe they were dead, after all. Two ghosts running around and around in this terrible castle, cut off from the rest of the world. That the two of them had done this a thousand times before.

Because that was the way she looked at him. As if she'd despaired of him in precisely this way too many times to count already.

He could have sworn he heard her playing then, though there was no piano in sight. Still, the blood in his veins turned to symphonies instead, and he was lit up and lost.

For the first time since he'd started this terrible journey, he honestly didn't know if he could complete it. Or even if he could continue.

And all the while, his seventh wife—and first love, for all the good it would do him in this long, involved exercise in futility—gazed back at him, an expression on her face he'd never seen before.

It made everything in him tighten, like hands around his throat.

"What if I choose a third option instead?" she asked. Quietly. So very quietly.

Outside, the sea raged and the sky cracked open, again and again. But all he could focus on was Angelina. And those unearthly blue eyes that he was sure could see straight through him and worse, always had.

"There is no third option," he gritted out.

"But of course there is," she said.

And she smiled the way she had when he'd been deep inside her, on that night that shouldn't have happened. The night he couldn't forget.

He heard a great roaring thing and knew, somehow, that it was happening inside him.

"I could stay here," Angelina said with that same quiet strength. "I could have your babies and truly be your wife. No games. No locked towers or forbidden keys. Just you, Benedetto. And me. And whatever children we make between us."

He couldn't speak. The world was a storm, and he was a part of it, and only Angelina stood apart from it all. A beacon in all the dark.

"We don't have to play games. We don't have to do…whatever this is." Angelina stood there and *shined* at him. He'd never seen that shade of blue before. His heart had never felt so full. "We can do what we want instead."

No one, in the whole of Benedetto's life, had ever looked at him the way she did. As if he was neither her savior nor her hero nor even her worst nightmare. He could have handled any of those. All of them.

But Angelina looked at him as if, should he only allow it, he could be a man.

He didn't know how he stayed on his feet when all

he wanted was to collapse to his knees. To beg her to stop. Or to never stop. Or to *think* about what she was doing here.

To him.

"Angelina," he managed to grit out. "You don't know what you're asking."

"But I do." And this time, when her lips curved, it looked like hope. "Benedetto, you asked me to marry you, and I said yes. Now I'm asking you the same thing."

"Angelina…"

"Will you marry me? And better yet—" and her smile widened, and it was all too bright and too much and his chest was cracking open "—will you *stay* married to me? I'm thinking we can start with a long, healthy lifetime and move on from there."

CHAPTER TWELVE

"You must be mad," Benedetto said, his voice strangled.

Angelina couldn't say she wasn't. Maybe the next step was searching out convicted killers and making them her pen pals, as he'd suggested. But she rather thought the only killer who interested her was this one, who'd only ever been convicted in the court of public opinion. And who hadn't killed anyone.

"There is no third option," he said, his voice like gravel. But there was an arrested look on his face that made her heart lurch a bit inside her chest. "I made certain promises long ago. Whether you carry my child now or not is immaterial."

She'd been talking about babies as if she was talking about someone else, but the possibility that it had already happened, that it was happening *even now,* settled on her, then. She slid a hand over her belly in a kind of wonder. Could it be?

This whole night so far had been like one of her favorite pieces of music. A beautiful journey—a tour of highs and lows, valleys and mountains, storms and sunlight—and all of it bringing her here. Right here.

To this man who was not a monster. No matter how badly he wanted to be.

Her heart had known all along.

"I could do it your way," she said softly. "I could sign up for the heir apparent program. I could keep signing up. We could make it cold-blooded and chilly, if you like. Is that what you want?" There was something so heartbreaking about that, but she knew she would accept it, if it was what he had to offer. She knew she would accept anything if it meant she could have him, even the smallest part of him—but she saw something like anguish on his hard face, then. "Or is it what you think you deserve?"

And for a moment the anguish she could see in him seemed as loud and filled with fury as the storm outside. It was hard to tell which was which—but her heart knew this man. Her heart had recognized him from the start.

It recognized him now.

"It's all right if you can't answer me, Benedetto," she said. She went to him then, stepping close and putting her hands on his chest, where he was as hot to the touch as she recalled. Hotter. She tipped her head back, searching that beautiful, forbidding face of his. "If you can't bring yourself to answer, you don't have to. But tell me how we got here. Tell me why you do all this."

He made a broken sound, this dark, terrible man who was neither of those things.

She didn't understand why she knew it, only that she did. Her heart had known it all along. That was why, though she'd feared for her loneliness and sanity here, she had never truly believed she was in actual, physical danger.

He wasn't any more a butcher than she was. And once that truth had taken hold of her in this empty chamber, all the others swirling around her seemed to solidify. Then fall in behind it like dominoes.

She didn't want to leave him. She didn't want to learn how to scuba dive or to live in a caravan. She didn't want to run a spa in a far-off city, or collect grapes and goats.

She wanted him.

Angelina wanted to look up from her piano to find him studying her, as if she was a piece of witchcraft all her own and only he knew the words to her spell.

Because only he did.

God help her, but she wanted all those things she'd never dared dream about before. Not for the youngest daughter in a family headed for ruin. The one least likely to be noticed and first to be sold off. She wanted *everything*.

"Benedetto," she said again, because it started here. It started with the two of them and this sick game he clearly played not because he wanted to play it, but because he believed he had no other choice. "Who did this to you?"

Then she watched in astonishment as this big, strong man—this boogeyman feared across the planet, a villain so extreme grown men trembled before him—fell to his knees before her.

"I did this to me," he gritted out. "I did all of this. I am my own curse."

Angelina didn't think. She sank down with him, holding his hands as he knelt there, while all around the tower, the storm outside raged and raged.

The storm in him seemed far more intense.

"Why?" she breathed. "Tell me."

"It was after Sylvia was swept overboard," Benedetto said in a low voice, and the words sounded rough and unused. She didn't need him to tell her that he'd never told this story before. She knew. "You must understand, there was nothing about my relationship with her that anyone would describe as healthy. I should never have married her. As much for her sake as mine."

He stared straight ahead, but Angelina knew he didn't see her. There were too many ghosts in the way.

But she was fighting for a lifetime. She didn't care if they knelt on the hard stone all night.

She held his hands tighter as he continued.

"Sylvia and I brought out the worst in each other. That was always true, but it was all much sicker after Carlota died. All we did was drink too much, fight too hard, and become less and less able to make up the difference. Then came the storm."

His voice was ravaged. His dark eyes blind. His hands clenched around hers so hard that it might have hurt, had she not been so deeply invested in this moment. In whatever he was about to tell her.

"It took her," Benedetto grated out. "And then I knew what kind of man I was. Because as much as I grieved her, there was a relief in it, too. As if the hand of God reached down and saved me twice, if in horrible ways. Once from a union with a woman I could never make truly happy, because she loved another, and then from a woman who made me as miserable as I made her. The rest of my life, I will have to look in a mirror and know that I'm the sort of man who thought such things when two women died. That is who I am."

"You sound like a human being," Angelina retorted, fiercely. "If we were all judged on the darkest thoughts that have ever crossed our minds, none of us would ever be able to show our faces in public."

Benedetto shook his head. "My grandfather was less forgiving than you are, Angelina. He called me here, to this castle. He made me stand before him and explain how it was that I was so immoral. So devoid of empathy. Little better than my own father, by his reckoning, given that when my grandmother died he was never the same. He never really recovered." His dark, tortured eyes met hers. "There is nothing he could have said to wound me more deeply."

"Was your father so bad then?" She studied his face. "My own is no great example."

He made a hollow sound. "Your father is greedy. He thinks only of himself. But at least he thinks of *someone*. I don't know how to explain the kind of empty, vicious creature my father was. Only that my grandfather suggesting he and I were the same felt like a death sentence."

"Did you point out that he could always have stepped in himself, then?" Angelina asked, somewhat tartly. "Done a little more parenting than the odd hour on a Sunday? After all, who raised your father in the first place?"

And for moment, Benedetto focused on her instead of the past. She could see it in the way his eyes changed, lightening as he focused on her. In the way that hard mouth of his almost curved in one corner.

"What have I done to earn such ferocity?" he asked, and he sounded almost…humbled.

"You saved me from a selfish man who would have sold me one way or another, if not to you," she said, holding his hands tight. "You gave me a castle. A beautiful piano. And if I'm not very much mistaken, a child, too. What haven't you given me, Benedetto?"

He let out another noise, then reached over, smoothing a hand down over her belly, though it was still flat.

She thought of the oddly heightened emotions that had seemed to grip her this last month or so. The strange sensations low in her belly she'd assumed were due to anxiety. She'd felt strange and out of sorts for weeks, and had blamed it on her situation.

But knelt down the hard stone floor of this tower with Benedetto before her, his shoulders wider than the world, she counted back.

And she knew.

Just like that, she knew.

All this time she'd considered herself alone, she hadn't been. Benedetto had been here in the shadows and more, she'd been carrying a part of the both of them deep inside her.

Her heart thumped in her chest, so severely it made her shiver.

"My grandfather reminded me that I have a distant cousin who lives a perfectly unobjectionable life in Brussels. Why should he not leave all this wealth and power to this cousin rather than to me if I found it all so troublesome that I had not only married the most unsuitable woman imaginable, but failed to protect her?" Benedetto shook his head. "He told me that if I wanted to take my rightful place in history, I must subject myself to a test. A test, he made sure to tell me, he did not imagine there was any possibility I would win given my past behavior."

"Did he want you to win?"

He took a moment with that. "All this time I've assumed he wanted to teach me a lesson about loneliness. But I suspect now it was supposed to be a lesson about love."

Benedetto gathered her hands in his again, tugging her closer, and all of this felt like far more important ceremony than the one that had taken place in her father's house. There were no witnesses here but the sky and the sea. The storm. No family members littered about with agendas of their own.

It was only the two of them and the last of the secrets between them.

"My grandfather tasked me with finding women like you," Benedetto said. "Precisely the sort my father had preyed upon, in his time. Women with careless families. Women who might want to run. Women who deserved better than a man with a list of dead wives behind them. I would marry them, but I would not make them easy about my reputation. I would bring them here. Then I would leave them after the wedding night and let them sit in this castle with all its history and Signora Malandra, who is always only too happy to play her role."

"She's a little too good at her role."

"She, too, always thought I ought to have been a better man," Benedetto said. He shook his head. "When they found their way to this tower I was to offer them a way out. One that kept them safe, gave them whatever they wanted, and made me seem darker and more villainous to the outside world. And he made me vow that I would continue to do this forever, until one of these women gave me a son. And even then, I was to allow her to leave me. Or stay, but live a fully supported, separate life. 'You had two chances and you blew them both,' he told me. 'You don't get any more.'"

"How many chances did he get?" Angelina demanded, her voice as hot as that flash of lightning in her eyes.

"But that was the problem," Benedetto said in the same way he'd told her, on their wedding night, that he missed the man who had created this prison for him.

"My grandfather was a hard man. I do not think he was particularly kind. But he loved my grandmother to distraction and never quite recovered from her loss. She was the best of us. He told me that he was glad she had died before she could see all the ways in which I failed to live up to what she dreamed for me, because after my father had proved so disappointing, they had had such hopes that I would be better."

Angelina frowned. "I'm not sure how you were responsible for Carlota's choices on the one hand—in the face of her own family's pressure, presumably—and an act of nature on the other."

"It was not that I was personally responsible for what happened to them," Benedetto said quietly. "It was that I was so arrogant about both of them. Boorish and self-centered. It never occurred to me to inquire into Carlota's emotional state. And everything Sylvia and I did together was irresponsible. Would a decent man ever have let her out of his sight, knowing the state she was in?"

"A question one could ask of your grandfather," Angelina said.

"But you see, he didn't force me into this. He suggested I bore responsibility and suggested I test myself. I was the one who had spent the happy parts of my childhood playing out involved fantasies in these walls. Ogres and kings. Spells and enchantments. I thought I was already cursed after what had happened to Carlota and Sylvia. Why not prove it? Because the truth is, I never got over the loss of my grandmother either, and she was the one who had always encouraged the games I played. In some twisted way, it seemed like a tribute." Benedetto reached over and touched her face again, smoothing her hair back with one big hand. "And if my grandfather had not agreed, because without her we were both incapable of loving anything—too much like my father—could I have found my way to you?"

She let go the breath she hadn't realized she'd been holding.

"I don't care how you got here," Angelina told him, like another vow. "Just as long as you stay here now you've come."

Outside, lightning flashed and the storm rumbled. The sea fought back.

But inside this tower, empty of everything but the feelings they felt for one another, Angelina felt something bright and big swell up inside her.

It felt like a sob. It felt overwhelming, like grief.

She had the strangest feeling that it was something else altogether.

Something like joy.

"I don't want to leave you," she told him. "I don't want to play these games that serve no one. I have always wanted to be more than a bartering chip for my own father, and you are far more than a monster, Benedetto. What would happen if you and I made our own rules?"

"Angelina…" His voice was a low whisper that she knew, without a shred of doubt, came from the deepest, truest parts of him. "Angelina, you should know. I had read all about the Charteris sisters before I ever came to your father's house. And I assumed that I would pick the one who seemed best suited for me, on paper."

"If you are a wise man," she replied dryly, "you will never tell me which one you mean."

And just like that, both of them were smiling.

As if the sun had come up outside when the rain still fell.

"I walked into that dining room and saw an angel," he told her, wonder in his eyes. In the hands that touched her face. "And I knew better, because I knew that no matter who I chose, it would end up here. Here in the locked tower where all my bodies are buried, one way or another. And still, I looked at you and saw the kind of light I have never believed could exist. Not for me."

"Benedetto..." she whispered, the joy and the hope so thick it choked her.

"I had no intention of touching you, but I couldn't help myself. How could you be anything but an angel, when you could make a piano sing like that? You have entranced me and ruined me, and I have spent two months trying to come to terms with the fact you will leave me like all the rest. I can't."

"You don't have to come to terms with that."

"Maybe this is crazy," he continued, wonder and intensity in every line of his body. "Maybe I'm a fool to imagine that anything that starts in Castello Nero could end well. But I look at you, Angelina, and you make me imagine that anything is possible. Even love, if we do it together."

And for a moment, she forgot to breathe.

Then she did, and the breath was a sob, and there were tears on her face that tasted like the waiting, brooding sea.

Angelina thought, *This is what happiness can be, if you let it.*

If for once she believed in the future before her, not tired old stories of a past she'd never liked all that much to begin with.

If she believed in her heart and her hands, the man before her, and the baby she knew they'd already made.

"Our children will fill these halls with laughter," she promised him. "And you and I will make love in that bed, where there is nothing but the sea and the sky. It will no more be a chamber of blood, but of life. Love. The two of us, and the good we do. I promise you, Benedetto."

"The sky and the sea are the least of the things I will give you, little one," he vowed in return.

And the stone was cold and hard beneath her, but he was warm. Hot to the touch, and the way he looked at her made her feel as if angels really did sing inside her, after all.

She wrapped herself around him, high up in that tower that she understood, now, wasn't an empty room at all. It was his heart. These stones had only ever held his heart.

Now she would do the honors.

Because she was the seventh wife of the Butcher of Castello Nero. The first one to love him, the only one to survive intact, and soon enough the mother of his children besides.

There was no storm greater than the way she planned to love this man.

Deeper and longer than the castle itself could stand— and it had lasted centuries already.

And she started here, on the floor of this tower, where he settled her on top of him and gazed up at her as if she was the sun.

And then, together, moment by moment and year by year, they both learned how to shine.

Bright enough to scare away the darkest shadows.

Even the ones they made themselves.

Forever.

CHAPTER THIRTEEN

THE SEVENTH WIFE of the terrifying Butcher of Castello Nero confounded the whole world by living.

She lived, and well, by all accounts. She appeared in public on Benedetto's arm and gave every appearance of actually enjoying her husband's company. As months passed, it became apparent that she was expecting his child, and that, too, sent shock waves across the planet.

The tabloids hardly knew what to do with themselves.

And as the years passed without the faintest hint of blood or butchery, Benedetto found himself becoming something he'd never imagined he could. Boring.

Beautifully, magnificently boring to the outside world, at last.

Their first child, a little boy they called Amadeo to celebrate some of the music that had bound them to each other, thrived. When he was four, he was joined by a little brother. Two years later, a sister followed. And a year after that, another little girl joined the loud, chaotic clan in the castle on its tidal island.

A place only Angelina had seemed to love the way he always had, deny it though he might.

And Benedetto's children were not forced to secrete

themselves in hidden places, kept out of sight from tourist groups, or permitted only a weekly hour with him. Nor were they sent off to boarding school on their fifth birthdays. His children raced up and down the long hallways, exactly as Angelina had said they would. The stone walls themselves seemed lighter with the force of all that laughter and the inevitable meltdowns, and the family wing was soon anything but lonely. There was an endless parade between the nursery at one end, the master suite on the other, and all the rooms in between.

Ten years to the day that Benedetto had brought his last, best wife home, he stood at that wall of windows that looked out over the sea, the family wing behind him. He knew that even now, the staff was setting up something romantic for the two of them in that empty tower room that they kept that way deliberately.

Because it reminded them who they were.

And because it was out of reach of even their most enterprising child, because Angelina still wore the key he'd left her around her neck.

They would put the children to sleep, reading them stories and hearing their prayers, and then they would walk down this very same hall the way they always did. Hand in hand. The bloodred ruby on her hand no match for the fire inside him.

The fire he would share with her up there where they had pledged themselves to each other. The fire that only grew over time.

Benedetto was not the villain he'd played. He was not the boogeyman, as so many would no doubt believe until he died no matter what he did.

But any good in him, he knew with every scrap of conviction inside him, came from his angel. His wife and lover, who he had loved since the very first moment he'd laid eyes on her. The mother of his perfect, beautiful, never remotely disappointing children. The woman who had reminded him of the child he'd been—the child who had believed in all the things he'd had to relearn.

And the best piano player he had ever had the privilege of hearing.

He could hear her playing now, the notes soaring down from the tower that was still hers. These days, there was often art taped to the walls, and the children lay on the rug before the grand piano so they could be near her. So they could feel as if they were flying, too, as their mother played and played, songs of hope, songs of love. Songs of loss and recovery.

And always, always, songs of joy.

These were the spells she cast, he thought. These were her enchantments.

The sun began to sink toward the horizon. Pinks and reds took over the sky. And still she played, and he could picture her so perfectly, bent over the keys with her eyes half closed. Her hands like magic, coaxing so much beauty out into the world.

He could hardly wait to have them on him again, where he liked them best.

Benedetto had so many things to tell her, the way he always did after time apart. Whether it was five minutes or five weeks. How much he loved her, for one thing. How humbled he still was, a decade on, that she had seen the good in him when it had been hidden from everyone. Even himself.

Especially himself.

She had a heart as big as the sea, his lovely wife. She maintained a relationship with her family, and he rather thought her quiet example made her sisters strive to be better than they might otherwise have been. Her mother, too, in those few and far between moments Margrete Charteris thawed a little. And if her father could never really be saved, it hardly mattered. Because Anthony Charteris had as a son-in-law a rich and besotted billionaire more than willing to spend his money on his father-in-law if it pleased his wife.

After all, there was always more money.

Benedetto would spend it all if it made her happy.

He heard the music stop and found himself smiling. He decided he would wait until they were alone to tell her that he had decided to share her piano playing with the world. Whether she wanted to perform or not, he could certainly share her music. He thought the world deserved to know that not only had Angelina soothed the savage beast with her playing, she was one of the best in the world. Accordingly, he'd bought her a record company.

But that would come.

First there was tonight.

He heard her feet on the stone and then she was there beside him, her eyes still the bluest he'd ever seen. Particularly when they were sparkling with music and love and light, and all of it for him.

"Happy anniversary, little one," he murmured, kissing her. He felt that same rush of longing and lust, desire and need, tempered now with these long, sweet years. "I have loved you each and every day. I love you now. And I only plan to love you more."

"I'm delighted to hear that," she replied, in that dry way he adored. "I love you too. And it turns out I have a rather bigger gift for you than planned."

Benedetto turned to look at her in some surprise, and Angelina smiled.

She took his hand in hers—her thumbs moving over the calluses there that it had taken her years to understand he got from performing the acts of physical labor he preferred to a gym membership—and moved it to her belly.

And he had done this so many times before. It was the same surge of love and wonder, sweetness and hope. Disbelief that she could make him this happy. Determination to do it better than his parents had, no matter what it took.

He was already better, he liked to think. If his grandmother could see him now, he was sure he would make her smile. And maybe even his grandfather, too.

"Again?" he asked, grinning wide enough to crack his own jaw.

"We really should do something about it," she said, her eyes shining. "It's almost unseemly. But… I just don't want to."

He pulled her to him, marveling as ever at how perfectly and easily she fit in his arms. "Angelina, my angel, if you wish to have enough children to fill this entire castle, we will make it so."

She laughed, her mouth against his. "Let's not get *that* carried away."

And he kissed her, because the future was certain.

That wasn't to say he knew what would happen, because no man could. Storms came. Sometimes they took more than was bearable. Sometimes they left monsters in their wake.

But he was not alone anymore.

He had Angelina, and together, they made their own

light. And Benedetto knew that no matter how dark it became, they would find a way to light it. And with that light, they would find their way through.

They would always find their way through.

And all the while they would stay here, in this ancient place where they'd found each other. When the tide was low, they would welcome in the world. There would be laughter in the halls, and deliciously creepy stories about disappearances both centuries old and more recent.

But soon enough the tide would come in, and the castle would be theirs again.

Like their heart made stone and cared for throughout time, they would love this place. They would love each other and their children. They would choose light over dark, hope over heartache, and they would do what no other Franceschi ever had across the ages.

They would make Castello Nero a home.

Their home.

And he kissed her again, long and deep, because that was how forever happened when it was made of love— one life-altering kiss at a time.

* * * * *

COMING SOON!

We really hope you enjoyed reading this book.
If you're looking for more romance, be sure to
head to the shops when new books are
available on

Thursday 11th June

MILLS & BOON

Coming next month

REVELATIONS OF HIS RUNAWAY BRIDE
Kali Anthony

'This marriage is a sham.'

In some ways, he agreed with her. Yet here he stood, with a gold wedding band prickling on his finger. Thea still held her rings. He needed her to put them on. If she did, he'd won—for tonight.

'You're asking me to return you to the tender care of your father?' A man Christo suspected didn't have a sentimental, loving bone in his body.

Thea grabbed the back of a spindly chair, clutching it till her fingers blanched. 'I'm asking you to let me go.'

'No.'

Christo had heard whispers about Tito Lambros. He was reported to be cruel and vindictive. The bitter burn of loathing coursed like poison through his veins. That his father's negligence had allowed such a man to hold Christo's future in his hands...

There was a great deal he needed to learn about Thea's family—some of which he might be able to use. But that could wait. Now it was time to give her something to cling to. *Hope.*

'You'll come with me as my wife and we'll discuss the situation in which we find ourselves. That's my promise. But we're leaving now.'

She looked down at her clothes and back at him. Her liquid amber eyes glowed in the soft lights. 'I can't go dressed like this!'

No more delays. She glanced at the door again. He didn't want a scene. Her tantrums could occur at his home, where any witnesses would be paid to hold their silence.

'You look perfect,' he said, waving his hand in her direction. 'It shows a flair for the dramatic—which you've proved to have in abundance tonight. Our exit will be unforgettable.'

She seemed to compose herself. Thrust her chin high, all glorious defiance. 'But my hat… I told everyone about it. I can't disappoint them.'

'Life's full of disappointments. Tell them it wouldn't fit over your magnificent hair.'

Thea's lips twitched in a barely suppressed sneer, her eyes narrow and glacial. The look she threw him would have slayed a mere mortal. Luckily for the most part he felt barely human.

'Rings,' he said.

She jammed them carelessly on her finger. *Victory*. He held out the crook of his arm and she hesitated before slipping hers through it. All stiff and severe. But her body still fitted into his in a way which enticed him. Caused his heart to thrum, his blood to roar. Strange. Intoxicating. All Thea.

'Now, smile,' he said.

She plastered on a mocking grimace.

He leaned down and whispered in her ear. 'Like you mean it, *koukla mou*.'

'I'll smile when you say *that* like you mean it, Christo.'

And he laughed.

This second laugh was more practised. More familiar— like an old memory. But the warmth growing in his chest was real. Beyond all expectations, he was enjoying her. For his sanity, perhaps a little too much…

Continue reading
REVELATIONS OF HIS RUNAWAY BRIDE
Kali Anthony

Available next month
www.millsandboon.co.uk

LET'S TALK
Romance

For exclusive extracts, competitions
and special offers, find us online:

 facebook.com/millsandboon

 @MillsandBoon

 @MillsandBoonUK

Get in touch on 01413 063232

For all the latest titles coming soon, visit
millsandboon.co.uk/nextmonth

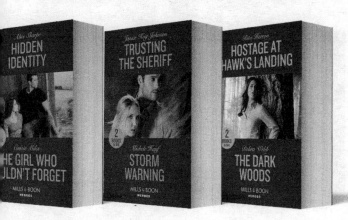

MILLS & BOON

THE HEART OF ROMANCE

A ROMANCE FOR EVERY KIND OF READER

MODERN

Prepare to be swept off your feet by sophisticated, sexy and seductive heroes, in some of the world's most glamourous and romantic locations, where power and passion collide.
8 stories per month.

HISTORICAL

Escape with historical heroes from time gone by. Whether you passion is for wicked Regency Rakes, muscled Vikings or rugg Highlanders, awaken the romance of the past.
6 stories per month.

MEDICAL

Set your pulse racing with dedicated, delectable doctors in the high-pressure world of medicine, where emotions run high a passion, comfort and love are the best medicine.
6 stories per month.

True Love

Celebrate true love with tender stories of heartfelt romance, the rush of falling in love to the joy a new baby can bring, an focus on the emotional heart of a relationship.
8 stories per month.

Desire

Indulge in secrets and scandal, intense drama and plenty of s hot action with powerful and passionate heroes who have it a wealth, status, good looks…everything but the right woman.
6 stories per month.

HEROES

Experience all the excitement of a gripping thriller, with an i romance at its heart. Resourceful, true-to-life women and str fearless men face danger and desire - a killer combination!
8 stories per month.

DARE

Sensual love stories featuring smart, sassy heroines you'd wan best friend, and compelling intense heroes who are worthy of
4 stories per month.

To see which titles are coming soon, please visit
millsandboon.co.uk/nextmonth

JOIN US ON SOCIAL MEDIA!

Stay up to date with our latest releases, author news and gossip, special offers and discounts, and all the behind-the-scenes action from Mills & Boon...

 millsandboon

 millsandboonuk

 millsandboon

might just be true love...